Preston brought his young wife to the party, not knowing he'd encounter his first love, the woman he jilted at the altar years ago. Margo's timeless beauty tantalized him once again, making Nicole wonder, *Is the honeymoon over?*

Alone on the fourth floor, Mr. and Mrs. Preston Phillips were having a marital spat. Having no clue that he had behaved boorishly throughout the evening, Preston had climbed the three flights of stairs feeling good about himself. He was sure Margo still had feelings for him, and he had to admit, he was still attracted to her. He had enjoyed the attention of Kitty Kelley, too. *I've still got what it takes to attract a woman*, he thought with a grin. *And I rather enjoy aggravating the men, as well.*

"What are you smiling at?" Nicole asked.

Her tone pierced Preston's reverie. He had been expecting her to fall right into his arms. "What do you mean?"

"Don't play innocent with me, Preston. I've been watching you with your friends all night. Frankly, I think you've made a fool of yourself."

"And how do you think I've made a fool of myself, Miss Expert? A few months of marriage, and you think you know me and my friends that well?"

"Totally. I know enough to know there's something going on between you and that Margo, and the others either detest you or barely tolerate you. I may not have been around for the back story, but I'm not blind."

Nicole sat at the dressing table and stared at her husband in the mirror.

Preston returned her stare in the mirror, aiming for sincerity. "There's nothing going on with Margo and me. I haven't seen her in forty years, for God's sake."

"Oh, yeah. Then what were you two doing for fifteen minutes when you both went upstairs?"

Preston turned away from the mirror, pacing. "Maybe we shouldn't have come this weekend. I didn't mean to upset you."

"Answer my question. What were you and Margo doing?" Nicole's voice rose in pitch, as if she were about to cry.

"Keep your voice down. We weren't doing anything. We were talking. We *are* old friends."

"You could talk to your old friends all night long, right in front of everyone. You didn't have to leave the table to follow that old hag. I asked you not to leave me alone with these people, but I never dreamed you would go off pussy-chasing. I'm mortified." She stood and paced around the room, brandishing her hairbrush.

"I'm not going to apologize to you, Nicole, because I didn't do anything wrong. I love you, and I married you. End of story. Now let's go to bed."

"Don't think this is the end of this discussion, Preston. If you do one more thing to upset me this weekend, you'll live to regret it." Nicole's voice trailed off at the end of the threat, as Preston grabbed her from behind, both hands sliding smoothly into the front of her panties.

Annoyed as she was with him, her first impulse was to push her husband away. On the other hand, this was how she and Preston communicated best. She moved against him, signaling that the argument was over, and the making up was underway. *Let them eat their hearts out*, she thought. *Preston Phillips belongs to me.*

"Mmmph," Preston groaned into her ear, feeling the full effect of the blue pill he had taken earlier. "Don't worry. You're the only woman I need, baby."

Someone comes to the party with murder in his heart and poison in his pocket...

A powerful and rich playboy, a rare but naturally occurring poison, a newly divorced woman with an axe to grind, and pressure from the former President of the US—these are just a few of the challenges that African-American Detective Oliver Parrott faces when he answers a routine call for backup and discovers someone died at a country estate the morning after an elaborate birthday party. When Parrott learns the deceased is the wealthy former US Secretary of the Treasury and just about everyone at the party had a motive to kill him, he realizes this will be the investigation to make—or break—his career.

KUDOS for *Murder in the One Percent*

"An Everyman detective is asked to solve a murder in a wealthy community in which ample motives and abundant resources make everyone a suspect. Detective Oliver Parrott, who takes charge of the case, is so struck by the partygoers' consensual impressions of the selfish businessman that he realizes the case may be more about who didn't kill Preston than who did." ~ Kirkus Reviews

"The twists unravel then turn around and bite you. Saralyn Richard's take on the classic murder mystery is fresh, fun, and deadly." ~ Bob Bickford, author of *Deadly Kiss*, ITW Best First Novel Award winner

"Some might call *Murder in the One Percent* an American cozy with nods to contemporary social issues. I call it a page turner packed with humorous lines that made me laugh out loud. Or maybe it's best to call this delightful mystery a satire about the upper class. However you describe it, Saralyn Richard successfully delivers a rollicking whodunit that will make you stay up late at night and leave you guessing until the very end. Move over, Dame Agatha Christie. There's a new kid on the block." ~ Ann Weisgarber, author of *The Promise* and *The Personal History of Rachel DuPree*

"Newcomer Saralyn Richard rolls out a swanky Rolls Royce of a novel in her debut mystery, *Murder in the One Percent*. It's no simple task to clothe a troupe of shallow, upper-crust characters in true-to-life garments, but with this one, you can smell the over-priced cologne and catch the atomic blast blinding glare of perfect teeth while you settle in for the slow burn—there's as much intrigue here and build-up as the best the genre has to offer. Ms. Richard has a modern winner in Detective Oliver Parrott, a real cop's cop. If there's a sequel coming, I'll want first dibs." ~ George Wier, author of the *Bill Travis Mysteries* and co-author of *Long Fall From Heaven*

"The festering secrets and grievances of the idle rich make for a combustible combination during a weekend birthday gathering in bucolic Pennsylvania horse country…With a crisp, felicitous prose style, and a vivid eye for the kind of detail that conjures a world and characters of dimension, Saralyn Richard stakes claim to territory pioneered by P. D. James and Agatha Christie…An impressive, page-turning debut…The perfect beach read." ~ Mark Valadez, Executive Story Editor, USA Network's *Queen of the South*, Crackle's *The Oath*

"In this Detective Parrot mystery, Author Saralyn Richard gives the reader convincing insight into the lives of twenty-first-century party-going one-percenters, many with a motive for murder, and a puzzle worthy of Dame Agatha." ~ Susan P. Baker, author of *Unaware, A Suspense Novel*

MURDER

IN THE

ONE PERCENT

Large Print

SARALYN RICHARD

A Black Opal Books Publication

MURDER IN THE ONE PERCENT ~ Large Print
Copyright © 2018 by Saralyn Richard
Cover Design by Rebecca Evans
All cover art copyright © 2018
All Rights Reserved
Large Print ISBN: 978-1-626949-99-7

First Publication: FEBRUARY 2018

Published by Black Opal Books
http://www.blackopalbooks.com

To Ed, the perfect partner in all things

But what is happiness except the simple harmony between a man and the life he leads?

~ Albert Camus

Chapter 1

Sunday, December 15:

Sundays usually meant good luck. Parrott had been born on a Sunday, and every important event in his life that he could remember had happened on a Sunday, too. He'd met Tonya on a Sunday in the fall of freshman year. It was Sunday when he'd scored the winning touchdown for Syracuse at the Texas Bowl. It was Sunday when he'd received the news of being promoted to detective of the West Brandywine Police. But this Sunday, Parrott just wasn't feeling it.

Why he'd thought being a detective in the affluent horse country outside of Philadelphia would be a rewarding job, he couldn't imagine. There was no way a young African-American was going to fit in with the elite WASP community there. Or maybe he was just rattled by all the racial tensions associated with being a cop these days.

As he prepared for the weekly Skype-date with his fiancée, he surveyed his two-bedroom bungalow, satisfied, at least, that all was scrubbed, folded, sorted, and arranged. *It might not be a mansion, but everything's exactly the way I like it,* he thought. Parrott put the final touches on the bird-cage, an immaculate microcosm of the house. Horace, the cockatiel, perched on Parrott's shoulder and whistled something over and over that sounded like, "Oh, dear."

"My sentiments exactly," Parrott replied. He'd had bad news last night from St. Louis.

Parrott looked at the clock. With characteristic efficiency, he polished the bars of the cage door and rang the little bell, signaling completion. "Let's go, Horace," he whispered to his pearl-and gold-feathered companion. "It's almost Tonya Time." Hearing the name of his faraway mistress, Horace nuzzled Parrott's neck. Parrott offered his index finger as a resting place, and the bird hopped aboard for a special petting of his orange cheeks.

Tonya's tour of duty in the US Navy had taken her to Germany, Iraq, and now Afghanistan with two stateside assignments between deployments. With the exception of furloughs the last few Christmases, she had been mostly gone since they graduated from college together five years ago. Parrott picked up her framed picture, seeking comfort from Tonya's smiling eyes. He closed his eyes and conjured images of her that neither photo nor Skype could provide—the firmness of her slender frame, the subtle smell of sandalwood, the way she fit against him. She was strong and brave and smart and witty, and she knew all of the ragged places in his heart and loved him anyway.

It was rough being apart like this. Parrott put down the photograph in its proper place, opened the laptop with his free hand, and pushed the power button. He tucked his brooding thoughts away and positioned himself and Horace where the camera would capture them both.

As the honking of the Skype connector pierced the air around the kitchen table, he patted Horace's head, wishing for something far from reach. When Tonya's face appeared on the computer screen, he pasted a smile on his face and tried to look normal.

"What's wrong, Detective?" Tonya said at once, one perfectly shaped eyebrow lifted in concern.

Parrott's baritone voice cracked. "Nothing."

"You can't fool me, sweetheart. I see it in your eyes. So c'mon. Out with it."

She looked so damn beautiful with those full lips and large brown eyes, those Hollywood eyelashes. Parrott felt like smashing the computer screen to get to her. Instead, he said, "It's nothing. I'm not going to gripe to you with all you're going through over there. Tell me about you."

"Everything's fine here. Quiet. Busy, but peaceful. Now you."

"Okay, okay. I didn't sleep much last night. Police shooting in Missouri last night—this time my cousin Bo got killed."

"Oh, dear," chirped Horace, a Greek chorus in the room.

"Bo Jones? The guy who showed me how to fix my bike when we were freshmen?"

"Yeah." Parrott stood and paced around the kitchen table, remembering Bo telling him then, "She's a keeper, Ollie. Better not let that girl get away."

"I'm really sorry. He was a good guy," Tonya said. "He sure doesn't seem like the kind to get mixed up with police, though."

"He wasn't. Apparently, an innocent bystander. Senseless. No details yet." Parrott stood and paced in front of the computer screen, oblivious to the fact that Horace now perched on his head.

"I can tell you're taking this hard. Don't blame you, either."

Parrot sat. "Yeah. Maybe I chose the wrong profession. I thought I could get the bad guys, make things better for the good guys. But now, seems like people think cops are bad guys, and I'm not sure who is who. I almost envy you for being in Afghanistan. At least the good guys and bad guys are better defined."

Tonya shook her head. "Oh, no. You aren't even making sense. Are you letting those rich folks mess with your head, Oliver? You've accomplished a lot, and you've earned respect from 'most everyone you've met."

"Maybe." He twirled the hairs in his moustache. "But there's not much to be proud of when all your cases involve stolen property, insured property belonging to people so rich they hardly even miss it when it's gone."

Tonya grinned, showing that endearing tiny space between her front teeth. "Are you saying you're hankering for something more gruesome—assault and battery, rape, or murder?"

Parrott ran his hands through his short-cropped hair and gave a sheepish smile. "The dilemma of a cop—the best opportunities come from other people's misfortune. Can't say I want someone hurt, but I sure would like to get something challenging, something where I can make a difference. And after what happened to poor Bo, I hope it happens soon."

ↄↄↄ

Just as Parrott disconnected from Skype, his cell phone jangled in his pocket. The caller ID showed W Brandywine PD, unusual for a Sunday.

When he answered, prickles traveled up his spine.

"Parrott, hate to disturb you on your day off. Need you to check out a death at the Campbell farm. Lots of important people at a weekend party. Looks like natural causes, but you need to make sure.

Be careful what you wish for? "Okay, Chief. I'm on it." Parrott shut down his computer, refilled Horace's water bowl, and escorted the little fellow

5

back into the cage. He put on his heavy coat. He glanced back at Tonya's picture before he stepped out and closed the door.

Chapter 2

One Month Earlier:

The invitation to what would be an unforgettable birthday party was postmarked precisely on November thirteenth, one month before the event. Examining it once again, the hostess ran her long fingers over the engraved ivory vellum, picturing the faces of the dozen invitees, imagining them as they opened the thick, lined envelope and read the simple, but elegant wording:

*Please Join Us for a Weekend Celebration
In Honor Of
John E. Campbell
On the Occasion of His
65th Birthday
December 13–15
Arrival at 7 p.m.
Bucolia Farm
RSVP Caro*

Caroline Campbell, or Caro, as her friends called

her, felt a *frisson* of excitement about welcoming their oldest and dearest friends for a weekend at the sixty-acre gentleman's farm in rural Pennsylvania.

She and John E. had just moved into the remodeled country mansion, and she was eager to fill its rooms with the laughter and reminiscences that only close friendships could provide.

Her plans, however, had been tempered by her genteel upbringing, which prohibited her from doing anything to show off. These days, with so much negative attention in the media, parties of the rich and famous had become *passé*, as, it seemed, the rich and famous, themselves, had become *passé*. So Caro had toned down her husband's birthday celebration. Instead of a full-blown dinner with live music and dancing, she had chosen an intimate gathering of John E.'s closest friends and colleagues. Even so, the bubble of anticipation rose from her core to her brain, and, like a heady champagne, it made her giggle.

కుణకు

Julia Winthrop dropped her jeweled, twenty-four-karat-gold letter opener into the lap of her suede skirt, as a throng of butterflies danced inside. What a coincidence that this invitation had arrived today, just as she most welcomed it. She grabbed her iPhone and speed-dialed her husband's office, knowing his personal cell phone would be turned off during the work day. Impatiently, she tapped her shiny salon gel-wrapped index fingernail, waiting for his assistant to answer.

One ring…two rings…three…

"Federal Reserve Bank, Marshall Winthrop's Office," the velvet-voiced Trudy answered.

Trying to keep the excitement out of her voice, Julia asked to speak to her husband.

"Oh, hello, Mrs. Winthrop," Trudy oozed. "He has just ended a meeting. Let me connect you."

Julia waited exactly two minutes, as usual. Marshall didn't believe in answering calls quickly. He felt eagerness would be interpreted as weakness, even when the caller was his wife.

"Hello, Julia. How's your day going?" Marshall's deep voice was one of the things Julia adored about him.

"Marshall," Julia began. "You'll never guess what came in today's mail." She paused before gushing on, "An invitation to John E.'s sixty-fifth birthday party. And this one is a weekend retreat at the farm."

"That's nice, dear."

Julia could hear the shuffling of papers.

"Don't you see the significance?" Annoyance crept into her tone. "This may be the opportunity we've been waiting for."

"Ahem." He cleared his throat. "Yes, dear. I look forward to hearing more about it when I get home tonight. I'll be on the eight-ten."

Julia caught the anticipation in Marshall's voice, just enough to let her know her message had been conveyed. She wouldn't push him to talk about this at his office. Tonight, they would have a very interesting dinner conversation, indeed.

ভৈতন্ত্র

In a lofty New York apartment, the yet-unopened invitation stood on end in a soldier-like array of the day's mail, where Francesca, the well-trained maid, had set it. Neither Libby nor Les Bloom, the youngest couple on the invitation list, had arrived home from work yet.

Their high-powered jobs—his at Sterling Martin Financial, and hers at Columbia University—kept them working at such a pace that they had hardly a moment to enjoy the trappings of their incredible wealth.

Libby's much older sister, Margo, recently divorced and visiting from her villa in Tuscany, glided past the entry hall, wearing earbuds and humming to the soundtrack of *Les Miserables*. She corrected her posture, barely averting a collision between her elbow and a Georg Jensen crystal vase of exotic fresh flowers. That was when she noticed the neatly arranged mail, particularly the cream-colored envelope with calligraphy on the front.

"Hmmm, it looks like baby sister and her hubby are invited to a fancy party." She turned the envelope over in her manicured hand, brushing the embossed return address with her thumb. Even without the name, Margo recognized the return address in Rittenhouse Square, the city home of Caro and John E. She had spent many happy and some not-so-happy times with the Campbells—she and Preston. It was years since Margo had allowed herself to think of Preston. Still, the pain that accompanied all thoughts of him stung, and her eyes filled in swift reaction.

I'll bet Preston will be in attendance at this little soiree, Margo thought, clutching the envelope to her chest. *Maybe I can find out from Libby just what he's up to these days. On second thought*, she chided herself, *I am much better off not knowing anything about Preston Phillips, now or ever.*

She hesitated before replacing the envelope into the line of Libby's mail. She wished she hadn't seen it. She wanted nothing to do with Preston Phillips—nothing at all.

၄୬၄୬

Caro was in a chatty mood as she and John E. packed for their ordinary weekend at their extraordinary Pennsylvania farm. "The invitations to your birthday party most likely arrived today, John E. I'll be eager to see how many of our friends accept."

"I'm still having misgivings about it, you know.

11

As big as the farm is, it might not be big enough for these twelve friends for an entire weekend." John E. tossed a cashmere sweater onto the pile on the bed.

"Don't be ridiculous. It's been years since all the friction over money and politics." Caro straightened the pile of clothes, toiletries, and reading material firmly and secured them with the inside straps. "I'm so glad we have doubles of everything at the farm. Makes packing so much simpler."

"Yeah, and don't forget Margo. Libby and Les probably haven't forgotten that," John E. added. "Besides, everyone I know is so on edge from the income inequality issues these days. No one seems to be in a partying mood anymore."

"I know, dear," Caro said. "That's why we decided to celebrate in low-key fashion. I'm sure the weekend at the farm will be relaxing and pleasant for everyone. We can indulge in good food, drink, and company without pressures from the outside world."

"Don't forget the cigars. The guys will definitely want Cohibas. We'll have to order new stock."

"You know how I feel about cigars, John E. Outside only. You take care of the wine and cigars. I'll focus on meals and bedroom accommodations. Deal?"

"Deal. You're really a sport to go to all this trouble for my birthday."

"My pleasure. After all, what good is Bucolia if we don't share it with our friends?"

❧❧❧

Caro's first cousin, Preston Phillips, was known as someone to admire, someone to fear. Raised among the ultra-rich in the Hamptons, Preston had the pedigree and experiences that opened doors. The best schools, the highest grades, the most prestigious positions, the highest salaries—all had been his for the taking. His athletic prowess was equally amazing. That and his striking good looks had made for a continuous parade of beautiful girls vying for his attention. He had lost count of how many women he had loved and discarded, Margo Martin, among them. He was on wife number four now, a pretty young thing he had met at the Lamborghini dealership.

Despite being raised with all of the social graces befitting his station in life, Preston had, over the years, developed quite a mercurial temper. Those who knew him as Chairman of the Congressional Ways and Means Committee in the 'eighties had witnessed some of his mood swings during times of economic crisis. When the pressure escalated, Preston exploded. The flip side was that once he blew up, his intelligence kicked in, and he was the best economic problem-solver in America. Still, even his closest friends never fully trusted him.

Now that he had been the US Secretary of the Treasury, and right-hand to the last president, he could add power with a capital "P" to his list of attributes. Of course, it was not an easy time for the rich and powerful, especially those from the previous administration. The backlash against the wealthy seemed to be growing and strengthening, a Grendel-like monster, with no Beowulf in sight, not even Preston Phillips.

For this reason, Preston was distracted throughout cocktail hour and the elegant dinner placed before him. Despite Nicole Phillips' attempts at conversation, he remained aloof and picked at his food. *Maybe I can relax with a cigar and some jazz music,* he thought afterward, as he recessed to his private man-cave, where he contemplated the serene movements of the tropical fish in his wall-sized aquarium.

"By the way," Nicole cooed a few hours later, as she seductively removed her silky blouse, revealing two perfect bare breasts, "we got an invitation to John Campbell's birthday party today."

"John E.?" He raised his right eyebrow. "It'll be another stuffed shirt affair at his country club, I guess. Maybe we can just make an appearance and duck out."

"No, I don't think so. I totally didn't *get* the invitation. It gives the date of the party as, like, December thirteenth to fifteenth? I think it might be a three-day party?" Nicole's sentences often ended with the high pitch of a question mark.

"I'll take a look at it later. First, I want to give you my undivided attention," Preston said, as he grabbed Nicole's blonde mane, and pulled it hard.

"Oooh, Preston," she gasped. "You really do want me, don't you?"

"Oh, yeah, baby. There's nothing I want more."

Chapter 3

The state-of-the-art, rhinestone-encrusted i-Phone rang from where it rested on the side of the marble bathtub, a whirlpool the size of Rhode Island. Vicki Spiller breast-stroked to answer it, careful not to spill a drop from the flute of crisp, cold *Veuvre Cliquot* on the ledge next to the phone.

Who would be calling me at this time of the afternoon? she thought. *My friends all know this is my meditation hour.*

The caller ID said, *Restricted* but something told Vicki she should answer. "Spiller residence," she answered with a slight Hispanic accent, careful not to slur her words. She pretended to be the upstairs maid, someone she had been forced to let go almost a year ago.

"Ta-ray-za," the voice said with over-familiarity, "is Mrs. Spiller in? This is Julia Winthrop."

"I believe she is in, Mrs. Winthrop. I'll check to see if she is available," Vicki replied, hoping the sound of moving in the bathwater wasn't giving away her play-acting. She muted the phone, set it down, and eased herself out of the tub. Ordinarily, she would have called her friend back later, but the

16

invitation from the Campbells had changed everything.

A full two minutes and a pat-down with a luxurious Turkish bath sheet later, Vicki unmuted the phone. "Julia, we need to talk."

"I know. That's why I'm calling. Did you get the Campbells' invitation?"

"Yes. I knew you must have been invited, too."

"I'm certain the whole crowd will be there, including ol' PP. This may be our best chance to finally confront the old bastard. It's not fair that he continues to breathe the same air as we do. As much as I hate to spend a weekend with him and his latest trollop, I must say I tingle when I think of what I'd like to do to him, and the weekend party will certainly give me an opportunity. What do you think?" Julia asked.

"I agree," Vicki replied. "If there is anyone who detests Preston more than you, it's probably me." As if to punctuate the thought, she took a long swig from the champagne glass.

"So you and Leon are planning to attend?"

"Yes, Leon's in, though he'd rather not be in the same zip code as that man. You know how he blames him for the horrendous tragedy."

"I know, and we've got our own reasons to hate him," Julia muttered. "It will be much simpler knowing you'll be at the party, too."

☙❧

Andrea Baker, crime writer and horsewoman, was riding her beloved Mustafa along the trails between her farm and the Campbells'. The crispness of air and the steady clopping of horse's hooves provided a soothing backdrop for her thoughts.

The invitation from the Campbells had prompted her to think about the long history the two couples had shared. They had become especially close since the Campbells had bought Bucolia. Before that, John E. and Stan had worked together at Baker, McCall, and Brewster, the notable Wall Street firm. Before that, they had collaborated on several books about finance in their days together at Princeton. Though Stan was a generation older than John E., he respected the younger man's intellect and ambition, and he felt an almost fatherly pride in John E.'s vast accomplishments. It warmed Andrea's heart to see the Campbells following in Stan's footsteps, moving to Philadelphia, buying the adjacent farm, and joining the ranks of horse owners.

Andrea, pronounced "On-dria," thought of herself as a no-nonsense woman. She managed her relationships as meticulously as she managed her waking hours. An early riser, she made a pot of decaf tea, donned her comfortable country clothes, and sequestered herself in her rustic office, where she conducted research and organized her current bestseller-in-the-making. The fact that she was now the premiere crime writer in America, and that stories came to her, instead of the other way around, didn't appear to have gone to her head, any more than the fact that she and Stan were listed on the *Forbes'* billionaire list year after year. She worked diligently throughout the day, rewarding herself with a late afternoon trail ride when she felt she had earned it. In the evening, she and Stan ate delicious, healthy dinners, and indulged in their passion for watching newly released films, mostly foreign, in their home movie theater. Most weekends, they hosted or visited their children and grandchildren, and, on rare occasions, got together with friends. It was a charmed life, Andrea knew, a blessed life, and she determined not to waste a moment of it.

Today, as the sun was melting into the horizon, spilling vibrant pinks and corals over the horse stables to the west, Andrea was debating about whether she should be straightforward with her friend Caro. The thought of spending a weekend at the Campbells' farm would ordinarily hold some appeal, since Stan and John E. were so close, and she and Caro had a lot in common. But the birthday celebration meant that she would have to suffer the company of some people whose values she truly disdained. Could she really tolerate it for a whole weekend? She didn't think so. But she also couldn't deprive Stan of participating in his protégé's birthday celebration.

At least I won't have to stay at Bucolia for the

whole weekend, she consoled herself. "Stan and I will be able to come and go as we please, Mustafa," she murmured, patting her favorite Arabian gelding. "Maybe it won't be so bad, after all."

Chapter 4

itty Kelley glided on the arm of her husband Gerald to the ivory leather booth in the center of the new Japanese restaurant in Manhattan. People were vying for reservations at Oishii, but the Kelleys walked right in. Kitty loved being married to the head man at Miles Stewart. Gerald had penned a nonfiction bestseller, *Essential Economics: Everyone Can Earn Millions*. The fortune that had come from authoring the book paled by comparison, however, to the perks. Dry cleaners, shoe salesmen, restauranteurs, golf caddies, car parkers, literally everyone Gerald encountered, all recognized his name, if not his face. Kitty was happy to tag along.

Tonight was Kitty's birthday, so Gerald had planned a special dinner for just the two of them. As they settled into the comfortable seating, Kitty looked around with curiosity. She loved being the first to try new restaurants, and she was especially interested in the décor, since it was a hobby of hers to decorate and redecorate each of their three estates.

"Hmm…" Kitty purred, as she assessed the sleek shapes and textures surrounding her. The delicate aromas combined with the visual motif to create a thoroughly pleasant *feng shui*.

"I hope you like it," Gerald murmured. "I wanted to do something special tonight." With that, he drew a silver-wrapped square box from his suit pocket and placed it before Kitty's rectangular service plate. "I hope you like this, too."

Kitty took her time opening the neat package. She loved imagining what treat lay in store almost as much as actually seeing it. "Oh, Gerald," she cried, "it's exquisite, and I love it." She donned the South-Seas-pearl-surrounded-by-diamonds ring, happy that she had left her right ring finger unjeweled when she dressed for the evening. *It's so lovely being Mrs. Gerald Kelley.*

After the waiter took their drink order, Kitty remembered to mention the upcoming weekend at John E.'s and Caro's. She toyed with her wooden eating utensils as she considered the upcoming party particulars. Secretly, she was looking forward to seeing Preston Phillips again, even though she hated him for standing her friend Margo up at the altar all those years ago. She had always felt magnetically drawn to Preston, maybe because they were both tiger-ish in pursuing what they wanted from life. She could never disclose those thoughts to anyone, however, especially not within earshot of Gerald, who had an even more compelling reason to hate Preston.

"Let's not ruin this beautiful evening talking

about John E.'s birthday party," Gerald said. "As much as I love John E. and Caro, I can't bear to think of who will be at the party."

"Oh, we'll have a fine time catching up with everyone, and that farm is so big, you'll be able to avoid being next to the person you don't want to talk to. I won't even mention his name."

Gerald wiped his hand across his forehead, as if to erase the thought inside. "It'll be a miracle if one of us doesn't wring his neck in those thirty-six hours. Now, what would you like for *your* birthday dinner?"

৩৩৩

John E. Campbell stood in his farm's vast temperature-controlled wine cellar, pondering which of his lovelies to select for the party. Despite Caro's desire to keep the party low-key, he couldn't entertain friends without treating them to samples of the many fine wines he had collected. *Let's see*, he thought, *we're having an eight-course meal, so I can uncork thirty bottles from my seven favorite categories.* He ran his fingers along the rows of reds and whites, sparklings and stills. Mentally reviewing Caro's menu for the eight courses, John E. pulled appropriate bottles to make superb pairings.

Many of the bottles evoked memories of his years at Baker, McCall, and Brewster when Stan Baker had taken him under his tutelage as both fi-

23

nancier and wine collector. Others reminded him of his partnership with Marshall Winthrop, which had taken them both to southern France. In fact, many of John E.'s most prized bottles were purchased at the time when he and Marshall were growing their herbed cheese import business that had taken America by storm. *It's funny how a specific brand and year of wine can elicit so many memories,* John E. reminisced. He moved the chosen bottles to the "on deck" shelves. There, they would recline in all their glory until called upon to impress the palates of some of the most sophisticated tasters in the country.

ероско

Upstairs, Caro sat at the long soapstone counter, head in her hands, trying to figure out which couple to place into which bedroom. She and John E. had designed the house to accommodate large groups of family and friends, so space was not the problem.

Let's see, she reviewed mentally, *we've got a total of six couples and nine bedrooms. The Bakers will stay at their own farm, so that leaves five couples. Why is this so hard?* There were three bedrooms on each of the three floors. Like most of the country manors in this part of the country, there was no elevator and no bedroom on the first floor. That meant everyone would have to climb stairs to get to their accommodations. Her ruminations were interrupted by the ringing of her cell phone.

Caro wondered who might be calling her so early on a Sunday.

"I hope I'm not calling too early?" Libby Bloom said. "Les told me John E. usually goes riding early on Sundays."

"Oh, hi, Libby," Caro said, glad to put down her pencil and paper. "I was just going over the room accommodations for the party."

"Well, actually," Libby began, "that is why I am calling you."

Oh, no, Caroline thought. *If Les Bloom isn't at the party, John E. will be upset.* Having mentored Les at Baker, McCall, and having introduced him to Margo's sister, Libby Martin, John E. felt a patriarchal attachment to both Les and Libby. "I hope you haven't changed your minds about coming."

"Noooo," Libby said. "In fact, we're really looking forward to John E.'s birthday. It's just that we have a problem with Margo."

An unexpected chill climbed up Caro's spine. "What about Margo?"

"Well, you know she's recently gotten divorced. She's been staying with us. We thought it would be temporary, but when the time came to go back to Tuscany, she just couldn't. She's been looking at apartments in New York and Philadelphia." She took a long breath. "Anyway, she'll be here through the Holidays, and I don't feel right leaving her for the whole weekend, especially when she's so close to practically everyone coming to the party."

Caro took a deep breath. A thousand thoughts tumbled in her mind, but her patrician upbringing gave her the good sense to suppress most of them. "Of course, Margo should come. Everyone would love to catch up with her, and we have plenty of room."

"Thanks, Caro. I hate to impose, but I just didn't know what else to do."

"Don't worry about a thing," Caro replied. *Let me do the worrying*, she thought ruefully. *How ever will I do the room accommodations now?*

"See you in two weeks," Libby said. "The three of us will be there with bells on."

❧❧

It was probably fortunate Caro couldn't hear how the excitement in Libby's voice dropped as she hung up the phone.

"Now," Libby thought aloud, "how am I going to break this to Margo?"

CHAPTER 5

The Winthrops were the first to pull into Bucolia's circular driveway Friday evening, December thirteenth. Julia unfastened her seat belt and opened the passenger door even before Marshall had come to a full stop. She was dressed fashionably in a citron charmeuse silk blouse, brown country tweed skirt, and high-heel Manolo Blahniks, with an Hermes scarf to complete the casual-chic picture. Her shiny black hair had been recently processed and trimmed to highlight the aesthetic facial enhancements she had treated herself to last month. There was no doubt in her mind that she looked good. She wanted to impress their old friends for Marshall's sake, if not for her own.

❧❧❧

In the spacious kitchen, Caro was putting finishing touches on the fresh flower arrangements, one to go in each guest bedroom, as she observed the Winthrops' arrival from the kitchen window. The host, hostess, and farmhouse looked ready for the big weekend. The antique ceiling timbers and floor planks glowed. The pastoral scenes, Andrew Wyeth originals, warmed every room with the natural beauty of the outside brought in. The dining table was set with casual linen placemats and napkins, multiple wine glasses, and centerpieces made from fragrant heather and rosemary. A pine cone-scented fire completed the scene. Caro called to John E., her voice amplified by the intercom system, "First guests arriving, Julia and Marshall."

"Coming up the stairs right now," John E. called from the wine cellar, where he had been reviewing the wine selections with one of the caterers. He rushed up the stairs nimbly for his age, almost colliding with Butch, his all-purpose farm-hand-slash-butler, as he emerged in the kitchen. "No need to stop what you're doing. I'll help them with their luggage."

"Happy birthday, John E.," Julia sang, as she breezed through the front doorway. "Did you realize it's Friday, the thirteenth?" She double air-kissed John E.'s cheeks as she handed over her Tumi overnight bag.

"Lucky day for me," John E. replied. "I was born on Friday the thirteenth." He held out his right hand, grasping Marshall's elbow with his left, as they loosely, but warmly, hugged. "So glad you could make it."

Marshall inhaled the aroma of *osso bucco* and sighed, as he stepped in from the frigid outdoors. "We wouldn't miss it. It's not every day you get to celebrate a big birthday with best friends. And, be-sides, I'm looking forward to some good food, good wine, and good cigars. In fact, I brought you some Cubans as a birthday gift. Don't tell anyone where you got them."

"My lips are sealed."

Caro rushed in to welcome the guests. "Julia, Marshall, so glad you could make it. I was worried that the Fed might not be able to spare you, Mar-shall, with the Holidays coming up so soon."

"I wouldn't miss John E.'s birthday, no matter what the Fed had to say about it," Marshall said, easing his burly frame onto a priceless Chippendale chair.

"Nor I," Julia piped in. "I've wanted to see Bu-colia for a long time." She peered at the antiques in the built-in vitrine cabinet. "I want the full tour."

John E. switched on the surround-sound system to play the golden tones of Lena Horne, backed by Blue Mitchell, one of his favorite CDs, while Caro, flowers in hand, showed the Winthrops to their suite on the second floor. "I hope you don't mind sharing the floor with the Spillers. At least every couple has a bathroom of their own."

Julia ran her fingers over the custom-made quilts on the beds. "I love how you've coordinated this fabric with the rug and draperies. Aren't these the British country colors of Farrow and Ball paint?"

Caro was about to answer when she heard John E. opening the front door downstairs. The noisy chatter of Vicki and Leon Spiller drifted upward.

"Tour is on hold for now," Caro said, smiling at Julia and Marshall. "Make yourselves comfortable, and come downstairs whenever you are ready. We'll have drinks and hors d'oeuvres by the family room fireplace."

∽∽∽

Caro descended the staircase with perfect posture as she welcomed Vicki and then Leon. "Come on in out of the cold," she said warmly, happy the party was finally beginning. She just hoped everyone would put aside their old grudges and jealousies for John E.'s sake. *If it weren't for Preston, I wouldn't have to worry. But my mother would kill me if I didn't include her dear nephew. She might be the only one who can't see his faults.*

"Is Preston coming?" Vicki asked, as if she had read Caro's thoughts.

"Yes, of course," Caro answered. *And so it begins. What will they do when they learn that Margo is coming, too?*

Leon and Vicki exchanged glances, which did not go unnoticed by Caro.

"Would you like to see the rest of the house?" she offered, hoping her internal radar was overreacting. *I do so want this to be a fun and relaxing weekend for everyone, even my crazy cousin, Preston.*

Gerald and Kitty arrived next, wearing matching mink coats. Tiny snowflakes dotted their collars, as if they were shooting a scene for an old trendy magazine. These days it was rare to see a mink coat in public, and even rarer to see one on a man. Seemingly oblivious to this shift in reaction to public opinion, Gerald and Kitty glowed with ostentatiousness.

"Hey, Ger," John E. boomed, engaging Gerald with a three-part handshake. "Welcome to my humble getaway."

It had been at least four years since the Campbells and the Kelleys had been together in person, certainly not since Preston had edged Gerald out of becoming the president's choice for secretary of the treasury.

"Wuhoo," Gerald whistled, as he looked around at the décor, "ain't it grand to be rich?"

Both men laughed. It was liberating, John E. thought, not to have to be self-conscious about their mutual wealth and good fortune.

"Happy birthday, John E.," Kitty said, as she threw her arms around his neck. "Did you realize it's Friday the thirteenth?"

"No worries," John E. replied, seemingly for the umpteenth time. "Just lucky to have friends helping me celebrate this big one." He took both coats, struggling to make room for them in the entry-hall closet.

⌖

The smoothness of Lena's voice and Blue's trumpet was overpowered by the pitches and rhythms of female and male voices. The whole group had not been together since…perhaps since John E.'s sixtieth birthday bash five years ago. *Has it really been that long?* thought Caro. *The ladies certainly look no older. Even Vicki has maintained her young appearance, despite the tragedy she and Leon have endured. If only Preston and his first wife Laura hadn't come up with that sailboat birthday party for their son Peter.*

"How is Lexie?" Caro asked, referring to the Kelleys' thirty-nine year old daughter."

Kitty replied, glancing at Vicki. "Doing well. She lives in Boston, teaches at the Helen Keller School for the Blind now."

Caro realized too late that it might be painful for Vicki to hear about anyone's grown children. "Come on, ladies. Let's have some hors d'oeuvres and drinks."

⌖

Vicki turned away, tears forming in her eyes. She still couldn't hear about Lexie without thinking of precious, smart, considerate Tony, her baby, who had been killed at Peter Phillips' sixteenth birthday party years before. *I detest you, Preston Phillips. I hope you rot in hell for what you did to my kid.*

Fortunately, there was a powder room on the way to the family room. "I'll just duck in here for a minute," Vicki said, her voice shaky.

Inside the small, but well-appointed room, she examined her reflection in the mirror, pleased that her inner turmoil was not revealed. She patted her brown pageboy and ran her finger under each eye, making sure no mascara smudges betrayed her strong feelings.

"You can handle this," she said to her reflection. "You are surrounded by friends, and besides, there's a good stiff drink with your name on it in the next room."

⁊⁊⁊

At precisely that instant in the circular driveway, Preston Phillips emerged from his pristine Lamborghini, ignoring the pop in his right knee, and strode around to help Nicole from the passenger side.

"I'm really nervous about meeting your friends, Preston. I'll bet they won't like me very much," Nicole whined. She flipped her straight blonde hair behind her right shoulder as she patted her collar, diamond necklace, and Gucci purse strap into their proper places.

"They'll probably be jealous of your youth and good looks, baby, but don't worry. They are all too refined to show their feelings. They've been holding them back for so long, their feelings are probably mummified. Just be yourself, and you'll do fine." *Besides, the guys will probably lust over you so much, you'll be the hit of the party.* "Truth be told, I'm not too thrilled about this weekend, myself. These old farts wouldn't know a good time if one slapped them in the face. If it weren't for Caro's being my closest cousin, I wouldn't be here at all."

"Promise me one thing, Preston?" Nicole grabbed her husband's arm. "Promise me you won't leave me alone with those barracudas?"

"Wish I could make that promise, but if I know Caro and John E., there will be certain activities that'll keep us separated at times. Just try to avoid the fangs and claws, and if you don't feel like talking, look pretty and stay quiet."

Nicole unlatched from her husband's arm and bit her lip. Preston pushed her toward the front door. Conversation time was over.

❦

As Preston and Nicole entered the house, the friendly chatter around the fireplace stopped abruptly, as if an invisible conductor had signaled for silence. Simultaneously, the Thelonius Monk piece on the stereo entered a quieter movement.

Marshall sat up straighter as he recognized the voice of his childhood neighbor and former best friend. His normally affable features took on a coldness, his gray eyes fixed on his highball glass, his mouth a thin, wide line.

He watched, as seemingly oblivious to the indoor change of climate, Caro rushed over to embrace Preston and meet his new wife. "Come on in, Preston. And you must be Nicole," she said in her most welcoming voice. "We're so glad you could come. Everyone's visiting in the family room, so take off your coats and come on in.

Marshall stared out the window at the gray landscape. The wind had kicked up, and the flurries had become full-fledged flakes. He tried to compose himself, but as Preston entered the room, all Marshall could think was that Preston looked like a coral snake, full of eye-appeal, but deadly.

I can hardly bear to be in the same room with him.

Preston smiled, showing dimples and the new veneers he had spent time and money acquiring. He greeted everyone as if there hadn't been a shred of animosity, jealousy, greed or tragedy in their shared past. "Hi, Everyone. This is my wife, Nicole. I've told her all about you, and she's been looking forward to meeting my old friends."

If you told her the truth, Marshall said silently, *she wouldn't even have dared to come. Boy, she looks like a cheerleader. If she only knew what that old bastard is really like, she'd dump him, for sure.*

A caterer entered with a tray of hot canapés, as the bartender took more drink orders. Preston settled into a chair by the window, framed by the now thickly falling snow. Nicole perched on the chair's arm, her shiny blonde hair swinging behind her cashmere-clad shoulder.

Preston looked around at the group. "So, how's everybody doing? Are we still all in the one-percent club?"

How obnoxious, Marshall thought. *Especially after you convinced my parents to let you tie up their money while I was in Viet Nam. If I hadn't gone into business with John E., I'd still be treading water financially, thanks to you.* "Preston, must you start every conversation with a reference to money? People like you are the ones who give one-percenters a bad name."

"Okay, Marshall." Preston switched topics. "How's your golf game?"

"Still holding onto my single-digit handicap. Played Pebble Beach in October. Sudden death playoff on the eighteenth hole," Marshall replied.

"Sudden death?" Preston repeated. "That's one phrase I just hate to think about."

ოჳღ

"Are all the guests here?" Vicki asked, as she plucked another brie bag from the tray of hors d'oeuvres. The smooth texture of the warm cheese and light crust in her mouth comforted her. It wasn't easy to sit in the same room with Preston Phillips. If she hadn't had that phone call from Julia, she might have declined the invitation.

"Actually, no," Caroline replied, twisting her linen cocktail napkin in her lap. "Stan and Andrea Baker will be coming from their farm for dinner." She paused, as if considering not answering further, then took a breath and spoke quickly. "John's protégé Les Bloom and his wife Libby are coming, and Libby is bringing her sister—"

"Margo? Margo Martin is coming here?" Vicki gasped. Her eyes involuntarily slid toward Preston, wondering whether he had heard this news. She was rewarded by the slightest flinch in Preston's handsome face.

"I thought Margo lived in Italy," Kitty Kelley piped up, her plumped lips turning up at the corners.

❧❧❧

Nicole leaned closer to Preston, adjusting her sweater to reveal a glimpse of her diamond-studded navel, and whispered, "Who is Margo?"

Kitty leaned forward, as if to eavesdrop on Preston's answer to the question.

"An old college friend of Caro's, someone I dated years ago." Preston picked at an invisible speck on his sweater.

Oh, no, not another one, thought Nicole. *It's already obvious that Kitty Kelley is hanging on his every word. Is there no end to the list of women who covet my husband?*

෨෨෨

Caro diverted the flow of conversation. "I can't imagine what is taking them so long to get here unless it's the snow. And the *osso bucco* is almost ready. I know—why don't we all go up to our rooms and freshen up a bit before dinner?"

"Good idea," John E. agreed, standing to stretch his long legs.

Relieved to have changed the subject from the impending arrival of Margo, Caro reviewed the assigned sleeping arrangements aloud: "The Winthrops and Spillers will occupy two bedrooms on the second floor, where our bedroom is. The Blooms, Margo, and the Kelleys will stay on the third floor, and the newlyweds, Preston and Nicole, will be on the fourth floor. The Bakers, of course, will stay at their own farm." Briefly, Caro envied them.

As the group gingerly climbed the stairs, Caro pointed out the various rooms. Though the farmhouse was newly constructed, the building materials and features were antiques, repurposed to give the grandeur of old money. The effect was a modern house with the charm and luster of an old country manor.

Kitty nudged Gerald as they turned a corner in the stairway. "Look at that brass horse door stop. It adds a perfect touch to the décor."

Gerald grunted, trying to suppress the fact that he was short of breath from climbing so many stairs. "Glad *we're* not on the fourth floor," he replied.

☙❦❧

"Knock, knock, we're here," came a voice from the entry hall.

"Anybody home?" Les Bloom looked about as he stamped his feet on the welcome mat and brushed snow from his Burberry.

The remaining five guests entered, unbidden, glad for the warmth and blended aromas of meat, garlic, and wine that greeted them just before the butler appeared from the kitchen to take their coats.

John and Caro rushed down the stairs in tandem. "I was just starting to worry about you," Caro said to Libby. She turned to Margo, her eyes taking in Margo's thick auburn hair and smooth complexion. She gave her a big hug. "Margo, you look marvelous."

"You, too, Caro. You never change."

The Bakers waited at the rear of the ladies' reun-

39

ion, having just seen John E. and Caroline the previous weekend.

"The roads are really slick out there," Les said. "My car was skidding all over."

"So we saw these kids on our way over," Stan said, pointing to Les and his crew. "We motioned for them to leave their car at our place and ride over with us in the van. I don't think anyone will be getting in or out of here without some serious snow plowing for the next few hours."

"Well, nobody's going anywhere for a while, anyway," John E. said. "Now my birthday celebration is complete."

The Spillers were heading down the stairs, followed by the Kelleys and the rest.

Les nudged John E. "Hey, did you realize it's Friday the thirteenth?"

"Yeah," John E. said, tired of explaining this was a good luck day for him. "Let the good times roll."

၈ၣ၄ၣ

Margo Martin Rinaldi shivered inside her sable jacket. She stamped her leather-booted feet on the entry hall rug, trying to lose the snow. It wasn't the weather that was making her cold, though. She needed to get her quivering under control immediately, before she faced Preston. The forty years since their last interaction melted away in remembered emotions. The conflicting feelings churned inside her belly like fire and ice. Love and hate.

I shouldn't have come, she thought, almost saying this aloud. *How did I ever think I could bear to see Preston again?*

Libby grabbed her older sister's hand. Margo lifted her youthful-looking chin, exerting the strong will that was a Martin family trait. *Libby's right. I'm going to make Preston Phillips regret the choice he made all those years ago. If I get my way, he'll be very sorry indeed.*

As Margo entered the family room, Julia and Kitty rushed to greet her, and the men rose to their feet. A shift in atmosphere, an electrical jolt, shook the dynamics of the group. The flash of Margo's magnetic asymmetrical grin and the careless toss of her auburn locks covered her insecurities. *On with the show*, she thought bravely.

On the opposite side of the room, Preston looked as though his insides were curling. "Hello, Margo," he managed to say, when she finally made eye contact with him.

"Why, Preston," Margo replied with more aplomb than she felt. "You finally show up, after all these years."

Dammit, she thought. *He still has those piercing eyes and that thick dark hair. And those dimples.* She couldn't bear to hold his gaze for one more second. She turned to Nicole, whose arm was draped behind the chair where Preston had been sitting, and extended her hand. "I'm Margo Rinaldi."

"Nicole Phillips," said Preston's young wife.

Oh, no, groaned Margo to herself. *If I didn't know better, I would think this girl is Preston's granddaughter, not his wife.* It was all Margo could do to nod and smile at Nicole and glide over to the tray of dirty martinis on the sofa table. "After all the traveling in snow and ice, I think a drink is just what I need," she announced to no one in particular. "Cheers, everybody!"

Just then, the butler sounded the golden notes of the dinner chime, and Caro beckoned everyone into the dining room. "Dinner is served. Sit wherever you'd like tonight—no place cards."

Chapter 6

Preston remained quiet as the birthday toasts began. He wasn't feeling the jolly mood, and he could tell Nicole wasn't either.

"Here's to us," John E. exclaimed, raising his wine glass high from the head of the long dining table. "We've earned it, we've got it, so let's enjoy it while we can."

"Happy birthday, John E.," came the reply of several voices, male and female.

The Batard Montrachet 1992 flowed in an endless stream, bottle after bottle, as the birthday celebrants smiled and ate and talked about old times. The *osso bucco* was perfect, tender and with just the right amount of garlic and rosemary.

"First speech." Stan Baker rose at his place. His age, combined with the large amount of wine he had imbibed, made him unsteady. Still, he was a commanding presence among this group. In many ways, educators like Stan had paved the way for all of their careers. "I've known John E. since he was a young, innocent guy, taking on his first classroom at Princeton. He's a good man, colleague, and friend. I couldn't care more for him if he were my own son. Many happy returns, my man."

"Hear, hear." The sound of wine glasses being touched punctuated Stan's words. Everyone took another sip.

John E. nodded thanks to Stan and smiled at Andrea, who seemed unusually quiet.

Marshall looked around before standing up. "I guess I'll go next. Well, John E., we've come a long way since the cheese business, and I'm glad we've come out on top, despite certain setbacks." He paused to glare at Preston. "It's been a great ride, Buddy. Here's wishing you sixty-five more good years. And, oh, yeah, thanks to Caro, too, for treating us to this fabulous weekend in your world."

Kitty leaned over to whisper to Gerald, revealing cleavage impossibly suntanned for the season. Gerald nodded and patted her on the shoulder. She stood up in a single, fluid motion, moving her napkin from her lap to the right of her plate. "Well, John E.," she began, "this shouldn't be an all-male tribute to you. I've known you at least as long as Stan and Marshall. I met you freshman year when you were dating Caro, and I—" She paused a moment to look around the room, her eyes landing fleetingly on Preston. "—I was Caro's pledge sister. I must say, you and Caro were the perfect couple then, as now. Gerald and I wish you a happy birthday, and we brought you a little something as a token of our good wishes." Kitty handed over a small package wrapped in bronze paper and bow.

John E. opened the box and laughed. He held up the Sterling silver money clip for everyone to admire. "Thanks, guys. I hope I'll always keep it full."

"I'll drink to that," said Les, rising from his seat as Kitty took hers. "I think I'm the newcomer in this group," he said, looking around and perhaps realizing that, in fact, Nicole Phillips was. "But my respect and friendship for you, John E., is no less. You were the best teacher I ever had, and the best mentor, too. If it hadn't been for your guidance, I never would have gone so far in my career, and I wouldn't have met Libby, either." He touched Libby's elbow to encourage her to stand by his side, which she did. "This has probably made me more sentimental than normal, but I want to thank you from the bottom of my heart for all you have done for Libby and me." Libby nodded, her eyes glistening in the candlelight. "I hope we will be together for many more of your birthdays, all of us."

Libby added, "And Les and I have an announcement to make. We are expecting a baby in July. It took us awhile to embrace the idea of parenting, but we're excited. Another thing that would never have happened if you hadn't introduced us, John E."

"Hey," Preston interjected, misunderstanding Libby's remark and leering at his host. "I thought you were a little old to be responsible for baby-making, John E."

Libby glared at Preston, ignoring his joke. Her look may have said that *he* was a little old to be marrying a young kid like Nicole.

John E. congratulated Libby and Les. "How nice that the Blooms are blooming. Let's drink to a happy and healthy baby." Only then did he notice Libby was drinking only water.

All eyes turned toward Vicki and Leon. Vicki was picking at her dinner, her eyes glazed, and eyelids half closed. She was in no condition for speech-making. Leon ran his fingers through his still-thick salt-and-pepper hair and stood at his place. "Vicki and I are saving our toast for tomorrow night. Our gift, too. It's something specially made for everyone to enjoy. Meanwhile, cheers to you, John E."

"Good idea, Leon," Preston called out more loudly than necessary. "I'll save my speech for tomorrow night, too."

To be honest, Preston was starting to feel really uncomfortable, staring at Margo's timeless beauty and thinking of how things might have been different if he hadn't been so stupid as to get involved with her best friend before their wedding. He was almost too distracted to follow the conversation. As he looked around the table and listened to the heartfelt tributes to his host, he realized that aside from Cousin Caro and Wife Nicole, there was no one whom he could call "friend."

John E. interrupted by raising an issue near and

dear to the hearts of everyone at the table. "Well, we have quite a financial think tank here. What do you folks think about the politicians' talk? First, we had Occupy Wall Street then income inequality and now dynastic wealth."

Everyone started to talk at once, words and phrases of indignation, fury, and outrage competing for dominance in staccato.

At last, there was something it seemed everyone could agree on.

ᴄᴐᴄᴐ

While Marshall and Gerald were expounding upon the largely unappreciated contributions the wealthy had made to this country, Margo quietly excused herself from the table. She headed for the second floor, where she could escape from the very personal tension she was feeling from being in the room with Preston. Was it her imagination, or had Preston been staring at her? As much as she told herself she hated his guts, she couldn't help thinking of how she had once adored him, had wanted nothing more than to feel his strong body next to hers. *I must stop thinking this way*, she reprimanded herself. *Preston is evil, and I won't be fooled by his charisma ever again! Besides, he is married, married, married—to that little girl with puppy-dog eyes.*

ᴄᴐᴄᴐ

Preston saw this opportunity to have a moment alone with Margo and wondered whether he should risk it. He wasn't so worried about Nicole. She was so enamored of him, he doubted she would even notice, or if she did, she would be too afraid to disrupt the fragile balance of their barely established marital rhythm. He wasn't worried about what the guys would think. He didn't care a whit about any of them anyway, and he knew the feeling was mutual.

No, the person he was most afraid of was Margo, herself. He knew he had wounded her deeply, and he couldn't predict what her reaction would be if he confronted her alone, even to apologize. His eyes had been drawn all night to Margo's face and body, her demeanor. Her attractiveness had only multiplied with age. His desire to tell her how much he regretted having hurt her welled up inside of him like a bitter syrup, heated to a slow boil. *Hell*, he thought, *if I don't go speak to her, I'll never forgive myself.*

"Excuse me," Preston mumbled a few minutes after Margo left the room. "I've got to get my pills. Be right back."

He squeezed Nicole's thigh as he rose from the table. It felt good to stand up after sitting so long. He headed for the staircase, ignoring the warnings from his right knee and his left brain.

꩜꩜꩜

Nicole remained at the table, an artificially cheerful smile glued to her face. She flicked her hair between her fingers, mentally counting the minutes Preston and that Rinaldi woman were away from the table. She might be young, but she wasn't inexperienced in the ways of men and women, and there had been some serious eye exchanges between Margo and Preston all night. Not that it was flirting—it was more worrisome than that. The two of them looked as though they were both miserable. Whether it was with love or hate, she wasn't sure, but the intensity of their feelings was all too apparent, and alarms were clanging in her head. *I'll be damned if I'm going to let that old woman get between my husband and me,* Nicole said silently. *I've worked too hard to become Mrs. Preston Phillips, and Mrs. Preston Phillips I will stay!*

Chapter 7

It was a huge relief to adjourn the dinner party after hours of food and drink and sometimes tense conversation. Andrea and Stan left for their neighboring farm, and, one by one, couples thanked their hosts and trudged upstairs to their assigned accommodations. As the party guests settled into their rooms and suites, the internal and external dialogue was intense. The very air in the house crackled. The long evening of toasts and conversation, instead of relaxing everyone, had seemed to spark annoyances and petty arguments, along with jealousies and worries. The sweet-smelling toiletries and plush downy bed coverings did nothing to assuage these.

Gerald, for example, was really annoyed with Kitty. "What is it with you, anyway, Kitty?" he muttered, as he rinsed his mouth of toothpaste. "I saw you looking at Preston all night. If I didn't know better, I'd think you have a crush on him, just like every other female in America."

Kitty put down her moisturizer and glowered. "Don't be ridiculous, Gerald." Her voice was low and even. "I think you just haven't gotten over

Preston's acing you out of your dream job. Not that I blame you for resenting that."

She patted the fluffy comforter next to her. "Let's go to bed. I'm sure you'll feel better tomorrow morning."

"I'll never feel better about Preston Phillips. He is a hundred percent slimeball. I won't feel better about him until he is six feet under."

"Keep your voice down, Gerald. Margo is right next to us."

"I don't give a damn if she hears me. She has an even better reason to hate the guy." With this, Gerald slipped, naked, into the queen-sized bed and put his arm over Kitty's silk-covered hip. "What d'you say we forget about Preston and concentrate on us?"

Kitty raised her negligee and slipped it over her head then snuggled into Gerald's embrace. Her soft reply was only one word, "Meow."

ᥱᤁᥱᤁ

Like the Kelleys, the Winthrops were having a fretful conversation. "That Preston," Marshall ranted, careful to modulate his baritone voice so only Julia could hear. "Did you see how that asshole throws around his money and power? All he talks about is money this, money that! I can't wait for him to be out of my life once and for all."

"We'll never get back all of those sleepless

51

nights when he had your parents' money tied up out of reach," Julia replied.

"Screwing me out of *my* parents' money. I'll never forgive him."

"Nor should you. Preston is the type of guy who will shake your hand and leave you with no fingers. It's time he paid for what he's done to you, to us, to Margo, and how about the poor Spillers?"

"Speaking of paying, where did you put the cigars?" Marshall whispered.

"Locked in the portable humidor."

"Good thinking, Julia." Marshall leaned over to kiss his wife on the lips. "Tomorrow should be a very eventful day. Let's see if we can get some sleep."

"No amyl nitrate tonight, dear?" Julia asked.

"No, let's save it for tomorrow night. I'm tired."

"Okay, I have a little headache, anyway."

Then as if on cue, Julia and Marshall turned toward the night tables on either side of the bed and donned their CPAP machine masks, and Marshall clicked off the lamp.

ତ୍ରତ୍ର

In the bedroom next to the Winthrops, Leon was helping Vicki undress for bed. Propped against the headboard, Vicki slumped, muttering four-letter epithets. Leon pulled on Vicki's sleeves, one at a time, until her elbows escaped the confines of her soft sweater. "I hate him. Hate, hate him." Her head shook drunkenly from side to side, perspiration glistening on her forehead.

"I know you do," Leon said, gently taking the sweater over her head. "But no amount of hate is going to bring Tony back."

"Don't tell me yer havin' second thoughts." Vicki smeared her mascara as she rubbed her eyes.

"No, Vicki. I hate him as much as you do. Maybe more." Leon considered his feelings, as he said this. He blamed Preston for the loss of his son, just as Vicki did, but he also blamed him for changing Vicki, and their lives, forever.

"That's good." And with that, Vicki passed out on the soft down comforter, leaving Leon alone with his dark thoughts.

※※※

Although Libby had not had any alcoholic drinks, her pregnancy at age forty-two was making her extraordinarily tired, and a little crabby, to boot. She didn't want to spoil the party for Les, Margo, or especially Caro and John E., but it wasn't easy listening to all of the one-percenters and their egotistical banter. She and Margo had always been rich. Their grandfather, Sterling Martin the first, had founded what had become the largest private banking enterprise in the country. Libby knew people envied her name, her wealth, her place in society, but few knew of the downsides that she had suffered from all three. Even as a young child, her life had never been hers to live. She was forced into friendships with "the right people," events she "must attend," clothes and accessories that "made the right statement," and the list went on and on. The baby of the family by many years, she was raised by nannies and given all of the material things she could dream of. Her sister Margo was at Princeton and hanging around with Caro, Julia, and Kitty when she was born. *I've had a bellyful of rich people,* she thought. *With all of the intelligence and wisdom at the dining table tonight, these people could join forces and save the world, but what do they talk about? Themselves!*

"What's the matter, Libby?" Les asked. "I can tell by the set of your eyebrows you're upset."

"Nothing, really. It's just hard for me to sit through one night of these old farts. I don't know if I can stand a whole weekend. And, I'm really worried about Margo. It's putting a big strain on her to be around Preston, and I can tell it's getting to her. Maybe we shouldn't have come."

"Come on, Libby. We've talked about this a hundred times. We owe it to John E. and Caro to be here for his birthday. You don't have to put up with anything you don't want to. This is a big farm. We can just excuse ourselves and go for a walk any time you feel overwhelmed. You don't want to upset the baby by working yourself up. Let's just try to get some sleep now."

"Okay, Les, but promise me one thing. That we won't become as arrogant and selfish as these guys when we're their age."

"Promise. And neither will our baby."

ﾟ◞ﾟ◞

Alone on the fourth floor, Mr. and Mrs. Preston Phillips were having a marital spat. Having no clue that he had behaved boorishly throughout the evening, Preston had climbed the three flights of stairs feeling good about himself. He was sure Margo still had feelings for him, and he had to admit, he was still attracted to her. He had enjoyed the attention of Kitty Kelley, too. *I've still got what it takes to attract a woman,* he thought with a grin. *And I rather enjoy aggravating the men, as well.*

"What are you smiling at?" Nicole asked.

Her tone pierced Preston's reverie. He had been expecting her to fall right into his arms. "What do you mean?"

"Don't play innocent with me, Preston. I've been watching you with your *friends* all night. Frankly, I think you've made a fool of yourself."

"And how do you think I've made a fool of myself, Miss Expert? A few months of marriage and you think you know me and my friends that well?"

"Totally. I know enough to know there's something going on between you and that Margo, and the others either detest you or barely tolerate you. I may not have been around for the back story, but I'm not blind." Nicole sat at the dressing table and stared at her husband in the mirror.

Preston returned her stare in the mirror, aiming for sincerity. "There's nothing going on with Margo and me. I haven't seen her in forty years, for God's sake."

"Oh, yeah. Then what were you two doing for fifteen minutes when you both went upstairs?"

Preston turned away from the mirror, pacing. "Maybe we shouldn't have come this weekend. I didn't mean to upset you."

"Answer my question. What were you and Margo doing?" Nicole's voice rose in pitch, as if she were about to cry.

"Keep your voice down. We weren't *doing* anything. We were talking. We are old friends."

"You could talk to your old friends all night long, right in front of everyone. You didn't have to leave the table to follow that old hag. I asked you not to leave me alone with these people, but I never dreamed you would go off pussy-chasing. I'm mortified." She stood and paced around the room, brandishing her hairbrush.

"I'm not going to apologize to you, Nicole, because I didn't do anything wrong. I love you, and I married you. End of story. Now let's go to bed."

"Don't think this is the end of this discussion,

Preston. If you do one more thing to upset me this weekend, you'll live to regret it." Nicole's voice trailed off at the end of the threat, as Preston grabbed her from behind, both hands sliding smoothly into the front of her panties. Annoyed as she was with him, her first impulse was to push her husband away. On the other hand, this was how she and Preston communicated best. She moved against him, signaling that the argument was over, and the making up was underway. *Let them eat their hearts out,* she thought. *Preston Phillips belongs to me.*

"Mmmph," Preston groaned into her ear, feeling the full effect of the blue pill he had taken earlier. "Don't worry. You're the only woman I need, baby."

∽∾∽

Left alone in her bedroom on the second floor, Margo looked out the window at the snowy landscape, her thoughts in turmoil. She didn't know what she had expected when she agreed to accompany Libby to this party, but she never expected this. Seeing Preston, hearing his voice, it cut through the layers of insulation she had protected herself with all of these years. While married to Roberto, it was easy to bury the bad memories of Preston's abandonment, but since divorcing Roberto, Margo was feeling vulnerable and lonely. In this state, seeing Preston, it felt as if the small pilot light in her deepest recesses had ignited into full flame.

It's his confidence, she decided. *More than his looks or his words. He is so sure of himself, so comfortable in his skin, that he intrudes into my skin, my body, my mind, taking them over completely. It's dangerous. I simply cannot let myself be dazzled by his charms again*

Margo punched her pillow and placed it where she thought it would soothe her into slumber, but this was a night that sleep would elude her. *I never expected Preston to follow me upstairs. And apologize so earnestly. And try to assert himself so urgently back into my life.* On the one hand, her mental filters were ready to send Preston's words to the spam folder. On the other hand, his flattery, his attention—it was all so overwhelming. *Admit it, Margo,* she thought miserably, *you still want him.*

"No, You. Don't," she blurted aloud. Her head was aching with the sound of warning bells so loud it was surprising the whole house couldn't hear them.

"You okay?" Libby called from across the shared bathroom.

"Yeah, fine, baby sister. I'll be just fine."

Chapter 8

The next morning the snow had ceased, and what remained had created a fairyland of Bucolia. The ground was sparkling from the early rays of the sun, and the white carpet erased any hint of imperfection in the landscape. The tree branches and stables were etched with white, as if a confectioner had outlined them with sugar frosting.

Inside, the birthday party guests awoke to smells of coffee, eggs, and Canadian bacon from the kitchen. One or two at a time, starting with Nicole and Preston, they drifted downstairs to re-convene, eat, and make plans for the day. Kitty and Caro laughed as Margo joined the group wearing the same heather tweed color from the Ralph Lauren collection they both had on. "Great minds shop alike," Margo said. "Shall I go upstairs and change clothes?"

Vicki and Leon were the last to come downstairs. Neither looked as if they had slept well. Vicki's expensive makeup worked wonders on minimizing the shadows beneath her eyes, but the puffiness from too much alcohol defied coverage. Leon poured two mugs of black coffee and handed one to Vicki, as he offered her the chair at the table next to Julia. "I'll sit at the counter," he said, perching his designer jeans-clad bottom next to Nicole. "How're the eggs?" he asked.

"Fine," Nicole answered, lost in thoughts about last night. She pushed her eggs around on her plate.

John E. suggested a morning ride for anyone who wanted to see the farm on horseback. He stabled more than a dozen horses to choose from, ranging in ages from three to eight, both mares and geldings. Neither Marshall, Gerald, Les, nor Leon considered themselves equestrians, at least not to the degree that John E. and Stan Baker did, but they were all game to enjoy a few hours of riding in the brisk, clean air at the farm. They all had brought riding clothes just in case.

"How about you ladies?" John E. asked, pausing to sip from his steaming coffee mug. "We have some smooth riders, and I know Andrea will be joining us on the trails."

Caro interrupted. "Ladies, don't feel you have to go horseback riding. I'll be doing some shopping in Kennett Square this morning, and I'd be glad to take any of you with me. There are some great antique stores and art galleries, as well as unique gift shops. We'll all meet for lunch at Longwood Gardens, regardless of what you choose to do this morning."

"I don't think I should go horseback riding," Libby said, touching her abdomen. "My doctor told me to be careful with high impact sports during the first trimester."

"I'll stay with you and Libby," said Margo.

"Me, too," said Julia. "It will give us a chance to catch up."

"Well, I'm not going to miss out on the college nostalgia trip," said Kitty, glancing at Gerald.

Everyone looked at Nicole to see what she would choose, since she seemed not to fit into either group. Panic flickered across her face as she seemed to consider, but finally, she put her arm through Preston's. "I'll go riding."

ↃↄↃↄↃↄ

The day couldn't have been more perfect. The group of seven from the farmhouse joined up with the Bakers, and the nine riders and their mounts made a striking picture as they trotted on the wintry landscape. The horses stepped lively, seeming as happy as the people to breathe the clean air and hear the rhythmic clopping of horseshoes on fresh snow. The trail was picturesque with evergreens and snow-laden tree branches on either side.

Andrea, looking almost regal in her DJ Bennett riding clothes, was enjoying her time with Mustafa, her favorite horse. She was so glad to have escaped Bucolia last night after the heavy meal and conversation. She would never say anything to Stan about his colleagues, but she found the men tiresome and the women insipid. *It's not that I'm a snob,* she argued with herself, *but these people really get on my nerves. Instead of being grateful for all they have, they vie for attention like third-graders trying to win the spelling bee. And, we get to enjoy another round of it again tonight.*

"Andrea," Nicole called out, interrupting her thoughts, "does it seem like my horse is having trouble?"

The two women had fallen behind the men. Nicole's horse, Sally Ride, was bringing up the rear and trotting with a slightly jerky side-to-side motion.

Andrea circled back. She could tell Sally Ride was uncomfortable. This was the horse Caro usually rode when she and Andrea went out together, so Andrea was quite familiar with her gait. "I think we'd better go back to the stables. We can get a different horse for you to ride today."

"Won't I fall behind Preston, though?" Nicole said, her voice a bit shaky.

"She's not acting the way she usually does," Andrea warned. "I'd take her back if I were you."

Nicole tried calling out to Preston, but the men had galloped too far ahead, and her voice vanished in the cold air. "Let's try to catch up to the guys," she said, the sound of panic cutting through her words. "I don't know why Preston let his horse get so far ahead of us."

Sally Ride had slowed to a near halt, and Mustafa was stamping his front hooves, eager to go ahead on the trail.

Despite her desire to let the horse go full throttle, Andrea's better judgment said Nicole shouldn't be left alone with a skittish horse. "Listen," she said. "The men are a good quarter mile ahead of us. We'll never catch up to them now. Let's go back and get another horse for you, and then we can all have a good ride."

As Nicole was deciding what to do, a pair of deer pranced into the path from a clump of bushes, startling both horses and riders. Sally Ride let forth a neighing shriek and reared, tossing Nicole onto the packed snow. Oblivious to the havoc she had wreaked, the horse began to gallop back toward the stables with the reins flying out behind her.

Nicole's scream of pain sliced the air.

Andrea calmed Mustafa and dismounted, adrenalin guiding her actions. She tied the horse's reins to a tree and rushed to Nicole's side. Andrea could tell from the torsion of Nicole's booted ankle that it was broken. She must have twisted it in the stirrup as she was thrown from the horse. Her body was curled in pain, her right shoulder and hip having borne the brunt of the fall, as well.

"You'll be okay," Andrea said to calm Nicole, hoping that this was true. Nicole was gasping and sobbing uncontrollably. Andrea pulled her cell phone from her jacket pocket and quickly called her stable manager. "A guest has been thrown from her horse. We're in the northeast quadrant of the Campbells' trails, several yards from the large sycamore trees. Call the paramedics, please. And is there someone who can come to take Mustafa back to the stables for me?"

Her next call was to Stan. She had no way of knowing Preston's phone number, and asking Nicole didn't seem to be a good option. Stan could notify Preston and send him back to help his wife. Her heart beat in her ears as Andrea listened to the phone ringing. After five rings, Stan's voicemail message came on, and Andrea hung up. Hopefully, Stan would see her missed call and call back. Andrea knew better than to try to move Nicole. Instead, she tried to comfort her. She crouched next to her, moving bits of dead foliage and dirty ice from her hair and mouth, murmuring words, hoping help would come soon. *Surely the guys have noticed by now that we aren't following them on the trail,* she thought. *Preston should be here with Nicole, not me.*

"Take a deep breath," Andrea coached, remembering her Lamaze from years ago. Nicole was gulping small bits of air at such a rapid rate that Andrea feared she would lose consciousness. "Deep breath," she repeated.

Soon the sobs softened to moans, and Nicole stopped hyperventilating. Meanwhile, her right ankle was swelling visibly through the soft leather of her boot. Andrea knew the boot should come off, would likely have to be cut off, but she would not dare to remove it.

What seemed like an eternity was only fifteen minutes, when two paramedics and Andrea's stable manager came into view in an all-terrain vehicle. The stable manager had met the paramedics at the nearest road and transported them to the trail in the Bakers' farm vehicle. The truck scrunched to a halt several yards from the women.

"Thank you, Jeff," Andrea cried with relief.

The paramedics jumped out and ran over to minister to Nicole, examining her pupils and taking her blood pressure.

Jeff, the stable manager, took Andrea's arm by the elbow, asking if she was okay, as he moved to untie Mustafa's reins. He patted the faithful horse.

"I'm fine," Andrea replied, "but I think Mrs. Phillips may have a broken ankle. Her horse was spooked by some deer, threw her, and took off. The mare is probably back at the Campbells' by now."

Andrea startled as Nicole howled, "Ohhh, ohhh, ow. You're killing me." The paramedics were moving her to a stretcher, and the slightest jostle drew fresh screams. "Call Preston," she shrieked. "I need Preston."

"I'll take care of calling her husband," Andrea offered. "You can ride Mustafa back home," she said to Jeff, "and I'll go in the truck with the paramedics and Mrs. Phillips." She dashed back to Nicole, finding a way to remove the cell phone from

Nicole's back pants pocket without interfering with the paramedics' work.

Before she could make the call, the sound of horses' hooves distracted her. *That will be Stan and the rest of the guys,* she dared to hope. As she looked up through the bare branches of the trees, she exhaled, tears stinging her eyes.

"Uh oh, there's been an accident," she heard Stan call out loud. "Preston, it's Nicole."

∽∾∽

Within seconds, the seven men galloped to the spot, halted their horses, and dismounted. Preston ran over to Nicole, who was being carried on the stretcher to the truck, her boot cut from her foot, and her right side supported by ice packs.

"Preston," she cried. "I need you, Preston."

"It's going to be all right, baby," Preston answered, trying to hide his annoyance. *I should have known better than to bring Nicole out here. She doesn't know anything about riding a horse,* he thought. *And I don't do well with 'needy.'* "We'll get you to the hospital, and they'll fix you up."

"I think I'm going to pass out," Nicole whined. "It really, really hurts."

"You need to be strong, Nicole. For your own good."

Andrea walked alongside the stretcher. "I'll go with you to the hospital. I know most of the staff there, and you'll be well taken care of."

John E., perhaps feeling that his birthday celebration was crumbling before his eyes, took charge. "Men, let's ride back to my stables, and I'll rush Preston to the hospital. If we hurry, we can get there almost as fast as the ambulance. Then the rest of us will meet up with the ladies and take it from there." As he mounted his gelding, he muttered aloud, "There goes my party. Unless it's a simple fracture, this'll put a damper on the rest of the weekend."

CHAPTER 9

After two hours of intense shopping in the high end antique stores, the ladies had been glad to get off their feet at 1906, the restaurant at Longwood Gardens. "Mmm, it smells wonderful in here," Caro commented, "cilantro, I believe. I must be hungry after all that shopping."

Julia rubbed her foot. "Remind me not to wear high heels next time."

"Right, and remind me not to wear clothes at all," Caro said, laughing. "You never set foot out of your house without high heels, Miss New York."

"Remember when you did that Miss New York parody at our rehearsal dinner?" Kitty reminded Julia. "I don't think I've ever laughed so hard."

Julia re-crossed her long legs, her black Christian Louboutin pump hanging daintily from her instep. "Well, it lightened up the tension between you and Gerald's mother at the time. I remember that."

Kitty rolled her eyes and examined her five-carat diamond ring. "I think that may have been the first time Gerald's mother realized that I was a real human being with nice friends and a sense of humor and not just a gold digger with hooks into her baby."

"How is Gerald's mother, by the way?" asked Vicki.

"Amazingly well, living in Sarasota with her third husband. Each time she's married, she's increased her portfolio, so who turned out to be the gold digger, I ask you?"

"Speaking of gold diggers, do you think that's why Nicole married Preston?" Julia asked.

"Let's not even go there," Libby said quickly, glancing at Margo.

"Oh, I almost forgot," Caro said, as she dug into her Louis Vuitton shopping bag. "I bought a little baby gift for you, Libby." She pulled out a square package with a pompon of frizzy yellow ribbon on top.

"How thoughtful," Libby said. She opened the gift wrapping to find a Sterling silver drinking cup. "Baby Bloom's first gift. Pretty exciting to picture our baby drinking from it."

"What else did everyone buy this morning?" Margo asked. The ladies had shipped most of their purchases home, so the "show and tell" became just a "tell."

For the next few minutes, everyone enumerated their purchases, everyone but Vicki, who pasted a smile on her face and listened absent-mindedly, gazing out the windows at the winter landscape.

"I wonder what's taking the men so long," Caro

interjected, looking at her Rolex for the third time in five minutes. "They were supposed to meet us here at one." The ladies were working on their second round of drinks, more than they usually allowed themselves at lunchtime.

"They'll probably be here any minute," Margo said. She was rather enjoying this time with just the girls. She felt a bit sorry for Libby, though, having to hang out with the older women, and probably not enjoying the nostalgic memories. *She probably would have been happier to ride horses with the other group. Oh, except I could never picture Libby and that Nicole having a single thing to talk about.*

❦❦❦

"Excuse me," Libby said, as she rose and headed for the ladies' room. Walking past the radiant fireplace in the center of the room, she decided it had been a nice morning, after all. It was good to see Margo laughing and having fun with her old friends, especially after last night. *I was ready to kill Preston for messing with her while everyone else was at the dinner table. She'd never admit it, but I know that was why she was crying when we went to bed. And why is he chasing Margo, when he and Nicole are newlyweds? I can't see what Margo ever saw in Preston anyway.* Libby shook her head in disgust. She was happy her life had taken a different path from her sister's.

When Libby returned to the table, Caro was just disconnecting from a call from John E. Her forehead furrowed, and her lips formed a tight line.

"Something wrong?" Libby asked as she settled back into her chair and lifted her glass of iced tea to her lips.

"It's Nicole. She was thrown from her horse, and she's at Brandywine Hospital."

"How badly hurt is she?" Vicki asked, stirring her drink.

"They think it's just a broken ankle, but they are still doing some tests," Caro replied. "The guys are going to leave Preston there with her and come over here to meet us for lunch. They'll be here in about ten minutes.

"It's a shame she got hurt. I got the feeling that she only went riding because she didn't want to spend the morning with us," said Julia.

"More probably, she didn't want to let Preston out of her sight," added Kitty.

Vicki popped her stuffed olive into her mouth. "She has her hands full being married to that one, all right. She'll be lucky if an ankle is the only thing broken—Oh, Caro, I just remembered Preston is your cousin. I wasn't thinking."

"That's okay. I understand how you feel about Preston. Besides, there are three ex-wives out there who would probably agree with you." Caro paused, still frowning. "I hope Nicole is all right, both for her sake and for the sake of our weekend. I wouldn't feel right going on with the party if she is in serious condition."

"Then here's to Nicole," Kitty proclaimed, holding her pomegranate martini aloft.

"And to more partying," Margo seconded. "I'm just getting started on catching up with all of you."

"Speaking of catching up," Caro said, "tell us about the restoration of your villa in Tuscany, Margo. I saw the photo shoot in *Vanity Fair*, and I was blown away."

"It was a fun challenge. You should all come play there some time, maybe next year for *my* milestone birthday." The thought of sharing her Italian residence with her college girlfriends gave Margo a warm feeling inside, and it had nothing to do with the alcohol she was imbibing. For the time being, Margo wasn't thinking about her divorce, apartment hunting, or even the disturbing encounter with Preston the night before. Margo smiled and then giggled. It was the happiest she had felt in a long time.

Chapter 10

Before contacting the wives, the men had taken over the small waiting room at Brandywine Hospital, waiting for news of Nicole's condition. What they knew was that she had sustained a trimalleolar fracture. The doctors had cast her leg to hold the bones in position.

"So what's going on at the Fed these days, Marshall?" Leon asked.

"Same old, same old," Marshall replied. "You have to love the chairman. He's got his own agenda, which may or may not jibe with anyone else's."

"I question his sanity at times," Preston said. "Doesn't he know we're in a recession?"

"Well, if the market would just make up its mind, things would be okay," Gerald said.

"Besides, some of the blame falls directly on the White House."

"Watch it, Gerald," Preston warned, pointing his index finger in Gerald's direction. "I'm hearing sour grapes."

"That was tacky, Preston," John E. said. "Let's all just get along, okay? Consider it my birthday gift."

"Easier said than done," Marshall replied. "Past

grievances have a way of affecting the present, as most of us are realizing. Anyway, aren't we supposed to meet the ladies at one?" Marshall pumped his knee impatiently. "It's five after already."

"Yeah, why don't you guys go ahead and meet the girls? No need for everyone to sit here all day." *Bad enough that I have to sit here,* Preston thought, *but I'd rather be alone than suffer the presence of these fools. Past grievances, my ass.*

"Okay, Preston. Here's my cell number. Call me when you have some news." John E. turned to the others and nodded his head toward the door. "Let's go have some lunch."

⁊⁊⁊

"Mr. Phillips?" the orthopedics resident asked.

"Yes?" Preston rose from the vinyl sofa and put down his fourth cup of bitter black coffee from the waiting room machine. *Jeez, this kid is the doctor working on Nicole?* "I'm Mr. Phillips. Do you have news for me?" He extended a firm hand to shake the doctor's.

"Let's sit down. I'll take you in to see Mrs. Phillips in a moment, but I wanted to talk with you first."

"That sounds ominous. Is she going to be okay?"

"Yes, she is not in any immediate danger, but she has sustained a bad injury to her ankle, and her situation is complicated. Her ankle bone is broken, but she also dislocated it, and it is extremely swollen."

"Well, you can fix that, can't you?" Preston asked impatiently.

"Yes and no. Your wife will need surgery eventually. We can't do it now because the swelling is so severe. We sedated her in order to X-ray it and set the bone in a cast. Then we X-rayed it again to make sure the bone was lined up correctly, but it wasn't."

"Who was doing this inept work on my wife?" Preston exploded. "I want to talk to your supervisor."

"Calm down, Mr. Phillips. I am the resident on call this weekend. I assure you I know what I am doing, and the ankle has now been properly aligned. We've been working on her for the past two hours, making sure the external fixation is perfectly in place."

"It'd better be. Now tell me what external fixation means." *I hate having to suck up to this pipsqueak.*

"Your wife has six pins in her bones that are connected to a bar. The bar holds the bones in place. She will have to wear this appliance for three to four weeks, until the swelling goes down enough for her to have surgery."

"You mean the kind of surgery that means permanent plates and screws?" As a football enthusiast, Preston was familiar with the process that would sideline a player for at least a season. He never dreamed he would have to deal with such an injury with his wife.

"Yes, that's exactly what I mean. It is an unfortunate accident, but Mrs. Phillips' prognosis is good. She's young and healthy, and she'll heal fast."

"We're just here for the weekend. We live in New York," Preston muttered, half to himself.

"Yes, Mrs. Phillips mentioned that. She can travel home with the appliance on her foot and see an orthopedic surgeon there. The important thing is that she not get an infection. You can see her now, but she is going to need to rest. She's still groggy from the sedation, and she will have to remain on oxycodone for the next several days. If all goes well, she'll be able to leave the hospital on Monday."

"Monday? Why can't she just rest at the Campbells' farm? We're here for a very important birthday celebration."

"I assure you, Mrs. Phillips is not going to feel much like partying. Your wife is in a lot of pain."

"Nevertheless, I think she would be better off resting at the farm. Unless she is in mortal danger, I want her discharged now."

"As you say, Mr. Phillips, but you'll have to sign papers acknowledging that this is against medical advice."

"Well, take me to my wife, Doctor. We'll have

to do the best we can." *I'll let Cousin Caro play nursemaid tonight. I'm sure she'll do a better job than I could. This entire weekend is a fiasco,* Preston thought, but then he remembered that if he hadn't come, he wouldn't have seen Margo and had the chance to apologize to her. *Hmmm…maybe the whole weekend isn't ruined, after all,* he thought, smiling wickedly to himself.

CHaptER 11

The men had joined their wives at the restaurant, where they lingered into the afternoon, waiting for Nicole to be released from the hospital.

"I hope Nicole is able to leave the hospital this afternoon," said Les. "It's after three already."

"Dinner won't be until late," Caro said. "I thought we could go back, rest from our day's adventures, and come down for cocktails at eight."

Marshall looked at his watch, pulled a pill case from his pocket, and downed a small white tablet. He glanced at Julia and shrugged. "With horseback riding, the hospital, and now lunch, it slipped my mind completely."

Julia didn't reply. She knew how much pressure Marshall had been under lately. Being a financial wizard wasn't easy, especially in these uncertain times. She worried about Marshall's health, his job, his investments. That was one of the reasons she had wanted to come to John E.'s birthday celebration. She wanted to confront Preston, to make him pay for hijacking Marshall's inheritance. Fortunately, Marshall had a good income, and they had wisely parlayed the cheese business profits into secure assets, but, in this economy, one could never be too sure about money. *Truthfully, it seems the more we have, the more we need. There is just no way to get ahead anymore.*

She was pretty sure Preston would want to do right by Marshall once she explained everything to him her way. She had spent years gathering information about her in-laws' estate and the way Preston had mismanaged it from the beginning. It was time to use that information now, before things got really nasty.

೧೨೮೨

Vicki was watching Julia. It seemed as if her friend had been talking to herself a lot this weekend. Except for the few hours of shopping and light conversation with the girls this morning, Julia had seemed tense, and Vicki knew better than most why. *Julia hates Preston almost as much as Leon and I do, although for different reasons. I can't blame our financial woes on him, although who knows? If Tony hadn't been killed, maybe Leon would have been more careful with risking so much in that bad deal last year. Maybe every single bad thing that has ever happened since Tony's death is Preston's fault.*

Vicki's eyelids felt like lead weights. "I think a nap is a great idea," she said in response to Caro's suggestion.

Just then John E.'s Polytron prototype cell phone rang. "It's Preston," he informed everyone, before answering the call. "Hello? Sure, we've been waiting for your call. I'll be there in about ten minutes."

"Let's go, everyone. Nicole has been released, though she's not going to be much in the mood to party tonight."

Everyone piled into the three SUVs that had brought them into town. Two headed straight to Bucolia, and one took a detour to the hospital to pick up Preston and Nicole. Les expressed what everyone was likely thinking, despite the accident and individual agendas, "No matter what's happened, we came here to celebrate a birthday, so we are going to party on."

ↄ⌀ↄ⌀ↄ

"So sorry, John E.," Nicole slurred, as she rode sideways in the back seat of the Mercedes SUV, her foot propped up on pillows. "Didn't mean to ruin your party, you know?"

"Not your fault," John E. replied. "And besides, the party isn't ruined. We'll all still have a great dinner tonight. I'm just sorry you are in so much pain."

Nicole didn't answer. Her head had lolled over to

the left against the soft leather upholstery, and her faint snore indicated that the pain medicine had kicked in.

John E. patted the seat next to Preston. "It's going to be hard on you these next few days, taking care of Nicole."

"Oh, I don't know," Preston replied. "Nicole is pretty tough. Once this pain medication wears off, she'll probably be hopping around on one foot and taking care of me."

"I wouldn't count on that," John E. said. "Those pins and that metal contraption look like pure torture to me. Also, I'm thinking we should make a bed for her on the first floor tonight. There's no way she can make it up to the fourth floor bedroom."

Preston smiled, revealing his trademark dimples. "Good idea, John. I'm sure that would be best for Nicole. And I won't mind sleeping by myself for one night, either."

John E. shook his head at Preston's lack of concern for his wife. *I'm just glad I'm not married to him.*

⁊⊶⁊

By the time John E., Preston, and Nicole arrived at the farm, the main floor was bustling with preparations by the army of personnel, overseen by Caro. Almost all of the guests had gone upstairs to rest before the evening's festivities. The florist crew, dressed in green and gray uniforms, was decking the house with fragrant arrangements. The catering staff, dressed in formal black and white, was preparing the table and serving trays, setting up the bar, and starting to cook. The impending feast promised to be a memorable one.

Julia had offered to stay downstairs to assist Caro with whatever needed to be done, though obviously there were more than enough people on hand. When Caro politely declined, she asked if she might read her novel downstairs. "I never sleep in the daytime, but I don't want to disturb Marshall's nap. Poor darling, he works too hard, and he needs his beauty rest." *Hopefully this way I might have a chance to talk privately with Preston once he gets Nicole settled*, she thought. She curled up in the office, where she had a view of the circular driveway and the warm family room.

When the Mercedes SUV pulled up in the driveway, she put her book down and jumped up, her rehearsed speech running through her head like the ticker tape at the Stock Exchange. She donned her mink sweater and joined Caro in front of the garage to greet the two men, who were trying to figure out the best way to transport Nicole inside.

"Why don't we use the caterer's dolly?" Julia suggested, pointing to the large flatbed stacked with aluminum containers.

"That's a *really* good idea," Preston said, as if

amazed that Julia could have generated it. "Let's move these pans somewhere, so we can get Nicole onto the dolly."

"I've already covered one of the sofas in the family room with pillows and bed linens," Caro said. "We just have to go through a couple of rooms to get her there."

Nicole had awakened when the car rolled to a stop, and she was looking about, her eyes half open. "I'm afraid, Preston, totally," she cried when he bent into the back seat to place her arm around his neck. "I don't want anyone to touch me, but you."

Despite Nicole's petite size, lifting and carrying her dead weight was not that easy. Preston felt every bit of his sixty-seven years, mostly in his right knee. "Hold on tight, and we'll do this as quickly as we can."

John E. had secured a dog ramp to the back steps. It was the perfect size for the catering dolly. Preston wheeled Nicole to the family room sofa, where she collapsed as if she had been the one doing the carrying. "I need another pain pill, Preston," Nicole complained. "This really hu—r—ts."

Trying to make herself useful, Julia went into the kitchen to get a glass of water. She carried it into the family room. "Here you go, Nicole," she cooed, hoping she sounded sympathetic. *I hope the pill knocks her out quickly, so I can have a little chat with Husband of the Year, here.*

Nicole gazed at Julia with puppy dog eyes as she grasped the glass of water. Preston held out an oxycodone, which Nicole swiftly gulped down with a swig. Preston hesitated before closing the pill bottle. On impulse, he removed an additional pill, popped it in his own mouth, and drained the glass of water.

Just then Caro walked into the room. "Preston, Julia, can you give me some time with Nicole? I want to make sure she is comfortable and all of her needs are taken care of." She shooed the two into the first-floor office and sat next to Nicole, careful not to jostle her. She'd never dreamed that hosting the birthday party would be this complicated.

෬ෙ෬

"Preston, may I have a word with you?" Julia began, as soon as they cleared the threshold to the office. She patted the loveseat to indicate where she expected him to sit, a few inches from where she then sat down.

Preston obliged, but he stared out the window at the snow, instead of making eye contact. A small vein throbbed near his eye.

"I was hoping we could talk."

"About what?" Preston asked.

"About the Winthrops' estate, that's what."

"That's ancient history, Julia. Your in-laws' estate has been closed for at least a decade." He rubbed his right knee, wishing the oxycodone would kick in.

"Technically speaking, you are correct," Julia replied, nonplussed. "But it's what happened in the thirty years before it was closed that I wanted to talk with you about."

"Julia, I've been above-board with Marshall about that, and I don't have anything to say to you about it today." *If I could,* Preston thought, *I would fly from this room and out of the county to get away from Julia's probing dark eyes. Besides, why is Marshall letting her do his dirty work, instead of talking to me himself?*

"Not so fast, Preston. I've been gathering documents from various sources over the years, and there are some discrepancies I've found related to the investments you made on behalf of their estates. I believe you owe Marshall and me an explanation, and I think we should set up a plan to address them. If I am correct, you owe Marshall a very expensive apology."

"I have no idea what you're talking about, Julia. Just what are you accusing me of?"

"No accusations at this point, just questions—many questions."

"Look, I'm a former secretary of the treasury, for God's sake. Why would I get my hands dirty with something like what you are implying?"

"These discrepancies pre-date your big power position, Preston. But unless we straighten them out soon, they may come back to kick you in the proverbial butt."

"That sounds like a threat."

"Take it however you wish," Julia retorted, trying to maintain a calmness she did not feel. "When can we meet to discuss this?"

"I'll think about it and let you know," Preston answered, trying to buy time. *I haven't a clue what Julia's grievance is, but if she and Marshall think they are going to get big sums of money from me, they've got another think coming.* "And now, if you'll excuse me, I have to check on Nicole."

"Don't make me wait too long, Preston. These are not easy times for money disputes, even if we are in the one percent."

Chapter 12

Caro stood beside the long dining table, fingertips grazing one of the menus, gold-embossed on sheer scalloped paper, that had been placed on every service plate. When she had first shown it to John E., he told her it was a culinary program fit for royalty.

Menu
Hors d'oeuvres
Champagne Krug, 2000
First Course
Bouillabaisse with Loupe
Chablis Grand Cru Les Clos, 1990
Second Course
Pate d'Foie Gras, Toast Points
Sauterne Chateau d'Yquem, 1990
Third Course
Fresh Halibut Cheeks
Corton Charlemagne Grand Cru, 2006
Fourth Course
Bibb Lettuce with Hearts of Palm, Vinai=

grette

Fifth Course

Wood Roasted Squab, Boysenberry Sauce

Richebourg Leroy, 1991

Sixth Course

Rack of Lamb Persillade

Chateau Lafitte Rothschild, 1982

Seventh Course

Selection of Fine Cheeses

Graham's Vintage Port, 1977

Eighth Course

Triple Chocolate Torte with Chocolate Ganache

Truffles a la Vicki

Hennessy Paradio Cognac and Other Cordials

Her pleasant reverie was interrupted by the sound of heavy treads emanating from the stairwell.

Preston barely glanced at the menu as he stormed past the dining room on his way to check on Nicole. His mind was a volcano, magma forming lava, about to erupt. *How dare that bitch insinuate that I stole from her and that mealy-mouthed husband of hers! If they think they could have done better investing the Winthrops' money, they should have...Well, they couldn't have invested it them-*

selves, because Mr. and Mrs. Winthrop entrusted me with it while Marshall was in Viet Nam. By the time he came back, the parents were both gone. And the money...damn if I can remember, it was so long ago. He ran his fingers through his hair, trying to recall the details. *I was just getting started, and I might have made some bad investments...Anyway, it really wasn't all that much money lost, at least by today's standards.*

Preston strode into the family room where Nicole lay on the sofa, her hair fanned out on the pillow, her eyes closed, and her breathing soft and even. He shook his head as if to clear it of all thoughts of Julia and Marshall. He tried to muster feelings of sympathy for Nicole. Her swollen foot looked so uncomfortable in that appliance. He knew how a devoted husband *should* feel, sorrowful to see her suffer, perhaps a bit guilty for having put her into the position of endangerment, solicitous of her comfort now. He just wasn't good at any of this. What he felt as he stared at his sleeping wife was annoyance. He was annoyed by the fact that Nicole's injury would provoke expectations of him, expectations that he couldn't or wouldn't live up to.

He exhaled with a deep sigh and sank into the chair next to Nicole.

Preston flexed his knee, suddenly aware that the oxycodone had taken effect. He felt a drowsiness beyond that of the drug. *It's been a long day,* he thought, as he ran his fingers through his hair again. *And it's going to be a long night, too.* He remembered the length of the printing on the scalloped menus. *Maybe I'll go upstairs and take a quick nap and shower before dinner.*

ↂↂↂ

On his way up the stairs to the fourth floor, Preston encountered Vicki, descending from the third floor with several white boxes in her arms. Preoccupied with his own thoughts, Preston was about to pass by her without comment, but Vicki had something different in mind.

"Oh, Preston. Would you mind helping me take the truffles downstairs to the kitchen? I made them as a birthday gift for John E., and I didn't want to bring them down until just before tonight's dinner."

"Why don't you get Leon to help you, Vicki? I'm really tired, and I'm going in the opposite direction."

Vicki gasped with disbelief, her mouth forming a wordless cavern for several seconds. She blurted back, "That's so typical of you, Preston. You are a Class-A Jerk."

Not unfamiliar with being called a jerk, Preston had no such delay in forming his response. "Well, I don't like you much, either, Vicki. You are a Class-A Drunkard."

Vicki set the boxes of candy on the landing, her fists clenched as if about to throw a punch. "You listen to me. Anything you don't like about Leon or me is all your own fault. If you hadn't insisted on having that idiotic birthday party for your son Peter, everything would have been different."

"Don't lay that on me," Preston countered. "I didn't kill your son. It was an accident."

"I begged Tony not to go to that party. I thought it was irresponsible from the get-go to allow sixteen year-olds to race sailboats on the Hudson, but Tony said you were making fun of him, making fun of me. You practically *dared* Tony to participate."

Oh, no. Not another crazy female verbally attacking me. What is this, Pick On Preston Day? "Vicki, I'm sorry about the accident, okay? I wish it had never happened, but no amount of talking will bring Tony back." He scooped up the boxes of truffles. "If it will make you feel any better, I'll carry these downstairs for you."

Before Vicki could say another word, Preston turned his back and moved toward the first floor with a speed and limberness that surprised even him. Following in his wake, Vicki shouted, "Nothing you could ever do would make me feel any better."

When he reached the kitchen, Preston deposited the boxes on the soapstone counter without a word, turned on his heel, and intended to resume his climb to the fourth floor, leaving Vicki in the kitchen with Caro. Before he crossed the threshold, though, Caro grabbed his arm and pulled him back.

"What's going on?"

"Why don't you ask your drunken buddy here, cousin? I'm sure she'll be glad to fill you in on all of the details." He pulled away from Caro as if her touch had stung. As he exited the room, he muttered, "I must say you and John E. have a bunch of losers for friends."

❦

He was just wondering how this day could get any worse when he encountered Margo in the second floor hallway.

"What's going on out here, Preston?" Margo asked. "Was that Vicki I heard yelling?"

Margo's concerned expression was a refreshing oasis. Preston wanted to drink in her soft voice, her classic beauty, and her silky lounging outfit. Why hadn't he married her when he'd had the chance? *Well, maybe I can make up for that now,* he thought. He touched Margo's shiny auburn hair with the reverence of a worshiper. "Margo, I'm so glad to bump into you. I've been thinking about you all day. We need to talk."

"Preston, I don't know," Margo replied, tossing her head as if to free herself from his touch, keeping her voice low.

"Can you come upstairs to my room, Margo? Please?" His pleading tone was uncharacteristic. "I don't want to disturb everyone's rest, and I do need to talk to you."

☙❧

Margo wavered. She knew better than to trust Preston, but she was flattered by the attention, and she was frankly curious about what might happen next. "Well, just for a minute, and just to talk. Understood?"

Preston looked into Margo's eyes, and his face lit up with that dimpled smile. He took Margo's hand in his, as he led her in a silent waltz up the two flights of stairs to his quarters. At that moment, Margo realized she was lost, whether in the past or in the future. When Preston touched her, she was powerless to say no.

CHAPTER 13

When they reached the fourth floor apartment, Preston pulled Margo into an embrace. Her silky loungewear had the lightness of a negligee, and he could feel the delicious curves of her body. She stiffened, though, and whispered, "Just to talk, remember?" She smelled of Shalimar perfume, a scent he had always associated with her.

He released her and moved to close the door. She perched on one of the chenille-upholstered chairs in front of the room's small window. The late afternoon light softened the very air in the room. Preston looked at the bed, willing her to relocate. When he saw that she was ensconced in the chair, at least for the time being, he sat in the matching chair and took her hand in his. He thought before speaking.

"Have you thought about our conversation from last night?" he finally asked.

"Yes, of course, I have," Margo answered, not meeting his eyes. Her other hand clutched a bit of fabric from her pants leg, and she rolled the material back and forth against itself.

"Well? What are your thoughts?"

"To be honest, Preston, I don't know why you want me, when you have a beautiful young wife in your life. You're newlyweds, for God's sake."

For a fleeting second Preston wondered, himself. There was no explanation, beyond the fact that he was driven to possess Margo Martin, here and now. "Why did Prince Charles want Camilla when he had Diana?" Preston replied. "I fell in love with you first. I've always loved you."

Margo bit her lip. "I think you've always wanted what you couldn't have." She removed her hand from his. "We could have had a wonderful life together, but you had to get involved with my best friend."

Preston leaned forward, elbows on knees, moist eyes seeking hers. "Please, Margo. I've grown up since then. I know what I want now. I've known since you walked into the room yesterday afternoon. It's all I can think of." He searched her face for confirmation that he was getting through to her. "Losing you was the biggest mistake of my life. I know that now. Please let me make it up to you. I know we could be very happy together."

"So, now, you're prepared to divorce Wife Number Four? To break her heart?" Margo rose and began pacing around the room, arms crossed. "Pardon me if I can't quite believe that."

"If that's what it takes, that's what I'll do. I want to spend the rest of my life with you, Margo. I feel that this weekend, John E.'s birthday, the whole thing, was fated to bring us back together. I don't want to waste another minute of our lives being apart."

Margo took a deep breath before allowing her thoughts to tumble out. "If you mean what you say, Preston, then you will have to prove it to me before we go any further."

"How can I prove it to you?" He held his breath—Hercules ready to accept his task.

"Tell Nicole you want a divorce, that you are going to marry me."

A struggle played out on Preston's face as he considered this request, his eyes never leaving Margo's. "Done. I'll tell her tonight."

Margo grinned, her asymmetrical smile making Preston want to ravage her right then. "Maybe you should wait until she gets through her surgery. And, besides, you may not have an opportunity to tell her with all these people around."

"No, I want to show you I mean what I say. And I want to show you in other ways, too. Meet me up here tonight after everyone has gone to sleep." Preston took her hand in his again and held it to his lips. "We need to be together. After our kiss on the stairway last night, I know you feel it, too."

"I'll think about it, but no promises." Margo shrugged and turned her back. "I need some time to think."

The sounds of running water and muted voices of guests preparing for the dinner party were drifting up the stairs. Preston stood up and drew Margo into an embrace. "We belong together, you and me. Don't think too long."

"How will I know if you have talked to Nicole?" Margo asked.

"How about this? If I've told her, I'll leave this door open for you to come in. If I haven't had the chance, I'll close the door when I come upstairs. That way you'll know before you come in. Fair enough?"

"Fair enough," Margo replied, looking pleased for the first time. She planted a chaste kiss on his lips and smiled. "Now, I believe we have to get ready for a very important party."

Chapter 14

Andrea and Stan were conversing across the wide expanse of granite between their his-and-hers dressing tables at their own country retreat as they dressed for the dinner party at Bucolia.

"You know, I feel sorry for Nicole," Andrea said, tilting her head toward Stan, as she threaded a simple gold and diamond earbob through her right earlobe.

"Why's that?" Stan replied, preoccupied with tying his Hermes tie.

"Well, she seems so out of place here. She clearly has had no experience with horses. I think the only reason she went riding was because she wanted to be with Preston. And then, he rode ahead with all of the guys, oblivious to her needs or feelings."

Stan smiled at his wife. "And leaving you to play nursemaid to her. Are you blaming Preston for the accident?"

"Not at all. It's just that I think she is head-over-heels crazy about him, and I get the sense that he regards her as nothing more than a pretty collectible that he can bring out of the showcase whenever he desires."

"Because she's so much younger?" Stan asked. "I don't have to remind you of *our* age difference."

"No, Stan. You have never treated me like that. And our marriage is nothing like theirs, thankfully. I just sense that she would like for there to be more substance to their marriage, that's all." Andrea put the final touches on her hair and used the hand mirror to check the back of it. "I called Caro to check on Nicole's condition this afternoon. She's left the hospital, probably against medical advice, with pins and hardware holding her ankle together. I'll bet that was Preston's doing, not hers. When she left in the ambulance, she was in a lot of pain." Andrea bent to place a black lace Jimmy Choo pump on each foot. "I'm dreading this evening for some reason. I just don't have a good feeling about it."

Stan stood, checked his reflection in the mirror, and walked over to Andrea, placing his hands on her shoulders. "Your instincts are usually pretty good. I'm glad Preston and Nicole aren't our problem." He paused, frowning, started to say something, and then apparently changed his mind. "About ready to go, sweetheart? You can check up on your young friend in person in just a few minutes."

♥❧♥

Nicole was dreaming about a handsome prince on a white horse. He had scoured the countryside, looking for the woman whose foot would fit into the Waterford crystal shoe that had been left behind at the ball. She waved him over to the plush sofa, where she was sitting, her right foot held aloft, toe pointed daintily. Determined to make the shoe fit, she pushed and pushed against the glass. The pressure was so great she was afraid it would shatter shoe and foot alike. She heard a voice from behind her, saying, "That's enough. You don't want it to turn to butter." *My foot, turn to butter?* she thought. As the whirring of the beaters ceased, Nicole opened her eyes to a flurry of sounds, smells, and, yes, pain.

"Ohhhh," she moaned, as she tried to sit up without jostling her foot. The pins fixed into her bones felt like molten javelins. She wanted to scream, whether from pain or terror, she didn't know. Instead, she cried softly, wishing she could return to the dream.

After helping Nicole to change out of her ruined riding clothes and clean up a bit, Caro had put a small table next to the sofa with tissues, a bottle of Pellegrino, a glass of ice, and Nicole's pain pills on it. Nicole poured herself a glass of water and took a sip, swishing it around in her dry mouth. *I must have slept for hours,* she thought. She checked her Baume Mercier watch and frowned. *Everyone will be coming down for dinner soon, I'll bet. I wonder where Preston has gone. Maybe he went up to get ready.* "I should have stayed in the hospital," she said aloud. "My foot is killing me, my back is stiff, and I probably look a total wreck. Why did I let him talk me into coming back here tonight?"

"Oh, are you awake, m'lady?" the British bartender asked, as he passed the sofa carrying a tray of polished crystal. "I hope I didn't rouse you."

"No problem," Nicole replied, stretching her arms and arching her back. *I just can't get comfortable. This is sheer misery. Must be time for another pain pill.* She opened the plastic container and poured the pale blue pills into her hand. There were enough to fill her palm completely. *I wonder if there are enough of these babies to get me through this horrible pain. Boy, being married to a rich guy isn't half as great as I thought it'd be. I've just traded old worries for new ones.*

The sounds of music and voices, the blended smells of seasonings, the energy of party preparations brought her no comfort. "Where is Preston when I really need him?" she mumbled to herself. As she drifted into another pill-induced sleep, she fought against the notion that perhaps marrying Preston had been a gigantic mistake.

℘℘℘

Kitty and Gerald were the first to descend the stairs for the party. "I Heard It Through the Grape-

101

vine" from the *Big Chill* soundtrack pulsed through the house. "One of my favorites," Kitty said, bopping her shoulders and ample chest to the music.

Gerald took her left hand in his right and swung her into a jitterbug step. The flounce at the bottom of her gold pencil skirt floated around her tanned legs.

"Ooh, it feels like a party for sure. Love this music," Kitty gushed. She stopped dancing as she caught sight of the sleeping beauty on the couch. "Oh, how insensitive of me," she said, "dancing while poor Nicole is in so much pain."

"It won't be much of a birthday celebration if we focus on Nicole, instead of John E.," Gerald said. "Besides, Nicole looks like she is in another world at the moment. Those pills must be very strong."

"Who's very strong?" John E. asked, as he entered the room. He was dressed in gray wool slacks of the finest thread, the collar of a white-on-white pinstripe shirt peeking through the V-neck of a soft red cashmere sweater. He was impeccably groomed, his hair and goatee as perfect as if he had been barbered just minutes ago. Even his fingernails were perfectly shaped and finished with a matte shine. He might be crossing over into Medicare, but he didn't have to look like it.

Gerald replied, "I was saying Nicole's medication must be very strong, since she seems oblivious to the music and our voices. It's such a shame about her injury."

Kitty said, "Don't you think she'd be more comfortable in a bedroom, away from all of the noise of the party?"

"Caro asked her earlier. We could have moved things around to accommodate her, but she insisted she'd be just fine on the sofa. Besides, she couldn't bear the thought of having her foot touched in any way. I can understand it," John E. said. "Anyway, she's probably in la-la land from that oxycodone. It's the strongest painkiller in pill form."

Kitty saw the bartender pouring champagne into crystal flutes and excused herself. Returning, she held the glass aloft. "Let me be the first tonight to toast you, John E. May all your birthdays be as joyous, and may we celebrate many more happy occasions together." She leaned over to plant a kiss on John E.'s cheek before tasting the fizzy libation. "Mmmm…this is go-o-o-d," she exclaimed. "I may forego dinner altogether."

"Better pace yourself, Kitty," John E. warned. "The best is yet to come." He chuckled with the confidence of a man who had memorized the nine-course meal and wine pairings.

CHAPTER 15

By seven-thirty, Andrea and Stan had arrived, and the party was in full swing. Everyone was dressed in winter finery, dressy casual, and aside from Nicole, whose locomotion had been all but non-existent, and Preston, who had been too busy in the afternoon hours, everyone looked refreshed and ready for fun. Everyone, except for Margo, who hadn't yet come downstairs.

Staff was passing steaming hors d'oeuvres and icy champagne. Nat King Cole's mellow voice filled the background with golden notes about love. Libby and Les, holding hands, approached to offer sympathy to Nicole, who decided she should have a little something to eat after so much medicine. She downed a large tidbit of tangy ramaki. "Better than hospital food," she mumbled.

"Well, I hope you get to feeling better," Libby said.

"Thanks. I'm sure I'll feel better when Preston and I get back home," Nicole said, suddenly realizing that Preston was nowhere to be seen in the roomful of people. "Preston knows the best doctors and hospitals. He'll make sure I get excellent care."

She flinched and grimaced as the pins dug into her flesh. *Just where is he, anyway?*

☙❧

Preston had wandered into the office, hoping to find Margo. Instead, he bumped into Andrea, who was stalling before having to mingle with the other guests at the long night's dinner party. She was flipping through a local magazine featuring Brandywine Valley events, *The Hunt.* In the latest issue were pictures of Bucolia.

"Oh, hi, Preston," Andrea said. "I've been wanting to ask you about Nicole's prognosis. They didn't tell me much when I left the hospital."

Just what I need, another busybody interfering with me and my life. "The doctor says she'll be fine. Don't forget, Nicole is young and healthy."

"Well, if she needs anything, I'll be glad to help out. After this morning's accident, I feel a bit attached to Nicole, and I do know most of the local physicians."

"Very nice of you," Preston replied, looking beyond her toward the staircase.

"Are you looking for someone in particular?" Her tone was that of a schoolteacher who'd caught someone cheating.

"Uh, um, no," Preston replied. "I just have a lot on my mind with Nicole and all."

☙❧

Just as Preston was about to climb the stairs to see what Margo was up to, she appeared at the top of the stairs. Her winter white dress was an off-the-shoulder embossed fabric that clung to her in all the right places. Her burnished hair was combed over her right shoulder, and her emerald eyes sparkled. *She is stunning,* Preston thought for the second time that day. *Maybe not in the way that Nicole is with her smooth skin and her athletic figure, but stunning nonetheless.* Margo's beauty defied her age. The feathery lines on her face were barely perceptible, and her eyes shone with some secret joy. Preston could hardly wait to get her into bed.

"Hello, Preston," Margo said, as if she were merely greeting an old friend, and descended the stairs, graceful long legs in the lead.

"I was just wondering what was taking you so long to come downstairs," Preston began, taking Margo's elbow.

Margo disengaged her elbow from his grasp and made eye contact. "I was putting the finishing touches on my makeup and outfit. By the way, how is Nicole feeling?"

"I haven't had a chance to talk to her yet," Preston whispered. "But I will. Don't worry."

"Oh, I'm not worried at all," Margo oozed with coolness. "Either you will, or you won't."

"Let me get you a glass of champagne," Preston offered.

"I'm perfectly capable of getting my own champagne." Margo walked around Preston and into the family room, where she made a grand entrance on the scale of Audrey Hepburn's at the ball in *My Fair Lady*.

☙☙☙

"Don't you think you should be in there taking care of your bride, Preston?" Gerald taunted, as he pushed his way past on his way back from the powder room.

"Mind your own business," Preston retorted, his eyes following Margo's shapely bottom as she sashayed over to speak to Kitty.

Following his glance, Gerald mistook the target of Preston's longing look, thinking it was Kitty. "Listen, you. Don't get any ideas about *my* wife. You won't live to see the light of day if you mess with her."

Preston grinned wickedly, revealing arctic white implants and deep dimples. "Be careful making threats, Gerald. You never know who might be listening." He headed for a waiter with an hors d'oeuvres tray. As an afterthought, he tossed over his shoulder, "Besides, you might jeopardize that big career of yours."

Gerald clamped his fists at his sides. *I really want to kill this guy,* he thought, not for the first time. He vocalized, more to himself than to anyone else, "This time, you have really gone too far— way too far."

107

CHapter 16

After Preston's remark about all of their friends being losers, Caro had reexamined the seating chart for dinner. With nine courses, the dinner would take approximately five hours, a long time for dinner partners to have to get along—or not. She wanted to preserve the boy-girl-boy-girl pattern as much as possible, and she wanted to split married couples up, just to make for more interesting dynamics. She knew she couldn't seat Preston next to Vicki, Margo or Julia, and probably Libby wasn't a good idea either. Nicole would probably not be at the table for long, if at all. Even then it would be best to have her placed at the end of the table, where she could prop up her leg. That left Kitty and Caro, herself. *What a shame,* she thought, *that I have to use a negative seating arrangement, instead of a positive one, but with Preston as a guest, that is how it has to be.*

The seating arrangement looked like this:

Andrea Leon Margo Gerald Julia Les Vicki
Caro   John E.
  Preston Kitty Marshall Libby Stan Nicole

As cocktail hour wound down, one of the servants sounded a miniature xylophone, calling everyone to the table. Vicki downed her champagne, taking Leon's arm with her free hand. "Let's go, darling. Believe it or not, I am starving."

Marshall had been talking to Gerald about the fluctuations in the futures market. Each was asking questions of the other, most likely trying to gain some insight that could be used to enrich his own personal portfolio. Both men gesticulated with enthusiasm, as though imparting economic wisdom with every sentence, but neither gave up anything of value in the exchange. That was one of the unwritten rules of the one percent. "We'll have to pick this up later," Gerald said, nodding his head toward the dining room to signal to Kitty that he would meet her there.

Libby, Les, and Margo were talking to Julia, who reported on the latest Broadway hit, *Strychnine*, at the Imperial Theatre. The three ladies rose from a grass-cloth sofa as if joined at the hip, the fabrics of their chic outfits falling sleekly about them. Together they headed in the direction of the dinner gong.

Andrea and Stan walked in with Caro. Stan commented, "What a lovely table, Caro, dear. You always entertain so exquisitely." Unlike the dinner of the previous evening, which had been country casual, tonight's place settings and centerpieces were pure elegance. The silver and crystal sparkled in the light that emanated from centerpieces consisting of water-filled tubes displaying floating orchids and protea flowers. Battery-operated lights shone at the bases, while floating candles topped each. The effect was fairyland.

Preston assisted Nicole into the rented, freshly delivered wheelchair and pushed her to the end of the table, where she could sit with her leg propped up on an ottoman. His manner was brusque as he lifted her from wheelchair to dining chair. As she eased her arm from around his neck, she whispered, "Preston, what's wrong?"

"We'll talk later. Now isn't the time."

"I have to know. Are you upset with me?" Her voice, dimmed by the oxycodone, came out as a soft whine.

"I just need to get through this night, Nicole. It's been a long day, and I just want to get this over with."

"Seriously?" Nicole replied. "*You* had a long day? You bastard!" The volume of Nicole's voice had risen from a whisper to an almost-normal utterance, causing everyone seating themselves around the table to suddenly silence their conversations and turn their eyes toward the head of the table.

Preston's anger traveled at the speed of light from his eyes to hers, and apparently getting the message, Nicole clamped her mouth, if not her feelings, shut.

Margo, overhearing the tail end of Nicole's remarks, smiled primly, certain Preston had done what she had asked. Preston was soon to be hers again. As much as this pleased and excited her, she couldn't help feeling sorry for Nicole. She remembered all too well how it had felt to be abandoned by Preston Phillips.

Gerald, seating himself on Margo's left, shot scathing looks at Preston as he took the seat next to Kitty. *Of all the people at this table, why did Caro have to put Kitty next to the devil incarnate?* Assessing the way Kitty tilted her head as she smiled at Preston, he felt the familiar tickle of jealousy.

Similarly, Preston gazed across the table at Margo, seated next to that jerk, Gerald, and wished his cousin had been more intuitive in designing seating arrangements.

Margo, catching the look of wishful thinking on Preston's face, and thinking that playing hard to get was working spectacularly well, decided to flirt a bit with Gerald. She knew her friend Kitty wouldn't mind. After all, Kitty was already flirting shamelessly with Preston.

Vicki held the impressive menu at eye level, candlelight flickering through the delicate paper. "Wow, John E.," she said to her table partner, "you and Caro have outdone yourselves this time."

"I hope everyone enjoys it," John E. replied. "Fine foods and wines for my fine friends."

Nicole, on John E.'s other side, inhaled to push

back the faint nausea that came from the smell of bouillabaisse as it was being served. "I'm afraid I don't have much of an appetite."

John E. wondered why Caro had placed him next to the two women who would be least likely to enjoy his company for this five-hour meal. Nicole would probably excuse herself from the table soon, and Vicki would likely imbibe enough to be there in name only. *So much for being the man of the hour. Well, I'm not going to let anything spoil this extravagant meal.* He lifted his soup spoon to signal for everyone to begin.

૯౨౯౨

Andrea was into the third course, halibut cheeks, when she realized with a sudden ping of insight that she was actually having a not-half-bad time. If she couldn't be seated by Stan, she at least had her second choice in Caro, one of the most gracious people she knew. Preston and Kitty, across the table, furnished an ongoing source of amusement with the kind of witty repartee rich, intelligent people specialized in. Kitty's lilting giggle at Preston's White House stories kept them rolling ceaselessly. Even poor Leon, seated to her left, served as an interesting dinner partner. His new protocol for electronic medical checkups might really take off. His optimism, at least, was refreshing. She noticed, too, how Leon kept leaning over to check on Vicki.

It was touching to see how solicitous he was of her needs after so many years of marriage. Of course, their mutual grief over losing their only son in that tragic accident had probably brought them closer than most couples their age.

Gerald and Margo were laughing about remembered fraternity pranks. "Do you remember the time someone put a fiber laxative into the barbecue sauce at Friday night dinner? Everyone had the runs for the next two days."

As the servers removed the fish course, replacing it with a light salad, Leon looked toward Vicki as if to signal something. She stood up, teetering a bit on her Stuart Weitzmans. Leon rushed to her side, putting an arm around her and holding her close. He was the keel to Vicki's ship. Her balance absolutely depended on him.

Leon looked at John E., silently asking the professor for permission to speak. John E. smiled and nodded, and Leon began. "Well, I know you'll agree with me this is quite a birthday celebration." The guests applauded softly. "Vicki and I can't thank you enough for including us." He looked back and forth from John E. to Caro. "Like most of you, our friendship with the Campbells goes way back, and it has survived some great and terrible times." Vicki's eyes filled at the mention of "terrible times," but she nodded. "John E., you are a brilliant professor, entrepreneur, and gentleman farmer, but most of all, you are a great friend. In over forty-five years of friendship, I can't think of a single bad moment to roast you with." He paused to look around the table, his eyes pausing when they landed on Preston. "Anyway," he continued, "you all probably noticed on the menu that Vicki and I brought a birthday gift for everyone to share at the end of this fantastic meal. We hope you enjoy the home-made truffles."

"Thank you, Leon and Vicki," John E. replied, lifting his glass in a toast-back. "I hope everyone is enjoying the food and drink. The secret is to go slowly and drink lots of water along with the wines. Of course, at our age…" And he paused to look at Nicole, Libby, and Les. "…well, at most of our ages, going slowly is not a problem."

As eating, drinking, and conversation resumed, Andrea noticed Nicole was pushing the pricey food around on her plate.

John E. must have noticed, too. "You really have no appetite, my dear," he said. "I'm sorry you can't enjoy this feast."

Nicole shrugged. "I guess I should've stayed in the hospital after all? I'm totally not hungry, and my foot is killing me. Back hurts, too, from sitting in this position so long."

"Why not excuse yourself from the table and make yourself more comfortable? We certainly understand."

"Yes, I think I will. You and Caro have been very nice."

"Preston, why don't you help Nicole get settled in the other room? She's had enough partying for tonight, I'm afraid," John E. called.

Preston looked up. "I'll be right back," he said directly to Kitty's cleavage then met Margo's eyes across the table as he rose to do his husbandly duty.

Nicole remained silent as she slipped her arm around Preston's neck, and he lifted her into the wheelchair. Every slight movement brought a grimace, but no cries.

Andrea sympathized with Nicole. In her shoes, she would have hated being a party pooper and a burden to her husband, so much so that she might have had to howl with self-pity.

ℰℐℰℐ

Once in the next room, out of earshot of the party, Nicole started in on Preston again. "Please tell me what's wrong?"

Keeping his voice as low as possible, Preston responded as he thought best under the circumstances. Their exchange was brief, under two minutes, and it ended with Preston's handing his wife two oxycodone tablets, and downing a third one, himself. When he returned to the dining table, it was as if Nicole had never been there. People were eating the savory roasted squab, complemented by sweet boysenberries, and drinking the Richebourg Leroy, and no one seemed to be feeling any pain, least of all, Nicole's. Only Margo met Preston's gaze as he took his seat next to Kitty. Her raised eyebrow was the only indication of the unasked, unanswered question between the two of them.

After the next course, the rack of lamb, Preston felt it was the right time to give his toast. Not one for flowery speeches, especially when the topic was a tribute to another man, he, nevertheless, knew decorum obligated him to extol his hosts. Therefore, he clinked his wineglass, which still had a few sips of Chateau Lafitte Rothschild in it, and stood at his place.

"I think I'm the last to toast you, John E.," he began. "Last, but never least," he added with a chuckle.

More than a few pairs of eyes rolled at this inauspicious beginning.

"I just want to say, 'Happy Birthday' to a great cousin. Thanks for the party. Cheers."

Those who hadn't finished their wine responded, "Cheers," and drained their glasses. Julia consulted her diamond-crusted Rolex and said, "It's twelve-thirty already."

Margo stood then, all eyes drawn to her. Despite the long evening, she still looked fresh and beautiful, her happy mood evident in her expression. "No, Preston, yours is *not* the last speech." She paused for everyone to stop their conversations. "I also want to thank Caro and John E. for this magnificent party. I appreciate being allowed to tag along with baby sister and her husband."

Caro murmured something to the effect that Margo would always be welcome at Bucolia.

"I know. We go way back, and I count both of you among my very dearest friends." She reached down under the table, where she had stashed a large box earlier in the afternoon. "This is a little birthday gift from Libby, Les, and me. We hope you like it." She carried the box to the end of the table and handed it to John E. with a kiss on the cheek.

John E. methodically untied and unwrapped the package. He held up the burgundy satin smoking jacket for all to see. "Perfect gift," John E. exclaimed. "I will put it to use as soon as we've finished dessert."

"We thought you'd be smoking cigars," Margo said, smiling. "And now you don't have to get your nice clothes all smelly."

"Actually," Marshall interjected, "*I* brought the cigars for after dinner, John E.'s birthday gift from Julia and me."

"Great minds think alike." Margo beamed at Marshall. "Then again, there aren't too many things one can buy for someone who already has everything."

☙❧

After the cheese course, everyone took a fifteen-minute break before sitting down to dessert. It was just past one a.m., and most were beginning to feel tired. At least no one had to travel far to get into their beds.

During the break, Vicki had insisted on helping to plate the dessert course. She had made specialty truffles for each of the guests, having coordinated with Caro well in advance. She arranged the candies decoratively on the plates bearing chocolate torte with ganache, and carried them in, announcing the flavor at each person's right side as she carefully placed it before him or her. Vicki seemed to have regained much of her equilibrium, or perhaps she was so proud of her role in creating the sweets, but she seemed only as drunk as everyone else at this point. "Raspberry," she announced when serving Stan. "Lemon," serving Libby. "Coffee," for Marshall. "Coconut," for Kitty. When she got to Preston, Vicki announced, "White chocolate. I knew you were allergic to chocolate."

Preston looked at Vicki with suspicion and down at his plate of lemon ganache with two white truffles. How did she know he was allergic to chocolate? *Caro, I suppose.* And why would Vicki be so nice as to cater to his allergy, anyway, given the way she had hollered at him earlier that afternoon? *Oh, well. I've got an aftertaste in my mouth from that oxycodone. Maybe the white chocolate will help.* He popped the first of two truffles into his mouth and rolled it around, melting the outside shell with the friction of his tongue. The smooth inside exploded with sweetness, removing all other flavors of pills or cheese from his palate. *Not bad— think I'll have another.*

Vicki continued around the table, serving each person with a favorite flavor. Caro bit into her dark chocolate truffle. "Now this," she said, holding the remainder of the candy between thumb and forefinger, "is heavenly. Thank you, Vicki, for such a mouth-watering gift."

Similar remarks were made around the table as everyone tried the truffles. Then everyone dug into their chocolate tortes, everyone except for Preston, whose torte was lemon, and Margo, who eschewed the calories.

ഗ୬ଓ

After dessert and coffee, John E. donned his new smoking jacket, wrapping it over his clothes and tying it with the satin sash. He invited everyone who wanted to participate to join him on the back porch for the final "course" of the evening. He knew he wasn't the only one looking forward to enjoying the Cohibas, hard to come by as they were.

Les politely declined. He had never taken up cigar smoking, and, besides, he didn't want to risk having the smell upset Libby in her condition. Preston loved cigars, but he didn't want to ruin his

119

chance with Margo, so he glanced her way for a sign of approval or disapproval. Margo flicked her wrist in the direction of the porch, telling him to go ahead. The other men: John E., Gerald, Leon, Stan, and Marshall, adjourned to the wide screened-in porch, the change of scenery signaling the start of the after-party.

The ladies, except for Libby, who went upstairs with Les, and Nicole, who was snoring in her makeshift bed, moved into the living room, where they de-briefed on the evening's festivities.

Marshall had brought his portable humidor downstairs, and made a show of opening the seal of the clean wooden cigar box. Devoid of the typical labeling, shrink wraps, or ring bands, these Robusto-sized puppies looked suspiciously like smuggled Cubans. No one dared ask. At forty dollars per stick, they were a real extravagance for the ordinary smoker.

Like a proud new father, Marshall handed out cigars with precise ceremony. The first on the left went to John E., the first on the right to Preston. He proceeded to hand cigars out, first from the left of the row then from the right. No one questioned his methodology in their eagerness to light up. Marshall took the last for himself, and then took a seat in a comfortable rocking chair.

It felt good to be outside in the early morning hours on the farm. The profusion of stars spattered across the inky sky provided a novel bit of scenery for the mostly-city folk. The night air was frigid, but the smokers were protected from the winter bitterness by the house and porch screen, as well as a portable heater, so they were not uncomfortable. As they puffed, they, too, de-briefed on the lavish dinner party.

"John E., I've got to hand it to you," Stan commented. "That was one phenomenal dinner. I won't eat again for a week."

"What about brunch tomorrow morning?" John E. teased his old friend.

"Ohhh, noooo, not more food," groaned Leon. "Tomorrow morning I'll be hung over for both food and drink."

"Anybody else feeling light-headed?" Preston asked. Suddenly he felt an unfamiliar dizziness. *Could it be the oxycodone? Or delicious anticipation of being with Margo?*

"I always said you were light in the head, Preston," Gerald quipped.

"At least I'm light somewhere, Gerald, which is more than you can say for you." *What did Kitty see in this guy, anyway? And Margo had seemed to enjoy his company tonight, too. No accounting for women's tastes.*

"I want to be on the guest list for your seventieth birthday party," Marshall said.

"We all want to be on the guest list, Marshall," Preston countered. "At our age, we all hope to be alive in five years."

John E. chuckled. "You can all come back for the seventieth, but you don't have to wait that long, either. You are invited back to Bucolia anytime."

Chapter 17

I hate to break up the party," Margo said, yawning, "but it's way past my bedtime." She rose from the loveseat she shared with Andrea, straightened the skirt of her ivory dress, and picked up the rhinestone-studded sandals, slinging them on her fingers behind her bare shoulder as she moved toward the staircase. "Wonderful evening, Caro. A wonderful weekend. I can't thank you enough." As excited as she was about meeting up with Preston, she wondered if she could muster the energy. After all, she wasn't twenty-one anymore, and it was already after two a.m.

❧❧❧

As if waiting for someone else to be the first to say goodnight, Julia, Kitty, Vicki, Andrea and Caro also stood and stretched. "I'll go stick my head out on the porch to see if Stan is ready to leave," Andrea said. "Go on upstairs, girls."

Caro replied, "I wouldn't dream of it. I'll just say goodnight to those of you going upstairs. Don't rush to come down for brunch tomorrow. Let's all just sleep till we wake up." She air-kissed each of her sorority sisters in turn and sent them on their way to their bedroom suites. "Let me check on Nicole while you go check on Stan," Caro said to Andrea.

Caro tiptoed into the family room, where Nicole was sleeping. Nicole had thrown off the down comforter, so both legs and her torso were exposed to the cool air. Caro felt a twinge of maternal concern for this miserable girl. She reached across the sofa to lift the comforter up and over Nicole's frame, causing her to stir.

"Ummm," Nicole murmured, her eyelids still shut. She tried to roll over to her side, but apparently felt a jolt of pain from her ankle. She shot up straight, eyes wide open, and looked about.

"I'm sorry I woke you," Caro apologized. "I was just checking to see if you need anything."

Nicole licked her lips then ran her tongue around the inside of her mouth. "Where's Preston?"

"The men are smoking cigars on the porch. I'm sure they'll be coming in soon, and I'm sure Preston will check on you. Is there anything I can help you with?"

"I'd really like to use the restroom, if you wouldn't mind."

"Not at all," Caro said. "Wheelchair or walker?"

"What great options. I think I'll try the walker this time?"

Caro was amazed by how nimble Nicole was, considering the severe swelling of her foot and the painful-looking fixation device. "I think you are getting better already," she ventured. "I don't think I'd be able to move that well if I were in your condition."

"Maybe all those hours of spinning and Pilates classes have paid off," Nicole mused, as she manipulated the walker. "I just wish I could go upstairs to sleep with Preston. We've never slept apart since we've been married. Somehow I think it's bad luck to start?"

"There will be plenty of time to sleep with Preston after tonight," Caro replied, patting Nicole lightly on the shoulder. "Right now you need to focus on getting that ankle healed."

☙☙☙

"Good night, Caro," Andrea and Stan said in unison, as they passed Nicole and Caro, coming out of the powder room.

They were en route to the entry hall, to fish their coats and boots from the closets. The last of the servants had left a half hour before.

"It's good to see you up a bit, Nicole," Andrea continued. "I hope you feel better soon."

"Thanks," Nicole said, as she hopped with the walker back toward her sofa. "And thanks again for calling the paramedics and all, Andrea. I don't know what I'd have done without you."

"You were very brave. Glad I was able to help."

"See you tomorrow, I guess," Nicole said, as she continued to hop and slide. She had to admit both Caro and Andrea had defied her expectations of one percent wives. Both had been kind and supportive.

As soon as Andrea and Stan departed, the smoke party broke up on the porch, and the men passed through the family room on their way to the staircase, the pungent odor of cigars permeating the parade.

Preston was surprised to see Nicole sitting up on the sofa, her soft blonde hair freshly combed and a smile on her face.

She waved him over. "Hey, Preston. Aren't you going to say goodnight?"

"Uh, sure, Nicole," Preston replied. He had been hoping to find his wife in an oxycodone stupor, so he could go upstairs and prepare for Margo. It was late, and he was tired. He also didn't feel so great after all of the eating, drinking and smoking. "I didn't think you'd be awake at this hour."

"I've slept so much all day and night. I guess I'm starting to feel a bit better."

"That's good, but don't you think you should take another pill and go back to sleep? Tomorrow is another day, Miss Scarlett."

"I want to come upstairs with you, Preston. If you help me, I think I can go up the stairs on my butt."

"Not in your best interests, Nic. I'd never forgive

126

myself if you knocked the pins loose and re-broke your ankle."

"Then you sleep down here with me," Nicole pleaded. "I think we should be together, especially after our little spat at dinner. Please, Preston? I'm feeling better, and I think we might even be able to fool around." She had never known Preston to pass up an opportunity for sex.

"Tempting offer, but I'm beat. I just want to go upstairs and go to sleep."

"But, Preston…" Nicole's wheedling turned into a whine. "I'd feel so much better with you here. What if I have to get up and no one is around?"

Preston closed his eyes and rubbed his temples. "Just call me on my cell phone, and I'll come down." He lifted her cell phone from the table next to the sofa, held it to his ear, and put it back down. "I'm only a phone call away." He smiled and kissed her lightly on the nose. With that, he turned and headed for his fourth floor suite, checking his watch as he mounted the first stair.

∽∾∽∾

Margo was debating about whether to go to Preston or not. Her head was pounding with dueling impulses. On the one hand, she simply could not bury the past, not entirely. Preston's infidelity all of those years ago had left an indelible imprint on Margo's life.

Her inability to trust him, and men in general, had made her relationships, even her marriage to Roberto, tenuous. How could she, in the space of two days, forgive Preston enough to go to bed with him tonight?

On the other hand, the past two days had awakened feelings in her that she didn't know she still had. Preston claimed to love her, promised to give up his young wife for her. Didn't that count for something? Besides, they weren't getting any younger, and opportunity like this may never come again. And then there was that boyish look of hunger in Preston's handsome eyes, those incredible dimples, and the supreme confidence that allowed Preston to go after whatever he wanted in life, even her.

I'll sneak upstairs, she decided, *check to see if his door is open, and then make up my mind.*

She smiled and nodded her head. Inside, she knew that, open door or closed door, she was going to play this out to its natural conclusion. Not to do so would be to die.

❧❧❧

As Preston passed the second floor on his way to the fourth, he slowed his step and strained to hear a sound that would suggest Margo's decision to come to him. He hoped to hear her showering, brushing her teeth, even humming a tune, anything to let him know that she was still awake. So much depended on this. It was not only lust that had drawn him to Margo. It was the chance to redeem himself for his brutish behavior toward her all of those years ago. *Finally,* he thought, *I feel ready to settle down and have a real relationship with a fine woman, not the flash and dash of fast cars and young women.*

All was quiet on the second floor, and on the third. Preston entered his fourth floor bedroom, turned on the Oriental lamp at the bedside, and left the door open. He knew it was dishonest. He hadn't, in fact, told Nicole he wanted a divorce. But he had laid the groundwork. And he couldn't stop himself from pursuing Margo any more than he could turn back time and undo any of the mistakes he had made, some of which were heavy on his mind since being confronted by Julia and Vicki today.

I wish I weren't so tired. Margo deserves the best love-making possible. Preston walked about the bedroom suite, picking up articles of clothing and toiletries. As he did, he felt a sudden dizziness.

Concerned that he might not be at peak performance, he opened his buttery leather Dopp kit and took everything out to search for the Viagra. *Margo should be here any minute,* he thought. He quickly swallowed the blue pill, chasing it with a couple of swigs of tap water. He leaned into the mirror to check for whisker stubble that might have sprouted since he had shaved hours earlier. Finding none, he combed his thick hair into place, brushed his teeth, and smiled into the mirror, admiring his dimples. All that was left to do was wait.

CHaptER 18

Dressed in a soft lime-green silk twinset and matching slacks, and feeling incredibly light and sexy with no underwear on, Margo pushed away her qualms as she padded up the stairs in the dark. The second floor was utterly quiet. The only sound on the third floor was a steady, faint whooshing noise coming from Julia's and Marshall's room. When she arrived at eye-level to the fourth floor, where Preston's room was nestled into the eaves of the house, her heart flipped. The door was open.

This is really going to happen, she thought, with both trepidation and delight. She took the final few stairs slowly. *Is this really what I want?* she asked herself for the millionth time. When she got close enough to see the golden slant of light coming from the lamp onto the bed, which had been neatened since the afternoon, she was overwhelmed with a feeling of finally coming home.

When she entered the room, Preston was not there. A strip of light and the sound of water emanated from the closed bathroom door. She took a seat in the upholstered chair and waited.

✿✿✿

When Preston opened the door and saw Margo, her auburn hair glinting in the lamplight, he felt inflated, like a happy, floating balloon, filled with joy, hope, perhaps love. He inhaled her scent, *floral*. In that moment, accomplishments in the financial world, his massive wealth, all were forgotten. *This, this is the ultimate triumph.*

Preston opened his arms, and Margo stood, opening hers in response. They met in the middle of the room, wrapping each other in a long, close, warm embrace, as if they would never let go. In a second, Preston remembered how well their bodies had fit together before, so many lifetimes ago. Wordlessly, they kissed—a long, deep kiss that spoke of nostalgia, regret, but also of promise.

This time will be perfect, Preston thought. No rush, no acrobatics, just two pillars of flesh, yearning, reaching, melting into one. He couldn't banish a fleeting thought of Nicole, how different it was with her. He smiled in amazement. *All the old guys who chase young girls have it all wrong.*

This might be the most passionate he had ever felt. For the first time in his life, he wanted to give more than to get. He would not let anything stand in his way.

☙❧

Afterward, there was little talk. There was so much to say, giggly, heady plans to make, but it was already after three a.m., and both Preston and Margo had reasons to keep a blanket around their relationship for now. They decided to meet in New York the following week, exchanged cell phone numbers, gazed into each other's eyes, and kissed one last time. Margo looked back at Preston as she left the room. Her eyes filled with tears at the sight of him, her first and last love.

She descended the stairs with caution, hoping she could avoid the eyes or ears of any of the other guests. She breathed a sigh as she closed the door to her room and hugged herself, trying to memorize the feeling of Preston's body against hers. She yawned and pulled open the plush coverings of her bed. She was just crawling between the crisp coolness of the linens when she heard the sound of metal against wood outside of her room. *It's nothing. I must be imagining things.*

When she heard it again, she pushed off the covers and swung her long legs out. Still wearing her lime silk outfit, she emerged from her suite into the hallway.

What she found was Nicole, scooting up the stairs on her butt, dragging the awkward appliance behind her.

"Nicole, what are you doing?" Margo uttered, holding back the shriek. She clutched the two sides of her jacket together in the center of her chest, as if to protect her heart.

Nicole stared at Margo, eyes lingering on the silk

outfit. She kept moving along the hallway toward the next flight up, peering around Margo into the open door of her room, as if to see if Preston were there.

"What are you doing?" Margo's sharp whisper cut through the thick air between them.

Nicole paused, curling back on her spine, her bent knees in the air. It seemed a difficult pose to hold. "I'm going to Preston."

"Up to the fourth floor? On your rear end?" Margo instantly regretted the incredulous tone of her outburst.

"Isn't that obvious?" Nicole replied. "He *is* my husband, in case you've forgotten it. I decided I want to sleep with him."

Margo's mind raced at the speed of light. If Preston had told Nicole he wanted a divorce, the last thing on earth she would want would be to scoot three stories up the stairs with a broken ankle to sleep with him. *He didn't tell you,* Margo almost shouted loudly enough for the entire house to hear. *I've been a fool!* She felt her new-found happiness draining away as she faced the truth. She stared at Nicole, so young and beautiful, so agile and strong, and she wondered how she ever could have competed with her for Preston's affections. *I was nothing but another conquest for him. It wasn't enough that he broke me once—he had to do it again.*

She wanted to clutch her side from the palpable pain that accompanied the shattering of her dream.

She wanted to shake Nicole's well-toned shoulders, warn her that her husband was the worst scoundrel ever, that he wasn't worth exerting herself and risking her ankle. Instead, she realized that she pitied Nicole. No one knew of Margo's liaison with Preston. She could go downstairs in the morning with her head held high, leave Bucolia, and forget all about this shabby interlude. But Nicole would have to continue to live with that two-faced two-timer and be subjected to his lies and abuse.

"Let me help you," Margo offered with convincing sincerity. She placed a gentle hand on Nicole's shoulder.

⁓⁓⁓

Nicole's eyes bored into Margo's. Truthfully, Nicole had braved the stairs on her butt mostly to find out whether Margo was sleeping with Preston. Now that she saw Margo's willingness to help her, as well as the fact that she was alone in her own bedroom, after all, Nicole had to admit it was an ordeal to have come this far. "Preston's probably sound asleep anyway," she answered. "Maybe you could help me get back down the stairs to the sofa?"

"Sure, I will," Margo replied, bending to help lift Nicole to a standing position on her left foot. She placed a supportive hand around Nicole's waist and let the younger woman's arm go around her neck.

Between Margo and the stair rail, Nicole was able to hop down the stairs to her walker.

"Thanks for everything," Nicole told Margo. *Thanks for being in your room, thanks for not sleeping with my husband, thanks for seeing past your sorority sisters to help somebody you hardly know.*

"My pleasure," Margo responded. She was surprised to find that she really meant it.

CHapteR 19

After the formality of the nine-course dinner the night before, Sunday brunch was designed to be laid-back and casual. No wake-up calls, seating arrangements, or fancy menus. It was a good thing, because everyone was tired from being up so late, their stomachs, livers, and kidneys still processing all they had devoured and imbibed.

John E. had set out an informal buffet of smoked salmon and venison, an antipasto vegetable tray, and some caviar and blini with chopped egg and capers to garnish. The aroma of spicy chili from a crock pot scented the room, as well. Bloody Marys and an ice bucket of chilled champagne sat on a shiny silver galley tray, where guests could serve themselves on their way into the dining room.

"I'm sort of glad the servants are off today," John E. remarked to Caro, who was arranging coffee mugs, sugar, and creamer at the end of the buffet counter.

"I know what you mean. Sometimes I find it hard to carry on a normal conversation with friends in front of the servants. I fear they will think badly of us."

"If that's your worry, I'm sure they've heard enough this weekend to keep their tongues wagging for months."

"What do you mean, specifically?" Caro asked.

"Well, there has been enough boasting and one-upmanship this weekend to satisfy any bystander's curiosity about how the other half lives."

Footfalls on the stairs interrupted the conversation. Seconds later, Libby and Les entered the room. "Good morning," they chirped in unison.

"Are we the first ones?" Libby asked, looking around.

"Mmmm...coffee smells great," Les said, eschewing the alcoholic drinks and heading directly toward Caro. He planted a kiss on her cheek as he grabbed a coffee mug and served himself a fragrant, steamy mug full.

"What a beautiful buffet," Libby remarked. "You two have outdone yourselves this weekend!"

"Yes," Les chimed in, "I'm going to hate to go back to my humdrum world after this weekend."

"Your world is anything but humdrum, Les," John E. laughed. "And anyway, you youngsters have to keep the economy going so us old farts can collect Social Security."

"Who's collecting Social Security around here?" Leon Spiller boomed, as he entered the room. "That's a laugh!"

"Shhh," Caro said. "Nicole's sleeping in the next room."

"Oh, sorry," Leon apologized. "I forgot about Sleeping Beauty."

"Where's Vicki?" Libby asked.

"Another sleeping beauty. She'll be down after a while. Whoa, look at this caviar."

"What's happening down here?" asked a freshly shaven Gerald, leading Kitty by the elbow. "That was quite a birthday dinner, John E., Caro." He patted his ample midsection as if to confirm its satisfaction with the previous night's menu.

"Morning, everybody," Kitty murmured as she, too, headed for the coffee. "Nice party last night."

"How did everyone sleep?" Caro asked.

"Fast," Gerald replied. "I don't think we got to sleep much before three. I think some of us forgot that we're not in college anymore."

"I slept like a baby," Julia claimed, picking up the conversation seamlessly as she entered the room, stopping to pick up a Bloody Mary on her way. "Loved the dinner, loved the company, great party."

She kissed John E. on the cheek and sat down at the table.

As more guests drifted downstairs, and the volume of voices increased, Nicole stirred on the sofa then sat up with a gasp of pain.

Caro excused herself from her conversation with Julia and called to Nicole, "I'm coming, Nicole. Be there in a second."

"I'm okay, Caro," Nicole said. I just need to go

to the bathroom." She fumbled with the bottle of pills then swallowed one before mustering the will to stand and use the walker.

"Let me help you," Caro offered.

"Thanks, but I'm going to have to manage on my own sooner or later."

Caro hovered, nevertheless. She felt so responsible for Preston's wife. After all, they were now cousins. "When you've washed up, come on into the dining room. We're having breakfast." *It's a shame we didn't build a bedroom on the first floor. Then Preston could have stayed here with Nicole and taken care of her. It's so awkward having her down here with almost strangers, while he sleeps away on the fourth floor.*

๛

By noon Andrea and Stan had arrived, and everyone had come downstairs for brunch, except for Margo and Preston. Nicole was sitting uncomfortably at the table, her leg propped up, pushing tiny bits of food around on her plate. "I wonder how long Preston is going to sleep," she mused aloud.

"Why don't you call him?" Caro suggested. "It's time he woke up, anyway, or he'll miss the tail end of the party."

Nicole tapped into her Smartphone and waited while it rang once, twice, three times. Four times. Then voicemail. "That's odd. He's not answering."

"He must be wasted after all of that partying last night," Marshall said with a laugh. "You know, he's not a spring chicken anymore, like the rest of us here."

"I'm going up," Nicole said, ignoring Marshall's implied dig. She used the table to stand and grabbed her nearby walker.

"No, you're not," Caro said firmly. "I'll go up and check on him for you." She took off for the stairs before Nicole could give her an argument.

As she mounted the stairs to the second floor, she encountered Margo, who was fully made up, her hair in a ponytail, and heading downstairs. "Hi, Caro," Margo said, yawning. "Sorry I overslept."

"No problem. Just go on down. Everyone's having brunch and getting in some last-minute visiting."

"Where are you headed?" Margo asked.

She replied over her shoulder, "Checking on Preston. He's still asleep and not answering his phone." She kept moving past Margo and up the stairs.

Margo shook off a fleeting thought of concern for Preston. *He's not my problem,* she repeated in her head, as she reached the first floor and moved into the dining room. "Hi, how's everybody?" She started to pour herself a glass of champagne, the bottle tilted in the air, when she heard Caro's muffled voice from the fourth floor, then knocking, then pounding. What she heard next caused her to set the bottle down on the table with a bang.

"Omigod! John E., come quick. Call for help."

John E. darted for the stairs, taking two at a time. He shouted over his shoulder, "Somebody call nine-one-one."

Pandemonium overcame the dining table as everyone began talking at once, speculating as to what was happening.

Nicole screamed, "I knew something was wrong with Preston. He never sleeps this late. I've got to go to him." She leaped up as fast as the appliance on her ankle would allow, grabbing her walker.

Andrea, sitting next to her, jumped up, as well, intending to put her arms around Nicole's shoulders. The young woman was too quick, however, and she slipped away, scooting and sliding toward the stairs. "Nicole, stop. You're in no shape to climb three flights of stairs. Trust me, I know about these things." Andrea shuddered as she thought of her previous night's premonition, and then of some similar experiences she had known from researching her true crime stories.

"You can't stop me," Nicole shouted, beyond all reasoning. "I've got to get to Preston." She abandoned her walker at the base of the staircase and began scooting up the stairs on her rear end.

"Well, at least let me help you," Les said. "I can carry you much faster." He formed a chair with his arms, scooping the slim woman aboard to ride sideways. Andrea followed, carrying the walker.

Stan put away his cell phone and gave instructions to the rest of the group, taking charge as captain of the teetering ship. "Keep calm, everyone. Clear the driveway and keep the stairway open for the paramedics."

಼ಿ಼ಿ಼

It took nine minutes for the paramedics to traverse the winding road to Bucolia, a very long nine minutes in which the party of fourteen struggled to remain composed in a most shocking situation. After the first moments of chatter in the dining room, everyone became starkly silent, each holding his or her own thoughts and feelings inside. While most held no love lost for Preston, it was nevertheless disconcerting at the very least and horrifying at the most to imagine that one of their own might be in mortal danger. Twice Margo jumped up from her place at the table, as if to run upstairs, but apparently thinking better of it, sat back down. Marshall rose and paced from the dining room to the stairwell and back, hoping to hear something to indicate what was transpiring.

Sounds of Nicole's screaming and crying, wafting down the staircase, had signaled that Preston was either in grave condition or beyond. Stan took it upon himself to organize the car clearance operation, so paramedics could park in the circular driveway immediately in front of the doorway. The only car that couldn't be moved was Preston's Lamborghini. Luckily, it was positioned at the far end. Just to have something to do, Margo began clearing dishes and putting food away. Whatever appetites anyone had before had vanished in the instant Caro had shouted, "Omigod!"

Just before the paramedics arrived, Les came barreling down the stairs and rushing into the dining room. Everyone crowded around him, anxious looks pressing him with questions. His pale complexion and the grim set of his mouth were enough to cause Libby to rush into his arms. He hugged her tightly, burying his face into her neck for a moment before looking around at the assembled group. "It looks bad. John E. is doing CPR. That's all I can say."

The paramedics arrived at the same moment that a police car pulled into the circular driveway, both having been routinely dispatched at the time of the nine-one-one call, both vehicles flashing and wailing in the frigid afternoon air. What was not routine was an emergency call from one of the upscale gentlemen's farms, which is why, despite their haste to attend to the patient, the service personnel gazed about them at the elaborate furnishings. Stan pointed the way up the stairs, and the trio moved quickly, the EMTs carrying triage equipment. They rushed into the bedroom, where John E. was straddling Preston, administering CPR. John E.'s face was flushed and dripping with perspiration. His own breaths were ragged from exertion. In contrast, Preston's face was pale, frozen in a grimace, eyes scrunched.

Nicole was hunched in an almost-fetal position on the floor, her ankle with its metal contraption pointing in front of her like an arrow, holding onto Preston's arm with all her might. She muttered unintelligible words and phrases, possibly prayers. Her expression and tightly closed eyes mirrored those of her husband.

Andrea and Caro were standing behind Nicole, two sentinels of silent support. They exchanged glances several times as they observed John E.'s ministrations. Unspoken fears were evident in their expressions.

The paramedics did a double-take when they saw Nicole. They were the same ones on duty yesterday when Nicole had been the patient they transported to the hospital. Nicole opened her eyes as they called for everyone to stand back, so they could assess today's patient. They immediately placed defibrillator tabs onto Preston's chest, trunk, and limbs, and the machine proceeded to shock his heart multiple times. Between shocks, the EMTs did CPR.

The patrolman frowned as he examined the room with a well-trained eye. Left to right, ceiling to floor. While it was extremely unlikely that foul play would be involved in a place like this, with people like this, one could never be too careful in assessing the details. *If this turns out to be a crime scene*, he thought, *it'll already be totally screwed up with the CPR, the woman on the floor, and now the paramedics.*

The early afternoon light coming in from the window was the only illumination in the room. The officer focused on the patient. *The guy looks normal,* he thought, *good looks, fit, mid-sixties, I'd guess. No signs of blood, vomit, ligatures, bruises. Maybe a heart attack?* He sniffed. Smells like designer cologne or perfume, and something else. He moved closer to the bed, and then he knew. There was an unmistakable smell of ejaculate mixed with sweat.

The first paramedic stood by the defibrillator, his body shielding it from view of the others. Failing to see improvement, he knew what he had to do. "We've got to take the patient to the hospital," he said to the group after several minutes of defibrillation and CPR. "We can only do so much with the equipment we have here."

"Please say he's alive," Nicole whispered hoarsely, tears shining in her round brown eyes.

"It doesn't look good, to be honest," replied the second paramedic, "but we'll do our best for him."

John E. looked at Caro and shook his head. "I'm going down to make way for the transfer." He looked at Andrea and Nicole then. "I think we should all go downstairs and let the paramedics do their work."

"I won't leave Preston," Nicole wailed. "It's bad luck for us to be apart."

"You won't be able to come with us in the ambulance," the first paramedic told Nicole. "With the defibrillator on, we need the whole rear space for the patient."

"The patient has a name," Nicole shouted. "The patient is Mr. Preston Phillips. He is the former secretary of the treasury. He's an important person. You have to save him. You have to."

Andrea put her arms around Nicole from behind, gently coaxing her to calm down. "I'll take you to the hospital, Nicole. We'll follow right behind the ambulance." She looked toward the policeman, a young man she recognized as someone she had interviewed in the past, as if to ask permission to leave with Nicole. He nodded. As the paramedics carried Preston down the stairs on the stretcher, the party guests spontaneously parted to create a solemn aisle through the house and onto the driveway.

The police officer followed immediately.

Once the wailing ambulance and Andrea's Land Rover had departed for the hospital, Officer Barton called for everyone to return to the dining room.

His sober gaze moved from one to another of the rich and beautiful assembled around the table before saying, "Except for Mrs. Phillips and Mrs. Baker, who will drive Mrs. Phillips to the hospital, we need everyone to remain in this house until we can ask some routine questions. Okay?"

Chapter 20

Officer Barton resisted whistling over the surroundings at Bucolia. The appetizing aromas of breakfast hung in the air; the well-dressed group sat among the antiques and oil paintings, as if sheer luxury ran in their veins. Having heard Nicole's mention of the patient's status as former secretary of the treasury, he knew he was in high-powered company. He knew of the Campbells—their presence in Brandywine Valley had caused a bit of a stir when they'd purchased the farm a few years back.

He assumed, correctly, that these were all heavy hitters in the financial arena. He hoped like hell that this guy had died of natural causes, because dealing with these people was not going to be simple. *Jeez, look at this place, even the air I'm breathing feels expensive.* He was determined to suppress his fascination, however. *Just stick to the protocols*, he muttered internally. Before making the decision to call a detective in, he began to orient the group as to what routine procedures were necessary in an incident such as this. He thought he might need backup, just to be thorough.

The table was buzzing with questions. The pregnant lady asked, "Is Preston alive or dead?" The guy sitting next to her said under his breath, but loudly enough for Officer Barton to note, "What could possibly have caused him to be ill?"

"Where are they taking him?" the lady with the straight, shiny hair asked.

"How soon will we hear anything?" another asked. No one appeared to notice that no answers emerged from the string of questions.

"It doesn't seem possible that my birthday weekend could end so tragically," Mr. Campbell said, rubbing his eyes with his hands.

Quite possibly, Officer Barton thought, people were wondering how long they would have to stay at the farm. It was Sunday afternoon, after all, and these were people with important schedules. But no one uttered a syllable about leaving.

He flashed his badge. "Officer Randy Barton."

John E. gestured for the officer to take a seat next to Kitty.

As he sat, he rolled off his typical introductory remarks. "It is routine procedure when there is a non-respiratory emergency call to take down information about the people on the scene."

"Non-respiratory?" Caro squealed. "Are you saying that Preston is dead?"

"It's possible, ma'am," Officer Barton replied, powering up his departmental iPad. "You heard the paramedics say it wasn't looking good."

John E. reached for his wife's hand and sandwiched it between his own. If Preston had died in their house, Caro would never forgive herself. And how would she explain it to her family? "We'll be glad to answer all of your questions, Officer."

"To start with, which of you are the owners of this farm, and what is the occasion here?"

"I'm John E. Campbell, this is my wife, Caroline, and this is my farm." He leaned across the table to shake hands with the patrolman. "We're all here for a weekend celebration. My sixty-fifth birthday, in fact."

"What is the full name of the…er, patient…and what is his relationship to you?" Officer Barton asked, his fingers on the virtual keyboard.

While John E. answered the officer's questions, his guests listened attentively, their facial expressions and body language anything but casual.

One guy was running his fingers through the thinning hair on his head, both elbows on the table in front of him, while his wife twisted her ultra-straight hair around her finger, let it go, and petted the still-straight locks. Another couple held hands under the table, squeezing so tightly that the tension showed in their shoulders and collarbones.

The heavy-set guy muttered something unintelligible under his breath. His wife's eyes were shiny with incipient tears. "Only a few hours ago, Preston and I were sitting at this table, laughing. He didn't seem sick at all."

A redhead sat to the left of a young blonde. The

redhead covered her face, and she seemed to be hyperventilating. Blondie patted Redhead's shoulder.

None of the body language escaped Officer Barton's attention. As much as he would have liked to wrap up his questions and let these smart people get on with their lives, there was something suspicious in the way everyone was so tense, notwithstanding the fact that one of them was most likely arriving DOA at Brandywine Hospital about now. "Excuse me a moment," he said. "I need to get something from my vehicle." He clicked off his iPad, closed its case, and rose from the table.

When he got to his car, he called for a detective. "Need somebody at Campbells' farm…Yeah, EMTs took the guy to Brandywine. I got fourteen people here and four floors of farmhouse…Yeah, I'll need help."

Caro's phone rang just as he was returning to the dining room. "Andrea?" she answered breathlessly. "Do you have news?" She paused for a second, her eyes closed in a kind of prayer. "Oh, no," she screamed, denial and genuine grief ripping through her voice. She dropped the phone on the table, her eyes meeting the policeman's.

Everyone at the table looked at everyone else. No words were needed to confirm their fears. Preston Phillips was dead.

Officer Barton was the only one who seemed in full control of himself and the situation. He dreaded having to work with these Wall Street types, but his role was clear: secure the scene, gather facts, recover evidence. "Let's all stay calm," he said in his most soothing voice. "Apparently Mr. Phillips has died?" He looked to Caro for confirmation, although his gut had told him so from the moment he entered the fourth floor bedroom. Her nod was the closing of a curtain on Preston Phillips' life, just as it opened a curtain on its aftermath.

"Now I need to take down the names, dates of birth, addresses and contact information of everyone here and everyone who came into contact with Mr. Phillips in the last twenty-four hours. We'll start with the hosts…"

CHAPTER 21

O fficer Barton was taking down the last bits of information from the guests. All semblance of party atmosphere had evaporated from the house, as the doorbell's chime perforated the somber mood.

"I'll get it," Caro said, glad to have a reason for standing. She felt like her body was moving through thick cotton as she walked to the door. *Preston dead? It just couldn't be true.*

"Afternoon, ma'am," the young plain-clothed officer said, his badge held at her eye level. "Detective Parrott of the West Brandywine Police Department."

"Come in, Detective." Caro opened the door, wishing she could exit through it, even as she ushered the detective inside. Her hand shook as she closed the door behind him, cutting off her transient dream for escape.

She led Detective Parrott, a tall, muscular African-American, into the dining room. He made eye contact with the guests, nodded to Officer Barton, and turned back to Caro. An impressive-looking metal suitcase was tucked under his arm.

"This is Detective Parrott," Caro announced to

153

the group. Turning back to the detective, she said, "Would you like to sit down?" She pointed to the chair she had just vacated.

"No, ma'am," Detective Parrott replied, his voice deep and resonant.

A preacher's voice, Caro thought fleetingly. *Seems out of place for a cop.*

"I'd like to take a look at the room where the deceased was found, if you don't mind," he continued.

"Certainly," Caro replied. "I'll walk up with you."

Detective Parrott followed Caro up the stairs, while Officer Barton wrapped up his remarks to the rest of the group. "I understand this has been a shock to you folks. I appreciate your cooperation. Now if you will remain here to give Detective Parrott and myself some time to look over the upstairs, we'll come back down and get you on your way home." He looked at John E., tacitly turning over leadership to him.

John E., shaky, but seemingly in control, nodded. He stood, stretched, glanced at his Patek Phillipe, and asked if anyone would like something to eat or drink.

"Not much of an appetite," Marshall said. "Sorry such a great weekend came to such a crashing end."

Others muttered similar sentiments.

"Don't think about me," John E. said, his voice

cracking. "Think about poor Preston. And Nicole. How is that poor girl going to manage with her ankle and now this?"

"Well, I can't be hypocritical, I am not President of the Preston Phillips Fan Club," Leon Spiller said. "On the other hand, I can't say I'm glad he's dead."

Vicki walked over to the galley tray to pour herself a bloody Mary. "Anybody else need a stiff drink?"

"None of us is overly fond of Preston," Gerald said, his eyes landing on Kitty, who had been crying off and on for the past half hour. "That doesn't mean we wished him harm. We aren't criminals."

"Do you think the police officers suspect foul play?" Libby asked. "Or are they really just following routine procedures?"

"How could it be foul play?" Julia retorted, her voice more shrill than normal. "That would mean that one of *us* would have to be a murderer."

☙☙☙

Having deposited Parrott at the doorway to Preston's room, Caro touched the detective lightly on the arm. "I'll leave you to your work, but before I go downstairs, I have a favor to ask. Preston Phillips is my cousin, as well as a public figure. Whatever you and Officer Barton find out about him, could you please share it with me first? I'm afraid this is going to become a media circus, and I worry about my aunt, Preston's family, even Nicole."

"I'll keep that in mind, Mrs. Campbell. I'm hoping what we'll find is just an unfortunate heart attack." Parrott thought about the recent violent death of his own cousin. Despite his personal bias against the very rich, he suspected Caro was a woman with a good heart.

He entered Preston's bedroom suite, where he donned gloves and booties to begin the methodical search for evidence. The rays of the afternoon sun spotlighted the same place where just yesterday Margo and Preston had planned their interlude. The pillows on the upholstered chair looked as if they had not been plumped up. Someone had been sitting there recently.

Parrott bent over the apricot-colored chenille of the chair, his eye caught by a fine lime green thread in the gutter where cushion met armrest. "Might ask around to see if anyone was wearing lime green this weekend," he muttered as he dropped the thread into a plastic evidence bag.

Barton was at the headboard, examining fingerprints under the ultraviolet lamp. Parrott crossed over to help.

"Smell like sex to you?" Parrott asked, sniffing the sheets. Without waiting for a reply, he rolled back the bed coverings, one layer at a time. The sheets were jumbled, but there could be any number of explanations for that.

"Yeah, I noticed the smell earlier. Campbell was doing CPR when I got here. He was all sweaty, so I smelled that, too."

"Well, what do you know," Parrott exclaimed, as he pulled back the thick comforter and the top sheet. "Two…no, three…pecker tracks. Not bad for an old guy. How many days had he been staying here?"

"Friday night arrival, so two. Vic was sixty-seven. Guess he still had it going on. His wife is a hot little number, young. Come to think of it, though, she's got a broken ankle, stuck in one of those metal things. I don't think she'd be much in the mood."

"Well, unless he was playing solitaire, he had a busy social life." Parrott shone a hand-held high intensity lamp over the sheets, looking for other bits of information. "Maybe the guy died while having sex, had a heart attack or something." *No blood, no urine, no feces, no mucous. But what's this?* The strong light cast a thread-like shadow near the middle of the bed. "Pubic hair. Hand me a bag, will you?" He bagged the hair and kept moving systematically across the sheets and from the head to the foot of the bed, looking for human traces. "Here's another one." He put the second hair in another plastic bag. With any luck, they would be from two different DNA types.

"No crime in having sex," Barton muttered. "I just don't think he was having it with his wife, that's all." He strode into the bathroom to check for drugs. "Maybe the guy overdosed. Looks like he was taking some stuff." He opened his iPad to list the contents of Preston's Dopp kit, as well as the items on the marble counter. Celebrex, Voltaren, baby aspirin, Restasis eye drops, Metamucil— nothing too out of the ordinary. "Nope, bottles are almost full, so no sign of overdosing."

Parrott straightened, turned off the lamp, and picked up a Smartphone from the nightstand. *Always pays to check these out*, he thought, scanning received calls first. He fired up his iPad to record names and numbers. "Hmm…last missed call was from Nicole at twelve-forty-five this afternoon."

Barton said, "That's the wife. Guess she was calling from downstairs."

"Calls made…nothing today or yesterday."

"It's the weekend. Even these financial big-wigs must take weekends off. Nobody works weekends anymore, 'cept the munis like us."

Checking the camera function, Parrott examined some of the saved photos. "Take a look at this," he said, holding the phone so Barton could see a picture of Nicole in a black lace pushup bra. "Is this the wifey?"

"Yeah. Young and pretty, just like I said. Some guys have all the luck."

"Guys like this—" Parrott paused. "—luck is a talent." His stentorian voice added, "Somerset Maugham, I think."

"Well, I'm impressed, Detective."

Parrott moved on to search Preston's contact list. In the Cs he found Caro, followed by an entry labeled "Chief." He wrote down the phone number with the 512 area code. "What area code is five-one-two?"

"Texas…Austin. My brother-in-law just moved down there."

"Austin, Texas…then 'chief' must be our favorite ex-president." He whistled his appreciation. "This guy must've been really connected."

"Yeah, his wife shouted something about his being former secretary of the treasury or something."

"Didn't keep him from the Grim Reaper, though." Parrott continued to scan the room with a meticulous eye. "I don't see anything to suggest foul play. We'll see what autopsy and toxicology come back with, but my bet is the guy had a coronary or stroke. What was your feel for the group downstairs?"

"Bunch of rich people, spoiled, shocked. None of them seemed to talk much, just answered questions. Mrs. Campbell and the red-haired lady seem the most upset."

"Let's eyeball the other bedrooms before we go downstairs and let them go home?"

"Sure thing."

᷉᷉᷉

The restless party guests were still in the dining

room when Andrea's SUV pulled up in the drive-way. From one person to the next, there was fidget-ing, nervousness, sadness, but mostly exhaustion. It had been a long weekend, a late night the night be-fore, and a stressful afternoon.

Kitty was pouring herself a glass of water near the sink, so she was the first to see the SUV pulling up in front. "They're back from the hospital. Here they are."

Her normally mellifluous voice sounded hoarse and gravelly. She had been thinking all afternoon that just about everyone there had a motive to dis-like Preston, but to kill him? She couldn't imagine anyone of their breeding and stature in the commu-nity would take their grievances that far. They all had so much to lose. Margo, who had remained si-lent for most of this time, was shivering in her seat, her hands wrapped around a mug of herbal tea. Her long cinnamon-colored hair shrouded her face as she leaned forward in her chair, leaving her expres-sion undecipherable. Kitty wondered what had transpired between Preston and her.

Kitty watched as Nicole, with Andrea's help, eased out of the car and onto her walker. Nicole moved like an old woman, the physical pain seem-ing the lesser of the two burdens she carried. Her glossy blonde hair hung in clumps, adhered by dried tears. Whatever makeup she had put on be-fore lunch was long worn off, and the purple curves under her eyes stood out like badges of grief.

☙❧

Caro greeted the pair at the front door, hugging Nicole and murmuring, "I am so sorry." She took their coats and led them into the family room, where a cozy fire brought little comfort.

Stan rushed from the dining room to hug his wife. He bowed his head toward Nicole. "Let me help you get comfortable," he said, helping Nicole to the sofa where she had spent most of the previous day and night.

Just then Officer Barton and Detective Parrott descended the stairs. They found John E. at the base of the stairs on his way to the family room.

"Mr. Campbell," Detective Parrott intoned. "Could we have a word with you?"

"Of course."

"In private?"

"Sure. Let's go into my office." He led the officers into the office, on the far side of the family room and closed the door behind them.

Detective Parrott took the lead. "Officer Barton and I have inspected the upstairs bedrooms, particularly the suite on the fourth floor where Mr. Phillips was found unresponsive. We have just a few questions for you, and then we can meet with your party guests briefly before letting them leave the premises."

"Okay."

"When did you last see Mr. Phillips alive?"

"About two a.m. We had a long dinner party last night, followed by a smoke on the porch. The guys started heading to bed between one-forty-five and two. Preston stopped to say goodnight to his wife, here—" He pointed in the direction of the family room. "—before climbing the stairs to the fourth floor."

"So his wife didn't sleep with him last night?"

"No, her ankle injury left her unable to go up the stairs."

"Did anyone, to your knowledge, see Mr. Phillips after two a.m., when he went up to his room on the fourth floor?'

"Not to my knowledge."

"Was Mr. Phillips complaining that he didn't feel well at any time during the evening or night?"

"Not that I remember. He was in good spirits at dinner and afterward when we were smoking."

"Did he have a heart condition or any other medical condition that you know of?"

"You would have to ask my wife. Preston was her cousin, and she knew him much better than I— but, no, I thought Preston was in the prime of his life."

"Okay, Mr. Campbell. Thank you for your cooperation. We'd like to meet with your houseguests now. We'll give them instructions and get them on their way home. I'm sure they're eager to get back to their lives."

"Okay," John E. said, "but before that can you just tell me one thing: do you think Mr. Phillips died of natural causes?"

CHAPTER 22

At this point, Mr. Campbell, we have more questions than answers. I'm sure you understand," Detective Parrott replied without making eye contact.

"Of course," John E. mumbled, sorry that what had preyed so heavily on his mind had rolled so easily from his tongue.

"I'd like to speak to everyone in the house, Mr. Campbell. Which room would be the best place to gather the guests together?"

"I'll ask them to step into the family room, so Nicole—er, Mrs. Phillips—won't have to move. She's got a rather severe ankle injury."

"So I've heard."

John E. went into the dining room, where he spoke to the group so quietly that his words were a series of unintelligible swishes, like the sound of a brush on the head of a drum. He returned to the doorway of the office, with his wife and guests in tow, and motioned for the officers to lead the way into the family room.

The scent of burning pine cones filled the room with a coziness that belied the occasion. The darkening snow-blanketed landscape seen from the

164

window matched it better. Nicole was sitting on the sofa, packing a few belongings, mostly toiletries, as Andrea handed them to her. Her movements were swift and mechanical, as if she could not bear to think. She looked up as the parade of people entered the fire-lit room.

"What's going on here?" Nicole asked, annoyance covering every surface of her voice.

Caro stepped in front of the officers and the others, hoping her relationship to Preston would give her more credibility in managing his distraught widow. "Nicole, dear, these gentlemen are police officers. They need to speak to everyone."

"I can't imagine what police officers would need to speak to me about," Nicole cried. "Can they bring Preston back? Can they help me in any way? My life is falling apart. What do I need with police officers?"

Caro looked back at the officers and John E. It was obvious Nicole was becoming hysterical.

Parrott stepped forward and insinuated himself between Caro and Nicole. "I'm Detective Parrott, ma'am. I'm very sorry for your loss." His deep voice exuded confidence and a rock-like strength, and Nicole responded by raising the curtain from her large eyes.

"Thank you, Detective." Nicole put down the toiletries she had been holding, her glassy eyes meeting the detective's sober ones. "I'm not myself right now. I just lost my husband."

"I understand, ma'am. Mr. Phillips' death has, I'm sure, come as a shock. I want you and everyone here to know that Officer Barton and I will do everything we can to expedite things, so you can all get on with your lives as much as possible."

"What 'things' are you talking about?" Nicole asked, the curtain rolling back down over her grieving expression.

"Autopsy, toxicology reports, police reports, ma'am." Detective Parrott spoke the harsh words as gently as possible. "All routine procedure in cases such as—"

Andrea interrupted to ask, "How long do you think these will take, Detective? I'm sure Mrs. Phillips would like to begin planning for Mr. Phillips' funeral as soon as possible."

"Autopsy usually takes two to three days, after which we can release the body for the funeral. Toxicology can take much longer, perhaps as much as three weeks. In this instance, though, because of— er, Mr. Phillips' standing in the community and such—we will push for quick processing. I would think you could have the funeral by mid-week, if you want."

The group of guests stood stock still as they contemplated the circumstances: Preston's death, the police presence, Nicole's predicament, an upcoming funeral, and the possibilities that might evolve from the medical examiner's findings.

John E. cleared his throat and spoke first. "I'm

sure we would all appreciate your expediency, as well as your discretion in handling these matters. I don't need to tell you that Mr. Phillips, as well as most of us here, was a public figure. You know how the press can be when they get wind of something they can play up as sensational. It would reflect inappropriately on Mr. Phillips, as well as the rest of us, if that were to happen."

Unfazed, Detective Parrott continued in silken tones, "Officer Barton here has taken down personal information from all of you, except for Mrs. Phillips and Mrs. Baker, whom I will interview. Here is my phone number." He paused to distribute business cards to each guest. "If you think of anything we should know, anything we should look into, please give us a call. Otherwise, you are free to return to your homes and get on with your lives."

Julia broke the silence. "Okay, guys, I guess we should start packing up."

Inwardly she was relieved. Having police gather everyone together like that had given her the impression that they were going to make some pronouncement or accusation. She still felt wary of Detective Parrott, though. Something in his authoritative manner reminded her of a fox. She took Marshall by the elbow and headed for the stairs. The others followed quietly, politeness holding them from chattering or rushing up the stairs.

"I can't wait to get out of here," Libby whispered to Les, once she was out of earshot of Nicole and the rest of the group. "Those policemen were giving me the creeps."

Les's brow furrowed. "I know. But they were just doing their job. I'm sure Preston just had an ordinary heart attack."

"It bothers me that Margo has been so distraught all afternoon. I wish I knew what she's been thinking."

"Maybe she'll talk once we get out of here and on our way back home."

☙❧❧

"Mrs. Phillips, ma'am," Detective Parrott began, sitting in the chair adjacent to the sofa, where Nicole had her packed belongings next to her.

Nicole looked up at the courteous man, her youthful energy depleted, her eyes lacking sparkle, her face drawn in tension. Her lack of response was less a result of indifference than of exhaustion.

"I hate to disturb you further, but I need to ask you a few important questions." He looked at Andrea and asked, "Would you please excuse us?"

Andrea nodded and glided toward the kitchen, leaving Nicole alone with the two officers.

Officer Barton had his iPad ready to record notes from the interview, while Detective Parrott did the

168

talking. "Mrs. Phillips, how long have you and Mr. Phillips been married?"

"We just celebrated our six-month anniversary last week."

"And have you notified Mr. Phillips' other family members?"

"I called his son Peter from the hospital. Peter told me he would contact Preston's mother and sister."

"And who, among Mr. Phillips' associates, did he refer to as 'chief'?"

For the first time all day, Nicole felt the twitching of an incipient smile, yearning to break forth. "Why, Detective, that is none other than the former President of the United States. I told you guys Preston was an important person."

"Fine." Parrott stole a glance at Barton. "Now, Mrs. Phillips, can you tell me when the last time was that you saw Mr. Phillips alive?"

"We spoke around two a.m. when Preston was getting ready to go upstairs to bed."

"You weren't sleeping together last night?" Neither officer made eye contact.

"I wanted to go upstairs with him. I begged him to let me, but he was tired and told me I needed to rest my ankle."

"So where did you spend the night?"

"Here on this sofa. I've been here pretty much non-stop since yesterday afternoon." She pointed to her ankle in its awkward appliance.

"Yes, we know about your accident," Barton interjected. "I was on duty yesterday when it happened."

"Did Mr. Phillips seem unwell to you at two a.m.?"

"He didn't say anything. He looked tired, but he had been eating, drinking, smoking cigars, and everyone was tired by that point."

"Had he taken any drugs that you know of?"

"Not that I know of..." Nicole said, her voice trailing off as she remembered Preston had taken several of her oxycodone tablets. "Well, he did take a couple of my pain pills." She rifled through her makeup bag to pull out the vial prescribed for her. She held it out for Officer Barton to inspect, and he made a note of the type and strength.

"Why would Mr. Phillips take your pain pills?" Parrott asked, keeping his tone of voice neutral.

"I don't know. I didn't ask him. I assume he was having some pain."

"Let's change the subject. Can you give me your date of birth, address, and contact information?"

"May 26, 1994. We live in the Dakota, One West Seventy-Second Street, Manhattan. I can give you contact information." Nicole thought for a moment, the reality of her situation hitting home again. "But why all this?"

"We will need to keep in touch with you about the autopsy and other reports, ma'am."

"Oh, yeah. I forgot for a minute." Nicole bit her fingernail and fought back tears.

Changing tactics again, Parrott asked, "How did you and Mr. Phillips meet?"

"I was a receptionist at the Lamborghini dealership where Preston bought his last car. It was love at first sight."

Officer Barton wrote "L@1S" in his notes, restraining himself from rolling his eyes at the young woman's naiveté.

If this turns out to be a murder, I'd peg this lady as the number one suspect, even with this contraption on her ankle.

"I want to make sure I have this straight, Mrs. Phillips," Parrott continued. "You and Mr. Phillips arrived here when?"

"Friday night."

"And you stayed together on the fourth floor?"

"Yes, Friday night we did. And then we went horseback riding Saturday morning, and I broke my ankle."

"So since Saturday morning, you have not been in the room on the fourth floor?"

"No. I've stayed down here in this room. Till this morning, when Les carried me up the stairs."

"You haven't been able to climb the stairs at all?"

Nicole bit her bottom lip, thinking of her early morning foray up the stairs, where she had met Margo.

Detective Parrott repeated, "You haven't climbed the stairs at all, Mrs. Phillips?"

"No, Detective. I haven't."

"By the way, Mrs. Phillips, what were you wearing on Friday night?"

Wondering what in the world her apparel would have to do with anything, Nicole answered, "Black low-cut pants, white cashmere skimmer, Stuart Weitzmans. Why?"

"It's our job to be thorough. That's all." Detective Parrott scratched his head before asking a final question. "Mrs. Phillips, how were you and Mr. Phillips getting along this weekend?"

Nicole's posture stiffened. "Just fine. We were practically honeymooners still. Why would you think otherwise?"

"Not saying I do, Mrs. Phillips. Sometimes even the most devoted married people have arguments."

"Well, Preston and I were very much in love." Nicole refused to let the niggling memory of her suspicions about Preston and Margo and what Preston told her on Saturday night during the dinner party creep into this now. She was Preston's wife, and she would be Preston's widow.

"Okay, Mrs. Phillips. Thank you for your cooperation. We extend our deepest sympathies to you and to Mr. Phillips' family. And I do need that contact information."

"Here. I'll write it down for you," Nicole said, and she pulled a Montblanc pen and notepad from her handbag and jotted down her phone numbers. She handed the paper to the now-standing detective. "Whatever you're thinking about me and Preston," she said, her voice becoming shrill, "Preston was my soulmate, and no one, not even Death, can take Preston Phillips away from me."

Chapter 23

*W*all Street Journal.
Monday, December 16th:
NEW YORK – Preston Phillips, 67, former US Secretary of the Treasury and Wall Street financier, died yesterday of an apparent heart attack at the farm of a close personal friend, John E. Campbell, where he was attending Mr. Campbell's 65th birthday party.

Mr. Phillips was the first-born child of (the late) Theodore and Penelope Bartlett Phillips of the Hamptons. He attended Choate Rosemary Hall and Princeton University undergraduate, where he was captain of the football team. He earned his doctorate in business from the Harvard Business School. Elected to Congress from New York's 22nd Congressional District in 1984, he became Chairman of the Congressional Ways and Means Committee in 1994 and served in that position until nominated by President Dalton to be secretary of the treasury. He returned to private life after President Dalton's re-election.

Former President Dalton issued a statement extolling Mr. Phillips' long and distinguished service to his country. "We are shocked and saddened by

Mr. Phillips' untimely death. America has lost one of its brilliant stars, and Mary and I have lost a close personal friend. Our deepest sympathies go out to Preston's family, along with our thoughts and prayers."

The White House has also issued a statement, noting Mr. Phillips' contributions to the United States, and extending the president's and first lady's personal condolences, along with the condolences of the American people.

Mr. Phillips is survived by his wife Nicole; his mother; his sister Frances Phillips Worthington; and his son Peter. Funeral arrangements are pending.

༒

Gerald and Kitty sat down at the breakfast nook in their primary residence in Chappaqua on Monday morning. Neither had slept very well. Their freshly ground Kona coffee filled the air with a delicious aroma but remained untouched. Gerald unfolded the *Journal,* placed as usual next to his linen napkin. Preston's obituary leaped from the bottom of the fold on the first page.

"Kitty, look. Preston's obit is on page one."

"That doesn't surprise me. Preston was a very important man, especially in financial circles."

"It says here he died of an apparent heart attack."

"Well, wasn't that what killed him?"

"If you ask me, he died from having no heart at

all, but that's just me. I know you feel differently."

"I do, Gerald. Preston wasn't as bad as all of you made him out to be. In fact, he had a certain charm about him. I, for one, am very sad that he's gone."

"You and probably a thousand other ladies who have thrown their panties at him over the years. I never could see what Preston's appeal was, but I have to admit he had it." Gerald took a first gulp from his coffee mug. "The thing is," he mused, taking a fork to his egg-white omelet, "Preston seemed to be in great shape. He wasn't sick, overweight, or old. I sure didn't see any signs of a heart attack coming, did you?"

"No. To be honest, I think of all the guys at the party, Preston was the last one I would have pegged to die first. I talked to him throughout the entire evening, and there wasn't the slightest indication he wasn't feeling well." Indigestion burned in her esophagus as she thought of how vibrant Preston had seemed. Breakfast, no matter how attractively presented, held no appeal for her. "Gerald, I feel sorry for Caro and John E., for Nicole, actually for all of us. It is quite traumatic when you think about it."

"Do you think the police suspect foul play?"

"That will probably depend on the results of the autopsy. We all had plenty to eat and drink Saturday night, and you guys smoked those god-awful cigars, but Preston was the only one who turned up dead, so who knows?"

"Hmm…I'm beginning to regret what I said that afternoon about wanting to kill him," Gerald said. His eyes bored into his wife's. "You know I was kidding, right?"

❦

Andrea was no stranger to deaths, especially un-explained deaths. Her work as a crime writer had taken her to crime scenes, courtrooms, police stations, and cemeteries. She had met face-to-face with family members and investigators, and she had a well-developed sixth sense for determining when someone had died under suspicious circumstances. With six books under her belt, all successful, she considered herself expert in reading the tea leaves. Now, sitting at her uncluttered desk in her wood-paneled writing studio on her spectacular farmland in the country's Northeast, her hands wrapped around a ceramic mug of cinnamon-spiced tea, she was harboring some definite pangs of conscience about last weekend's party at the Campbells'. Even before the guests had assembled on Friday night, Andrea had felt misgivings about participating. She had been glad to have another place nearby to sleep, so she wouldn't have to spend hours upon hours with the other guests. Her words to Stan as they were dressing for the party Saturday night echoed in her brain, '*I'm dreading this evening for some reason, Stan. I just don't have a good feeling about it.'* Now she wrapped her arms around her middle with regret. Was there something she could have said, something she could have done to prevent Preston's death?

Andrea picked up the phone, intending to call Nicole. Perhaps she could help with the funeral arrangements. Poor Nicole had so much on her plate with her ankle, on top of the pressures of planning a funeral. She was so young and inexperienced, and clearly out of her league when it came to dealing with Preston's stature in the financial community. *Maybe she would welcome some help from me, and maybe I could find out whether she's had any news from the police.*

The dial tone hummed as she contemplated what to say. When the fast busy tone came on, Andrea replaced the receiver into its cradle. She was, after all, not what one would consider a close friend, either to Nicole or to Preston. She was just a true crime writer whose antennae were humming with the premonition that Preston's death might make quite a fascinating book.

☙❧☙

Vicki was trying to keep busy this Monday morning. Leon had left for work, and there was no one in the house but her. Since she had let Tereza go, it was up to Vicki herself to keep the house clean, except on Fridays, when the regular cleaning service came. It was not too big a sacrifice, because it gave Vicki the privacy she craved to do whatever she wanted during the day. Today she embraced the quiet. She busied herself with lightly dusting the family room. She hadn't slept more than an hour last night, thoughts of Preston rolling through her brain like a silent film.

She ran her dust cloth over the framed pictures of Tony, remembering the joyful young man, and trying to block out the pain of losing him. She moved on to the fish tank. The vivid creatures were going about their day, some languid, some purposeful, but all with an enviable peacefulness. Vicki adored her fish tank. The beautiful creatures inside required so little, but gave so much. She could watch the brilliant shapes for hours. Presiding over the indoor biome gave her a sense of timelessness, as well as a sense of power.

She shuddered, still thinking of Preston's death, replaying her ugly encounter in the stairwell with him just hours beforehand. She was right to blame him for Tony's death and the destruction of her dreams. For all the accolades Preston would receive in the newspapers in the coming week, he had been an arrogant, reckless, even cruel bastard. She could not feel sorry for him now.

ඏඏ

Marshall sat at his desk at the Federal Reserve

Bank on Liberty Street in New York. He and Julia had taken their private plane into the regional airport near their waterfront manor on Kirby Pond in Rye. They hardly spoke the entire way, each lost in thought. The weekend had been a roaring success, in Marshall's opinion, up until Sunday afternoon, when Preston's death had put a definite pall over the festivities.

It was hard to concentrate on his latest report for the Beige Book, because images of Preston kept popping into his frontal lobe, clamoring for attention, much the same as Preston himself had. Marshall's feelings about Preston had always been jumbled. When they were kids, neighbors, Marshall had looked up to Preston with an almost-brotherly admiration. They had been best of friends until adolescence, when Preston's athletic accomplishments and preference for female company created a rift. Still, Marshall remained loyal, enjoying being an active observer in Preston Phillips' seemingly charmed life.

All of that changed when Marshall went to into the service. With his low lottery number, Marshall was forced into service, and he chose not to take the National Guard route, as so many of his friends had, because he had hoped for an eventual career in politics. His hero had been General Dwight D. Eisenhower, whose leadership in World War II and afterward inspired patriotism and confidence. In Marshall's absence, his parents had remained enthralled by Preston's intelligence and emerging financial expertise.

By then, in 1969, Preston was starting at Harvard Business School. While Marshall was committing murder-under-orders in the hot, miserable jungles near Khe Sanh, Preston was charming Mr. and Mrs. Winthrop with his talk of doubling and tripling their sizeable wealth.

By the time Marshall was honorably discharged after his parents' deaths, in 1972, Preston had his doctorate in business and was working on Wall Street. He had tied up the Winthrops' portfolio, tighter than Scarlett O'Hara's corset. He was the sole trustee of their trust fund, so in addition to controlling the money, he'd received a hefty compensation all of these years. *He ripped us off with bad investments and then ripped us off some more. Not that we've starved, but I've had to work twice as hard to earn what we have, and, by all rights, I should have had those two hundred million dollars.*

All that is water under the bridge, Marshall thought now, gripping his computer mouse and gazing at the blank screen. The tension building in his head was getting the best of him; the skin above his right eye visibly throbbed.

৽৵৽

Caro was puttering around the kitchen at Bucolia, unable to sit, unable to think clearly. She had

181

waved away the downstairs housekeeper, sending her to help the others with laundering linens and cleaning bedrooms and bathrooms. After any such party, there was a let-down when it came to cleaning up after the guests. The preparations had kept her busy for months, and now it was over in a flash.

This party, however, had ended horribly, and it had left her with an unending nightmare, a mind full of regrets. She took over operations in the kitchen, sorting through leftovers, boxing up most of them for the servants to take home. Now, unloading the dishwasher, she dropped a still-hot coffee mug. With a loud clink, it shattered into hundreds of shards.

John E. rushed over to put his arms around his wife, who had covered her face and was racked with silent sobs. "It's okay, Honey. It's going to be okay." He held her tightly.

It took Caro a few long minutes to catch her breath enough to talk. When she did, her voice sounded unnaturally high and child-like. "I don't know if I'll ever get over this."

"I know. I feel devastated, too."

"I feel even worse, because I worry about my Aunt Penny and my mother. Neither of them is in good health. Oh, why did this have to happen in our house? I feel so responsible!" Fresh sobs erupted, as Caro broke away from John E.'s embrace. She turned this way and that, looking for, but not finding, consolation in this room.

"I need to clean up the mess," she muttered.

"Leave it," John E. said. "The housekeeper can take care of that."

"I wish someone could fix everything else," Caro cried. "I can't believe Preston is gone."

⁕⁕⁕

After treating herself to a lavender-scented bubble bath, Margo wrapped herself in a cotton candy-colored fleece robe. She was so touchy that even the softest of her clothes felt scratchy. She retreated to the quiet of Libby's guest bathroom, where she was perched on the side of the Jacuzzi, one knee drawn to her chin. She desperately needed a pedicure, but the thought of having to talk to someone at the other end of her feet was unbearable.

"I'll just do it myself," she muttered, dabbing the cuticles of her toes with soothing oil. She needed time to think, although she had done nothing but think since the previous afternoon. She relived the events of the weekend, from the time she entered Bucolia on Friday evening until the moment when she knew Preston was dead. So much had transpired in those few hours. Preston had made her feel young, desirable, yes, even happy. He somehow melted her resolve to ignore him, and she had given him her trust. The wee hours of Sunday morning had been sheer ecstasy. Being loved by

Preston had filled her with a giddiness, a wholeness, that she hadn't felt in years.

On the other hand, colliding with Nicole on the stairway afterward, and realizing that Preston had deceived her about divorcing his wife, cut short her happy feelings, as surely as a sharp needle taken to balloons. That was when she had decided to go back to Preston's room, one last time, to give him a piece of her mind and to tell him that no way was she going to be made a fool of again.

Ouch, that hurt. Pushing back her cuticles with an orange stick, Margo jabbed herself. A drop of blood appeared on the skin above her big toenail. She wiped it away with a cotton ball, wishing she could wipe away the larger pain consuming her.

Now, with Preston dead and policemen sniffing around the farm, Margo was on edge. If the autopsy and toxicology reports indicated foul play, it would only be a matter of time before she would be questioned. There had been ample hints of flirtation going on between Preston and her all weekend. Nicole had probably already conveyed her suspicions to the police. Besides that, her fingerprints were probably all over that fourth floor room. *If the police seek me out, what am I going to tell them?* Tears of anger and fear welled in Margo's green eyes. In all her life, she had never felt so alone.

CHaptER 24

Nicole hung up the phone, proud of herself for maintaining her composure throughout her conversation with President Dalton. She had never felt quite so alone as she did now that Preston was no longer the ruler of her domain. The past twenty-four hours had challenged her in ways she'd never dreamed of. Not only did she have to manage the pain of her broken ankle, imminent surgery, and the logistical trials of everyday life, but she also had to converse with people from Preston's family, career, and social circle, people whose intellect and lifestyles were vastly different from hers.

Jeez, even the way I talk is different, she thought, feeling thoroughly inadequate. *Well, at least I got through talking to Preston's mom and sister and son, and the former President of the United States, for gosh sakes, without bursting into tears.*

"Preston," she intoned, looking upward, "I had no idea you were this important. So many famous people are calling to give their sympathy and ask about funeral arrangements." Nicole picked at the skin around her fingernail. "I wish the police would release your body, so we could move forward.

Both of us are in limbo right now."

The brring of the phone pierced the air and Nicole's thoughts once more. She regretted having sent her personal attendant to run errands.

She leaned over her lunch tray to answer it. "Nicole speaking, may I help you?" This was the same way she had answered the phone at her desk in the Lamborghini showroom.

"Mrs. Phillips?" the voice said. "This is Ted Lambert, your husband's personal attorney. I wonder if I might have a moment of your time?"

"Sure, Mr. Lambert. How can I help you?"

"I was wondering if you could come into my office sometime this week to discuss the matter of your husband's will."

Nicole felt a chill, hearing the word "will." She knew, of course, that Preston had been worth a lot of money, and she knew that as his wife at the time of his death, she would be a major beneficiary, but the reality of becoming an heiress, of actually having lots of her very own money to spend, overwhelmed her in a way that the broken ankle and Preston's death had not. She glanced at the gooseflesh on her forearms before finding her voice.

"Mr. Lambert, I don't know whether you know or not, but I have a broken ankle? It's in a halo contraption while I wait to schedule surgery. I have all of the funeral arrangements to make, as soon as Preston's body is released for burial, and—"

"Oh, I am so sorry to hear that, Mrs. Phillips.

186

Would you like for me to wait a few weeks, until things settle down for you, before discussing Mr. Phillips' will?"

Not wanting to seem greedy, but with her curiosity getting the best of her, she replied, "I didn't mean I'm not interested, Mr. Lambert. I was just wondering if you could come to me."

Nicole could hear the tongue in the lawyer's cheek, as if he had her pegged as a money grubber. "*Of course.* What would be a good day and time for you?"

"How about tomorrow at one p.m.?"

"That would be fine."

"Do you know where we—er, I—live?"

"Yes, ma'am. It's right here in front of me. I'll see you tomorrow afternoon."

"Thanks so much." Nicole paused before hanging up the phone, and then impulsively said, "Oh, Mr. Lambert?"

"Yes?"

"Could you give me a rough idea of how large Preston's estate is?"

"Certainly, Mrs. Phillips. Your husband was worth over three and a half billion."

Nicole tried, but couldn't suppress a soft gasp into the phone. "That much? I had no idea."

"Yes, well," Mr. Lambert replied. "We will have much to discuss at tomorrow's meeting."

"Okay, see you tomorrow." Nicole put the phone down slowly, the words "three and a half billion" echoing in her brain. That was more money than she had ever dreamed of. Even with the pre-nup she had signed, at least ten percent of that three and a half billion would soon be hers. Suddenly, the broken ankle, impending surgery, and funeral plans seemed like minor inconveniences. Three and a half billion had released adrenalin in Nicole's brain. She needed to call her hairdresser, manicurist, and personal shopper. She would need a gorgeous black outfit for the funeral, something that would look good on television. Maybe a hat or a veil, too. "Preston, I want to look good, so you'll be proud of me," she said aloud, looking heavenward.

Another telephone ring interrupted thoughts of fashionable splendor. "Hello?" Nicole answered, still in *nouveau riche* mode.

A familiar tenor voice, carefully modulated, greeted her. "Well, hell—oo, baby."

"I told you never to call me here," Nicole whispered into the receiver. Though hushed, her voice had a strident quality.

"That was when the old man was alive. And I tried to respect your wishes. But it's a new game now, baby, a very, very rich game."

"I don't know what you're talking about. I don't want to talk to you, Billy. Not now, not ever."

"Oh, come on, now. I'm sure you haven't forgotten about me, Nicky. I'm the only one who's ever understood you, the only one who can really make you happy. And now that you are the young and beautiful widow of a very rich old man, we can be together again."

The voice continued on, though Nicole heard nothing more. Her mind was speeding down a track, turning corners here and there, hoping to find the right thing to say to disengage herself from this call, this caller. "Billy, you can't call me here. I'm not alone, and I'm not free to talk. I've got a million things on my plate to deal with, and I can't have you interfering."

"Yeah, I'll bet you have a million things, even more than that, baby. I'll let you go, but I just wanted you to know I'm here, waiting for you, and sending you love every day."

Desperate to hang up, Nicole said, "Okay, thanks. Now don't call me. I'll call you." She slammed the phone down this time, suddenly frightened about what the future would hold. No sooner than the prospect of becoming rich in her own right had appeared, so had the specter of people from her past who would come swarming around her, seeking to benefit from her pot of golden honey. She knew how the game was played. She, herself, had played it for years.

Her mind wandered to Preston's death. She was still in shock, most likely, from the suddenness of it all. One moment she had been worried about losing Preston to Margo, and the next moment she lost him altogether. *I wonder what the medical examin-*

er is going to find, she thought, picking again at her cuticle. Suddenly she straightened her back and stared ahead, a chilling thought striking her for the first time. *Isn't it always the wife who is the first suspect in a murder investigation? Oh, Lord, what have I gotten myself into?*

Chapter 25

The first phone call Nicole made on Tuesday morning was to Detective Parrott. She was surprised how difficult it was to get through to him. He seemed to have more personnel guarding his privacy than she did, since she preferred to answer her own calls.

"No, I do not want to leave a message," she insisted. "Officer Parrott gave me this number and told me to call him if I need anything, and I need something, now."

"I'm sorry. Detective Parrott is in the field at the moment."

"Tell him Mrs. Preston Phillips needs to talk to him ASAP." She stirred her hazelnut coffee with a vengeance, spilling some onto the tray.

"Mrs. Phillips, I am not in immediate contact with Detective Parrott. I will have to relay your message."

"Okay. Have him call me on my cell phone." Nicole slammed the phone down. *I'll bet Preston never had to go through all this hassle to get people on the phone. Just his name opened doors. Why not for me?*

Thirty-six minutes and several phone calls later,

Nicole's desk phone uttered its brring. The caller ID showed *West Brandywine Police*. Nicole grabbed the receiver with equal parts of eagerness and dread. "Nicole speaking, may I help you?"

Parrott's baritone voice momentarily soothed her ruffled feathers. "Parrott returning your call. I understand you needed me urgently."

"Uh, yes, Detective. Thanks for getting back with me." *I sound so pitiful. Preston would tell me to get that subservient tone out of my voice.* She sat up straighter and cleared her throat. "Ahem. I've been receiving phone calls from people in high places who want to know what the funeral arrangements for Mr. Phillips are. Are you any closer to releasing the body?"

"Let me see, Mrs. Phillips. May I put you on hold?"

"Of course." Nicole tapped her newly manicured nails on her desk, annoyed to have to wait. For some reason, the tune to Adele's "Someone Like You" was running through her mind.

ᥱᣞᥱᣞ

Parrott, whose case load consisted of Preston Phillips' unexplained death and several other matters, was just as eager as, if not more than the Widow Phillips, to hear from the coroner. The longer it took, the colder the case would become, if there was a case at all.

He hated to pester her, but his intuition had been working overtime, and he wanted to be ready to jump in with both feet if death was not from natural causes. It wasn't every day that he had a murder to investigate, least of all, one with such a prominent victim.

He rubbed his dry hands in anticipation.

With Nicole holding on line one, Parrott punched line two and speed-dialed Maria Rodriguez, Coroner for Chester County. He didn't expect to get through, especially at this early hour, when Maria would likely be up to her elbows in body fluids. He was pleasantly surprised, then, when she answered the phone with a cheerful, "Coroner's Office, Rodriguez speaking."

"Maria, Oliver Parrott here, Brandywine PD."

"Hey, Parrott. I'll bet you're calling about Preston Phillips."

"Yes, indeed. Any word on when his body will be ready to go?"

"I just sat down at my desk to call you. We can release the body now. Toxicology won't be back for a few more days at best, though."

"Anything I need to know from the autopsy?"

"Just the usual. Patient stopped breathing. Organs in good shape, no obvious bruises or puncture marks."

"Do you have an estimated time of death?"

"Somewhere between four and seven a.m. I can't be more specific. The heated room slowed the

193

cooling of his body temperature somewhat."

"I've got the widow on the other line. Everyone's impatient to arrange the funeral. Patient was high up on the political food chain, so lots of media attention." The detective rubbed his hands over his cheeks as he thought. "Any chance you could put a super rush on toxicology? I have a feeling we're going to get hit with a sucker punch."

Maria shrugged. "I've already put a rush on it, but I'll call and remind them it's a high profile case. No problem."

"Thanks. You're the best." Parrott rubbed the sides of his freshly barbered head before returning to line one.

"Hello, Mrs. Phillips?"

"Yes?"

"Sorry to keep you waiting so long. I've just spoken with Maria Rodriguez, the Chester County Coroner."

"And?" Nicole realized she was holding her breath, the aftertaste of hazelnut coffee rising in her throat.

"You can proceed with funeral arrangements now. Mr. Phillips' remains will be released for burial tomorrow morning."

Nicole felt a surge of energy, either from the prospect of progress or the caffeine in her system. "So does that mean there's a report? Do you know what caused Preston's death?"

"You can discuss the autopsy results when you

call to arrange for the body transport. It will only be a preliminary report, since the toxicology studies haven't come back yet." Parrott's well-trained ear listened for an auditory tell, any unusual intake of breath or vocalized pause that might reveal the widow's frame of mind.

Hearing none, he proceeded, "Mrs. Phillips, have you selected a site for the funeral yet?"

Nicole wondered why he was asking. *Surely the police wouldn't be interested in attending Preston's funeral.* "I can tell you that Andrett Funeral Home on Second Avenue is who I am working with. I need a very large space, most likely Trinity Episcopal Church on Wall Street. I know President and Mrs. Dalton are coming, and probably some people from the current administration, too." Nicole fiddled with her gold filigree letter opener.

"Well, Officer Barton and I would like to extend our deepest sympathies to you and your family."

"That's very kind of you, Detective."

ᘓᕹᘓᕹ

Caro read to John E. from the *Wall Street Journal,* "'Funeral services for Preston Phillips, Wall Street financier and former secretary of the treasury, will be held at Trinity—Visitation, Friday at two p.m. Service at three. Interment will be private.'"

"It's going to be a circus," John E. said, as he

scraped the bottom of his bowl of steel cut oatmeal.

"I spoke with Nicole yesterday, and she's received calls from the White House, former presidents, and news anchors. She was even approached by a publisher to write a book about her life with Preston." Caro looked at her husband over her readers. "Can you imagine that?"

"It would have to be a very short book, I would think." He chuckled and took a swig of coffee. "Maybe we should go into New York tomorrow morning, spend the day and night with the family. We could stay at the Peninsula for a couple of nights. What do you think?"

"That's a marvelous idea. Let's see if Mother and Aunt Penny want to stay with us. If we can get the Peninsula Suite, it would be ideal."

John E. gazed lovingly at his wife. This was the first time since Sunday that she had sounded enthused about anything.

"But, of course, there isn't anything ideal about Preston's funeral." Caro crumpled her napkin in her lap and looked downward, her eyes filling with tears. "How could I forget, even for a minute?"

"I know, Caro. I feel terrible, too." John E. recalled the remarks about his birthday having been on Friday the thirteenth. "I guess this birthday was a bad luck birthday, after all."

CHAPTER 26

The Friday morning of the funeral dawned with a brilliance of oranges and blues that made Nicole think of the Tropics, rather than the brittle urban landscape that it was. A cold front had clenched the city in its fierce grip, making the grim prospect of a funeral even more uncomfortable.

Eager to provide the perfect funeral for Preston, Nicole had arranged the location at Trinity Episcopal Church. The elegant medieval building stood at the head of Wall Street, its graveyard housing the remains of Alexander Hamilton, the first secretary of the treasury. Preston would have loved that.

Outside, the media surrounded the church, running film as people streamed into the entrances, trying to get in from the cold and away from publicity.

There were strict orders not to film the funeral itself, but reporters, bundled in layers of outerwear, had been on assignment since early in the morning, hungry for details that would make for good copy. Preston Phillips had long been a favorite of the media. He was one of the few one percenters who had relished being photographed and quoted.

Like Nicole, they wanted to give Preston a media send-off that would do him justice. The catalogue of family members and those coming to pay their respects was extensive. Andrett's had set up velvet ropes and multiple memorial books, so that visitors could move through the lines as efficiently as possible. The entire front of the sanctuary, from pews to apse, was filled with a profusion of floral arrangements, perfuming the chilly air with delicate sweetness.

One of Nicole's sisters had come in from Albany to assist her with the logistics. Nicole felt conflicted over this. On the one hand, Francine was both capable and trustworthy, qualities desperately needed right now. On the other hand, Francine's simple earthiness was no match for the genteel society types that would be gathered around. *I might have been able to bridge the class gap,* Nicole thought*, but Francine—no way. I'm half-tempted to pass her off as a servant.*

"When we get to the church, I'll just make myself scarce, Nicky," Francine said, as if she had read her sister's mind.

"Don't be silly," Nicole said, ashamed of herself for being ashamed of her own background.

❧❧❧

Andrea and Stan stepped out of a silver Tesla limo, having come into the city from their home in Greenwich. Not one to dress ostentatiously, Andrea wore fine wool pants and a charmeuse blouse, both black. Her black and gray hounds-tooth vest and black cashmere coat completed the outfit. She held onto Stan's suede-clad arm as she entered the church, her posture erect and her demeanor appropriately somber.

Inside, her brain was a pinball machine, tossing questions about at odd angles and varied speeds. She couldn't help feeling Preston's life had been cut short, not by sudden illness, but by nefarious means. And if it were true, then someone at Caro's party was responsible. But who?

For the first time, Andrea regretted not having stayed at Bucolia with the rest of the group. The times she was at her own place, and away with Nicole, were times she might have developed a clearer picture of the dynamics.

As it was, there was suspicion enough to put her on high alert at the funeral. In her experience, murder was a possibility in every young person's death, and at sixty-seven, Preston qualified.

And if it was a murder, Andrea was itching to write about it.

჻

Les, Libby, and Margo were sitting in the plush leather space of a chauffeur-driven limousine as they approached the elegant old church. Margo appreciated the fact that her sister and brother-in-law did not try to engage her in conversation or even chatter away in their own dialogue today. Her mind was occupied with thoughts of Preston, memories of things he had said or done, both good and bad. As much as she had tried to dispel the images of his dimpled grin, his trim physique, his pursuit and abandonment of her throughout the years, she seemed to be fixated on nothing else. *One minute I feel profoundly sad, and the next minute I feel relieved. No more will I be under the spell of Preston Phillips. But if that's true, then why am I thinking of him every waking moment, even now?*

ೂ

The Spillers and the Winthrops stood together in one of the two slow-moving lines leading to the mourners. Julia and Vicki had arranged for them to go together. "I can't believe we had to go through metal detectors to get in," Julia remarked to Marshall, talking over her shoulder.

"I'm sure it's Secret Service protocol. Remember, it's likely President Dalton will be here, if not the current president."

Vicki gazed ahead at the crowd beginning to fill every seat, every pew. There were five rows on each side of the center aisle roped off, presumably for family and dignitaries. The lines reminded Vicki of the ones at the airport, where a certain etiquette was required in taking your turn to check bags.

Nicole, her ankle still in the protective metal circle, was sitting, instead of standing, in the front pew near the coffin. There was a strange woman sitting behind her, apparently tending to her needs as she greeted the vast numbers of people, most of whom were strangers. Of course, Vicki recognized Penelope Phillips, Preston's mother, standing next to Nicole and looking quite dignified and composed, despite her age and grief. Next in line was Frances Phillips Worthington, Preston's sister. Wearing a classic Chanel suit with stylish gold buttons, and holding a lace handkerchief in her hand, Frances concentrated her attention on her mother, even as she shook hands with each person in line. At the end of the receiving line stood Peter, Preston's only child. Tall and handsome like his father, he welcomed people warmly, thanking them for coming to pay tribute to his famous father.

Vicki bristled when her eyes fell on Peter. She hadn't seen him since the ill-fated sixteenth birthday party, when Tony was killed. Her throat thickened, her breath constricted, and she felt briny tears filling her eyes. *You're so grown up. My Tony never had the chance to grow up like you.*

Leon, always attuned to Vicki's demeanor, heard her gasp, and he focused his gaze in the direction of hers. *Oh, no. Shaking hands with Peter Phillips may be more than either one of us can stand.* He put his arm around Vicki's waist and whispered into her ear, "Maybe we should get out of the line and take a seat."

Vicki nodded, unable to speak. She tapped Julia on the forearm and motioned toward the seats.

Julia nodded, and she tapped Marshall, indicating for him to follow their friends. The four of them maneuvered their way out of the receiving line and into the tenth row of seats, where they made themselves as comfortable as possible to await the beginning of the ceremony.

It was only then that Marshall startled, turning to Julia with an amazed voice. "Look, Julia," he said *sotto voce*, "look at what's sitting on the coffin behind Frances."

"Oh, my Lord," Julia replied. "Is that an urn?"

"Yes," Marshall said. "Apparently Preston has been cremated."

❧❦❧

Gerald and Kitty, in their matching fur coats, were among the last to make it through the line and take their seats near the back of the church. "Amazing how many people are here," Gerald whispered through tight lips. "Don't think I'd have this many at my funeral."

Kitty started to chide her husband for his continued jealousy of Preston, but her attention was caught by a formal procession of dignitaries entering from a door at the apse. "Look," she said. "There's the guy who won the Nobel for Economics...is his name Rubin? And that's the President of Princeton, isn't it?"

☙❧☙

At the last moment before the Secret Service cleared the way for the top-clearance attendees to enter, and unbeknownst to Nicole, Preston's three ex-wives slipped into the row behind her.

Then the dignitaries began filling the five rows across from Nicole from the back, leaving the front row empty. Within minutes all but the front row of the church was packed with people. A hush traveled through the church as people noticed who was walking toward the empty row, first the secretary of the treasury, Andrew Kahn; then former President Dalton and his First Lady; and finally current Vice-President, Jason Ryan.

Nicole glanced with satisfaction at the number of people who had come to honor her husband. She felt special pride that even the vice-president came, especially since the current administration was of the opposite political party.

She leaned over to her mother-in-law to say, "Preston would be really glad to see so many people here."

Penny Phillips clasped her daughter-in-law's arm

in a rare gesture of affection. "You know what they always say, 'It's a shame that the best party of your life is on the one day you can't attend.'"

Chapter 27

Monday morning, December twenty-third, Nicole Phillips was wheeled into surgery to repair her ankle, her sister Francine left in the waiting room with Nicole's cell phone. Nicole's parting words as the gurney moved away were, "Well, Preston, wherever you are, life goes on."

At the West Brandywine Police Station, life was going on, as well. Parrott had immersed himself in the media coverage of the Phillips funeral. With his usual methodical precision, he had read and re-read the stories, played and re-played the clips.

The funeral was the closest thing to a state funeral as one could get without being a state funeral. All those dignitaries, hundreds of people.

He couldn't shake the feeling that something was fishy. He rubbed his head as if to elicit the answer to his most worrisome question: If this guy was so darned important, why didn't anyone seem that upset that he was gone?

Eager to move forward either to clear the matter or open the case, Parrott called Maria Rodriguez' office. "Any news on toxicology for Phillips yet?"

"Just came in by fax. I think you may want to sit down before I tell you."

"Sounds ominous." Unconsciously, Parrott rubbed his palms together, his nerves taut.

"Just a very unusual bit of information from toxicology, Detective. Your guy had a good bit of rare poison in his system—it's called palytoxin. Never encountered it before."

"Polytoxin?"

"P-A-L-Y, not P-O-L-Y. It's really sophisticated. Symptoms mimic a heart attack, respiratory failure, so it can easily go undetected. Whoever administered it must have figured to get away with it. You're going to have a very interesting case on your hands, Detective."

Parrott shook his head, unsure whether his worst fears or his best hopes were coming true. "Maria, where can I get information on palytoxin?"

"I'm pulling some together right now. It's all new to me, too." Maria whistled softly, as if in amazement at what she was reading. "By the way, we might want to take another look at the body now that we have this report. You want to file to exhume?"

"I hate to tell you this, but the body's been cremated. I saw the urn in some of the media shots."

"Well, that makes me wonder about the person who ordered the cremation," Maria said, "but then again, I'm just the coroner."

"I'd like to see what you have on palytoxin. How

about if I come over by lunchtime? I don't think I'll be very hungry after I've digested this news you've given me. And I've got to inform Chief Schrik right away."

"No problem, Detective. See you in a few hours."

"Oh, one more thing. Can you sit on this information till I get there? Assuming you are going to rule homicide, this is going to leak like the Johnstown Dam. I need to involve my boss before it gets past your desk."

"No problem. My lips are sealed."

Parrott thought for a moment before punching line one. He wanted to plan his next steps very carefully, now that he apparently had a murder investigation on his hands.

℮℮

Francine Rafferty was enjoying a Marlboro in the hospital parking lot when she saw *West Brandywine Police Department* on the caller ID of her sister's cell phone. Should she answer it or let it go to voicemail? At the last second, she decided to put out her cigarette and push the green receiver. "Hullo," she said, with a voice that sounded like a rake scraping rocks.

"Mrs. Phillips?" the smooth baritone voice asked.

"No, I'm her sistah," Francine replied. She

shouldn't have taken the call, after all. *I'm not any good at pretending, and Nicky's so far out of my league now.* "Who's cawlin'?"

"Detective Parrott with the West Brandywine Police Department. Is Mrs. Phillips available?"

"Naw, she's havin' h'surgery."

"Oh," Parrott replied, "her ankle."

"Any message?" The gravelly voice sounded so unlike that of the young widow.

"Just tell her I called, and…" Parrott let his voice trail off, just to see whether the sister would fill in the gap.

"And?"

"And I'll call back sometime tomorrow." *What I have to say to your sister can't be left in a message,* he thought. *In fact, it can't be said over the telephone at all.*

☙❧

The West Brandywine Police Department occupied a quaint stone-sided building with a bright red roof and lots of windows. Parrott gazed out at the frozen landscape from his second floor office, his feet glued to the floor. He had just this one last moment of peace and quiet before his whole world turned upside down.

Homicides in the township of Brandywine were as rare as soup kitchens. In fact, the last one had been three years ago, and that, eventually, had been found to be a wrongful death, two kids playing with a gun. *This sleepy little town has probably never seen a case the likes of this one, public figures, weird poison. It's going to be a heater, and the chief is going to shit a brick.* Parrott took a steadying breath, the kind he'd learned to take before pulling the trigger of a firearm. He couldn't afford a misstep from here on out.

He could have sworn the path to the chief's office was layered with quicksand. "Chief, got a minute?"

"Sure, Parrott. Have a seat." Chief Paul Schrik was leaning backward in his red leather chair, his belt buckle reflecting the overhead light, and an uncurled paper clip hanging from his mouth like an unsmoked cigar. Parrott knew Schrik had just quit smoking a few months ago. The office still had the trace aroma of nicotine, probably in the walls and curtains.

Parrott closed the door before seating himself in the red plaid conference chair. "Chief, this death at Bucolia, Preston Phillips. ME called just now with toxicologies. The guy was poisoned."

"Poisoned? You've got to be kidding me." Schrik jolted to attention; the paper clip fell from his lips to the floor. "What kind of poison?"

"Something called palytoxin, P-A-L-Y. Mimics heart attack, so the perp probably thought he'd get away with it."

"Holy shit, Parrott. This is going to be a heater.

Guy is connected all the way up to the White House, for God's sake. Is Rodriguez ruling it homicide?"

"Not yet, but probably soon. I asked her to keep a lid on it. I'm meeting with her in the next two hours. Thought you might want to come."

"We can't handle this case here. Too much publicity and pressure for our little department. I'm going to pass it off to the state police like a hot potato, maybe even the feds." Schrik stood and began pacing. "Shit. And tomorrow is Christmas Eve. Just the right time to kick off the bloodthirsty public's curiosity." He smacked his fist into his other palm. "Go to Rodriguez without me. Ask her to give me a chance to break the news to the feds before she files her reports."

Parrott remained quiet. He knew from past experience that this was the chief's way of thinking out loud, and, in this case, there would be no easy answers.

∽∾∽

Parrott showed up at the medical examiner's office at the stroke of noon, eager to find out as much as possible about palytoxin.

Even if the chief kicked the case upstairs, the local department would have to be involved. He knew once word got out that Preston Phillips had been poisoned, all semblance of peace at West

Brandywine would fly out the window.

He found Maria in her spartan office space. A manila folder lay open on her desk, her indigo-framed glasses laid across the stack of papers, her chin cupped in the palm of her hand. She looked up as Parrott rapped with two knuckles on the door frame. "C'mon in," she said, "Prepare to be amazed and bewildered." She pushed a half-eaten granola bar out of the way, next to a cold cup of lemon zest tea.

"That good, eh?" Parrott asked. "I guess we'll have our hands full."

"Well, your job might be easier if you can find out which suspects have access to fish tanks."

"Fish tanks?" Parrott parroted. "How do you figure that?"

Maria donned her glasses and held up the journal article. "Palytoxin is, and I quote, 'One of the deadliest poisons known to man.'" She continued, "It is produced by certain zoanthid species...coral reefs...readily available in the aquarium trade."

Parrott eased himself into the chair at the side of Maria's desk and leaned over to see what she was reading. The page was full of diagrams of what looked like molecules.

"Palytoxin targets the sodium-potassium pump proteins in cells and effectively shuts down the ion gradient essential for cell function. Symptoms are angina-like chest pains, breathing difficulties, unstable blood pressure. Just like a sudden heart attack."

"How does it get from the fish tank to the victim?"

"In a few reported cases the poisoning occurred from inhaling microscopic bits during tank-cleaning."

"I'll be damned," Parrott exclaimed. "Anybody with access to an aquarium could harvest this stuff, and no one would ever be able to trace it."

"That's the thing. Whoever used palytoxin to kill Preston Phillips must have thought the crime would never come to light. Heart attack symptoms, no blood, no vomit, just the total shut-down of the body's cells. A clean and neat way to get rid of someone."

How fitting for the rich, Parrott thought. *You wouldn't even have to get your hands dirty.* "How was it administered?"

"Hard to tell. Could be dermal contact, could be ingested or inhaled. There have been only a few documented cases of palytoxin poisoning. The only sure thing we know is this is really nasty stuff. It's readily available in the home aquarium trade, and its potency is so lethal that a tiny amount can kill a healthy human being in less than two hours." Maria pushed away from her desk and stood. "Because this is such a rare finding, I've got special paperwork to do, notify authorities. We've both got our work cut out for us."

"Chief wants to be the one to control information. He's thinking about involving the state police. He asked if you can give him some time before you file your reports."

"How much time?"

"We need to notify the widow, who's in surgery right now. Time to get the ducks in a row. Say twenty-four hours? And he asked you to put the lid on the people at the state lab, too. The potential for leaks here is very high."

"Okay, Parrott. Tell Chief Schrik I'll talk to the guys at Harrisburg. Nobody wants to be responsible for screwing up this case. I do need to notify the Bureau of Labs in Exton, the CDC in Atlanta, NIH, and others, though."

"Are there any tissue samples left? I'm just thinking ahead that the FBI may want to do their own tests."

"Now you're thinking like a medical examiner, Parrott. I'll check and let you know."

"One more question: wouldn't it be dangerous for the perp to mess with palytoxin to get it to the victim? I mean, how could he be sure that he wouldn't kill himself?"

"That's a very good question, and one I've been thinking about myself. Whoever killed Preston Phillips was taking a very big chance. So whoever it was must have really wanted him dead."

Chapter 28

Monday afternoon John E. and Caro entered their apartment in Rittenhouse Square after having spent the weekend of the funeral in New York with Preston's family. By noon they had deposited each of the family members in the appropriate locations. Tomorrow was Christmas Eve, and Preston's funeral had diverted attention from the usual holiday plans. Caro removed her leather gloves and stuffed them in the pockets of her lynx coat.

Standing in the foyer, she glimpsed the crisp ivory, green, and gold decorations dangling from the Christmas tree in the corner of the living room. "It's good to be home, even though I'm not in the mood for Christmas this year."

John E. held the collar of her coat as she slid her arms out. "Maybe we should cancel our plans with my cousins. They'll understand. We could drive out to Bucolia and just spend a quiet Christmas there." He hung both coats in the closet.

Caro shuddered at the thought. "No, not Bucolia. The memories of the party are just too fresh."

"Well, what would you like to do?"

"I'd like to turn back time. I just can't believe

my cousin is gone. Or that he died in our house."
Caro didn't know which was worse. Sadness and
guilt churned inside of her, creating a whirlpool of
negativity.

"You know, it could have happened anywhere,
Caro." John E. hated to see his wife so torn up.

Caro walked into the kitchen and sat down on a
padded barstool. She ran her fingers along the cool
granite counter at the base of the tropical fish tank.
"Yes, but it didn't. It happened in our home. I
know it's not rational, but I just can't forgive myself. I keep replaying the weekend in my head, trying for a different ending."

John E. pulled out the adjacent barstool and
placed his left flank on its square seat. "Hey, I wish
it were that easy." Then he remembered what today
was and asked, "Isn't Nicole's surgery today?"

"Yes, this morning, in fact."

"Well, maybe that's one thing we can do for
Preston. We can check in on Nicole and see if we
can do something to help her."

Caro leaned over to give her husband a peck on
the cheek. "Good idea. You are so practical."

೮⁃ა೮⁃ა

Andrea hesitated for a moment before calling
Caro. She knew Caro was taking Preston's death
hard, and she didn't want to say or do anything to
make it worse. On the other hand, with its being

215

almost Christmas, all of Caro's other friends were probably busy with festivities. If she recalled correctly, Nicole's surgery was scheduled for today. *Maybe Caro and I can go visit her together.*

She picked up the telephone and dialed Caro's cell phone number.

The ringtone, the theme from "Downton Abbey," came to Caro's ears from the interior of her handbag, left in the foyer. She sauntered toward the sound, reaching her handbag just in time. Caller ID showed it was Andrea. Somehow Caro felt a slight lifting of the heavy thoughts weighing her down.

"Andrea."

"Hi, Caro. Just wanted you to know I'm thinking of you."

"Thanks. It's been rough. I'm mostly worried about my mother, and Aunt Penny, of course."

"I'm sure it's been a huge shock for everyone. What are you and John E. going to do for Christmas?"

"We were just talking about it. We just aren't in the Christmas spirit this year."

"You are welcome to join us at the farm. We're just having a small group this year, very low-key."

"Thanks, but I think we're going to stay in the city."

Andrea had expected this response, but at least she'd offered. She shifted to another topic. "Caro, wasn't Nicole's surgery scheduled for today?"

"Yes, this morning."

"How'd you like to go into New York together tomorrow to visit her, take her some get-well gifts? With all of the Christmas festivities everywhere else, I'll bet she's going to feel very alone." *And I would give anything to spend some time with the grieving widow. In addition to cheering her up, I bet I'll be able to get a read on how she's bearing up. And who knows? Maybe she'll have the autopsy results by now.*

"Funny you should suggest that, Andrea. John E. just mentioned that visiting Nicole is one thing that we could do for Preston. I think I'd like to do that."

∽∾∽

The next afternoon, Nicole was propped up in her bed in her Dakota unit, dressed in a peacock blue velvet warm-up suit, its right leg sliced open at the seam to accommodate the thick cast from her toes to her hip. Still taking hydrocodone, she had the lethargic appearance of Cinderella long after the ball. She was cautious, however, not to let her guard down in front of Andrea and Caro. She would never let Preston's family or friends see the Old Nicole. She had worked too hard to polish her act, her speech, her demeanor, her wardrobe. Now she would be wealthy in her own right, and she would never go backward. She had sent Francine out with a list of Christmas gifts to buy for the servants, a task that would occupy her for hours on

217

this last afternoon before Christmas.

Caro and Andrea sipped their lattes as they made small talk with each other and with Nicole, whose droopy eyelids betrayed her lack of interest.

"Have you spoken with Aunt Penny since the funeral?" Caro asked Nicole.

"She called to see how I was feeling this morning." Nicole suppressed a yawn. "Very thoughtful."

"How long will you have to be in the cast?" Andrea asked.

"Three weeks, and then I'll start physical therapy. I just want all of this to be over with."

The house phone chimed its security tone. "I wonder who that could be," Nicole said aloud.

Sounds of the maid answering the phone drifted up the stairs. A moment later Rosa appeared at the doorway. "Mrs. Phillips. It's a Detective Parrott here to see you, ma'am."

Caro and Andrea exchanged glances. Andrea felt a chill. In her experience, this could only be bad news.

"Perhaps we should leave," Caro offered.

"Don't be silly. I'm sure Parrott will be glad to see you both again, and I don't want you to leave yet." Nicole told Rosa to allow security to admit the detective.

✧✧✧

Rosa opened the door to the spacious foyer, and

Oliver Parrott stepped inside. While she placed his coat and hat in the closet, he took the opportunity to look around the Phillips apartment. What caught his immediate attention were the high ceilings, the spectacular view of Central Park, and the media room to the left of the entry hall. Paneled in dark walnut with parquet flooring, the room was decorated in leather and suede. Framed pictures of Phillips with President Dalton and other mucky-mucks. Obviously Phillips' retreat, no feminine touches. In fact, the only vividness in the room came from the back corner, where a large aquarium lit up the room with tiny moving splashes of color. He wasn't certain from this distance, but it looked like there were plenty of coral reefs in there.

Before he could look into other rooms, Rosa summoned him to climb the staircase to the second floor. "This way, Detective. Mrs. Phillips will see you upstairs." He followed the crisp uniform up the staircase, still mulling over the fish tank.

Before he entered Nicole's bedroom, Parrott considered asking Rosa to remain in the room. In his experience, police business was best conducted in public areas of homes, and he didn't want to take the chance of being alone in the bedroom with the victim's wife, even if she was just out of surgery. As he approached the room, however, he heard soft feminine voices.

"Hello, Detective," Caroline Campbell said, rising from the chaise lounge and extending her hand.

Parrott shook her hand then Andrea's and moved toward Nicole's bedside, where he shook hands with her, as well.

"Please be seated," Nicole said, emulating Bette Davis in one of those Turner Classic movies. As tired as she was, she knew she had to be on her guard. The Brandywine detective wouldn't be coming to her home for something frivolous. She pointed to the Queen Anne chair next to the bed.

"I'd prefer to stand, if you don't mind," he said, moving in front of the chair, where he could observe all three ladies. Looking down on people in situations like this one gave him a visual, if not strategic, advantage. "Mrs. Phillips," he began, "I am here on police business. Would you like for me to speak with you privately?"

Nicole liked the polite way the detective was treating her. His smooth voice and his confident demeanor impressed her. Still, she was wary and thought it best if Caro and Andrea remained. "It's okay. Mrs. Campbell is family, and Mrs. Baker has been a great help to me with my ankle. You can talk in front of them."

"Yes, ma'am," Parrott replied. "It's about Mr. Phillips' death, of course." Parrott was on full alert, realizing that three of the fourteen suspects were in his presence, about to be told that the death had been ruled a homicide. "I've brought you the autopsy report from the ME's office. I know you have a lot on your plate right now, with your surgery and all, but I need to interview you again. In fact—" He turned toward the chaise lounge, where Andrea and Caro were sitting. "—I need to interview you again, as well."

"Interview me again? For what? I've already told you everything I know. Is there something you're not telling me about Preston's death?" Despite her desire to appear in control of herself, Nicole found her voice sounding like a violin, playing a melancholy *vibrato*.

"Mrs. Phillips, when you read the toxicology report, you will learn that your husband did not die a natural death. He was poisoned."

CHaPtER 29

Back at the West Brandywine Police Station, Parrott sat in Chief Schrik's office, while the chief paced, looking at, but not seeing, the snowy vista outside the window. Preston Phillips' laptop computer sat in his lap.

"...she appeared to be shocked. All three women did. When I said the word 'homicide,' Mrs. Phillips flinched then cried out, 'Omigod.' The other ladies went to the bed where she was sitting. Mrs. Campbell put her arm around Mrs. Phillips, and Mrs. Baker took her hand. It was a picture of grief and sympathy. The only thing is—"

"What?" Schrik interrupted, biting down on his paper clip with the sharp final T sound.

"It seemed artificial. As if the ladies were following stage directions in a play. But the most interesting part was the huge fish tank in the study. Plenty of coral, too. I could see it from the front door. This lady really interests me. Married to the guy for just six months, she probably inherits big-time. She's got means, motive, and opportunity."

"Yeah, but what about that metal contraption on her foot? Didn't you tell me she was sleeping on the first floor, while the vic was on the fourth floor the night of the homicide?"

"Yes. At first, I thought that would alibi her out, but now I'm not so sure. What if she poisoned him before he went upstairs, at dinner or afterward? And she's young and fit. Maybe she managed to scoot herself up the stairs, anyway."

"Newlyweds, eh? May-December marriage?" Schrik made another turn around his desk and back toward the window. "Why would she want him dead so soon after the wedding?"

"I'm not sure, but I have a theory. Phillips was a known playboy. What if she married him for his dough and then felt insecure about holding onto him? Maybe she suspected he was losing interest in her, looking for someone else? She could have decided to get rid of him before he got rid of her and left her with nothing."

"Well, you've got a lot of holes to fill, Parrott. Do you think this gal's sophisticated enough to know about, much less handle, such a deadly poison? How did she administer it to him with a broken ankle holding her back? How much does she inherit, anyway? This guy's a billionaire. I don't see him going into a marriage with a young chick without a pre-nup." The chief punctuated this last word by pounding his hand on his desk. He then sat in his chair and swiveled side-to-side, deep in thought. "We just don't have the manpower to investigate this case on our own, Parrott. You're a good man, but the people who were at the Campbells' farm that weekend are very smart, very rich, very influential people." He raised his voice. "Phillips was so connected. My phone's been ringing off the hook with 'inquiries' from people in high places. I just don't like it." He stood again and returned to fashioning a pattern of footsteps in the carpet. "And we're contending with the calendar, too. Nobody wants to answer questions from police this time of the year. Offices are closed. It's a mess."

"Well, anyway, I brought you this," Parrott said, placing the victim's laptop on the chief's desk. The technology expert would open it up like a juicy watermelon then offer slices of information for the investigation. That was, if there were any. Parrott picked up a snow scene paperweight from the chief's desk and turned it over, watching the artificial flakes drift onto the plastic ground. He felt a chill.

"I contacted the FBI and the state police," the chief continued. "Feebies say they don't have jurisdiction. If Phillips were still in office as secretary of the treasury, it would be different. State police offered the support of their labs. I'd give my right nut to be able to get more samples from the victim's body, but, 'No. The body's been cremated.' We can't seem to catch a break."

He pulled the paper clip from his mouth and pointed it at Parrott.

Parrott knew better than to interject his thoughts when Schrik was on a tear, and this might be the worst one yet. The louder Schrik's voice became, the more Parrott wrapped himself in imaginary insulation. Yes, this was a tough case, and yes, there would be a lot of pressure to solve it quickly, but he had ideas, and ideas led to questions, and questions led to answers. He was up for the challenge, despite his boss's pessimism. At twenty-six years old, Parrott was experienced enough to know how to proceed and energetic enough to embrace the challenge. He was glad the feds didn't want to touch this case. Like the cheetah, he was crouching behind the brush, waiting to leap into action. He could just imagine his cockatiel chirping, "Oh, dear."

೮ๅ೮ๅ

Christmas morning Parrott spent researching palytoxin. Maria had given him a folder full of information, along with the autopsy and toxicology reports. He spread them out over the maple breakfast room table and studied them, a pot of chicory coffee beside him on the counter. Every so often he glanced at the framed picture of his fiancée, in full dress Navy uniform. It felt wrong to be apart on Christmas. While she was fighting her battles, he would fight his own.

When he finished making notes from the reports, he roused his computer from sleep mode and took it on an internet adventure. There wasn't a lot of information about palytoxin yet, just some horror stories of how people accidentally poisoned themselves, cleaning their fish tanks, and some scientific explanations of what palytoxin does to the cells of the body. *What if one of the suspects had been looking for a discreet way to get rid of Preston Phillips, and read one of these articles?*

After hopping around the table as Parrott worked, the bird had fallen asleep, using Maria's folder as a pillow. The quiet served as a counterpoint to his roiling thoughts. At two he showered, shaved, and dressed in neat khakis and a plaid shirt. He organized his notes and straightened up the kitchen before leaving for a family gathering in Cain. *I'll spend a few hours doing Christmas, and then I'll get back in the saddle.*

‍ℰ∞ℰ∞

Early the next morning, Parrott presented Chief Schrik with a list of investigative tasks. It included the usual bank, credit card, phone records, daily planner information that would build a picture of what Preston Phillips had been doing in the days and weeks before his death. It also included questions about Phillips' will, marriage, pre-nuptial agreement, and property. The most unusual items on the list had to do with the guests at John E. Campbell's birthday party, who they were, what they did, where they lived, how they connected to

Phillips, and, most importantly, whether they owned or had access to aquariums.

Schrik sighed as he read over the list. He flicked his paper clip as though dropping an ash from a cigarette. "Okay, Parrott. We'll get the grunt work done. You interview the party people. Oh, and one more thing. These party people, the ones who are suspects, be sure to Mirandize them before you interview them. Even if it tips them off, you need to dot your *Is* and cross your *Ts*, or what they say may not be admissible in court. And for heaven's sake, keep in touch. I'll be the one getting all of the phone calls from ex-presidents and government officials."

⚜

Parrott had hoped to start off with a return visit to Bucolia first thing, but Caro and John E. were still in Philadelphia and wouldn't be at the farm until later that afternoon. He decided to pay a visit to Andrea Baker at noon, and then swing over to interview the Campbells.

A break in the weather made the fifteen-minute drive to the Bakers' farm, Sleepy Hollow, a pleasant experience with blue skies and melting snow. Parrott cracked his car window, so he could feel a slice of fresh air, and he hummed a tune as he reviewed the questions he had for the crime writer. *She's a sharp one. I'm sure she picked up some vibes throughout the weekend. I just hope she's willing to share what she knows. For all I know, she could be protecting the details for a book she's writing.*

It took another five minutes to drive from the front gates of Sleepy Hollow, follow the curvy lane, and pull up in front of the massive taupe brick home.

Parrott felt as though he had been transported to the English countryside as he gazed up at the antique structure. He was standing next to his car, shielding his eyes from the bright sun, when Andrea's cheerful voice brought him back to reality.

"Welcome, Detective. I hope my directions were clear." Andrea was dressed in her riding clothes, slim-leg pants, blouse, checked vest, and velvet blazer, with a cashmere scarf tied around her neck. She shook Parrott's hand with the firmness of someone who felt comfortable with her place in the world. "Come on in."

Parrott crossed the threshold into what could only be described as a palatial manor house. The high ceilings and stone walls belonged to another century. He recalled that the money came from her family, not his. A bright fire was gobbling the wood in the fireplace in the center of the living room, where three rust-colored chenille sofas and a coffee table created an inviting space.

Andrea held out her arms. "May I take your coat?"

Parrott wiped his boots on the Oriental rug at the door. He looked around, amazed Andrea had met him at the front door, and not a servant in sight. He shed his coat and handed it over.

"Paula's got the week off to be with family over Christmas," Andrea explained, as if she had read his mind. She lifted a monogrammed wooden hanger from the entry hall closet and dressed it with the detective's wool-lined trench coat. She filed it in the closet between a shearling and a full-length man's leather coat. "My husband is still out riding, but he'll join us within the next few minutes. Why don't we sit down?" Andrea pointed to the seating arrangement.

Parrott sat at the end of the center sofa. Andrea took a seat on the adjacent one. An end table served as a buffer between the two people, between their different worlds. Parrott removed a mini-iPad from his jacket pocket. Pleasantries completed, he was ready to begin with his prepared questions.

Parrott positioned himself sideways, so he could observe facial expressions and body language better. He hated these perpendicular seating arrangements. "I hope you don't mind answering a few questions. As a crime writer, I'm sure you have an excellent memory for details, and I'd appreciate your help in this homicide."

"Glad to help. After all, Caro's one of my closest friends, and Preston was her cousin. I'm as anxious as you to see this matter resolved successfully."

"Well, then, what was your relationship to Mr. Phillips, beyond being friends with his cousin?"

"Oh, I knew Preston for several years, of course, because of Caro and John E., but my husband and I were not part of the crowd that grew up and went to college together. Stan was John E.'s graduate business professor and mentor at Princeton, and that's how we met the Campbells originally. We didn't become close friends until they moved out here a few years ago."

"Can you give me a recap of all of the activities and events that occurred this weekend at the Campbells' farm?"

"Sure, but Stan and I weren't staying at Bucolia, so you might want to get that list from someone who was." Andrea untied the scarf around her neck and began playing with the ends.

Parrott leaned forward and raised an eyebrow, indicating he wanted her to answer the question.

"Well, we all gathered Friday night for drinks and dinner. Friday the thirteenth. That was John E.'s actual birthday. Saturday morning the men and Nicole and I went horseback riding. That's when Nicole was thrown from her horse and broke her ankle."

"What were the rest of the guests doing while you were riding?" Parrott asked.

"Shopping and having lunch, I think. Libby is pregnant and didn't want to ride."

"Go on," Parrott said.

"Saturday afternoon Nicole was at Brandywine Hospital. I went there with her in the ambulance. Once Preston got to the hospital, I called for a ride and came back home. Stan and I went back to Bucolia around seven. We had an elaborate evening of food and drink that lasted well past midnight."

"What was the seating arrangement at dinner?" Parrott asked.

Andrea was not surprised by any of the questions thus far, including this one. "Boy-girl-boy-girl. We did not sit with our spouses."

Parrott's right eyebrow lifted.

"That's not unusual in our circle, Detective. Party hostesses often mix up couples in order to spark livelier conversation. Anyway, Nicole couldn't sit at the table for long. She was in a lot of pain."

"Who sat on either side of Mr. Phillips?"

"Let me see," Andrea fiddled with her scarf, trying to remember. "I think it was Kitty Kelley on one side. She and Preston seemed to be talking and laughing a lot throughout the evening. I'm not sure about the other side, unless it was Caro. Oh, yes, that was it. Preston was at the corner of the table, and Caro was at the end. I'm sure that was the only place Caro could seat Preston."

"What do you mean by that?" Parrott asked, eyes narrowing ever-so-slightly.

"Well, Preston was not exactly Mr. Popularity. There was bad blood between him and some of the other guests, and he had the kind of abrasive personality that just rubbed people the wrong way, especially men."

"Can you elaborate? Who, exactly, didn't get along with Mr. Phillips, and why?"

Andrea re-tied her scarf then untied it again. She knew her answer would be of importance to establishing a motive to poison Preston. In truth, she didn't know all the back stories, at least not in detail, but she would tell the detective what she knew.

In her experience, cooperating with police officers made for the kinds of relationships that led to juicy details for fascinating books. "You'll have to ask Caro for particulars, but I think just about everyone there had some reason to dislike Preston. And it showed. There was a lot of verbal sniping going on from the moment the party started on Friday night. Oh, and heavy flirting, too."

"Oh? Who was flirting?"

"Preston was flirting with Margo Rinaldi. He left the dinner table when she did on Friday night, and everyone noticed."

"I imagine that didn't go over too well with Mrs. Phillips," Parrott murmured.

"I'm sure not." Andrea muttered, "I'm starting to feel like the town gossip. I hate talking about people this way, but, of course, a murder investigation requires us to open up."

At that moment the whoosh of a door opening and a blast of cool air interrupted the conversation.

Stan Baker, slim and attractive in riding breeches and leather boots, strode over to his wife's side, putting his arm around her shoulders. He reached out to shake Parrott's hand. "Hello, Detective. I hope your conversation with my wife has been helpful."

"Very helpful," Parrott replied. "And now I'd like to ask a few questions of you, sir."

Stan perched on the edge of the sofa next to his wife. "Go ahead."

Parrott asked some routine questions about how Stan was connected to the Campbells and to Preston Phillips. Had he noticed anyone expressing ill will toward Mr. Phillips during the weekend?

Stan's answers were short and unremarkable.

Parrott made eye contact with Stan before verbalizing his next question. "Mr. Baker, do you or your wife have, on any of your properties, an aquarium?"

Stan's expression was, in Parrott's opinion, one of genuine surprise. A quick glance at Andrea showed a similar expression. The couple looked at each other as if they weren't sure they had heard the question correctly.

"An aquarium?" they said simultaneously. "Why, no. We collect horses, not fish."

Chapter 30

The Campbells drove in silence to their Pennsylvania farm, lost in thought. Caro dreaded returning to the farm. She felt it was a bad luck place since her cousin had died there. Now they were going to have to submit to questioning by Detective Parrott, a nice enough guy, but still. It would be very intrusive and painful.

John E.'s thoughts were slightly different. The farm was his indulgence, his favorite place on earth. Usually, the drive from Philadelphia to Bucolia was a delightful anticipation of peaceful and joyful days and nights away from the city and its pressures. Today John E. worried about his wife. Would she ever recover from the trauma of her cousin's death? The poison that killed Preston may have also killed the Campbells' pleasure in their country home. Moreover, his friends—this meeting with the police detective would certainly churn up details about his friends' lives, their relationships, their privacy.

I hate it that my birthday party was the catalyst for what will surely become a dirty and ugly chapter in all of our lives.

John E. rolled up the car windows that had been

cracked to provide fresh air, so that he could be heard. "Caro?"

"What?" Caro broke from her thoughts about playing board games with Preston as a child and never being able to beat him.

"I contacted Harry Southfield about this meeting with the detective."

"Our attorney? But why?"

"The detective is going to ask us a lot of questions about the party, about our friends, about Preston. I wanted to get advice about what we should and should not say to him."

"But we don't have anything to hide. Maybe Preston's poisoning was accidental and had nothing at all to do with the party. And if not...if not, then whoever did poison him needs to be found out and brought to justice."

"Caro, did you ever stop to think that Detective Parrott might suspect you and me?"

"Of course not. That's completely ridiculous." Caro twitched and shifted her posture in the Thunderbird's bucket seat. "I like Detective Parrott. He seems very straightforward and honest."

"His job is to investigate a homicide, Caro. Harry says we shouldn't talk with him without having a criminal defense lawyer present."

"Do we have a criminal lawyer?"

"Of course not. We've never needed one before now. Harry is going to get us one."

Caro picked at a fleck of dust on the sleeve of

her pink angora topcoat. "Well, is he going to be present in the next hour, when we are meeting with Detective Parrott?"

"No, these things don't happen that fast. We'll just have to tell Detective Parrott to come back another time."

Caro pulled down her visor to shield her eyes from the powerful mid-day sun. "Don't you think that's rude? We shouldn't have made this appointment with Parrott if we weren't going to talk with him. Besides, if we tell him we want a lawyer present, won't that make him suspect us even more?"

John E. tapped the steering wheel with his thumbs. He didn't like to be disagreeable, but her penchant for proper manners could end up getting them or their friends into big trouble. "Listen, Caro. This isn't some television show, where things all come out right in the end. Police interviews have a way of trapping innocent people into saying the wrong things sometimes. I'm worried this will get nasty, if not for us, then for some of our friends. I just want to do what I can to minimize the damage."

"Well, what do you suggest?" Caro asked, annoyance curling around the individual syllables of her words.

"Invite him in, offer him coffee. When he starts asking questions, defer to me. I'll know when to cut him off."

"Okay. But promise me you'll be gentlemanly. I

couldn't stand it if word got out that we were arrogant or uncivilized. I wasn't brought up that way."

∽∾∽

As Parrott started his engine and eased down the long, winding road from Sleepy Hollow, he marveled at the fact that the Bakers had spoken to him without an attorney present. Most of these rich people had their lawyers on speed dial for occasions like this. *They must feel they are peripheral to the case. Otherwise, they wouldn't have been so confident.* In fact, he hadn't found anything in their comments that would indicate anything at all suspicious. They were friends with the Campbells, but merely acquaintances with everyone else. They were there for the dinners, but didn't spend the night. With all of their money, they couldn't be interested in Phillips' wealth, and even if they were, they weren't connected to him in any way that would give them a reason to inherit. No aquariums, either. *No, the only thing at all suspicious is Mrs. Baker's career. It wouldn't be beyond the realm of possibility for a crime writer to plan and execute a murder, just to be able to write about it.*

Now, as he approached the Campbells' farm, he hoped this couple would be as easy to interview. Somehow he doubted it. He mentally reviewed his list of questions. His plan was to address as many as possible to Mrs. Campbell. His first impression of her had been so positive. He just wasn't sure about the Mr.

☙❧

"Won't you have a seat, Detective?" Caro asked in her most gracious voice, ushering him toward the upholstered seating arrangement in front of the fireplace in the family room.

John E. was tending the fire, using the bellows to pump air into the incipient flames.

"Thanks," Parrott said, as he took a seat in the spot where Nicole had been reclining the last time he had been there. "I appreciate your seeing me on such short notice, especially at holiday time." *I suppose the Campbells have let their servants off for Christmas week, too.*

Except for the three of them, the house seemed deadly quiet.

He rubbed his hands together for warmth, then, thinking the gesture might be misinterpreted as over-eagerness, he stopped and rested his hands in his lap.

"May I bring you some coffee?"

"That sounds good, sure." Parrott could hardly believe his luck. No lawyer and coffee. It seemed like this would go as smooth as glass.

As Caro went into the kitchen to get the coffee, John E. put away the fireplace tools and drew the screen to a close. He used the hearth to off-load weight as he rose from a squatting position and turned to the detective, grinning sheepishly. "It's not as easy as it used to be," he said, "You'll see. One day you can stand and sit and walk and run, no problem, and the next day, you need a little help moving the ol' body."

Parrott thought to muster a polite reply, but anything he could think of might sound flattering, condescending, or downright insulting, so he merely nodded. He had never been very good at chit-chat, and they had so little in common.

Caro re-entered the room, carrying a small tray with mugs of steaming coffee. The aromas of the burning pine and the rich Colombian brew mingled to create an illusion of coziness, like that of friends enjoying a holiday afternoon together.

A gold-rimmed plate of Madeleine cookies added to the party-like atmosphere, and if it hadn't been for the grim occasion of his visit, Parrott might have been seduced into enjoying the Campbells' hospitality.

"Did you have a nice Christmas?" Caro asked the detective, as she handed him a mug.

"Yes, ma'am. And I hope you did, too. Despite the circumstances. I'm sorry for your loss." He took a sip of the black coffee. It was just the way he liked it, strong and just on the underside of scorching. "Mmm…it's good."

"Thank you, Detective."

Parrott watched as John E. dressed his coffee

with sugar and cream then stirred it with the same deliberation as he'd shown when nurturing the fire. He wondered if Campbell did everything with such precision.

Though he hated to spoil the pleasantness, Parrott was here to do a job, and it was not in his nature to drag these things out. "Mr. and Mrs. Campbell, I appreciate your cooperation. I assure you the West Brandywine Police Department is here for you at this difficult time, and we promise to do our best to get to the bottom of what happened to Mr. Phillips."

Caro's lips closed into a curve that only resembled a smile. The pain of Preston's death, sometimes lulled into a dull ache, sharpened inside of her and stabbed at her with renewed vigor.

John E. gripped the handle of his mug more tightly, preparing himself for what he knew would be, at the least, uncomfortable.

Parrott noticed these small tells. He knew that questioning these two would be difficult, but he had to start somewhere, and the Campbells were central to the whole investigation. They were the hub that connected all of the spokes to the wheel. As if to bolster his resolve, he lifted a cookie from the plate and popped it into his mouth. He thought he might never have tasted anything so soft and delicately sweet. *Vanilla.* "Delicious," he murmured, as he swallowed and washed it down with another swig of coffee. He placed his mug down on the napkin on the tray, wondering if it was polite to do so.

"I understand the party you had the weekend of the thirteenth through the fifteenth was for your birthday, Mr. Campbell. Is that right?" He wanted to start off with a simple yes or no question.

John E. answered, "Yes, it was."

"And did you send written invitations to this birthday party?"

"Yes, we did."

"Can you tell me when the invitations were mailed?"

Caro looked at John E., wondering when he might stop the questioning. These first questions seemed innocent enough. Hearing nothing, she answered, "They were postmarked on November thirteenth, one month prior to the date of the party."

Parrott thought about whether one month was enough time for someone to plan a murder like this one. He supposed one day would be long enough if someone was motivated and clever enough. He picked up his coffee mug again and leaned forward. "I understand the main event of the weekend was a dinner party on Saturday night. Is that right?"

John E. answered, "That's right."

"And the guests stayed here in this house over the weekend?"

John E. nodded. "The Bakers stayed at their own place, but everyone else stayed here."

"Can you tell me which houseguests stayed in which rooms?" Parrott asked as he pictured the walk he and Officer Barton had made up to the victim's fourth floor bedroom.

"Sure," John E. replied. "In fact, I'll draw you a diagram." He went to the office for a piece of copy paper, a pen, and a clipboard.

While he was gone, Parrott turned to Caro and asked, "Can you tell me what was served at the Saturday night dinner party?"

Caro glanced at the spot where John E. had been sitting before answering, "If you wait just a moment, I can get the menu," she offered. "I still have a few copies left." She rose and went into the kitchen where she opened the desk drawer. There, on top of the receipts from the party, was the gold-embossed menu on sheer scalloped paper.

She returned to the family room and handed the menu to the detective. "You can keep it, if you'd like."

John E. returned to the family room, sat down, and began drawing a rough sketch of the second, third, and fourth floors of the house then labeling the bedrooms with the names of who had slept in each. "I'm sure you're considering who might have had the least conspicuous access to Preston's fourth floor suite."

Without responding, Parrott put down the menu and took another Madeleine, while John E. completed his task. Parrott's mind was accelerating beyond the maximum speed limit. He mentally rehearsed at least a dozen more questions.

"Here you go," John E. said, handing the page to the detective. "You can see that Preston's was the only occupied bedroom on the fourth floor. He and Nicole were both there on Friday night, but after her accident on Saturday, Preston stayed there alone."

Not quite alone, Parrott thought, remembering the stained sheets and the lime green thread in the chair. "I appreciate this," he stated. He picked up the fancy menu and put it on top of the room diagram in his hand. He ran his eyes over the curlicued words on the menu. *Lots of unfamiliar terms, lots of booze.* One item at the end of the menu caught his eye. "Truffles a la Vicki?" he asked. "Is that dish named after Vicki Spiller, the party guest?"

John E. set his coffee mug down with a firm *clunk* onto the tray, and he stood up, his arms crossed in front of his midsection. "Detective Parrott, I hope you understand, but my wife and I have been advised not to answer any questions of a personal nature without having an attorney present. Since you've mentioned one of our party guests, I think we should halt this meeting. It's not that we don't wish to be cooperative. We do. It's just that this whole thing has come as a shock to us, and we don't want to say or do the wrong thing."

Parrott stood and mimicked Campbell's body

language, confrontation without ugly words. "I assure you, Mr. Campbell, there is no wrong thing, as long as you tell the truth. You and Mrs. Campbell have knowledge and perspectives that are important to solving this case."

"Yes, we know that. But just the same, I'm afraid we will have to reschedule this interview so we can have an attorney present."

"Okay," Parrott conceded, dropping his arms to his side. He removed a card from the plastic case in his pocket and handed it to Campbell. "We'll meet at the station, then. Call me and let me know when. The sooner we can get statements from you both, the better chance we have of solving the case. Do keep that in mind." He started walking toward the entry hall, where Caro had hung his coat.

Caro rushed ahead of him, bright red spots dotting her cheeks. "Let me get your coat."

Parrott made eye contact with her, and he knew she was uncomfortable with the way her husband had ended this meeting. "Don't worry, Mrs. Campbell," he said. "My promise still holds. We will get to the bottom of this incident." He donned his coat and turned to open the door. Then he remembered his manners. "And thank you very much for the coffee and cookies."

CHAPTER 31

M arshall Winthrop slumped in the buttery leather executive chair in his newly redecorated office at Thirty-Three Liberty Street in New York. He had a splitting migraine and had already taken 100 milligrams of Imitrex. He had skipped lunch, too nauseated to entertain the thought of food, and too preoccupied to converse with his colleagues from the Fed. Even watching the vivid tropical fish in his tank, normally so soothing, today made him want to smash the glass. *If I'm not careful, I'll end up with a stroke over all of this. Wouldn't that be ironic?*

What was troubling him was Preston's death. Well, not precisely his death. His death, after all, was something Marshall had often fantasized about over the years, to be honest. The Winthrop estate trust, thanks to Preston's clever manipulation to become its trustee, had been written in such a way that upon Preston's death, the assets would be distributed by the successor trustee, Metropolitan Bank and Trust, to the beneficiary, namely Marshall, free of trust.

That meant, at long last, Marshall would gain control of several hundred million dollars, and

Preston's hands would no longer be in the pot, so to speak.

For the past forty years, Preston had been paid a handsome fee to manage the money, which was bad enough in and of itself. But there was more. Marshall had been gathering evidence for over a year now that proved Preston had systematically looted the trust. Properly invested for forty years, that money would have been well over a billion by now. He had been preparing to go to the authorities within the next few weeks. Knowing a scandal would ensue—after all, it was the former secretary of the treasury he would take down—Marshall had been focused, discreet, and organized. In the week before John E.'s party, Marshall had been suspicious that Preston knew what he was up to. He had worried about Preston's ability to thwart his plans. Now there was no need for any of it. The money would shortly be all his. Instead of being overjoyed, Marshall was shaken. It was like climbing to the peak of a mountain, only to find that the air up there was noxious.

Preston's death solved one problem for Marshall, true enough, but it created several others. Now he would have to decide whether to bring his suspicions to the successor trustee, Metropolitan Bank and Trust, so inquiries could be made into past accountings before distributing the assets. Would it be prudent to do so, now that Preston was dead? Marshall rubbed his painful right temple. Julia had heard from Caro that Preston had been poisoned. The fact that Marshall would benefit financially from Preston's death would give the police reason to suspect him. It would only be a matter of time before they would be on his doorstep. *And what am I going to do about that?*

બ્રબ્ર

Kitty Kelley also had a headache. She could not stop thinking about Preston, how much they had laughed together at dinner, how handsome and charming he had been. It was inconceivable that all of the brilliance and energy that had been Preston Phillips for sixty-seven years could possibly be contained in an urn and put away, never to be enjoyed again. It would have been bad enough if Preston had been ill, suffering, or met his end through a dreadful accident, but Caro said he had been poisoned—poisoned—and that single word wrapped itself around Kitty's mind in a virtual pressure bandage.

She poured herself a cup of strong black tea, its acrid smell and taste distracting her from the pain. "Ah, caffeine, do your thing," she murmured aloud. *If Preston had been murdered*, she thought, *almost any one of the party guests might have done it. The only ones who didn't have a reason to dislike him were the Campbells, the Bakers, and Gerald and me.*

Just as she mentally excluded herself and Gerald from her list of possible suspects, Kitty remembered the angry and jealous comments Gerald had made about Preston that weekend. Gerald had always been envious of Preston, even before Preston had been named secretary of the treasury, when Gerald had so wanted the job. *And he had been jealous of Preston's attention to me.*

With a jolt, Kitty remembered Gerald's comment to Preston when he thought Preston was flirting with her, "Listen, you. Don't get any ideas about *my* wife. You won't live to see the light of day if you mess with her."

Could it be possible? Could Gerald have killed Preston? Kitty didn't think so, but everyone had heard him say those threatening words to Preston just hours before he was killed. *Would someone repeat them to the police?* A sour taste rose in Kitty's throat at the thought that Preston's demise could, quite possibly, not only touch, but also overturn the very comfortable life she had built for herself.

Kitty had half a mind to go to the police and tell them about all of the back stories, the grievances that everyone, especially the Winthrops, the Spillers, and Margo and her sister Libby, had against Preston. If she didn't tell them, how would they ever find out?

It wasn't natural for people of their wealth and stature in the community to discuss such things, and she was certain that everyone would huddle together to protect themselves and their friends from exposure. It wasn't right.

⌒ↄ⌒ↄ

Leon was worried about Vicki. He was used to her hangovers and nights of fitful restlessness, but ever since the weekend at Bucolia, she had seemed withdrawn in a way that he hadn't seen since Tony's death twenty-five years ago. She had closed herself up in the bedroom, pulling the darkening shades to keep out sunlight, unplugging the telephone to keep out noise. "Headaches," she cried. "I can't stand these headaches."

Even Christmas couldn't tempt Vicki to rejoin the living. After cajoling, pushing, and even threatening to go without her, Leon caved in and canceled their plans to be with his brother's family.

"I can't understand it," Leon tried again in a pleading tone of voice. "What is causing you to have these headaches?" He had hoped Preston's death would have helped Vicki bury the past and move on.

Vicki turned over in bed, facing Leon. Her hair was a jumble of yarn. "I hate to admit it, but I probably need to go to rehab again. I know this isn't a good time, financially, and I detest the prospect of it, but I'm so sick. I'm so sorry."

Leon stroked his wife's face from ear to chin. Even at this age, in this condition, she was still beautiful. They had been through so much together, the trauma of losing Tony, but lots of fun and exciting times, too. When Leon looked at Vicki, he still saw the cheerful, capable young sorority girl he had fallen in love with. "Don't worry," he murmured. "I'll take care of everything. All you have to do is get well."

ଓଽଓଽ

The workmen were hammering, sawing, drilling, and Lord knows *what-ing* in the Blooms' Park Avenue condominium, converting an office into a nursery. Both Les and Libby were at work, leaving Margo alone. The noise was giving her a pounding headache, as if her thoughts weren't enough to cause her head to throb. *I've got to get out of here and get a place of my own,* she thought, not for the first time. *Libby has been gracious enough, but she and Les need their privacy, and frankly, I can't stand this noise for one more day. It's time I got on with the rest of my life.*

With that self-proclamation, Margo threw off the downy bedcovers, rolled onto her side, and lowered her legs toward the floor, pausing to slide her feet into the mink slippers next to the bed. She yawned, ran her hand through her auburn locks, and made her way to the bathroom, where she examined her face in the mirror.

The face that looked back at her was frowning,

tired, unhappy. She examined it closely for wrinkles, knowing she could trust her recent procedures at Dr. Friedman's to keep them at bay. She swallowed two Excedrins and reached for her toothbrush. Her life was a mess, and she hardly knew where to begin to fix it. She could go back to Tuscany. She had a beautiful life there—home, friends, things to occupy her time. But Tuscany was also filled with memories of Roberto, which left a discouraging aftertaste.

It was strange how just those few happy hours with Preston had colored her mind with anticipation of a new life in New York. Once planted in her brain, they had continued to germinate, despite Preston's death. Margo had pictured herself as a bride once again, whole new vistas of the future projecting on the wall of her brain, and she had been happy.

Now she was left with a dream unfulfilled. The pain of it was not dissimilar to the way she had felt when Preston abandoned her the first time; only this time, she supposed, he had left unwillingly. She couldn't help believing that even if he hadn't told Nicole he was divorcing her, Preston's love for her was real, and it would have resulted in their marriage.

I can't believe Preston was poisoned. Who might have done it? How? Margo rubbed her expensive anti-aging cream into her forehead, as if to divine the solution to the mystery. *Whoever it was com-*

mitted a crime, not just against Preston, but against me, too.

The whirr of the buzzsaw carved into Margo's thoughts once more. *That's it. I'm moving to one of the condos at the AKA Central Park until I can find a place to buy in New York. Meanwhile, I think I'll call Caro and see if she wants to come with me to look for a place. Maybe she'll know something about the police investigation, and maybe, just maybe, I'll tell her about the plans that Preston and I were making. I'm sure I can trust her to keep them secret.*

Chapter 32

Chief Schrik was chewing his paper clip and rubbing his brow, while he held the telephone receiver to his ear with the other hand. "Yes, President Dalton. Of course we are 'on the case.'" He listened to several run-on sentences about how important Preston Phillips had been to the country, how he deserved better. "Of course, Mr. President. Detective Parrott is young, but I see that as a plus. He's hungry. And he's working hard."

His door was cracked open, just enough for Parrott to hear his name being said in an apparent verbal volley on the phone. His fist was poised to knock, but he held back.

"No sir, I don't think he's too inexperienced. He's got more energy than any ten experienced officers put together. Just give us another week, ten days. We'll have something solid by then. Yes, I know it's my reputation on the line. Thank you, Mr. President. I appreciate your confidence in us." Schrik put down the receiver quickly, as if it had scorched his hand.

He looked up as Parrott rapped on the door and beckoned for him to come in, not failing to notice the tired lines around Parrott's eyes. Had his praise for Parrott's energy been misguided? "My new best friend. He wants to know if we are making progress in the Phillips case." He paused. "So, what do you have to report?"

"Not nearly enough," Parrott replied. "These rich people are hard nuts to crack, Chief. First of all, they're very smart—not just book smart, but cagey-smart. I get the feeling they are three steps ahead of my questions all the time. On top of that, they are so powerful. They're masterful at throwing up roadblocks. The Campbells, they just lawyered up on me, man."

Schrik stood, walked around his desk, and placed his hand on the detective's shoulder. "That's to be expected. I'm not worried about their lawyers. If anything, that just shows they are feeling insecure. And insecure is what we *want* them to feel." He sat down in the adjacent client chair and made full eye contact. "Don't let me see you get discouraged, Parrott. You heard me telling Dalton how much faith I have in you."

"I know. I appreciate that, Chief."

"Anyway," Schrik went on, "you'll be glad to know we made some progress here today."

Parrott tilted his head, his eyes brimming with hope.

Schrik reached across his desk for a folder, turned it 180 degrees and opened it. "Three things. The Phillipses' pre-nup. The victim's will. And

Marshall Winthrop's family trust agreement. Phillips was trustee. These are your copies." He closed the folder and slapped it against the edge of the desk. "Basically, the new Mrs. Phillips is sitting pretty as a result of her husband's untimely death. The pre-nup is typical. It provides way more for her in his death than it would have in divorce. But the will says she gets lifetime use of their principal residence, that gigantic co-op in the Dakota, and ten percent of his estimated three and a half billion dollar estate, about three hundred fifty million."

Parrott whistled. "Think that's enough to motivate her to bump him off?"

"It's more than she could have earned as a receptionist at the Lamborghini dealership in a thousand lifetimes. That's for sure."

"Who else benefits?"

"The son, Peter Phillips. He gets two billion after taxes and administrative costs. We checked him out, too. Aside from the fact that he was in Santa Monica, California, at the time of the father's death, he's living comfortably, no addictions, no scandals, no apparent need for more money."

"Geez, I can't believe we are talking about that much money. But what about the rest?"

"Charities—Choate, Princeton, Harvard—the Guggenheim."

"What about the Winthrops, did you say?" Parrott asked.

"It seems Marshall Winthrop's parents left several hundred million in trust with Marshall as the sole beneficiary, but with Phillips as the trustee."

"Why would they do something like that?" Parrott asked.

"Usually to protect the money till the beneficiary is capable of managing it on his own. The parents died young—while Marshall was serving a stint in Viet Nam."

"Still, he must have resented having Phillips control his inheritance. When did he get the money?"

"He *doesn't* get the money until after Phillips' death. The parents must have placed a lot of trust in Phillips, not so much in their son."

"So you're saying that as a result of Phillips' death, Marshall Winthrop will get his hands on several hundred million dollars?" Parrott's voice rose an octave on the last three words.

"That's right. You and I are on the same wave length now, and you know I promised Dalton, just one more week. So what do you propose we do next?"

Parrott took a deep breath and plunged into the plan he had been crafting. "I've been thinking I'd like to know more about Phillips. I thought I'd see if I could get an interview with the person who's known him the longest—his mother."

"Good idea. And I'll bet she doesn't bring in a criminal defense lawyer, either."

Penelope Phillips met with Parrott in the parlor of her mansion in the Hamptons, where she had lived with her husband and raised her children. The house was way too large for a family of one, and she had closed off five of its seven wings. It was becoming more and more difficult for her in her eighty-ninth year of life to manage the stairs, the long hallways, the wide expanses within the first floor rooms. Still, she hated to sell what had become almost a third child to her. She couldn't imagine turning over her home, with all of its personally chosen antique furnishings, to just anyone. She had hoped that Preston or Frances, his sister, would take up residence there upon her death. Meanwhile, the home glowed with impeccable style and meticulous care.

Mrs. Phillips took no less care of her person. At eighty-eight, she was slim, perfectly outfitted in a russet-colored silk suit with low-heeled alligator Ferragamos to match. Her silver hair was freshly coiffed, and she wore just the right amount of makeup to enhance her blue eyes and rosebud lips. Her dimples remained a distinctive part of her beauty, still evident despite time and sorrow.

As Parrott was announced then brought into the parlor, Mrs. Phillips rose from the pastel loveseat perpendicular to the fireplace, her spine straight and surprisingly tall.

"Welcome, Detective," she said, extending her right hand for a warm and firm grip before motioning for him to sit in the opposite loveseat.

Parrott expressed his condolences.

Mrs. Phillips' eyes shone glossy with unshed tears, but her voice remained steady as she thanked him. "Truthfully, I don't think it has hit me yet that Preston is gone. I go to call him several times a day before I realize that I can't. I'm afraid it will take a long while to adjust."

"I understand, ma'am. And I want you to know the West Brandywine Police Department will do all we can to solve the case in a speedy and respectful manner."

She considered a reply, but merely nodded.

"Mrs. Phillips," Parrott began, modulating his voice volume to fit the cozy space they occupied in this large room, "I wondered if you could tell me something about your son: his personality, his values, his relationships."

"That's a monumental opening question, isn't it? How to sum up a person's whole life in one paragraph." She thought for a minute, glancing at the portrait hanging over the mantle of Preston as a young man. His piercing gaze and confident posture conveyed an invincibility that caused her to shudder She lifted her chin and spoke softly. "Preston was extremely clever, almost from birth on. He was constantly asking questions, pushing the proverbial envelope. Some people didn't appreciate the way his mind worked. But he was brilliant." She paused to dab at her mouth with an embroidered handkerchief. "I suppose you might say Preston valued money and the things it could buy. He loved fast cars, beautiful women, expensive clothes. He also loved money for its own sake, just the accumulation of it. He was proud of having earned his own way, instead of relying on his family fortune, which he very easily could have done."

"What about his marriages?"

"Well, he had four of them, you know." For a second, a smile traversed her lips, and the dimples showed themselves fully. "Five, if you count Margo Martin, Preston's first true love. I assume you know their wedding was called off because Preston had fathered a baby with another woman." Parrott nodded. "That baby was Peter, Preston's only child as far as anybody knows," she said. "The marriage was never a good one, and Preston never wanted to have more children. I think he took care of that risk medically. The wives were all decent people, no messy divorces or anything. Preston just wasn't lucky in love after Margo."

"What about the most recent marriage—Nicole Phillips?"

Mrs. Phillips spoke as if choosing her words carefully. "I really don't know Nicole very well. She and Preston were only married a few months. I don't know what the two of them had in common. She is quite a bit younger than Preston, but I do think she loved him."

"Mrs. Phillips, do you know anything about

Preston's relationship with Marshall Winthrop?"

"Marshall? Well, yes. We were neighbors of the Winthrops, and the boys grew up together. Preston is a couple of years older than Marshall, who always looked up to him. Our families were close, and Marshall's parents treated Preston like a second son. In fact, they loved him so much they put Preston in charge of their finances. Then they died in a tragic accident, so young."

"Were you aware of any animosity between Preston and Marshall over the money, or otherwise?"

"No, but both boys chose careers in finance, very competitive, so I would imagine there might have been some friction from time to time."

"Who would you say were Preston's closest friends?"

"I would have to think hard on that one. Preston didn't have close friends, *per se*. He was close to his sister, his cousin Caroline Campbell, and me, of course. Former President Dalton was a close professional colleague, but that's not the same thing as a friend. Preston spent a lot of time with the ladies, but, except for playing sports, he was never one to socialize with the guys. He would prefer to spend his time making money."

"What about Leon and Vicki Spiller? Do you know anything about Preston's relationship with them?"

"Oh, that's the couple who lost their son at Peter's sixteenth birthday party. Tragic, that was. They were college friends of Preston's and Margo's, but I don't think there's been much of a relationship with them since the tragedy, which is understandable, don't you think?"

Parrott nodded. "How about Gerald and Kitty Kelley?"

"College friends. I think Kitty had a crush on Preston way back then, but no, they are better friends with my niece, Caroline."

"Is there anyone you know of who might have wanted to harm Preston?"

"To kill him, you mean? You don't have to sugarcoat things with me, Detective. I've already suffered the loss of my only son, and to imagine that someone took his life makes it all the more horrible."

When Parrott didn't respond, she went on. "I know Preston has made enemies. Anyone who has had the financial and political success Preston had couldn't have gotten there without stepping on toes or offending. What are the reasons people kill other people? Envy, greed, a desire for revenge? All I know is Preston deserved better. He worked hard to get where he did, and to have his life cut short before he could enjoy it—" Her voice broke off and her midsection began to shake with silent sobs. "Forgive me, Detective. I'm afraid I have lived too long."

"You deserve better, too, Mrs. Phillips. I appreciate your meeting with me." He drew a card from his jacket pocket and placed it on the coffee table between them, next to a delicate-looking Faberge egg. "If you think of anything else I should know, please call. I'll see myself out."

❧❧❧

On the way to his car, he thought of Mrs. Phillips' graciousness and affability, especially considering the circumstances. As she spoke about her son, he had wanted to give her a sympathetic hug, but he knew the differences between them were too great. It was as if a clear plastic wall ran between them. They could see and hear one another, but touching was out of the question.

What echoed in his mind most was this remarkable lady's list of possible motives for killing— envy, greed, and a desire for revenge. Those pretty much summed up what he had been thinking about the way the guests at the party may have felt toward Preston Phillips. The problem was that almost *all* of them had motives.

CHaPtER 33

Upon leaving Preston's mother's house in the Hamptons, Parrott punched previous destinations for the Phillipses' co-op, into his GPS. The chief had arranged for him to swing by and pick up certain of the victim's belongings, including his cell phone, his daily planner, and a list of the boards and committees he served on. Parrott hoped to have a chance to interview Nicole, as well. He was counting on her limited mobility to keep her at home, and her inexperience with police procedures to loosen her tongue. He had been reviewing his notes and coming up with more questions for the new heiress.

It was two p.m. by the time he pulled up to the entrance of the posh co-op, where a white-gloved doorman greeted him by name. Parrott nodded and concealed a smile. *Guess I've come up in the world.*

When he reached the penthouse hallway, Rosa met him at the door. "Hello, Detective." She ushered him inside with a broad flourish of her arm. Her uniform looked so crisp he expected it to crackle when she moved. "May I take your coat?"

Parrott stuffed the Burberry-knockoff scarf into

his coat pocket and shook his arms out of his wool-lined trench coat. He handed it over to Rosa, who hung it with almost as much care as he took at home.

"Mrs. Phillips, she is waiting for you in the breakfast room. This way, please."

Parrott followed Rosa at a respectful distance, gazing into the study with the aquarium as he passed through the entryway. They passed the living room, where a cinnamon-scented fire was blazing. It reminded him of those contemporary lithographs of interior scenes, all architecture and furnishings, but no people.

As they approached the kitchen, he heard Nicole saying, "Have to hang up now. Detective's here. Bye." As he walked into the sunny kitchen with adjoining breakfast room, he saw Nicole, dropping her iPhone onto the table.

"Mrs. Phillips," Parrott said. As he took her hand in his, he marveled at how strong it seemed, despite its petite size.

"Would you like to sit down?" She indicated the salmon leather chair opposite hers. Between them on the table was a bowl of fruit and a plate of cheese and biscuits. "Can I offer you something to eat?"

Parrott's stomach grumbled at the smell of the ripe brie. He hadn't eaten since five a.m., but he declined. He wanted to keep focused. Food could wait.

His eyes took in Nicole's appearance and demeanor. She looked good, considering she was recovering from trauma, both physical and emotional. She seemed vibrant and fit in her low-cut tank top and velvet loungewear that matched her eyes. He wondered whether her ankle or her heart would heal first. Either way, she'd have enough money to ease the pain.

"How is the investigation going?" Nicole asked, her tone inscrutable.

"We're moving forward, bit-by-bit," Parrott replied, removing the mini iPad from his jacket pocket. He opened it and glanced at the notes on questions he wanted to ask her, most just single words on each line. "Thanks for seeing me today."

"Well, it's not like I have something better to do," Nicole answered. "I'm pretty much grounded for the next coupla weeks at least. I asked my doctor when I could go back to the health club. I can't stand not exercising."

"What did he say?"

"Not for another six weeks. Six *weeks*," she moaned. "I don't know how I'll be able to stand it. I may have to get a personal trainer to come to the house." She shifted in her chair to get more comfortable then shrugged.

She was perfectly made up, and she had done something drastic to thin her eyebrows since he was last there. It seemed she wouldn't have to wait six weeks for spa services. "I'm sure it's very hard

265

on you," he managed to say with a note of sincerity in his deep voice. He was hoping to gain this woman's trust, though he was skeptical about it.

"Yes, it's been hard, but life goes on. Well, except for Preston's life, of course." Nicole took a tiny bite of cheese and rolled it around in her mouth. "I've boxed up the things Chief Schrik asked for. I hate turning loose of Preston's things, though. Will I get them back once this is all over?"

"Sure you will. I appreciate your cooperation. I wonder if I might ask you a few more questions."

"Go ahead. But first, I have a question for you. Am I a suspect?"

Skilled in reading people's facial expressions, Parrott controlled his own. "At this point in the investigation, everyone who was at the Campbells' place the weekend Mr. Phillips was killed is a suspect."

"So, you're saying, yes. Well, I didn't do it. I loved my husband."

"I'm sure you do." Parrott paused. Rushing into his questions might spoil the tenuous balance between concern for the suspect and concern for the investigation. "Ready for the questions?" When she nodded, he went on. "Had Mr. Phillips complained to you about any health ailments recently, either before or during the weekend at the Campbells'?"

"No, but Preston wasn't a complainer. I know he had a bad knee. He took some of my oxycodone that Saturday. Preston was a very private person, even moody. I learned not to ask too many questions."

Parrott wondered if the moodiness also applied to his widow. "This next question is rather delicate, Mrs. Phillips, but I have to ask. Were you and Mr. Phillips intimate during the weekend at the Campbells'?"

Nicole's thin eyebrows rose a fraction of an inch. "Why, yes, Detective. What does that have—"

"It's a routine question, Mrs. Phillips. Can you recall how many times you were intimate?"

"Well, Friday night, for sure, maybe twice. I broke my ankle Saturday morning, so after that, I slept downstairs, and we didn't have any privacy."

"Was it usual for you to have relations every day, or twice a day?"

"Yes, it was. Remember, we were still newlyweds."

"I understand, Mrs. Phillips. But Mr. Phillips was not, exactly—"

"—young. And you wonder if he could keep up with me in the bedroom. Well, he had help from the little blue pill, and he did just fine."

"So the fact that you broke your ankle meant that you were not having relations for thirty-six hours before his death. How were you two getting along during those hours?"

"What do you mean by that?"

"I mean, were you and Mr. Phillips intimate in other ways during that time? Was he attentive to you, did you spend time together, what did you talk about?"

"It all seems such a blur to me, to be truthful. I was in a lot of pain and discomfort, taking meds, sleeping a lot. And we were surrounded by those people. As I said before, we didn't really have any privacy."

"Did you notice Mr. Phillips' interactions with any of the other people at the party?"

Nicole flinched at the memory of Preston's eyes on Margo, his leaving the table when Margo did on Friday night. She was determined to blot out the memory of their last conversation—when Preston said he didn't think their marriage was going to work out. *That*, she would never tell anyone.

"All of those people are just bullshitters."

"What makes you say that?"

"They all have a lot of money and power, and they love to hear themselves talk. The guys, I mean. The women, well, Preston called them barracudas, told me they were probably jealous of me." She flipped her shiny blonde hair behind her shoulder. "If you ask me, those women were jealous that Preston was mine. He was by far the best-looking guy there, and who knows what their history with him was a thousand years ago. Probably he slept with all of them."

Parrott changed the subject. "Mrs. Phillips, were you aware that Mr. Phillips was the trustee of the Winthrop Estate?"

"Marshall Winthrop's money, you mean? I know Preston gets mail addressed to the trust, and there's a file on it in the desk drawer. In fact, I saw it as I was packing up the items Chief Schrik requested."

"Would you mind if I took a look at that file?"

"Not at all." Nicole lowered her right leg to the floor and lifted herself from the chair without bearing weight on her ankle. It was a fluid motion, reminiscent of a dancer's gracefulness. She propped her knee on the cushion of her mechanized scooter and moved it into place. "I probably won't need this device much longer," she said, perhaps as much to herself as to Parrott. "This way to Preston's study."

Parrott walked a few feet behind the widow, admiring the view, despite himself. He was delighted that the questioning had led to an opportunity to enter the study without directly asking. As they passed, he noted the fire in the living room was past its prime. *What a waste of a good fire.*

Nicole paused momentarily before entering the study. "It feels strange to go into this room, even now. It was Preston's sanctuary. I almost never bothered him here."

Parrott was arrested by the spacious size and vivid colors of the aquarium, even more impressive up close. The movement within was at once frenetic and graceful, a microcosm for life in this neighborhood of New York. The fish and corals were the focal point of the otherwise colorless room. "Beautiful aquarium you have here," he commented. "Does it require a lot of work?"

Nicole looked at the big tank, as if seeing it through Parrott's eyes. "I really don't know. Preston took care of it himself. Fed the fish, cleaned it. It was one of his few hobbies, collecting fish. I suppose Rosa's been doing it since—" She moved toward the massive roll-top desk in the corner of the room. She switched on the pharmacy lamp and sat down in the comfortable padded chair. Large file drawers had been fashioned from the stacks of drawers on each side of the chair opening. Nicole flipped through the files in the right-hand drawer until she came to the Ws. "Here it is, 'Winthrop Trust.'"

The Redweld file was thick and heavy, a big envelope with lots of manila files inside. Parrott could see the neatly printed titles on some of the tabs: Correspondence, Paid Bills, Unpaid Bills, Tax Information. Nicole thunked it onto the desk. Parrott looked over her shoulder at the contents.

"May I?" he asked, as he started to lift the unpaid bill file out of its alphabetical position.

He adjusted the lamp to improve the light and flipped through the short stack of bills. *Wow*, he thought, as his eyes trailed the bottom lines with amounts due. Airplanes, home maintenance, artwork—every one of them was more than Parrott earned in a year. He dropped the file back into its place and picked up the paid bill file. The top one was from a hospital stay at Mount Sinai Hospital for Marshall Winthrop. The itemized charges filled up the entire first page with several pages behind it. "Mrs. Phillips, I'd like to take this file with me and copy it. I need some time to study the contents."

"I don't mind. It's of no use to me. Do we need to ask the Winthrops, though?"

"No, the trust has provided for a successor trustee, and I will make sure that entity knows we have custody of it." Parrott clasped the file under his arm, eager to get a better look at the types of things Marshall Winthrop spent money on, as well as what had taken him to the hospital three months ago. "Now I have another question. Do you still have the toiletries and medications Mr. Phillips took with him to the Campbells'?" He hoped against hope that Nicole's surgery and impairment had kept her from cleaning out her husband's personal belongings.

"Yes, I do. I haven't had time to go through them, for obvious reasons."

"Officer Barton and I examined them earlier, but I just want to verify something."

"Okay, Detective. Follow me." Nicole led Parrott into the "his" section of the "his and hers" dressing rooms. The long marble vanity was gleaming, the cabinetry polished to a high gloss, as well. Nicole opened several of the many drawers next to the sink. The first contained sections for razor, toothpaste, dental floss, and hairbrush. Everything was perfectly placed in its proper section, as if the person they belonged to had arranged them as recently as this morning. The second drawer was a deep one. It contained prescription and over-the-counter medications, standing upright.

Parrott slipped a pair of plastic gloves on. "May I handle these?"

Nicole nodded.

He recognized the prescriptions he had seen in the bathroom at the Campbells'—Celebrex, Voltaren, Viagra, Restasis eye drops, Metamucil—in keeping with an older guy who had arthritis and a young wife. He looked at the labels of some of the other bottles. Acetaminophen, Aleve, nothing that unusual. "Are these the same bottles that were in Mr. Phillips' Dopp kit that weekend?"

"Yes, I believe so. I brought it back, and Rosa unpacked it."

"I'd like to take them with me, as well."

"Okay. Preston won't be needing them anymore, and neither will I."

"I appreciate your being so cooperative, Mrs. Phillips."

"Sure." This time it came out sounding like, "Shoo-ah." The woman still had occasional traces of her not-so-wealthy past in her accent. Parrott couldn't criticize. His own past had been not-so-wealthy, and his speech patterns had also been cultivated to fit in with the people and places where he worked.

"Anything else?" Nicole asked, a bit of weariness creeping into her voice.

"No, let's go back to the breakfast room, and I'll gather up the items and leave."

As they walked back past the living room, whose glass wall overlooked Central Park, Parrott realized the day was drawing to a close. He would be stuck in horrible traffic, tired and hungry, but he felt satisfied that he had made some progress. He looked forward to a full night of homework.

Just as he was placing the Redweld file and the handful of medicines into the box on the kitchen counter, a triple buzzing sound issued from his pants pocket. Parrott pulled his cell phone out and saw Chief Schrik's name on the caller ID. He swiped the green dot. "Yes?"

"Parrott, are you still at the victim's house?" Schrik's voice boomed.

"Affirmative, Sir."

"Well, you don't need to come back quite yet. Go to Mount Sinai Hospital while you're still in the city. It's at East Ninety-Eighth between Madison and Fifth Avenue."

Parrott's stomach grumbled, but he did not. He wanted to ask questions, but he was keenly aware that the lovely Mrs. Phillips was listening. "What's there?"

"Gerald Kelley is there. He's had a stroke."

Chapter 34

Kitty Kelley had been worried about her husband ever since John E.'s birthday weekend and Preston's death. Of course, it had been unpleasant and shocking to all of them, but Gerald, it seemed, had suffered a personality change. Kitty had tried to tease out of him what was causing him to be so withdrawn, taciturn, even morose.

"It's nothing. I'm just pre-occupied with things at work."

Kitty knew better. Gerald's position at the top of Miles Stewart had its ups and downs in the past, but she had always been able to navigate a life raft through the rough waters and save Gerald from drowning. This time, though, she wasn't sure. Last night she had employed her ultimate tool in the form of her sexiest lingerie, and even that had failed to get a rise out of him.

I don't get it, Kitty mused. *Why would Preston's death affect Gerald so deeply? They weren't even friends. In fact, they were more like rivals.* Kitty knew Gerald had been angry and frustrated when Preston was appointed secretary of the treasury. Gerald had worked hard to develop the expertise and skills, intellectually and politically, to hold that position. Even the journalists had seemed surprised when, at the last moment, President Dalton had named Preston instead. But that was five years ago, and for goodness's sake, Preston was dead.

Gerald had been reluctant to go to Bucolia to begin with.

He went for my sake. And I wasn't very sensitive to his discomfort, either. Perhaps I should have gone horseback riding with him, instead of out to lunch with the girls. Perhaps I shouldn't have been so flirty with Preston at dinner.

Trying not to brood, Kitty put on her newest outfit, a burnt orange Oscar de la Renta skirt, blouse, and sweater, and went into the city to take Mr. Melancholy out to lunch at McCormick and Schmick's. She was going to shower him with attention until he returned to his comfortable, normal self. Maybe she would propose a spur-of-the-moment weekend trip to Boston to visit Lexie. Surely Daddy's little girl would be a tonic.

"To what do I owe the pleasure?" Gerald asked, as they made themselves comfortable at his usual table.

"I just thought you might need a break from your routine," Kitty said, smiling. "And I needed to spend some quality time with the man in my life."

A doubtful expression passed over Gerald's face, but he didn't probe. Instead, he inhaled the aromas of garlic and fine herbs, and the wavy lines across his forehead seemed to fade. Kitty was glad she had brought him here.

The waiter delivered their usual drinks, wine and Grey Goose vodka, neat, along with a basket of warm, fresh rolls. Gerald pinched off a sizeable piece, buttered it, and popped it into his mouth with a sigh of pleasure.

Kitty lifted her glass of Chardonnay. "Here's to us."

Looking embarrassed that he had started eating before Kitty's toast, Gerald mirrored the gesture and clinked his highball glass with his wife's wineglass. "To us." He downed the contents in one smooth swallow.

Kitty frowned, worries about Gerald's state of mind renewed, but rather than spoil the mood by questioning him, she kept quiet.

Gerald had ordered his favorite, the dry rubbed Black Angus ribeye steak, center cut, topped with lump crabmeat and butter, while Kitty ordered the chilled shrimp cocktail appetizer as her entrée. When their meals arrived, Gerald dug into his juicy and aromatic steak and crab.

Kitty picked up her cocktail fork and addressed the first of her four jumbo shrimp when she noticed Gerald's mouth drooping on the right side. In the next few seconds, her whole life flipped. "Gerald! What's the matter?"

Gerald dropped his fork onto the china plate. The clatter drew the attention of people at adjacent tables, including their waiter, who turned around and stared. Gerald was drooling. He held a napkin to his mouth with his left hand, but he slumped over onto the table, his right cheek barely missing the au jus gravy boat and saucer.

"Help him," Kitty shouted to the waiter. "Call nine-one-one."

❧❧❧

An hour later, Kitty was sitting in the surgical waiting room at Mount Sinai. Someone told her a team of doctors was performing an intravenous recombinant thrombolysis on Gerald's artery infarction. New vocabulary words were the least of Kitty's distressful problems. She called Lexie, who promised to come in from Boston as soon as she could hire a plane, but she held off calling Gerald's mother, who, she knew, would freak out and somehow make it to be all Kitty's fault.

Why was *this happening? Why Gerald, and why now?* Kitty's ruminations of the last few weeks returned to rumble around in her brain. *Was Gerald under so much stress at work? Was Preston's death weighing on him, and if so why? Or was it the high cholesterol meal he was eating, along with the fact he was probably thirty pounds overweight?*

Strokes were something that happened to old people, not people like us in the sixty-is-the-new-forty generation. What if the effects of the stroke

277

didn't reverse themselves? Gerald was such a control freak. Kitty didn't want to think of how he would cope if he were incapacitated. Or what if he died? All of the homes and cars and clothes and jewelry in the world couldn't make up for his absence. The fact that what was happening in the surgical room at this very moment was critical to her future made her want to scream. She realized she had been clenching her teeth so tightly that both jaws ached. She needed someone to talk to, if only to push away the "what if" thoughts echoing in her head. She grabbed her cell phone and pushed the number for Caro at the farm. She knew Caro would understand.

℘℘℘

Caro, as fate would have it, was on the phone with Chief Schrik when Kitty's call beeped into call waiting. Schrik was attempting to follow up with her on the source of the seafood used in the bouillabaisse and the halibut cheeks served in the Saturday night dinner. Palytoxin had been known to appear in tainted seafood. He doubted this was how the victim had been poisoned, since he seemed to be the only person affected, and everyone there had eaten the fish. Still, it was good to be thorough.

"Can you hold on a minute, Chief?" Caro asked. "I'm getting an important call." Caro could see that the call was only from Kitty, but she was eager to jump on any excuse to get away. Since John E. had warned her not to talk to the police, she was skittish about saying the wrong thing. She was supposed to refer him to the attorney immediately, but that seemed rude, and contrary to the way she had been raised. Of course, her mother probably never dreamed she would be in the position of being a suspect in a murder.

⟅⟆⟅⟆

Schrik took a pretend-drag of his paper clip cigarette as he waited for Caro to come back to the phone. He had a few more questions to ask about the items consumed at the party, and he hoped she wouldn't cut him off and refer him to her attorney. Of all the people involved in the case, he found Mrs. Campbell the least suspicious.

Despite the slight tremor in her voice that betrayed nervousness, she was polite and kind. His thoughts were interrupted when she patched back in with a click.

"Chief, would you please contact our attorney, David Louis of Anderson, Glasser, and Louis? That was Kitty Kelley on the other line. Gerald has had a stroke and is at Mount Sinai Hospital. I need to get into the city to be there with Kitty while Gerald is in surgery."

⟅⟆⟅⟆

Parrott stopped at Corner Café and Bakery after slugging his way through rush hour traffic and parking in the hospital lot. He ordered a build-your-own sandwich and two large peanut butter cookies. "Give me a half dozen more cookies, different kinds," he said, as an afterthought.

It couldn't hurt to take a bag of goodies into the hospital with him. In his experience, people under stress appreciated gifts of food.

The cookies might make up for what might be considered the rudeness of his appearance there while the Kelleys were in crisis. He knew why Schrik wanted him there, but he hated barging in on people when they were at their worst.

He chewed and swallowed on the run, barely tasting the advertised whole wheat goodness and freshness of his combination lunch and dinner. What would he find when he got there, what would he say, and what might he be able to learn? Truthfully, the Kelleys had not been high on his list of people to interview. He would have gotten around to them eventually, but so far he hadn't learned anything that would serve as a motive for either of them. He had been more concerned about Nicole Phillips, the Winthrops, the Spillers, and Margo Rinaldi. But fate had a way of throwing curve balls into investigations, and he might as well swing at this one. Besides, he doubted either of the Kelleys would even think about having an attorney with them at the hospital.

The woman at the information desk directed him to the eighth floor, where neurosurgery and its waiting room were located. As he stepped off the elevator he could see Kitty Kelley in her bitter orange outfit, her legs crossed, one pumping rhythmically. Blobs of mascara encircled her eyes, making her otherwise attractive face ghoulish. The blank stare on her face gave the impression that she was sitting there in body only.

Parrott approached tentatively, bending down to make eye contact. "Mrs. Kelley," he said in his most soothing voice.

Kitty startled, her arms flying upward like a baby's. "Yes?" She tried to remember where she had seen this young black man's face before. *Oh, yes, at Caro's. The policeman. What on earth is he doing here?*

"Mrs. Kelley, I brought you some cookies from the Corner Bakery." He handed her the crisp white bag of cookies. "I'd be happy to get you some coffee, too, if you'd like."

Kitty accepted the cookies in an automatic response, much like that of a robot programmed to take what was given. "Thank you," she said. "How did you know I was here?"

"Mrs. Campbell was talking to my boss when you called her. She told him about Mr. Kelley's stroke. I'm very sorry." He let his words sink in. "I was already in the city, so I decided to stop by and see how things are going, see if there's anything I can do to help."

"Very nice of you," Kitty responded, though she couldn't imagine how he or anyone else, for that matter, could help. "They're working on Gerald now, trying to open his artery. Luckily, we got here pretty quickly. This procedure has to be done within four hours in order to work." She dug into the bag, pulled out a chocolate chip cookie, and took a bite.

Parrott sat next to Kitty on the cool vinyl sofa, but he turned his body to see her face clearly. He maintained a sympathetic expression on his face, but he didn't disrupt her thoughts with questions.

Somehow she found his presence comforting, though she hardly believed he was there as a friend. "Detective, have you ever loved someone whose life was in danger?" she asked.

"Yes, ma'am," Parrott replied. "My fiancée is in the navy in Afghanistan. I think about her all the time."

"Then you know," Kitty said, "how hard it is to even think straight. I've been sitting here wondering about things, and all I can come up with is questions. No answers."

"I understand. Sometimes I just have to box up my feelings about her and put them aside, so I can go about my everyday life. But the box is never far from me—no farther than my left front pocket." He tapped the spot on his chest where his heart was beating.

After a long minute, Kitty asked, "How's the investigation into the Phillips death going?"

"It's coming along. I was planning to interview you and Mr. Kelley later this week."

"I don't know what Gerald or I could possibly tell you that could help you."

"Oh, everyone who was at Mr. Campbell's party is a valuable resource to us. The things you observed that weekend. Sometimes it's the tiniest detail that will crack a case."

"Like what, for instance?"

"Are you sure you feel like talking about it?" Parrott leaned forward.

"Yes, it's okay. It's hard to wait out here by myself, anyway. Caro and my daughter Lexie will be here later, but right now you are all the company I have, and it'll help me get my mind off of my problems."

"Well, can you tell me a little about your relationship with Mr. Phillips?"

"I've known Preston since I was seventeen years old. I met him when I was a freshman in college. He was driving a shiny blue Corvette convertible past the University Center, and he offered me a ride. I shouldn't have gotten in the car with a stranger, but he just seemed so clean-cut and friendly. I didn't see any harm in it. I went to a fraternity party or two with him, nothing serious. I was the one who introduced him to Margo, and that was history."

"So you've been friends for all these years? How about Mr. Kelley?"

"Gerald didn't go to school with us, so he didn't meet Preston until after we were married. They weren't close friends."

"Yet they were both in the same field, finance. Is that right?"

"Yes, we all have that in common." Kitty raised her chin as she said this. Despite the circumstances, Kitty felt proud to be part of the elite group, the money people.

"I understand you were sitting next to Mr. Phillips during the Saturday night dinner party. Is that right?"

"Yes, Caro split up the couples, so I was seated next to Preston and not Gerald." Kitty felt a pang of something like guilt as she said this.

"Did Mr. Phillips seem unusually talkative or quiet? Did he complain of feeling ill?"

"No, Preston was his usual sparkling self. He could be quite charming when he wanted to, and that night he was reminiscing, telling stories from the good old days, when we were in college, fraternity pranks and such. He seemed happy."

"Did he seem worried about his wife's injury?"

Kitty thought before answering. The truth was, Preston had pretty much ignored Nicole, who seemed so miserable at the end of the table with

John E. If anything, he was making goo-goo eyes at Margo throughout the evening. She said, "Not overly worried. I guess he figured Nicole was young and strong, and she would heal."

"How well do you know Mrs. Phillips?"

"You mean the *new* Mrs. Phillips?" Kitty asked. "That was the first time we had met her, at John E.'s birthday party."

"Yes. Well, what did you think of her? Of their marriage? Having known Mr. Phillips for so many years?"

"She's okay. It's too bad she got thrown from the horse and broke her ankle. I think she was in a lot of pain."

"How did she fit in with the group?"

"Well, she's quite a bit younger, as you probably know. She was at a disadvantage, since we all know each other quite well, and she was the newcomer. Then she had the accident, and she was all doped up after that. She was Preston's wife. That was all."

"What did you think about their marriage?"

"Oh, she was his fourth wife, you know, and younger than his son Peter, so we figured he married her for sex, and she married him for money." She took another bite of cookie.

Parrott made no comment. Instead, he went on, "Let me shift gears for a minute. Do you recall any of the women wearing lime green during the weekend?"

"Lime green?" Kitty had a marvelous memory for detail when it came to clothes and furnishings, and especially for color. She thought of all of the outfits she had seen the guests wearing, but she could not recall any of them being lime green. "I don't think so, Detective. Lime green is more of a spring color. I'm sure I would have remembered it if anyone had worn that color in the winter."

Parrott wished Gerald Kelley were available to answer some questions. He thought Mr. Kelley might have a more objective view of the victim, since he wasn't one of the Princeton crowd, and it was time to hear some things from a man's perspective. "Was there any time when Mr. Kelley interacted with Mr. Phillips during the weekend, either in your presence or outside of your presence?"

"Y—Yes," Kitty said. "We all had different conversations with one another, and the men went horseback riding on Saturday morning—well, Andrea and Nicole went, too—and the men smoked cigars late Saturday night. Who knows what they talked about?"

"Well, I hope Mr. Kelley recovers soon."

℘℘℘

The elevator just outside of the place where they were seated *pinged*, and the doors opened to let out a gaggle of young men and women carrying notebooks and photographic paraphernalia.

"Oh, no, reporters," Kitty cried.

"Are you Mrs. Gerald Kelley?" the first of them asked.

Before she could answer, they formed a tight circle around Kitty and Parrott, and a bright light blinded her.

"Is it true Mr. Kelley has had a stroke?"

"Have you had any word about his condition?"

"Can you verify Mr. Kelley's age and position at Miles Stewart?"

The questions kept coming, as if the frenzy were about asking questions, instead of receiving information.

The door at the opposite side of the room opened, and a man in scrubs with a mask hanging by a string from his neck entered the waiting room. "Mrs. Kelley?"

"Yes?" Kitty asked, jumping up from the sofa and pushing through the crowd to rush across the room, leaving Parrott to deal with the press. "Is Gerald okay?"

The surgeon surveyed the group of rubberneckers and pulled Kitty into the private room adjacent to where they were crowding. "Mr. Kelley is in recovery now. The procedure went well, and we were able to open up his artery. We are hoping he will recover the use of the right side of his body by tomorrow morning. And, of course, we hope he will regain his ability to speak."

"How long will he be in the hospital?"

"We'll know more after tomorrow morning. We got to him fairly quickly after he was stricken, so that's in his favor. He will most likely need to go to rehab for a while. A lot will depend on the next twenty-four hours."

"Can I see him?" Kitty asked. Her voice sounded strangely distant, as if coming from deep within a well.

The doctor looked through the blinds at the place where Kitty had been surrounded by the press. The swarm of people appeared to be increasing with each elevator stop on the floor. He looked back at her and said in his gentlest voice. "You may go in to see him, but I want to prepare you not to expect too much this soon. Your husband has suffered a major stroke. He'll be able to hear you, but he won't be able to talk. This will be frustrating for you, and also for him."

The young doctor's kind voice pierced the bubble of shock that had insulated Kitty from the full reality of her husband's condition. A sob escaped from her lips, and she began to shake uncontrollably. "Oh, Gerald," she cried.

CHAPTER 35

The next morning was Vicki's first at The Caron Foundation, an alcoholic rehab facility. Leon joined her for breakfast. Family involvement was an important facet of the Caron recovery method, and Leon intended to be there for Vicki every step of the way. Wearing a soft plaid skirt and pastel angora sweater over a raw silk pleated blouse, Vicki was already seated at the glass-topped table for two when he leaned in for a kiss on the cheek and plunged himself into the seat opposite her, a folded newspaper under his arm.

The room smelled sweet, like vanilla French toast and maple syrup. Waiters dressed in starched uniforms carried polished silver serving pieces on linen-lined trays. The scene was reminiscent of a breakfast room in a fine hotel, except for the hushed atmosphere.

No voices from the dozen other diners at the scattered tables could be heard above Brahms's "Tranquil Yearning," obviously meant to soothe.

Vicki looked tired already. Day one of a week-long detox had kept her awake most of the night, thinking about what had brought her here and what lay ahead.

Her highlighted pageboy hairdo, carefully applied makeup, and candy apple red fingernails could not disguise the stress. It showed in the dullness of her hazel-flecked eyes and in the firm set of her lips.

"Good morning," Leon fairly chirped with false cheer. "How was the first night, my angel?"

"Oh, Lee," Vicki moaned. "I am so sorry for what I've done."

"You don't have anything to be sorry for, Vicki." Self-recriminations were a necessary first step for alcoholics, he knew, but he hated witnessing them. Even though he'd been through this before, Leon felt his gut seize. Sometimes, it felt as if his entire life had been jammed into a beaker and subjected to unthinkable degrees of heat.

Vicki's hands moved from silverware to napkin to tablecloth and back again. It was as if she wanted to run away, but only her fingers had the strength to make the journey. In an almost-whisper, she said, "I've brought us both to ruin. Physical. Financial. Moral. Ruin."

"Vicki, you'll get past this. You know you will. It will be okay."

"How much is this costing us?" Vicki raised her voice, waving her hands about, as if to include the room, its furniture and furnishings, the food.

Leon was stung by his wife's reference to their recent financial setbacks. It was true they had made some decisions to cut back on spending, but not when it came to this. "We can afford it. Not to worry." Leon removed the handkerchief from the breast pocket of his fine wool jacket, and used it to clean his wire-rimmed glasses.

"It's so hard...so hard to live with myself, knowing that..."

"Knowing what?" He was familiar with the torments of a person in detox, but Vicki seemed to be beating herself up about something, in particular, this time. If only she would bring it out.

But as surely as if she had changed channels on the television set, Vicki's mood shifted and so did the topic. "Are you eating breakfast?" She pointed to her open menu. "They've got poached eggs and homemade sausage, just the way you like them."

A waiter with gloved hands appeared at their table, offering Leon a second menu, as if they were in the swankiest venue in New York.

Leon ordered for both of them, as usual, and then he opened the morning's *Journal*. A headline grabbed his eyes and held them. "Oh, no..."

"What's the matter?" Vicki asked, her fingers teasing her collar and the tiny pleats in her blouse.

"It's G—Gerald K-Kelley. He's had a massive stroke."

Vicki dropped her hands to the table, pressing hard, as if to use them to keep herself from falling over. Her mouth formed an O.

Leon read from the paper. "'Wall Street Journal, Friday, December twenty-seventh. NEW YORK.

Gerald Kelley, sixty-seven, CEO of Miles Stewart, suffered a stroke yesterday. Mr. Kelley is being treated at Mount Sinai Hospital. A statement released by the hospital characterizes Mr. Kelley's condition as serious, but stable. News of Mr. Kelley's condition sparked concern over its effect on the stock market, but thus far, the only stock expected to be affected is that of Miles Stewart itself, which opened at—'"

"Poor Kitty," Vicki murmured.

"Poor Gerald," Leon said. "He seemed fine just two weeks ago."

"Yes, we all seemed fine two weeks ago."

Leon regretted bringing the newspaper. He made a mental note not to do so again during the next twenty-seven days. Vicki didn't need any worries from the outside world to distract her from getting well. Her inner demons seemed to be more than enough for her to handle.

"We have Miles Stewart stock, don't we?" Vicki asked. "I think we bought it when Gerald became CEO."

"Yes, we do," Leon said, resisting the impulse to pat his wife's hand in what she would likely frown on as patronizing. "But not so much that we need to fret about it right now."

"But my private room. It must cost a fortune."

"Shhh," Leon said under his breath as the waiter approached with their breakfast. "I've got it all taken care of. You just get well."

MURDER IN THE ONE PERCENT

Julia and Marshall lingered over bagels and coffee in their Kirby Pond home before Marshall departed for his last day of work for the week. It was five a.m., but they were used to rising early, a routine made easier now that both had been diagnosed with sleep apnea and gone on CPAP machines at night. Most wives wouldn't get up so early to see their husbands off to work, but Julia wasn't that way.

He was a lucky man to have such a woman. Julia had stood with him through the rollercoaster ride of the past year, hospitalization and all. She never complained.

"More juice?" Julia leaned over Marshall ready to pour from a crystal pitcher. The clean smell of his aftershave drew her in for a quick nuzzle of his neck.

Marshall reached up to press his wife's face against his own, smiling at her show of affection. They weren't completely free of the constraints of the Winthrop trust yet, but now they would have more financial autonomy.

"I can't stop thinking about poor Gerald," Marshall said, as he took his last bite of bagel. He reflected on the call from John E. the previous night to tell them the news.

"Me, either," she replied. "I keep thinking about the weekend at the Campbells'. I never dreamed

293

John E.'s birthday would be such a turning point. First Preston, and now Gerald."

"Well, let's hope Gerald doesn't end up like Preston. Supposedly they got him to the hospital in time." Marshall rose from the table, dabbing his mouth with a linen napkin.

"I'm going to sit with Kitty at the hospital today," Julia said. "Is there anything you need me to do in the city while I'm there?"

"Nothing I can think of," Marshall mumbled, as he packed his leather satchel with reading material for the long ride into work.

His chauffeur was waiting in the warmed limousine on the circular driveway. Marshall donned his Burberry and cashmere scarf then bent to kiss Julia on the lips after she put the breakfast dishes in the sink.

He tapped his coat pocket to make sure he had a fresh supply of cigars on hand.

"Oh, one more thing," he said on his way out the door. "If you hear from the West Brandywine Police today, don't say anything about anything."

ȔȔȔ

Libby sat on the bed in her guest room, watching Margo pack the last of her things in her Louis Vuitton suitcases. "I hate to see you leave, sis."

"I appreciate that," Margo said, as she zipped up the rolling carry-on bag. "But you and Les have been more than hospitable, and it's time to give you back your privacy before the baby comes. Not that I know about these things first-hand, of course."

Libby ignored her sister's reference to her childlessness. She knew it was not of Margo's own choosing, and she guessed it was enough of a rub to see her younger sister's expanding belly. "Are you sure you'll be okay at the condo at the AKA?"

Margo laughed, a light tinkling sound. "The AKA? They'll wait on me hand and foot. Besides, I won't be there long. After the holidays, I'll find a permanent apartment. And maybe I'll go back to Tuscany for a while."

"I just feel so bad about everything—" Libby said.

"You feel bad? Why?"

"I should never have taken you to the birthday party. I should have declined the invitation."

"Don't be ridiculous," Margo replied. "How did you know it would turn out the way it did?"

"But I knew that seeing Preston again would be difficult for you. I feel like I opened Pandora's box, and now I can't put all of the troubles back in." Her hands motioned opening a box then trying frantically to close it.

"Listen, Libby. In a way, I'm glad I got the chance to see Preston again one more time. If I hadn't gone to the party, I wouldn't have ever known..." Margo's voice drifted off into the air.

She thought of Preston's saying, '*Why did Prince Charles want Camilla when he had Diana?*' "Anyway, nothing was *your* fault, little sister."

Libby shivered from her sister's words. "I hope you're not blaming *yourself* for anything. Whoever killed Preston, I'm sure it had nothing to do with you." She picked up a pillow and rearranged it on the bed. "And now with Gerald in the hospital, it seems like there's a cloud over us all."

"Well, at least Gerald is being treated, and hopefully will recover. And no one appears to have poisoned *him*." Margo bit her lip, and tears welled up in her emerald eyes.

How awful when the man you've loved dies from poisoning right under the same roof. Not for the first time, Libby wondered how much Margo knew, how much any of them knew. She could never ask those questions, although she was sure the time was coming when the police would be asking those questions, and more.

CHAPTER 36

Andrea had gone for an early morning ride on Mustafa and now was sitting cross-legged in her executive chair, across from the toasty fireplace, reviewing the notes she had made about Preston and Nicole, Marshall, Leon, and Gerald. *The internet makes it so easy these days,* she thought, as she recalled the rigors of information-gathering when she was writing her first crime books.

She ran her fingers through her short curls, lifting them to allow air underneath. Her organic pomegranate tea let off comforting waves of steam and a delicate aroma. If it hadn't been for the subject matter of her notes, she would have felt cozy.

She felt a bit like a snoop, investigating Caro's family and friends, people she held more than a passing acquaintance with. On the other hand, this was what she did—delve into crimes, filling her mind and pages with details that, put together in certain configurations, might lead to solutions, and ultimately to good books. No one had asked her to spend hours searching through various websites, and no one had to know what she was doing, at least not yet.

The unopened New York *Times* was sitting next to her iPad. Her Mac was opened to a *Financial Times* article about Marshall Winthrop's views on inflation.

She had read countless articles such as these, learning very little that she didn't already know, but she believed in meticulous research, and that meant reading and interpreting facts and quotes, so the subjects felt real to her. She smiled at the contrast between Marshall's everyday speech from the weekend at Bucolia and the esoteric quotes attributed to him in these articles.

Undoubtedly, Marshall was a financial wizard, nominated by the president and unanimously approved by congress for his position at the Fed, one of the country's heavy-hitting leaders in the field of economics. Yet her one outstanding memory of his presence at Caro's table was that he seemed hypersensitive to anything that Preston had said or done. Andrea had noticed a small tic, a barely perceptible twitch of Marshall's right eye whenever Preston spoke or laughed, even if the acts had nothing to do with Marshall.

This had piqued Andrea's curiosity, so she searched for "Marshall Winthrop *and* Preston Phillips." She took notes about a long-standing personal and financial relationship between the two, leading up to some recent information in a gossip column about a rift the size of the Atlantic Ocean. Fortunately, the columnist, Hedy Steininger, was a personal friend, so Andrea decided to lean on her for the deets.

Brrrrrring. The phone rang only once before Hedy picked up. "Andrea, how terrible about Gerald Kelley!"

"What about Gerald Kelley?" Andrea asked, a chill starting at the base of her spine and moving upward.

"Haven't you heard?" Hedy said, her words rushing out faster than Niagara Falls. "He had a major stroke yesterday. He's at Mount Sinai. Don't you know him through Caro Campbell?"

Andrea gripped her mug of tea, her thoughts returning to John E.'s ill-fated birthday weekend. "Yes," she replied. "What is his condition, or do you know?"

"Serious, but stable, according to my sources. The city is in shock. Man of his stature, it affects the stock market, the news, even politics." Hedy's voice bore the tone of someone who was trying to curb her enthusiasm for gossip in the face of someone else's tragedy. "Anyway, if that's not why you called me, what is?"

"Maybe I just called to say hi," Andrea responded, teasing.

"Yeah, and maybe the Tooth Fairy will abdicate in favor of the Easter bunny. Seriously, what's up?"

"Actually, I wondered whether you knew anything about the bad blood between Marshall Winthrop and Preston Phillips."

"Uh-oh, you must be playing sleuth again, princess. I must admit that the late Mr. Phillips' untimely death makes for interesting drama, and all of the world is dying to know what happened to him. Actually, I do know a little bit about the feuding. I'll show you mine if you show me yours."

"I don't have anything to trade yet, Hedy. Just a hunch that it might be important information. If you help me out now, I'll get back to you later if it turns out I'm right." She dug her toe into the plush chocolate-colored carpet, hoping this promise would be enough bait to catch a shark. She could hear the clicks of Hedy's computer keyboard.

"Okay. You've never disappointed me before, so here goes. Pretty Boy Preston was apparently controlling Marshall's parents' estate for the past several decades, much to the chagrin of Marshall, who certainly was competent to take care of his own money, since he—oh, that's editorializing—anyway, the word through the grapevine is that Preston had abused his power, taken large fees for himself, made some bad investments. Who knows why he'd want Marshall's money when he had plenty of his own, but you never know. Anyway, supposedly, Marshall had hired attorneys and begun proceedings to break the trust and have Preston charged with malfeasance.

And then Preston died. So, I guess we may never know whether Pretty Boy was dipping into the

Winthrop well or not. A pity from my point of view."

Andrea sipped her tea and petted her Siamese cat, Hermione, who had leapt onto the desk. "Interesting rumor," she murmured, releasing her leg from under her and tapping some keys of her own. "Do you know the name of Marshall's attorney?"

"Nope. Not for sure, but it's probably someone from that Ballenger firm. I've seen the Winthrops and the Ballengers together at many affairs lately."

"Thanks, Hedy. You're an angel."

"Don't forget me when you start writing. One pen washes the other in this business."

Andrea pushed the red button to end the call. As usual, after talking to Hedy, she felt compelled to wash her hands with antibacterial soap. The shock of Gerald's stroke was still making background noise in her head.

I've got to call Caro, she thought. She re-fired her iPhone and thrust her feet into the fuzzy green slippers beneath the desk. She began pacing back and forth in front of the fire, for the moment forgetting about Marshall Winthrop, and remembering what she had uncovered about "Gerald Kelley" *and* "Preston Phillips." She wondered if Preston's death had brought about Gerald's stroke.

After four rings, Andrea was rewarded with the sound of Caro's voice. Breathless, she sounded as if she had run to answer the phone. "Andrea? Hi."

301

"Caro, I just heard about Gerald. Why didn't you call me?"

"I was going to. Actually, the phone's been ringing constantly, and I'm trying to get dressed. I'm in Philly today, and I'm going in to New York to be with Kitty at the hospital."

"Want some company?" Andrea offered, wondering how fast she could get ready and drive the fifty minutes to Rittenhouse Square. "I feel just terrible for Kitty, and I don't have anything planned for today that I can't cancel."

"How soon can you get here?" Caro asked. "My driver is supposed to be here in an hour."

"I'm on my way," Andrea said, dashing to her bedroom to get dressed. The thought that landed in her frontal lobe was that today's research would not be the kind done on the internet.

ೞೞ

Parrott had left the hospital and driven the three and a half hours home, most of it plagued by slanting snow and wind. He had plenty of time to think about the case as he drove. Normally he listened to WCBS, particularly to the news, weather, and traffic, but last night he had snapped off the radio and luxuriated in the rich silence and solitude.

He needed to compile his notes, not the written ones, but the ones floating around in his head after meeting with the Bakers, the Campbells, Nicole

Phillips, Penelope Phillips, and now Kitty Kelley.

He knew the chief was under constant pressure from the media, not to mention former President Dalton and other big-wigs. The interviews with the Winthrops, Spillers, Blooms, and Margo Rinaldi would be set up in the coming days, but right now he wanted to review the information and impressions he had been collecting. Forming some opinions would guide him in developing questions for the others.

Okay, what do I have here? He considered the cast of characters and the relationships that had been described to him. The love angle, of course, involved Nicole and possibly Margo, although Preston seemed to have been popular with the ladies in general, and even with Kitty Kelley going back to the college days. *Could any of the three be characterized as a woman scorned? Angry enough to kill someone she had loved? And who had the victim had sex with several times in that fourth floor room? Who might have been wearing a lime green garment, leaving a thread behind on the upholstered chair?*

The money angle applied mostly to Nicole, who benefited financially from Preston's death. However, the Winthrops certainly benefited, as well, since they gained control over the estate of Marshall's parents. No one in this group needed food stamps, but that didn't mean they couldn't be greedy for more wealth. The pre-nup made it clear that being divorced from Preston Phillips would not be as lucrative as being married at the end of his life. This guy had already had three divorces, so he'd been financially armored before he married Wife Number Four. The question was, would this marriage have been his last if he hadn't been killed? And just how bad was the squeeze Preston was putting on the Winthrops? Several hundred million dollars would pass from trust into Marshall Winthrop's hands as a result of Phillips' death. Parrott glanced at the stars through the windshield and tried to fathom that much money.

His thoughts were interrupted by the buzz of his cell phone. He punched the answer button without taking his eyes from the road. "Parrott here."

"Parrott. Schrik. Where are you?"

"Not quite halfway back. It's snowing pretty hard, and traffic's slow, too."

"How'd your meeting with Mrs. Kelley go?"

"Informative, despite the circumstances. Looks like the husband's stroke was pretty bad. He won't be talking any time soon." The windshield wipers kept rhythm to Parrott's words, as if he were singing a mournful tune.

"We're working late here. Think you can come in for an hour before you head home? I know you've been working hard all day, and that drive is a bitch."

Something was up. Schrik rarely worked into the night. When he did, there was always a good reason. Hope flickered in his gut. "I'll come straight there, Chief. What's cooking?"

"I don't want to discuss it over the phone, but we've got a something from Nick."

Named after St. Nick, who brings gifts to children for Christmas, Nick is the code name for the police department's computer expert. It must be Phillips' computer. "Okay, Chief. See you in another hour and a half." Parrott disconnected from the call, again without taking his eyes from the road. He couldn't let his weariness take over. He had to stay sharp, apparently for several more hours, at least.

He turned on the radio, hoping to get a weather report, but what he got was a truncated story about how Miles Stewart stock was expected to react to the news of its CEO's stroke. He snapped the radio off again. *Back to my mental notes. Schrik will want a status report, and I need to be prepared. Now where was I?*

Parrott remembered Mrs. Phillips' words, '*What are the reasons people kill other people? Envy, greed, a desire for revenge?*' The desire for revenge was the most complex. *I just don't know enough yet,* he thought, hitting the steering wheel with the heel of his palm. *I know the Spillers held a grudge against Phillips, something about the tragic death of their son. Margo Rinaldi most likely resented him for ditching her at the altar, too.* His thoughts circled back to the woman scorned, and again he felt irritated by the way the details of this case kept shifting. He thought of being at the beach when the ebbing tide would leave the soles of his feet on unsteady ground.

What about professional reasons? These guys were all in the money business, all wildly successful. Were they caught up in power struggles and competitions that may have boiled over into rage? Phillips was secretary of the treasury. Can't get much higher than that. Were Messieurs Campbell, Kelley, Winthrop, Spiller, Bloom, or Baker envious of Phillips' success? Enough to commit murder?

Parrott chortled out loud at the situation he was depicting in his mind. *It seems like everyone and his aunt is a suspect. At this rate, I'll be working on this murder till next Christmas.*

Finally, Parrott considered opportunity. Who had access to zoanthids and their deadly by-product, palytoxin? Certainly, Nicole Phillips did. Who had access to Phillips' fourth-floor bedroom suite at Bucolia? Again Nicole Phillips, but was she the only one? Somehow Parrott doubted that. How might Phillips have ingested the poison? Through food, drink, pills, smoking? He thought again about the toxicology report, the pretty scalloped paper of the menu the Campbells had given him. Who knew about palytoxin? Who might have slipped it into Phillips' hands or mouth or lungs, causing his cells to decompose and die?

Whoever it was, Parrott thought, needed to be identified and brought to justice, no matter whether the victim was honorable, brilliant, or well-loved— or a total bastard. A man's life had been cut short by another person's hand. It was his, Parrott's, mission to find out whose, and, by golly, he would.

Chapter 37

Nicole had just returned from a physical therapy session, and she was feeling hopeful. As she shirked off her shirred mink coat and brushed the melting snowflakes from her thick blonde hair, she inhaled deeply. She was healing ahead of schedule, according to her surgeon and physical therapists. Her spirits were healing, too, as she settled into a routine of life without Preston. New Year's Eve was tomorrow, and it reminded her of last year, when she and Preston had gone out for the very first time. It filled her with amazement at the way her life had changed in just one year.

She recalled how Preston had stopped by her desk after buying his new car. He'd leaned in to introduce himself, almost kissing her on the lips. His brazen confidence had stolen her attention, and the invitation to attend one of the most exclusive New Year's Eve celebrations in New York had given her that Cinderella moment she had been waiting for all her life. Within weeks they were featured in society columns and magazines, and soon she was wearing a five-carat engagement diamond on her left ring finger. She couldn't believe her luck in landing one of America's most desirable men.

Of course, the whirlwind romance was not without its costs, one of which was Billy Bartosh. Nicole had been considering moving in with Billy at the time Preston so suddenly injected himself into her life. She and Billy had been together for almost three years, and they had had lots of good times, but surely even he could see that this was an opportunity no girl could refuse. Now, a little more than a year later, she plopped down on the bed in the master suite and surveyed her plush surroundings. She considered, then decided against, popping one of the homemade white chocolate rum balls into her mouth. While Preston had enjoyed having the delicious treats on his nightstand, and the staff was taking pains to keep the household routines in place as much as possible, Nicole was determined not to allow temptation to rule. *I'll bet there are over three hundred calories in each one.* She remembered how Billy would tease her with Hershey bars, knowing how partial she was to dark chocolate.

"Is there anything else I can get for you, Mrs. Phillips?" Rosa broke into Nicole's reverie and brought her back to the present.

"Oh, Rosa, is it time for you to leave already? I've been meaning to ask you whether you'd like to have the next few days off to spend with your family."

"That's very nice of you, Mrs. Phillips, but I

think you'll need me to help you still."

"I'm much better, now, really. And I know you gave up Christmas to take care of me. Besides, my sister is coming in again, and she will help me with whatever I need."

"Are you sure? I don't mind working the holiday, and I appreciate the extra money."

"I'm sure," Nicole said with a firmness that didn't allow for further debate. She reached for her wallet to retrieve five hundred dollar bills, which she handed to Rosa with a flourish. "Here is a little extra for being so helpful over the past few weeks. I will see you on Thursday morning, the second."

Rosa accepted the tip with a nod of the head and a murmur of thanks. After Preston's death, Nicole hadn't been sure of her servants' continued loyalty, but she had learned during her short marriage to Preston Phillips that hundred dollar bills went a long way toward building relationships.

"Bless you, Mrs. Phillips," Rosa said. "I will see you on Thursday, and if you need me before, just give me a call."

Nicole leaned back against the comforting firmness of the Tempur-Pedic pillows on Preston's side of the bed and sighed. It was nice to be waited on hand and foot, but that came with costs, too, chiefly a lack of privacy. She felt a glimmer of conscience at having to lie about Francine, but then she supposed that any woman in her position had to do such things now and then; otherwise, how would she ever have a life?

She reached into her pocket for her smartphone and went to the "B's" on her contact list. As the phone rang, she examined her manicure as she thought, *This year's New Year's Eve celebration will be much different.*

❧❧❧

Parrott pulled up to the station, put the car into park, and placed his forehead against the steering wheel before killing the engine. It had been a long day, and, apparently, it was going to be an even longer night. The growl of his stomach reminded him that the sandwich from Corner Bakery had long since metabolized. He hoped there was something lying around the station to snack on. And hopefully some strong coffee, too.

The falling snow and biting wind ushered him into the station, where he was greeted by bright lights, the metallic smell of day-old coffee and the chief's booming voice. "Come on into the conference room, Parrott. We've been waiting for you."

Schrik clasped him by the elbow and led him into the spartan room, where "Nick," whose real name was Sylvester Riley, gazed at a computer screen, scrolling constantly. He rose as Parrott entered the room, and offered his hand in greeting.

"What have you got?" Parrott asked, his deep

preacher voice sounding like Charleton Heston's from *The Ten Commandments*. Sylvester's ability to extract jewels from motherboards was the stuff of a detective's dreams, and Parrott rubbed his hands together in anticipation of a break in the case.

"More than I expected to find," Sylvester replied, grinning to show a gold star in his second incisor. "The victim definitely was no stranger to his computer. We've got a trail of emails, internet searches, purchases, favorite websites, you name it."

"Meaning?" Parrott didn't mean to cut off the commentary, but it was late, and, excited as he was to hear the report, he was yearning for home.

Schrik broke in. "Listen, before we get started, I know you've been on the road, and you must be hungry. I saved you some General Tso's chicken, egg rolls, and shrimp fried rice. You want me to heat it up?"

Parrott began to salivate at the mere mention of his favorite take-out menu. "Thanks, Chief." Parrott's desire to go home drained away. He pulled a chair up to the computer and let its light bathe his face with the same glow as that illuminating the face of his new best friend. "Sylvester, my man, make my day."

ⒺⓈⒺⓈ

The next ninety minutes passed quickly. Sylvester had made catalogues of the victim's computer use for the six months prior to his death. There were thousands of pieces of data to log. Both Parrott and Schrik were impressed that Sylvester had been able to accomplish so much in just a few days' time. The report was just over four hundred pages, too much for the policemen to digest in time to keep moving forward with the case. That was why Sylvester was presenting this late night "show and tell."

"See these?" Sylvester said, pointing at a group of icons inside of a file. "These are files that Phillips saved, documenting information he found about Mrs. Phillips before he married her. It seems he didn't fully trust the pretty package enough to marry her without investigating her background first. Then he hid the information inside of folders within folders."

"Anything suspicious in there?" Parrott asked. The Chinese food had made itself at home in his digestive system, and the new blood sugar had made him fully alert again.

Schrik, who had looked this part over while waiting for Parrott to arrive, answered. "What you would expect—pretty girl, lots of boyfriends, a few serious, but no marriages. Ambitious enough to get a job at a fancy car dealership, where she would be likely to meet rich men. High school education followed by one semester at ju-co. Not dumb, but not a rocket scientist. Certainly not a naïve little girl, but nothing that screams 'criminal' either."

"She's still looking suspicious to me," Parrott said. "Can you get me information about *her* computer use, her cell phone calls, social media postings?"

Sylvester said, "Sure thing, as long as you approve, Chief."

"Sure, go ahead. Do the easy stuff first, and I'll tell you whether we need to go further. A victim this prominent, I'm sure I wouldn't need to do much to get a warrant."

"Okay, what else did Phillips do on this fancy machine?" Parrott asked.

Sylvester clicked out of one folder and opened another. "Something interesting here. In the weeks before the party at Bucolia, it seems our guy was busy researching."

"Researching what?" Parrott and Schrik asked in unison.

"Oddly enough, he was researching the people who were at the party. Well, not all of them. Just the Spillers, Kelleys, Winthrops, and Campbells. It's as if he wanted to know what each of the couples was doing currently before he met up with them in person."

Parrott commented, "Those were the ones he had known for most of his life. The Bakers and the Blooms were newer friends of the Campbells."

"What about Margo Rinaldi? Wasn't she part of that group?" Schrik asked.

"Yes, but she was living somewhere in Italy. She came to the party with her younger sister, Libby Bloom. Maybe Phillips didn't know she would be there," Parrott said.

"So what's in the folders?"

"Copies of news articles, postings on Facebook or Twitter, a few pictures. The biggest folder is about Marshall Winthrop. Seems Winthrop was not happy with Phillips' management of the Winthrop Estate Trust. Can't blame him, myself. Who would want to answer to an outsider for money at the age of sixty-five?"

"What's in there about the trust?" Parrott asked, leaning forward to look.

Sylvester clicked on more files, some of them requiring passwords. Parrott was doubly amazed to be able to look at copies of correspondence from Marshall Winthrop's attorney, Rodney Ballenger, to his client. *First of all, how did Phillips get hold of them? Then, how did Sylvester get to them?*

"It seems," Sylvester said, pointing to one of the letters, "that Winthrop had engaged Ballenger to represent him in a lawsuit against Phillips."

"If the suit had been filed, the news sharks would have gone into feeding frenzy mode," Schrik remarked. "Two guys that rich and powerful?"

"Nothing about a filing date," Sylvester went on, "but evidently they had been preparing to file."

Parrott thought out loud. "I can see why Phillips would want to keep an eye on Winthrop. Phillips' reputation might have been ruined by that kind of lawsuit, but why did he snoop on the others?"

Sylvester clicked out of and into other folders. "I can't answer that, Detective," he said, "but I can tell you Leon Spiller has suffered big financial losses in the past twenty-four months, all documented here." He pointed to the information saved in the Spiller file.

Again Parrott was amazed at how thoroughly Phillips had been able to obtain personal financial information on another person.

"What about Kelley?" Schrik asked. "He's the guy from Miles Stewart who just had a stroke."

"Lots of docs on Kelley, but nothing that stands out. Mainly financial articles about Miles Stewart and social stuff. The guy has three homes, if that means anything."

"You think these finance wizards play a tight game of one-upmanship?" Schrik asked.

"Probably," Parrott guessed, "but in this case, I think there is more to it. The vic did a lot of things to piss off his old buddies. He knew he was going to encounter them at the Campbell party. I think he wanted to be prepared for what might come up over the weekend."

"Well," Schrik said with a low chuckle, "I don't guess he was prepared enough, given what happened to him."

Sylvester clicked out of several folders then and flipped to another screen. "Now, I have to show you something even curiouser. I stumbled upon this by accident."

Something in Sylvester's tone of voice caused Parrott to perk up, despite the lateness of the hour and the tribulations of the day. He stood up and bent forward, his head almost touching Sylvester's ear.

"This is a list of the computer's search history for the past sixty days. Easy to access. Lots of searches, mostly financial. But look at this one from November sixteenth." Sylvester pointed to the spot on the screen where a single word was listed.

"Omigod," Parrott exhaled. "How can that be?"

The paperclip cigar fell from Schrik's mouth as he, too, exclaimed, "My God."

The word that Preston, or someone who had access to his computer, had searched just four weeks before he died was "palytoxin."

Chapter 38

After feeding Horace and cleaning out his cage, and giving him some time to fly free in the house, Parrott had trouble getting to sleep. He was still bummed about the violent death of his cousin, gone from the news, but still fresh and painful for him. His mind was also a constant feed of snippets from the interview he'd had with Kitty Kelley and the meeting with Schrik and St. Nick. More and more his focus was narrowing, like that of a microscope honing in on protozoa. Impressions were important, and while he didn't have anything against anyone he had interviewed, he was not so naïve as to think that he was hearing the whole truth and nothing but from any of them, either.

A thin line of melted marshmallow ringed the inside of the mug on his nightstand. It was a sign of frustration that he left it for tomorrow. He tried in vain to plump up his old, flat pillows, trying to get comfortable in the double bed. His flannel pajamas did little to ease him into dreamland, either.

He tried to erase the details of this case from his brain, focusing instead on the picture of Navy SEAL, Tonya Collins, by his bedside. The slight gap between her front teeth and her velvety eyes seemed to speak to him from worlds away. "These rich folks don't have nothing on you, Detective. Just follow your instincts, and you'll crack this case."

Parrott held the picture in both hands, wishing he could hold the real thing. He remembered last New Year's Eve, just before Tonya was deployed to Afghanistan. They had whooped it up bigtime with four days in the Big Apple, Times Square, the whole ball of wax. This New Year's Eve would be really different with Tonya a million miles away and this clunky case pressing in on every waking moment.

He clutched his pillows, imagining they had the warmth and shape of his girl, and eventually he drifted off.

 దిబిద

At six a.m., Parrott's radio alarm, set on the news station, burst into the commercial of a foreign-accented insurance mascot. He reached for the "off" button, tempted to push "snooze" instead. The year was getting away from him, and this made him feel even more pressured to jump out of bed and get going. His goal was to interview the remaining suspects before the New Year balloons lost their helium.

He lumbered out of bed, completed his toiletry

routine and a set of vigorous exercises, then made himself a gigantic bowl of oatmeal. When he arrived back at the station, he logged onto his computer and typed summaries of his notes from the past day's investigations. By then it was seven-thirty, and with no time to waste, he called the Spillers' home phone number.

Leon answered on the third ring, a cuckoo clock chirping its two syllables in the background, followed by a cheery Swiss tune. "Hello," Leon said, not particularly friendly.

"Mr. Spiller?" Parrott asked, his deep voice several octaves lower. "Oliver Parrott here, West Brandywine Police. I hope I haven't called too early."

"Well, I'm not used to getting calls at seven-thirty a.m., Detective, but you didn't wake me."

"I apologize, sir. I just wanted to set up a meeting with you and Mrs. Spiller to talk about John Campbell's birthday weekend."

"I'm sorry, Detective, but my wife is unavailable right now."

"What do you mean unavailable?"

"I mean, she is not available to meet with you or anyone. She's in the hospital."

Parrott donned his most sympathetic tone of voice. "I'm sorry to hear that. Which hospital is she in?"

"Not that I think it's any of your business, but she is in an alcohol rehabilitation hospital, The Caron Foundation." He added, "She's not in any condition to meet with you, and I would appreciate it if you could respect her privacy."

Not surprised by the sharp tone, Parrott took on a similar tone of his own. "Need I remind you, that we are investigating a murder? Of a public figure, no less. My orders are to interview every guest who was at the Campbell birthday weekend."

"*I* am more than willing to meet with you, Parrott. Ask me as many questions as you can think of, and I will answer them. Just please leave my wife out of it, at least for the time being. She's very anxious. Her doctors don't want her to have any visitors—except me—and I have strict orders not to bring up any topics that may upset her."

First Gerald Kelley, now Vicki Spiller—will there be no end to suspects who are unable to talk? Parrott leaned toward the computer screen and pulled up his Outlook calendar. "Okay, Spiller, I'll meet with you at your place. What's the best time?"

"I'm working from home today. Have to take some clothes to Vicki later this afternoon. How about ten a.m.?"

Parrott looked at his watch. It would be cutting it close to get there by ten, but he didn't have much of a choice. He wished he could earn frequent driver points for all the miles he was racking up in this case. Before he agreed, he realized he wanted to make a stop on the way. "How about eleven?"

One of the benefits of being a cop was being able to speed without penalty when necessary, and on this day, it was necessary. Parrott was blessed with less-than-normal traffic, blue skies, and some jaunty, jazzy tunes on the radio as he traveled to the Caron Foundation Hospital. If he timed it right, he might just be able to work his way in to having a private visit with Vicki Spiller before her husband intervened with the hospital authorities.

He pulled up in the circular driveway of the beige building with maroon awnings. It looked like a five-star hotel. "Nothing but the best," he muttered to himself, amazed at yet another reminder of the wealth and power of the people he was investigating. He patted his hair and smoothed his glossy mustache before entering the sumptuous lobby.

He strode confidently to the reception desk. He had to remind himself this was a hospital, as the beautiful appointments, soft background music, and faint aroma of furniture polish seemed more in keeping with a resort. Across from the desk in a large paneled room with a fireplace, a few well-dressed people were sitting on upholstered furniture, surrounded by antiques and floor-to-ceiling shelves of books. Cozy.

"May I help you?" a plump, gray-haired woman with purple glasses on her bosom asked.

Parrott introduced himself, drawing his badge

from the breast pocket of his sport coat and placing it on the marble counter. "I'm here to speak with Mrs. Vicki Spiller about a police matter. Just a few questions. Won't take but a few minutes."

"Just a moment, Detective," the pleasant-sounding woman replied. "You will need to speak with Dr. Stander." She withdrew from Parrott, walking backward, like an awkward geisha. She glanced over her right shoulder as she moved backward. It was as if she didn't trust Parrott not to bolt into unauthorized areas while she turned her back on him.

Within seconds, she returned to the desk with the giant from Jack and the Beanstalk in tow. The giant extended a beefy hand. "Dr. Alfred Stander. How can I help you?"

Parrott shook his hand, amazed to find his fingers and thumb intact afterward. "I need to have a few minutes with Mrs. Vicki Spiller, Doctor Stander. It's part of a murder investigation."

"Sorry, Detective, but our patients are not allowed to have visitors, most particularly—" He grunted. "—visitors that may upset them in any way, as I imagine you might."

Unfazed, Parrott went on, "I assure you, Doctor, I have no intention of upsetting Mrs. Spiller. I simply have a few questions to ask her about a party she attended two weeks ago. In fact, you or any of the hospital representatives may be present to assure yourselves of Mrs. Spiller's complete safety and comfort during this meeting."

"There will be no meeting, Detective. We have a strict policy to protect our patients from these types of intrusions."

"I would hate to have to resort to having her brought before the grand jury, but tha's what will happen if you don't allow me a few minutes with her now."

Stander chuckled with sarcasm. "Go ahead and get your subpoena, Detective, but you will not have access to Mrs. Spiller while she is at Caron. And that's final." He crossed his arms and stared at Parrott, cold and immobile as the marble of the counter.

Parrott realized there was no point in arguing with the human guard dog. "Thanks anyway," he replied. "I'll be back after I meet with the district attorney." He retreated through the lobby and back to his car, where he turned up the volume on the radio, determined not to let anything deter him from his mission.

♋♋♋

Twenty-five minutes later Parrott pulled up to a three-story brownstone in a distinguished old neighborhood of New York. *I thought houses like this didn't exist anymore.* His gaze swept over the neat row of brick homes with spacious porches. How this street had escaped being torn down in favor of skyscraper condos confounded him. *And these are the poorest of the bunch.* He imagined the houses in this location would sell for several million dollars each.

It was two minutes to eleven when Parrott rang the doorbell. He heard a molten golden *ding-dong*, followed by the yapping of a dog.

Spiller opened the door. By his side was a wise-looking standard poodle with piercing eyes and a long nose. Spiller unlocked the storm door and said, "Come on in, Detective."

Ignoring the negative attitude, Parrott nodded. "I'll try not to take up too much of your time."

The house had a typical floor plan with a staircase in the entryway, living room to the left, dining room to the right. Spiller ushered Parrott into the former, a high-ceilinged room with windows facing east and catching the day's strongest sunshine. The room's furnishings were elegant, although more casual than what he expected from such old construction—a circular sofa covered in forest green leather; green, eggplant, and ecru print chairs, and a glass and chrome coffee table that must have weighed a ton. The grouping was held together by a thick Aubusson rug with swirling patterns and silky fringe. Parrott's eyes landed on a large item behind the sofa. Though his heart skipped a beat, he was careful not to react.

It was a sparkling fish tank, about eight feet across and six feet tall. Inside were multi-colored swimmers, beautiful corals, and slender plants.

"Have a seat," Spiller said, pointing to a spot on the leather sofa. He lowered himself into the chair opposite, never taking his eyes from Parrott's. "Now what can I do for you?"

Within a matter of minutes, Parrott extracted from Spiller how he and Vicki related to the Campbells and the rest of the group. Spiller explained how his son Tony had been killed in a boating accident while participating in Phillips' son's birthday festivities. "I'm afraid it is something we will never get over," he said, "particularly my wife. Every time she thinks about that accident, she rips the scab from her grief."

"I understand," Parrott said, "terrible loss." He caught a glimpse of several photos of a good-looking teenager across the room. "I suppose in such a situation it would be easy to blame Mr. Phillips and hold a grudge."

Spiller jerked his gaze from the floor to Parrott's eyes. "What are you implying?"

"I'm merely speculating that the incident in which your son was killed would most probably also kill any friendship that existed between the two of you and Preston Phillips."

Spiller squeezed his hands together in a tight ball. "It would be fair to say so, Detective, but that doesn't mean we wanted him dead."

Parrott changed the subject. "You say Mrs. Spiller is in alcoholic rehabilitation?"

Spiller nodded, the corners of his mouth drawn downward.

"How long has she had an alcohol problem?"

"She's been drinking on and off for twenty-five years. She's been to rehab twice before."

"Does that twenty-five years coincide with the year of Tony's death?"

"Y—Yes, it does," Spiller responded. "I'm sure you can imagine, Detective, how a tragedy like that could put someone over the edge. Tony was our only child."

"I understand, of course," he replied. Changing course once again, Parrott said, "I'd like to ask you a question about the Saturday night dinner at the Campbells'." He pulled the folded calligraphic menu from his pocket. He pointed to the dessert item, *Truffles a la Vicki*. "Mr. Spiller, can you tell me about this item on the menu?"

Leon started to shake. This was the tell Parrott was looking for. Whether there was a connection between the candies and Phillips' death or not, this guy was scared.

"M—My wife's specialty is candy-making, Detective. She finds a great deal of satisfaction in making the world sweeter. She used to sell her truffles to hotels, wedding planners, restaurants. Now she just makes them for family and friends. Everyone loves her chocolates."

Parrott asked several questions about the truffles, the varieties, the recipes, the kitchen where they were made, how they were stored. Each question brought a tiny flinch.

Parrott made a mental note to question Mrs. Spiller thoroughly about the candies she had brought to the party, whenever he had the chance. He wondered if there were any leftovers at the Campbells' farm, as well.

Preying on what he thought was a chink in Spiller's composure, Parrott pushed on. "I wonder if I might see the kitchen where the truffles were prepared."

Spiller shrugged, as if it didn't matter, but the damage was done. He led the detective to the spacious modern kitchen. He pointed out the copper pots and pans hanging over the stovetop island where the candies were made. He opened the sub-zero freezer where boxes and boxes of truffles were stored. "Here, Detective. Why don't you take a box of truffles with you, back to the station? I'm sure you and the other officers would enjoy them."

Parrott accepted the box of candy with gratitude. He had plans for the truffles, but his plans had little to do with eating them.

CHAPtER 39

itty smiled at her friends who had come to the hospital to cheer her after Gerald's stroke. They were sitting at a round table for four in the hospital cafeteria, the remains of their breakfast growing cold. "I'm so glad you girls came in today. I can't tell you how hard it is to sit here hour after hour, not knowing if or when Gerald will recover."

"What was that pledge we made all those years ago, 'Sisters Forever'?" Caro replied. "You know we love you, Kitty, and Gerald, too. Oh, I asked Julia to come in with us, too, but she couldn't make it. She's got a thousand things to do to get ready for her annual New Year's Eve party. She said to give you her love and tell you she'll be here one day next week."

Kitty looked across the cafeteria table at Caro and to her left at Margo. She saw both women not as they looked today, but as they had looked in college with their long, straight hair, parted down the middle, colorful scarves woven through the belt loops of their bell-bottoms. Her eyes moistened with the memory. "I never realized back then how important those sorority bonds would be later on in life."

Andrea reached across the table to touch Kitty's forearm. "Even though I wasn't your sorority sister, Kitty, I hope you know how sorry I am that you are going through all of this."

"Thanks, Andrea. I know you mean it, and I'm glad you're here." She looked around the room at the other diners, many of them dressed in hospital garb, but others obviously family members of patients, like her. "Some way to end the year—first Preston and then Gerald. Makes you wonder, doesn't it?"

Margo curled the paper wrapper from her straw around her index finger, first in one direction then in the other. She had never been the talkative one.

Picking up the baton without missing a beat, Caro responded. "I suppose we're getting to the age where we can expect to see our peers become ill and die, but this has been such a shock. I think I'm in denial over the whole thing."

"Exactly," Kitty said. "But every time I see Gerald, all that brain power locked up in his head and unable to come out, it becomes a little more real." A barely-contained sob caused the last three words to be uttered in two octaves higher. "I can't help wondering whether he'll ever recover. Whether he'll ever talk or walk again. Or what will happen to Lexie and me." A parade of tears spilled over the rims of her eyes and marched down her cheeks.

Margo leaned over and gave Kitty a long hug. Kitty clung to Margo. After a quiet moment, their table a silent oasis in the hubbub of the busy cafeteria, Kitty spoke. "Hey, Margo. I was thinking the other night about you and Preston the Friday night of John E.'s birthday. Was it my imagination, or did he leave the table to follow you when you went to the bathroom?"

Margo winced, as if a two-ton stone sat inside her windpipe, suffocating her.

Caro broke in. "Kitty, leave it to you to be thinking about Preston and Margo, even now, when you have so much else on your plate."

"Well, it helps to change the mental scenery sometimes, and besides, I don't think I'm the only one who noticed how Preston couldn't take his eyes off of Margo the whole weekend. It was like old times. And, remember, I sat by Preston at dinner Saturday night. He was staring at you the entire evening."

Margo swallowed before speaking. "I—I don't know what to say. You know I've hated Preston for all these years. I've blamed him for everything that didn't go right in my adult life."

Sympathetic nods and murmurings encouraged Margo to go on.

"I didn't know how it would feel to be face-to-face with him again. I imagined all sorts of confrontations, put-downs, accusations, but it wasn't like that at all." Margo expelled a sigh that bordered on crying. "It turned out to be more like a re-union with a long-lost friend. So...I guess I'm grateful to have had that weekend." She made eye contact with Caro. "Thanks for letting me come."

Andrea was taking in Margo's words and body language. She could tell there was more to the story than Margo was letting on. She wanted to press her, but she was the odd-woman-out in this group, so any probing would need to be very delicate. She cleared her throat, and everyone's eyes shifted to her. "I've been thinking a lot about Preston's death, myself," she began. "It's distressing for all of us, even for Stan and me, to have a death in the midst of a wonderful birthday celebration among friends. But the thought that Preston may have been mur-dered has been haunting me. Who among us could have done such a thing?"

Caro stared at her hands, clasped together around her now-cooled cup of hot chocolate. "I've thought of little else. It actually feels good to be able to talk to you girls about it. I think John E. is sick of my moping and crying, remembering Preston this and Preston that. I keep thinking if we hadn't had the party, none of this would've happened."

"It's not your fault, Caro," Kitty said. "You had a magnificent party."

"I shouldn't have invited Preston. Too much bad blood between him and the others. He had words with both Julia and Vicki that Saturday. I just thought that enough time had gone by, and, honestly, I thought my mother and Aunt Penny would have killed me if I'd left him out."

"And then there was Nicole's accident," Andrea added.

"Do any of you know whether the police have any suspects?" Margo asked.

"Detective Parrott met with Stan and me."

"John E. and me, too."

"He was here at the hospital the day that Gerald was struck." Kitty looked at Margo. "Has he interviewed you yet?"

"Not yet, but I expect it will be my turn soon. I really don't have anything to tell him."

Andrea's right eyebrow lifted. She said gently, "Don't you?"

"Look," Kitty added. "Preston was obviously smitten by you, Margo. We all noticed it. Pretty young wife or not, he was drawn to you like the tide to the moon. I'll bet the detective is going to want to know what you and he talked about. You might as well tell us first."

The curled straw cover was in shreds. Margo looked each woman in the eyes, one by one, then nodded as if she had made up her mind to trust them, at least a little. "Preston, as all of you well know, was full of hot air." She looked at Caro, who slightly nodded. "I learned the hard way not to trust anything he ever said."

"So?" Kitty said. "What did he say that weekend?"

Andrea leaned forward, as if taking notes directly onto her brain.

Margo swallowed again, and the biting sting of tears overtook her. "He said," she started and then stopped, her voice shaky. "He said that he still loved me."

"I knew it," Kitty said. "I could just feel the vibes, just like old times."

"So," Andrea prompted, "the plot thickens."

Everyone looked at Andrea. After all, she was the most expert sleuth among them.

"What are you thinking?" Caro asked.

"Well," Andrea replied, "obviously someone in the group had it in for Preston enough to kill him."

Margo burst into tears and put her head on the table. Kitty patted her on the shoulder. She knew eventually it would come to this—everyone looking at one another and wondering who among them was the killer.

Between sobs, Margo lifted her head and took in air. "I just feel so terrible. I should never have come to the party."

Caro studied her dear friend whose distress so closely mirrored her own. "I think we all have regrets, Margo. But all of the crying in the world won't bring Preston back."

"I know that. But what if Preston's attention toward me is what brought about his death? How can I live with that?"

"What are you thinking?" Andrea asked.

"I'm thinking the same thing that probably all of us are thinking," Margo moaned. "I'm thinking that Nicole saw what was happening between Preston and me, and she killed him."

CHAPTER 40

*T*here's something about New Year's Eve, Parrott thought, as he pulled up to the station that morning. *It's as if the whole world screeches to a stop to evaluate the events of the last twelve months. When you're in the midst of a murder case, though, New Year's Eve is just another day.*

Parrott had hoped to interview the Winthrops, the Blooms, and Margo Rinaldi before the end of the year. His determination to solve this case dominated every waking moment, but he was learning that interacting with the rich and famous was like treading through rough territory and trying to avoid land mines. The comparison reminded him of Tonya, whose duty in Afghanistan was equally treacherous. He touched his chest the way she always did to show her love. Then he opened the door of his car and stepped out into the world of the murder case.

Normally a murder investigation would take precedence over suspects' daily activities, even New Year's Eve parties. Parrott was itching to interview Marshall and Julia. He had lots of questions about the family trust, which had conveniently ended with Phillips' death. The cigars Marshall brought to the party also piqued Parrott's interest. His plan was to show up at the Winthrop mansion in Rye, but Chief Schrik had other ideas.

"These rich folks are different," Schrik said. "We can't just turn up on their doorsteps and expect them to confess. They're gonna lawyer up on us, and turn this case into a comedy of errors. Better to make an appointment, act as if they are not suspects, just witnesses."

"I hate to lose two days of investigation time, though, Chief," Parrott complained. "New Year's Eve and New Year's Day."

"Society columns show blurbs about annual New Year's Eve parties hosted by the Winthrops. You wouldn't get much out of them, anyway, if they're preparing for a party."

"Isn't it sort of crass to give a party when you've just had a murder among your circle of friends?" Parrott asked.

"Maybe for you and me," Schrik commented. "The Winthrops live by different standards. Besides, they apparently have a lot to celebrate this year. Anyway, you have an appointment to interview them on Thursday morning at Winthrop's office at the Fed. Meanwhile, Maria Rodriguez wants to meet with you today. She's got results from the goods you took in."

Parrott rubbed his hands together. Maybe Maria would give him another gold nugget today. And afterward, he had big plans for ushering in the new year.

∞

"Hey, Oliver," Maria called, as Parrott entered her tiny office. "Happy New Year."

"Good to see you, Maria. My new year's happiness depends on what you have for me," Parrott replied.

"Well, grab a cup of coffee, and we'll have a chat about palytoxin, shall we?"

Parrott spun his chair around to face the Mr. Coffee machine. He poured a cup of hot java into a Styrofoam cup. He took a first sip. "Mmm, thanks." He turned back around, the cup of coffee held in his lap. "Maria, I've been reading up on palytoxin. It exists in fish tanks, but isn't toxic when wet. Is that right?"

"Absolutely. It has to be processed into a powder form. The person using it would have to be careful not to inhale or ingest it."

"Well, there's an aquarium at the victim's house. His widow might have harvested the poison and figured out a way to administer it to him. She doesn't seem sophisticated enough to have done it on her own, though."

"Well, maybe she had an accomplice. You might want to look into that, especially after you hear my latest report."

Parrott felt his pulse quicken, and he squeezed

the edge of Maria's desk. "What is it?"

"Well, first of all, let's talk about the truffles."

"Okay."

"The labs analyzed them thoroughly. They contained, as expected, large amounts of chocolate, caffeine, sugar, and some alcohol. But no poison."

"Doesn't mean that the truffles weren't the source of the poison. Just that the ones Spiller gave me were clean."

"Yes, but you brought in five types of medications from the victim's Dopp kit. Celebrex, Voltaren, Viagra, Restasis eye drops, Metamucil."

"Right."

"We tested each of them under carefully controlled conditions in our lab. The Celebrex, Voltaren, Viagra, and Restasis were all exactly what they were supposed to be."

Parrott's right eyebrow lifted and held. "And the Metamucil?"

"The powder in the Metamucil container was not Metamucil. It was palytoxin."

Parrott jumped out of his chair and slammed the coffee cup on the medical examiner's desk, spilling a bit. "You're not shitting me?"

"The state labs never lie."

The wheels in Parrott's brain were churning at full speed. "So the murder weapon has been found. In the victim's room. Now all I have to figure out is how it got there, and how it got into Preston Phillips' body."

Parrott returned to the station to give the news to Chief Schrik. "It's looking more and more like the palytoxin came from the victim's own aquarium, Chief, don't you think?"

Schrik smiled around the paper clip in his mouth, pleased by Parrott's enthusiasm. "Careful now. Anybody could have carried the Metamucil bottle into the victim's room and left it in his bathroom after they used it."

"Don't rain on my parade, Chief. I'm finally beginning to move on this case." Parrott rubbed the sides of his head with both hands.

"Okay, Parrott." Schrik had been careful not to pressure his detective toward a quick solution, despite the enormous pressure being brought to bear on him. "What are your next steps?"

"It's New Year's Eve, right?" Parrott began. When his boss nodded, he went on, "I'll be welcoming the new year in New York City."

Schrik looked at Parrott with surprise. "I thought your girl was overseas."

"She is," Parrott replied. "I'll be celebrating by myself. Or actually observing how the other half lives."

"Oh?"

"I'm going to stake out the Dakota. Find out how the new Widow Phillips celebrates."

CHAPTER 41

O n his way into the Phillipses' co-op building, Parrott decided to take a short detour to Mount Sinai Hospital to look in on the Kelleys. If there was any good thing about Gerald's stroke, from the standpoint of the investigation, it was that Gerald would likely be in the same place for a while, and no lawyers would be hovering to prevent the asking of questions. The bad thing, of course, was that Gerald might not be able to answer.

Gerald had been moved to a private room at the end of a hallway, where private duty nurses surrounded him twenty-four/seven. Parrott showed his badge to get there. As he approached, he saw a small nook twenty feet from the doorway, where Kitty and a young woman sat in two Naugahyde chairs. Kitty was needlepointing as if her life depended on it. The young woman's thumbs were flying over her hand-held device. Both looked up at Parrott.

"Hello, Detective," Kitty said, folding the needlepoint, placing it on a Formica end table. She looked as if she hadn't slept in a month. "Have you met my daughter Lexie?"

Parrott extended his hand to the young woman. "Oliver Parrott."

"Nice to meet you." Lexie shook hands, giving her mother a questioning look.

Reading her daughter's mind, Kitty explained, "Detective Parrott is investigating the death of Mr. Phillips, Peter's dad."

"Oh, yeah," Lexie said. "With all that's happened to Dad, I forgot about Mr. Phillips."

Lexie's resemblance to her father is uncanny. A shame, Parrott thought, *since her mother is quite attractive, even in her current state of distress.*

"Would you like to sit down?" Kitty asked Parrott. She pointed to the empty chair. "We're waiting while they do physical therapy."

"If you don't mind," Parrott said. "How's Mr. Kelley doing?"

"He's about the same. One side paralyzed, still not talking."

"I'm sorry to hear it," Parrott said. "Does he seem to understand when you talk to him?"

Kitty thought before answering. "It's hard to say. He nods and shakes his head, makes eye contact. But who knows what is going on inside his head?"

"Do you think I might have a few minutes with him?" Parrott asked. Mentally, he crossed his fingers, hoping the answer would be yes and he might get a bit of information from this witness, impaired though he may be. "I only have three questions."

"I don't know," Kitty said, "Gerald is still very

ill. The likelihood of subsequent strokes is high after a major one like this, and we don't want him to
be upset in any way."

"I understand," Parrott replied. "But this is a
murder investigation, and we really need everyone's cooperation. I doubt I'll upset him. And I
promise to be quick."

Kitty sighed but led Parrott to the door, where
she rapped lightly with a knuckle. She pushed the
door inward and stuck her head inside. "Is Mr. Kelley asleep?" she whispered.

The afternoon nurse was holding a cup of water
with a straw to the mouth of the patient, who was
tilted into a sitting position in the hospital bed. The
room was filled with afternoon sunshine and floral
arrangements on every available surface. The aroma of flowers and greenery masked the usual hospital smells, making for a cheery ambience. If it
weren't for the blips and beeps of the machines
keeping track of Gerald's vital signs, Parrott might
have been in someone's solarium.

Gerald was clean-shaven and neat in starched
bedclothes and maroon silk pajamas. It looked like
he had lost at least twenty pounds in the past week.
His sparse sandy-grey hair was cleanly parted to
one side, recently trimmed around the ears. His
blue eyes lacked the clarity Parrott had noticed
previously, but they were fixed on Parrott's face in
an eerie fascination.

"Honey," Kitty cooed. "Do you remember Detective Parrott? He is investigating Preston's death. We all met him that day at Caro's house?"

Gerald's nod was almost imperceptible.

"I'd like to ask you some questions, Mr. Kelley." He paused to observe any medical reaction. Noting none, he proceeded. "Do you know if anyone at the party had a reason to kill Mr. Phillips?"

Gerald looked at Kitty but didn't respond in any other way.

Disappointed, Parrott paused for a full minute before asking his second question. He had hoped for a better response, either from Kelley or from Kitty as interpreter. Seeing that no answer was forthcoming, he proceeded with his second question. "Are you aware of anyone's having seen or talked to Mr. Phillips after the gentlemen smoked cigars?"

Again, Gerald looked at Kitty then back at Parrott.

Parrott paused again, thinking this whole interview would be a waste of precious time. He hadn't expected a verbal answer, but he had at least hoped for a tell.

He leaned forward, blocking Gerald's view of his wife, as he asked his final question. "Mr. Kelley, have you ever heard of a poison called palytoxin?"

With this question, Gerald's eyes widened, and the heart monitor blips increased in frequency.

Either Kelley was familiar with palytoxin, or

something else was causing him to become excited, or maybe fearful.

The nurse inserted her narrow body between patient and detective. "I think that's enough questioning for today," she said. "Mr. Kelley needs to rest." She waved her skinny arms about, shooing the visitors away toward the door and out into the hall.

❧❧❧

Parrott retrieved his car from the hospital parking attendant. He couldn't shake a sense of gloom. The sadness over his cousin's violent death in St. Louis still hung over him, but this case was occupying him day and night. Kelley's reaction to palytoxin made him wonder. Would competition between Kelley and Phillips have been so intense as to lead to murder?

The more he investigated, the more it seemed everyone was a suspect. Still, most clues pointed toward Nicole. It stuck in his craw that she had cremated the body so quickly, besides having the money motive, and access to palytoxin and that computer with palytoxin searches. On the other hand, while gut feelings were potent, it was important to maintain objectivity until all of the facts were available. And there were a lot of missing facts.

Who, for example, had processed the palytoxin and placed it into the Metamucil container? How did it get into the victim's body in the wee hours of that Sunday morning? And wouldn't Phillips have been worth more to his wife alive than dead? As much as he wanted to pin the murder on her, Parrott had to admit he had doubts about her being able to pull it off, especially with that metal halo on her leg. Then there was the matter of the green thread on the chair. It might mean nothing, but in a place like the Campbell farm, where servants must have taken meticulous steps to prepare the rooms for company, he felt it might still offer a meaningful clue.

By the time Parrott considered all of this, he was approaching the Dakota, and it was five-thirty in the afternoon. The Victorian building had a grandeur and reputation that might have been intimidating, had Parrott not focused his thoughts solely on the task at hand. He parked on the Central Park West side, where he had a view of the formal entrance to the building. He was counting on the fact that his Toyota Camry would not attract too much attention, despite its placement in a no parking zone. On the seat beside him sat a knapsack filled with provisions and equipment for a lengthy stakeout.

There were already a few people going in and coming out of the Dakota. Parrott fished the mini-camera from the knapsack. Using the zoom feature, he took a picture of a middle-aged man hurrying into the building, his face covered by the low brim of his hat, and carrying a gift bag from Bergdorf Goodman. He was aiming for another shot when he heard a tap on the car window. A New York City policeman motioned him to roll down the window.

"This is a no parking zone," the stocky officer said, leaning his freckled face in for a look.

Parrott put down the camera and reached into his jacket for his police badge. He knew how it must look to the officer, seeing a stranger taking pictures outside of the Dakota. Security there had been thick ever since the Lennon assassination. Now another famous tenant had been murdered, albeit not on the premises. "West Brandywine Police," he offered, showing the badge. "Investigating the death of Preston Phillips. Want to see who comes and goes on New Year's Eve at his residence."

"I gotta call it in to verify," the cop said. "Just take me a minute."

"No problem."

The cop stepped away from the car, Parrott's badge in one hand, cellphone in the other. A minute later he returned to the side of the Toyota. "Checks out. You can stay."

"Thanks," Parrott replied, relieved that this one obstacle had been eliminated.

"Here's my card. If I can help you in any way, just call. Oh, and by the way," the policeman said. "That guy you just photographed? That was the mayor. You might want to delete that one."

Surveillance during winter in New York meant sitting in an uncomfortably frigid automobile, trying to stay alert, and pushing all thoughts of nature breaks aside for as long as possible. Parrott took photos of several people entering the Dakota; others he gave passes to, based on gut instinct. He was looking for a male of a certain type, someone who might appeal to a young widow. He ignored people in pairs and groups, as well. If his hunches served him well, Nicole Phillips would not want to spend New Year's Eve alone, but he didn't imagine she would be hosting a party either.

When the clock on the dashboard read eight-twenty-eight, Parrott noticed a young man striding quickly toward the Dakota's entrance, his collar turned up, and his hat turned down. He was carrying a paper bag in the shape of a champagne bottle, and a bouquet of flowers that he might have bought in the train station. The belted all-weather coat and rubber snow boots he wore shouted "tawdry," and Parrott fired off several photographic shots of him.

It was time for the second stage of his plan. Parrott swung open his car door, took a West Brandywine Police Department placard out of his knapsack, threw it onto the dashboard in hopes of avoiding a ticket, pocketed the mini-camera, and dashed across the street toward the famed co-op building.

The doorman looked him over as he opened the massive door into the spacious lobby. Parrott remembered the security station from his previous visits, but this time there were two uniforms behind it. The taller, older-looking one greeted Parrott with a superficial smile. "May I help you, sir?"

Parrott removed his badge from his jacket pocket for the second time that evening. "Oliver Parrott, West Brandywine Police Detective. Investigating the death of Preston Phillips."

"What can we do for you, Detective?" the shorter, younger-looking guard asked, confident in his ability to cooperate with police, while still maintaining security for the building's residents.

"Can you tell me if the guy who just entered the building was going to Mrs. Phillips' unit?"

The two men looked at each other, the glance giving away the answer to Parrott's question.

Parrott went on, "What was the name he gave you?"

Tall-old said, "I believe it was Bartosh, Bill Bartosh." He looked to Short-young for confirmation and received it in the form of a nod.

"Bill Bartosh," Parrott repeated, fixing the sound of it into his brain. "To your knowledge, has Mr. Bartosh visited Mrs. Phillips before?"

Shrugs from both.

"Not to my knowledge," said the tall guy. "Shall I call Mrs. Phillips to announce you, Detective?"

"No, sir," Parrott replied. "I'll just leave quietly

for now. No need to alarm her." He was mentally planning his next steps, almost giddy with the results of his watch. He made an about-face and had almost reached the heavy glass door when he remembered to call over his shoulder, "Thanks, guys. And Happy New Year."

Finally, Parrott was in a mood to celebrate.

Chapter 42

Libby hadn't wanted to go out this year on New Year's Eve. She and Les had been invited to several parties, but considering what had happened at the last party they'd attended, and her doctor's admonitions about hers being a high-risk pregnancy, she just felt like nesting in her Manhattan mansion-in-the-sky. Besides, Margo had offered to come over and cook an authentic Italian dinner for three.

Les had taken advantage of the low-key plans to put in a dozen solid hours at the office. The uncertainty at Miles Stewart had sent lapping waves of business to the other big houses on Wall Street, and as the up-and-coming CEO at Sterling Martin, he needed to harness the forces and nurture the tide. "Not that I mean any harm to Miles Stewart," he'd said to Libby earlier, "I really feel for Gerald Kelley." He glanced at his Rolex as he stepped into the apartment and saw Libby moving toward him in the spacious entryway. "It's six-forty-seven. Just enough time to shower and change." He sniffed the air. "Mmmm, garlic and tomatoes. Makes my mouth water."

"Hi, Les." Libby stood on tiptoes for a kiss. "Happy New Year."

Les removed and hung up his coat, remembering the servants were off for the holiday. He kissed his wife and patted her stomach, marveling once more at the miracle of gestation. "Boy, it smells wonderful!" He pointed toward the kitchen and dining area. "Is Margo working her kitchen magic in there?"

"Absolutely. And I am the cheerleader," Libby said, taking a bow.

"Can't wait to taste it," Les said. "Let me go freshen up first."

He disappeared into his personal bathroom, and Libby returned to the kitchen, perching on one barstool with feet propped up on the foot bars of another, while Margo moved gracefully from island to stove to refrigerator, her auburn curls twisted in the back and held by a barrette, her Lilly Pulitzer outfit partially covered by a frilly apron.

"I hate it that you are doing so much work on New Year's Eve," Libby said to her sister. "Maybe I shouldn't have given Sylvia the holiday."

"Don't mention it," Margo replied without looking up. She was rolling the paper-thin veal with onions and breadcrumbs into kebabs and securing them with toothpicks. "I love cooking, and it's the least I can do after you let me stay with you for so long. Besides, none of us is in the mood for partying this year."

Libby inhaled the aromas of spadinis and the accompanying dishes. She picked up the crystal toothpick holder from the counter and rolled it around in her hands, thinking. "Sis, I hate to bring up a sensitive subject, and you can tell me to mind my own business if you want—"

Margo stopped stirring the simmering home-made tomato gravy, thick and spicy, and shot her sister a glaring look. "But you want to ask me something about Preston."

Libby lowered her gaze. "Well, I was right there all weekend. I saw how he showered you with attention. And I heard you crying in your room that Friday night."

"And I've been mopey ever since," Margo continued. "So what's your question?"

"It's not so much a question as a statement. I worry about you. I know your feelings for Preston bordered on hatred. But since the party and Preston's death—"

"Not so much. Who was it who said, 'There's a thin line between love and hate'? After Preston stood me up at our wedding, I never wanted to see him again. I married Roberto, moved to Italy, and thought Preston was totally out of my system."

"Until I took you to that party," Libby said.

"Yes, until I walked into Caro's family room and saw him beaming at me, the way he had when we were young. I had forgotten how a smile from Preston could ignite a flame inside of me. I guess the pilot light never went out."

"Well, obviously the feeling was mutual," Libby said, scooching her bottom into a more comfortable position on the bar stool. "It was hard to miss how he was drawn to you all weekend."

"So what is it you want to know?"

"Margo, I'm concerned. You haven't been right since that weekend. You have circles under your eyes, and you don't sit still. It's as if you're afraid to confront your thoughts or feelings."

"All true."

"It's just a matter of time until we are questioned by the police. Probably the only reason it hasn't happened yet is the holidays. Maybe it would help to talk to me before you have to talk to them."

Margo stared at Libby. "I'm nineteen years older than you, old enough to be your mother. I'm not used to being the one who needs emotional support." She inhaled sharply and shuddered, dropping the wooden spoon and covering her face with her hands.

"I didn't mean to make you cry, honest I didn't," Libby said, rushing over to hug her sister. "But if you do feel like crying, do it with me. You can let it all out in this kitchen, and I promise I will never tell anyone."

Margo clung to her sister and sobbed. It seemed as if she would choke with all of the gasping for air. After several minutes, she broke from the embrace and returned to the pasta machine on the counter. Somehow it was easier to breathe, to talk, when her hands were occupied.

"I don't know what I'm going to do," Margo began. "My life is a shambles." The long strips of dough that would be the evening's linguini were emerging from the machine in slow, dignified order. "P—Preston told me he loved me, he always had. I thought he was just playing around with me, hoping for another conquest."

"But he wasn't?" Libby asked, resettling herself at the counter.

"I don't think so. He told me he was going to leave Nicole. He wanted to make it up to me for what happened in the past. He spoke with such urgency, such sincerity."

"So you believed him."

"Well, not at first. And then I did. And then I didn't." She threw up her hands. "I sound demented, I know."

Libby started to say, "Not demented," but Margo went on before she could get the words out.

"I slept with him, Libby. He led me to believe he had told Nicole he wanted a divorce. I slept with him, we made plans for the future, and I loved every minute of it. Then I went back downstairs to my room to go to sleep."

"What time was that?"

"Around three-thirty or four. My head was spinning with happy thoughts. I could still feel Preston's body on mine, and I was relishing it all. Then I heard a noise coming from the staircase. I was still dressed, so I went out into the hall. It was Nicole coming up the stairs with that metal thing on her ankle."

Libby took in a gallon of air before saying, "Omigod. She was on her way up the stairs to kill Preston?"

"I don't think so. At least not then. She seemed surprised to see me in my clothes. Said she wanted to go to her husband. She didn't seem to be angry with him, just desperate to be with him. It infuriated me, because I thought Preston hadn't told her about the divorce at all. He had lied to me." Margo paced back and forth as she spoke.

"So what did you do?"

"I talked her into going back downstairs, even helped her get settled on the sofa."

"So she didn't kill him?"

"Not unless she came back up the stairs later. After I left Nicole, I tried to go to sleep again, but I was so worked up. At that moment I almost wanted to kill Preston, myself, for ruining my life a second time. I felt like a fool."

Libby gasped. "But you didn't. Tell me you didn't."

Margo shook her head. "I wanted to go back upstairs, kick, scream, throw something at him, but I couldn't do that to Caro and John E., and I didn't want to awaken the whole household. I tried to calm down, took a thousand deep breaths. Then I went back upstairs to have it out with him, but—"

Libby muttered, "Oh, no, how is this going to sound to the police?"

"—when I got there, Preston was sound asleep."

"Are you sure he wasn't dead?" Libby asked.

"No, he was definitely breathing, and he had a smile on his face, as if he could still feel my body on his, and he was happy. I sat in the chair and watched him for a while, my fury subsiding into mere anger. I used his bathroom, thinking he might wake up from the sound of the flush, but he didn't. I decided whatever I had to say to him could wait." She uttered a laugh that sounded like a bird's caw. "Of course, I never got to have it out with him the next day—or ever."

Libby was turning the details of Margo's narrative over in her mind when Les's footsteps presaged his arrival into the kitchen. He walked in smelling of expensive aftershave lotion, a jolly smile on his face. "Happy New Year," he said, walking over to the Subzero and pulling out a bottle of Dom Perignon. "When do we eat?"

Chapter 43

This was the second New Year's Eve that Vicki had spent drying out. The first was twenty-four years ago, six months after the tragic accident. Vicki shut her eyes, trying to block out the memory of that excruciating pain, the remnants of which burned inside her still. "Funny," she remarked to Leon, stirring her steaming mug of cappuccino, "that New Year's Eve all I could think of was Tony and how I would someday make Preston pay for our loss. This year, Preston's gone, and the only one I keep punishing is myself."

Leon swallowed the bite of chocolate-covered biscotti and chased it with a swig of black coffee. "I know. I hope this will be the last time."

"Intellectually, I realize that drinking to cope with grief just causes more grief. Emotionally, it's hard to accept. I'm really going to try to be strong this time. I promise." She rubbed the fabric of her silk wrap dress between her thumb and forefinger. The smooth texture gave her the feeling of control.

"I know you will. I have confidence in you."

"I just hate what this does to you, Leon. The stress, the cost. Having a hag for a wife."

"Just stop, now. You're still the same beautiful

girl I fell in love with in college. And don't worry about the cost. You are worth every bit of it." He grabbed her hand and squeezed. "Besides, you've stood by me through tough times."

"You know, I've done a lot of thinking. Maybe Preston's death will give me the closure I need to move on."

"I hope so, Vicki, but if I were you, I'd be careful saying that to anyone but me."

"Why?"

"Because the wrong person just might think you're the one who killed Preston."

❧❧

In the double dressing room of the Winthrops' mansion in Rye, Julia and Marshall had a few moments alone before guests would arrive for their annual New Year's Eve party. They and their four servants had been preparing all day. A few hours ago the consultant from the exclusive Parties Perfect Company had arrived with her crew of ten to complete the preparations. Now, all that was left to do was get dressed.

"How is it that no matter how much help we have, my feet hurt before the first guest crosses the threshold?" Julia complained, crossing her long legs and peering into the dressing table mirror.

"Maybe we should have cancelled the party this year, with all that's been going on," Marshall replied, a worry line deepening between his eyebrows. He took a sip from the crystal glass of Dewar's he had brought in with him.

"And what would all our friends on the boards of the opera and art museum have done for New Year's Eve? They count on us for this, just like we all count on the Greshams for July fourth." She pushed the three-carat emerald stud through her ear and fastened it. "Besides, I think it would have been a tactical error to cancel. It would have drawn too much speculation. Better to act as if everything is normal."

"Even when it's not," Marshall replied. He was playing with the matching emerald studs and cufflinks that went in his tuxedo shirt. He had bought the jewelry for them both as a Christmas gift just ten days before.

"I know you're worried about Thursday's meeting with the police. I am, too. But at least we have competent legal representation. Bally's idea of presenting them with a proffer, instead of having us talk to the detective, gives me hope we can get through it smoothly. It was well worth the time we spent at his office yesterday, preparing it."

Marshall brushed his dark hair straight back from his forehead and used a small comb to smooth his graying sideburns. He looked like a Mafia don, preparing for confrontation. "Just because we use the proffer, doesn't mean that will be the end of it.

In fact, I'll be surprised if the police stop there. High profile case, and all."

Julia finished applying her lipstick in a four-step process then pouted to admire the results in the mirror. "Let's put it out of our minds for now. I'm sure Bally will take good care of us. And really, we shouldn't have anything to worry about."

She gazed at her reflection in the full-length mirror. *Not bad,* she thought, turning this way and that. *But I'll have to snack on the sushi appetizers and skip the Beef Wellington if I want this dress to look right all night.*

She pecked Marshall on the cheek and swooped out of the room, calling, "See you downstairs," over her shoulder.

⌒⌒⌒

In rural Pennsylvania, another couple was getting dressed in a lavish master bedroom suite. Stan and Andrea had cancelled their plans to attend a house party in New York, in favor of having Caro and John E. over for drinks and dinner.

"Are you sorry we aren't going out fancy tonight?" Andrea asked.

"Not at all. I'm sorry for the reason, but, actually, I'm relieved not to have to make such a big deal out of ushering in the new year. After so many years, that has grown old."

"It was the least we could do to help our friends

at this difficult time," Andrea said, sounding as though she had rehearsed it. "Caro is still taking Preston's death very hard." She readjusted the Hermes scarf around her neck and tucked the ends into the V-neck of her sweater.

"Yes, and I suppose it is even worse for them because Preston was murdered in one of their bedrooms—"

"And likely by one of their friends. Really, I don't know how either of them can stand it."

"What choice do they have?" Stan said, always the practical one. He slipped his feet into soft loafers the color of melted chocolate.

"The best thing we could do for them tonight, I think, is to take their minds off of the whole thing. Let's agree not to talk about anything having to do with Preston all evening." She sprayed two puffs of Paloma Picasso into the air in front of her then walked into it. "Mmm, I love that aroma."

"Me, too," Stan said, wrapping his arms around her from behind and nuzzling her neck. "But since we're all alone now, can I ask you one thing I've been dying to know?"

"What's that?"

"Who, do *you* think, murdered Preston?"

"Seriously? You know I'm not privy to many of the details of the case."

"Yes. With all of your experience with murders, I'd bet that you have a pretty good idea."

"Well, this is the first time a murder has happened this close to home, thankfully. The obvious suspect would be Nicole. She has the most to gain and the least to lose by killing him. And she's the most palatable choice for all of us, because she's the outsider."

"Interesting. Do I hear a 'but' coming?"

Andrea looked amused. "You know me so well, Stan. But—I don't think it was Nicole."

"Why not?"

"Gut feeling, I guess. I was with Nicole quite a bit when we went riding and after her accident. I got the distinct impression that she was a person who really loved her husband. Idolized him, even. I'm guessing she'd pinned a lot of hopes and dreams on becoming Mrs. Preston Phillips, and I don't think the honeymoon was over yet. I think she needed him too much to kill him. Besides, she'd have had a very hard time overpowering him, even with poison, with her foot in that contraption. She was so drugged out she couldn't even stay at the dinner table the whole time, remember?"

"So if she didn't do it, who, do you think did?"

"Between you and me?

"Of course."

"Confidentially, I think it must have been the other person who benefited most from Preston's death. I hate to even think this about one of John E.'s closest friends. But the more I think about it, the more I'm convinced that the murderer was Marshall."

CHAPTER 44

A quick search for white males aged twenty-one to thirty-five, height five-ten to six-one, in the New York metropolitan area named William, Bill, or Billy Bartosh had yielded nine hits, two with misdemeanor records. Parrott examined the nine summaries on his desk, combing through the details for something that would attract his sixth sense: suspicion. No matter what, the fact that the grieving widow was entertaining a male suitor just two weeks after her husband's death was enough to solidify her place on the Likely Killer List.

It was New Year's Day, and the office was quiet. If it hadn't been for this case, Parrott would probably have driven to his mother's in Connecticut. He would have put his feet up on the cushioned coffee table and snacked on Chex Mix while watching his alma mater, Syracuse, in the afternoon bowl game. That, not fancy homes and cars and parties with gourmet food, was his idea of celebrating a holiday.

He thought of his Aunt Rachel, celebrating the holidays without her only son from now on. The wound of Bo's death was still fresh for them all.

He wondered what Tonya was doing right now. He looked at his watch. *It's almost seven p.m. there. What kind of New Year's Day did you have, my love?* Whatever it was, he knew that giving up the Syracuse game would have been the least of Tonya's sacrifices. He allowed himself to daydream about the brave young woman, so full of fire and light and life. *Only fourteen more months, and she'll be back here in my arms for good. Wedding, kids, the whole nine yards—*

Brrrinnng, brrrinnng. Parrott's direct line interrupted the pleasant reverie, causing an abrupt return to reality. "West Brandywine Police, Detective Parrott speaking," he answered, his voice deepened even further from the morning's lack of use.

"Happy New Year, Parrott," Chief Schrik boomed from the receiver.

"Same to you," Parrott replied.

He could hear the tiny click of Schrik's shifting the paperclip from one side of his mouth to the other. *Guess he does that even at home.* "Thought I'd catch you in the office, despite its being a national holiday."

"I know, Chief, but if I don't keep going on this case, it's going to freeze up on me real fast."

"Well, I do have President Dalton on my tail, making ugly threats. Did you see that report we left for you on Bartosh?"

"Looking at it right now. I hate putting you in the position of having to stall Dalton."

"Well, keep me posted. I think you're onto something with this guy. Good bit of detective work last night."

"Thanks, Chief."

"Well, don't feel you have to work all day. Even *we* need to have holidays now and then."

"I'll be okay. I've got to see where this lead takes me, holiday or no holiday."

"Okay, I'm impressed. Don't think I've forgotten that little sporting event of interest to you on TV this afternoon."

"Don't remind me," Parrott groaned.

⚜

Ninety minutes later, Parrott had absorbed the information on all nine of the Bartoshes on the list. Nothing stood out, so he decided to do more research on the two Bills with police records. One had been convicted of petit larceny in 2013, and the other had been charged with auto stripping in the third degree. Plea bargain, sentenced to time served, just last year.

*Auto stripping, hmmm…*he wondered if the auto in question had been a Lamborghini. He dug further into criminal justice websites. His police user ID and passwords unlocked doors and windows faster than days and weeks of old-fashioned footwork could do. "Bingo," he shouted aloud for no one else to hear. Billy Bartosh, last on the list, had worked at Manhattan Luxury Cars on Tenth Avenue, the same place where Nicole had worked and met Preston. *This has to be the one. Ambitious boy meets ambitious girl. The rest is history.*

His pulse racing, Parrott dialed the number of Nicole's cell phone. In the time it took for the ringing to start, he planned his work for the rest of New Year's Day.

"Hello?" Nicole answered on the fourth ring, out of breath.

"Mrs. Phillips?" He knew his baritone voice would give him away instantly, even if she didn't examine the caller ID.

"Detective Parrott?"

"Yes, ma'am. Sorry to bother you, but can I stop by and talk to you this afternoon?"

Nicole hesitated, and Parrott could almost hear cogs and pulleys in her brain. "You are aware, of course, that this is New Year's Day?"

It sounded like Nicole was covering the receiver with her hand and shushing someone. "Yes, ma'am. But murder investigations don't take holidays. I have just a few questions."

"Well, can't you ask them over the phone, Detective? I'm pretty busy."

I'll bet you are, Parrott thought. He felt sure that Billy Bartosh, auto stripper, was right there at her side. "No, ma'am. I'm coming into the city anyway. I can come at your convenience, sometime after noon?"

"I just don't know."

"Your cooperation means a lot, you know. I'm sure you want to get to the bottom of who killed your husband as much as we do."

Sighing as if purging the carbon dioxide from her lungs were painful, Nicole agreed. "How about I meet you here at noon?"

"Perfect. I'll see you then." Parrott pressed the button to disconnect the call, but held the receiver near his ear, contemplating the meaning of the exchange. Something told him Billy was still there, he had spent the night, and those two were up to no good. *Boy, that lady doesn't waste any time. Even a broken ankle hasn't stopped her from getting a date for New Year's Eve. Unless—unless she and Bartosh never split, despite her marriage to Phillips. Oh, this might be an interesting interview indeed.*

❦

The noon bells at All Souls Church were tolling when Parrott arrived at the Dakota. Last night's doorman and security staff had been replaced by new faces in fresh navy uniforms with gold buttons. Parrott announced himself, producing his badge and a business card for them to keep.

"Mrs. Phillips is expecting you," the security officer said. His nod and grin spoke of complicity, as if he were about to add the word, "brother."

Parrott was used to such familiarities from other blacks, but he didn't need them. *It's all about the work,* he thought. Adrenalin pumped through his system. The next few minutes could possibly crack this case wide open. He shook his head at the mental picture of Nicole's pretty head splitting in two like an overripe melon.

❧❧

Expecting Rosa to meet him at the door, Parrott was surprised to see Nicole, dressed in a sexy-looking velvet jumpsuit with holes exposing her shoulders and midriff. The large diamond stud in her bellybutton vied for attention, despite Parrott's determined professionalism. Though still not weight-bearing, Nicole had graduated to crutches, and she was nimble enough with them to take his coat and lay it over the staircase railing. All of this occurred without a word being exchanged. The two stared at each other. Parrott couldn't imagine what, from Nicole's point of view, had changed since their last meeting, enough to erect frosty walls, unless it was a guilty conscience.

She led him into the sunlit breakfast room, decorated with glass and chrome and a view of Central Park. He looked at the spot where his Camry had been parked the night before and wondered whether she had spotted it there. A bouquet of flowers nestled in a vase on the counter.

When both of them were seated in leather and metal chairs, facing each other across the circular table, Nicole finally broke silence. "Okay, Detective. What is it this time?"

Parrott cleared his throat and said, "Mrs. Phillips, I appreciate your cooperation with this investigation."

"Yes, you've said that. But what's going on now? Do you have a suspect?"

"We are making progress, yes. But we have a long way to go still."

"What does that have to do with me?"

"I have some follow up questions for you. Some things have come up."

"I really don't like having my New Year's Day interrupted." She picked at an invisible thread on her lap.

Parrott had a few ideas about what he was interrupting. "I know how you feel. I don't usually work on New Year's Day, myself. But time is precious in a murder case."

"You know," Nicole responded, "I've been thinking. How do we know Preston's death was actually a murder? Maybe it was a suicide, or—or a freakish accident?"

Parrott held the young widow's gaze. Her heavily made-up eyes were opaque, *hiding what?* "What makes you think it might not be a murder?"

"Well, I just don't know who would have done that to Preston. The people at that party are all really smart, really rich, really famous people. Even if they didn't like him very much, I just don't see people like that stooping to *killing* him. You know what I mean?"

"Yes, but someone did." Parrott took his mini iPad from his shirt pocket. "Is there some reason Mr. Phillips may have been suicidal?"

"No—o—o," Nicole answered, drawing the syllable out as long as humanly possible. "I don't really think so. He seemed happy enough. But he was acting a little strange during the weekend."

"Strange in what way?"

"Mmmm, it's hard to say. I really never spent time with Preston and his friends before. We mostly went out just the two of us, as a couple, you know."

"So what struck you as different in this situation?"

"I don't know. He acted like he was showing off. His money, his success, even me. But—"

"But?"

"Well, I was pretty drugged at the time, but I felt Preston was distancing himself. He didn't like it when I was needy. It worried me. Now I'm just trying to forget it."

"Sorry to make you go through it all again. Let's talk about the desktop computer that we took from Mr. Phillips' office there." He pointed in the direction of the entryway. "Who else besides Mr. Phillips had access to that computer?"

"Preston's computer? Just Preston."

"Did you ever use it?" Parrott asked, noticing the dilation of Nicole's pupils.

"Once in a while. I mostly use my iPhone and iPad, but I'm not that much into electronics. That room was Preston's hideaway. I rarely went in there, especially if Preston was at home."

"Were you forbidden to use the PC?"

"No, nothing like that. Just didn't need it except once in a while. I maybe used it a half a dozen times?"

"Can you remember when you used it last, what you used it for?"

"No, why?" Nicole flipped her smooth blonde hair behind her mostly-bare shoulder. "Did you find something on it?"

Parrott did not intend to answer questions, only ask them. However, before he could formulate a response, he heard a muffled sound coming from the kitchen pantry. "What was that?"

"I didn't hear anything," Nicole said.

Parrott was sure he'd heard something—or someone, but he let it go in favor of more questions. "I want to talk to you about those pills you gave me the last time I was here."

"What pills?"

"The ones that had been in Mr. Phillips' toiletry kit at the Campbells' farm."

"Oh, those," Nicole replied, her voice whiny as a plucked violin string.

"Who, besides Mr. Phillips and you and I, had access to those pills, either before or after the weekend?"

A frown line appeared between Nicole's ultra-skinny eyebrows. "Nobody, I don't think. Maybe Rosa helped me unpack everything when I got back from the farm. Maybe my sister Francine. I really don't remember."

"How about Bill Bartosh? Did he help you un-pack?" Parrott's eyes were riveted on the face of his suspect, hoping for a flinch.

Nicole didn't disappoint. Her eyes moved in the direction of the kitchen pantry. *Aha! He's hiding in the pantry,* Parrott thought. Nicole's mouth opened to respond, but no words passed through her pouty lips.

"Mrs. Phillips?" Parrott prodded.

"Uh, I—no, Billy did not touch Preston's pills, Preston's computer, or anything else of Preston's."

"How about Preston's wife?" Parrott asked. The word "wife" fairly echoed in the tension between the two.

She gave a sharp intake of breath. "Just what are you implying, Detective? And, and how do you know about Billy, anyway?"

"Look, Mrs. Phillips. I know you and Billy Bar-tosh both worked at the Lamborghini place. I know you spent New Year's Eve with him last night. And I know he is still here in this house. Shall we take a look in the pantry?" Parrott stood up and held his arm out in the direction of the pantry, as if to say, "I'll follow you." He held his breath, praying his hunch was accurate.

Before Nicole could decide what to do, the creak of a door opening in the next room caused her to freeze in place at the table. In a matter of seconds, footsteps announced the appearance of an athletically built young man with thick brown hair tipped with blond; dark, snappy eyes; strong chin. Rosy cheeks were either natural or induced by the precarious situation. Regardless, the man seemed composed and confident, perhaps foolishly so, under the circumstances.

Striding up to the table, he extended his hand. "I'm Bill Bartosh," he said, as if networking at a cocktail party. "I know it seems strange, my being here and in the pantry, but I promise you it's not. We can explain everything."

CHaPtER 45

D riving back to the station, Parrott ruminated on the facts of the case. The two-hour drive was becoming a familiar setting for sorting out puzzle pieces, turning them this way and that. The deck was certainly stacked against Nicole now, especially with the new twist of an accomplice in the picture. What bothered him most, though, was the lack of hard evidence—everything he had was circumstantial at best. And he knew better than to rush to judgment in a high profile case like this, where arresting the wrong person could send his career careening into the dumper.

Bartosh's so-called explanation fell short of satisfying. Claimed they fell in love three years ago, broke up when Phillips entered the picture. Didn't speak for over a year, till Phillips' death was publicized.

You bet I'll be checking the phone records, Parrott thought, remembering the young man's suggested proof of innocence. *Not that that proves anything. Today people knew multiple ways to communicate without using cellphones.* He made a mental note to look into burner phones, emails, and social media, as well.

The two really seemed to connect with each other. He could tell by the way they avoided voluntary eye contact, but when their eyes did meet, the magnetic force between them was almost palpable. Could it be they were just reconnecting after a long separation while Nicole was married? Parrott thought of how it would be when Tonya came home from Afghanistan and knew he wouldn't be able to take his eyes from hers, either.

The case against Nicole was a house of cards, none of them aces. He had the money motive, the quick cremation, the home aquarium, the internet searches on palytoxin, the Metamucil container filled with the poison, and now the boyfriend. Working against him, though, was Nicole's ankle injury and narcotics.

Murder by palytoxin had to have been premeditated. If the newlyweds had been unhappy, no one had mentioned it. Bartosh notwithstanding, Nicole had seemed to be in love with her husband at the time of his death. Parrott remembered hearing about her high-pitched screaming when the paramedics were attempting to revive the victim. He wished he could place her in the upstairs bedroom after the dinner that Saturday night.

The fact that her fingerprints were on the Metamucil container meant nothing. She had handled the small canister on its journey back to the co-op, and again when she had given it to Parrott. As she had put it herself this afternoon, "If I had known there was poison in it, why wouldn't I have gotten rid of it when I had the chance? I certainly wouldn't have given it to you to analyze."

Parrott shook his head as he drove, doubts ricocheting inside. Eighteen days into the case, and he still didn't have a clear solution. Neither time nor an impatient public were on his side.

ဢဢ

Parrott reached his office by five p.m., tossing a bag of Chinese carry-out onto his desk. The smell of spicy vegetables permeated the space. His plan was to organize his notes and draft the questions for the Winthrops. He would meet with them and their attorney at Marshall's office at the Fed first thing tomorrow morning.

He kicked off his shoes and stretched his long legs under the desk, leaning his head back against the padded vinyl chair. He opened the first of three food containers, inhaling the steamy aroma.

The phone rang, piercing his gastronomic reverie. "Officer Parrott?" the strong, but crackly voice asked. "I hope I'm not interrupting anything important."

He glanced at the caller ID, though he was almost certain he recognized the voice—Phillips' mother. He re-sealed the insulated food container.

"Mrs. Phillips? Of course not. Nothing more important than whatever you have to say." His mind was spinning with possibilities.

"You gave me your card and asked me to call if I remembered anything significant. I know it's New Year's Day, but I guessed you'd be there."

"Yes, ma'am. What is it you remember?"

"I've been thinking about the last conversation I had with Preston. He'd called me from the car, on Bluetooth, the Thursday before his death. He was always checking up on me that way, when he was alone in the car. I had just had a minor medical procedure, and he wanted to know how it had gone. I told him I was fine, never better, and I asked him how things were going with him. I didn't think much of his answer at the time, but in light of what's happened since, I can't stop thinking about it."

"What did he say, Mrs. Phillips?"

"He said, 'Couldn't be better, Mom. New wife and all. Keeps me young. Just one more hurdle, and I'll be on top of the world.' I should have asked him what he meant, what the hurdle was. What if it had something to do with his death?"

Parrott replied, "You were right to tell me about this. Perhaps it is significant. What possible hurdles can you think of that Preston may have referred to?"

"Well, I know he'd been putting off a knee re-placement. At first, I thought that might be it, or something having to do with Peter. But the word 'hurdle' made me think it might be a business matter, something time-sensitive."

"Any particular business matters that you know about?"

"I can't say. Preston was a financial wizard, as you know. He had so many business interests, the stock market, bond market, international investments, and that doesn't even include his stint in politics as treasury secretary. Preston knew so many people, had so many business interests—it would be impossible to identify just one."

Parrott tried to narrow the woman's thinking. "Remember, there were just fourteen others at the Campbell house that weekend, though—the Campbells, the Bakers, the Spillers, the Winthrops, the Blooms, the Kelleys, Margo Rinaldi, and, of course, Nicole. Do any of those people sound like they might be a "hurdle" in Preston's life?"

"I—I just don't know—I wouldn't want to falsely accuse anyone—" Mrs. Phillips' voice faltered.

"It wouldn't be an accusation, ma'am. It would be a lead, a way to guide our focus as we continue the investigation."

"I guess you're right. In that case, I would eliminate Caro and John E. Caro has always been like a sister to Preston, and I know she would never harm him. The Bakers and the Blooms are Caro's friends and associates, not Preston's, so I doubt they had any motive, either."

Parrott nodded, though no one could see.

"The rest are long-time connections. Of them all, Marshall Winthrop would be the only one I'm aware of with a business tie to Preston. Except for Nicole, of course. Oh, this is all so upsetting. I've known Marshall all of his life, and I just can't imagine that he would be a murderer."

"You've been very helpful, Mrs. Phillips. Please call me again if you think of anything else."

"I will, Detective. And thank you. It's comforting to know that you are working so hard to solve this case. Goodbye, now."

As Parrott put down the receiver, a shudder took hold of him. The questions he was about to draft for Marshall Winthrop had just become even more important.

Chapter 46

Thursday, January second, in New York City dawned with a celestial brilliance uncommon for that time of year. It was as if the sky were introducing the world to new possibilities on this first business day of the new year. Parrott, driving into the city once more, chose to take it as an omen of good things to come in his interview with the Winthrops.

Once he arrived at Thirty-Three Liberty Street, in the heart of the financial district, he felt a bit less confident. The fortress-like appearance of the Federal Reserve Bank of New York gave a counterpoint to the sunny day. Over a quarter of the world's gold was reputed to dwell there, but Parrott's focus was not monetary. It would take more than luck to come away with the treasure he was seeking. On his way to Marshall's office on the fourteenth floor, he reviewed the questions he had prepared. He knew the interview would be tricky.

He wasn't daunted by people with money anymore, but he had been warned the Winthrops would have legal representation on hand, and he knew of their association with Rodney Ballenger, whose reputation for shrewdness both in and out of the courtroom was famous.

Parrott had timed his arrival for ten o'clock, instead of eleven. He hoped he would get there before all of the players assembled and reviewed their strategy. Even the slightest diversion could be parlayed into an advantage, and with its being three against one, he needed every advantage possible.

"Isn't the meeting scheduled for eleven?" Winthrop's young bespectacled assistant asked, glancing at the clock on her desk. The nameplate on the desk said *Trudy Cunningham*.

"Traffic wasn't as bad as I expected, Ms. Cunningham," Parrott muttered.

"Why don't you have some coffee, make yourself comfortable? I'll tell Mr. Winthrop you're here." She pointed to a well-appointed cupboard filled with fine china. Its wide serving shelf had linen placemats, a crystal vase filled with sunflowers, a bowl of summer fruit, a pot of coffee, cream and sugar, and a plate of pastries.

Parrott took a pass on the food and drink in deference to his jittery stomach. He took the seat closest to the assistant's desk, hoping to overhear or observe something interesting.

"Detective Parrott is here," Trudy said into the telephone receiver. "Yes, he knows. He said traffic was light." She examined a fingernail. "I'll tell him." She hung up the phone and thumbed through some papers on her desk.

Parrott checked the knot in his tie and leaned forward, hoping to get a glimpse of the papers Trudy was holding.

After a minute she met Parrott's gaze and said, "Mr. and Mrs. Winthrop won't be available to meet with you until eleven, as planned."

"Quite all right," Parrott replied. "I have some work to do while I wait." He pulled a list of questions from his folder and began to look through them. He noticed the curious expression on Trudy's face, her turn to be nosy.

At ten-thirty the double glass door rolled open, and a tall figure crossed the threshold. Rodney Ballenger made a strong first impression with his long silver-gray mane, Roman nose, impenetrable eyes, and perfect posture. Wearing an Italian suit that matched his hair, he carried an alligator briefcase in one hand, a Burberry coat on the opposite arm. Reading glasses hung from a lanyard around his neck.

Parrott made eye contact with Ballenger, whose pictures in the *Times* social columns and on the local news had made him a recognizable icon. *He looks like a former underwear model.* Parrott laughed inside, bemused by his surprising new attitude toward the very rich. *Probably has his own problems and insecurities, just like everyone else.*

Showing no sign of insecurity, Ballenger strode up to the receptionist and received immediate clearance to enter Winthrop's inner sanctum, leaving Parrott to reconsider his magnanimous thoughts. *It's really no surprise,* he said to himself. *Any good lawyer would prepare his clients for a meeting with the police in a murder case. Glad I'm prepared, as well.* He reviewed his notes once more then leaned his head back and breathed deeply. He pictured himself as a strong and powerful samurai, perfectly poised to attack.

✦✦✦

Once admitted to Winthrop's office, Parrott could hardly contain himself. An aquarium filled with plants and animals, some of which were large-branched corals, adorned one wall. The tank looked clean, the colorful fish active. A few feet away sat a round conference table and four chairs covered in oxblood leather. Marshall and Julia Winthrop sat across from each other, dressed like Fifth Avenue models, with Rod Ballenger between them. "Please have a seat, Detective," Marshall said, without standing or using Parrott's name.

Parrott took the seat, made eye contact with each of the participants, and opened his iPad. He cleared his throat. From his football days, he believed in being the first to score.

Before he could utter a syllable, however, Ballenger usurped the floor by introducing himself and saying, "Detective, I'm sure you realize Mr. and Mrs. Winthrop have hired me to represent them in speaking with you today. Before we get started, may I ask whether Mr. or Mrs. Winthrop is a suspect in this investigation?"

Realizing the meeting was not off to the best start, Parrott broke eye contact. "At this point in time, I am not able to exclude them."

The attorney nodded. "While I am sure you have a list of questions, I have recommended to the Winthrops that they not submit themselves to questioning at this time, unless they are granted full immunity. Unless they are granted said immunity, I have recommended that they invoke their Fifth Amendment rights. However, since the Winthrops don't want your trip to be wasted, we have met to discuss their perceptions and insights regarding the unfortunate demise of Mr. Preston Phillips, and we have prepared a proffer, which I will read to you at this time."

All charitable thoughts toward the rich and powerful fled from Parrott's mind at the thought of being stifled, but outwardly he showed no rancor. "All right, let's hear the proffer." He crossed one long leg over the other knee and sat back, adopting the body language of a guest at a barbecue.

Julia and Marshall exchanged edgy glances then gazed at their attorney as if hypnotized.

Ballenger began to read from a formal document. "If the Winthrops were called upon to testify before a court of competent jurisdiction with regard to the death of Mr. Preston Phillips and were duly sworn upon oath, they would state, as follows: Mr. Winthrop has known Mr. Phillips all of Mr. Winthrop's life, having grown up in the same neighborhood, attended the same schools, and pledged the same fraternity. Mrs. Winthrop first met Mr. Phillips during college when she began dating Mr. Winthrop. Mr. and Mrs. Winthrop are close friends with John E. and Caroline Campbell. The Winthrops met the Campbells during their college years together. The relationship between the Winthrops and the Campbells is both a business and personal relationship. Mr. Winthrop and Mr. Campbell were partners in a gourmet cheese import business from 1975 to 1993."

Nothing new here, Parrott thought. The attorney's monotone invited him to zone out, but he steeled himself against doing so. *There might be a nugget of information worth having in here.*

"In 1972, while Mr. Winthrop was serving in the United States Army, stationed in Viet Nam, his parents were killed in an automobile accident. The terms of their separate wills left their estate, valued at the date of their deaths at two hundred million dollars, in trust for their only child, Mr. Winthrop. The document creating the trust stipulated that Mr. Phillips was to act as the sole trustee of said trust."

Parrott uncrossed his legs and leaned forward.

"While both Mr. Winthrop and Mr. Phillips held prominent positions in the nation's financial markets, Mr. Winthrop did not consider himself and

Mr. Phillips to be close personal friends, and as such, the Winthrops and Mr. Phillips rarely met on social occasions. The Winthrops would further testify that one such rare occasion was the house party to celebrate John E. Campbell's birthday at the Campbells' farm in Pennsylvania, the weekend of December thirteenth through fifteenth. The Winthrops were not aware that Mr. Phillips and his new wife Nicole would be among the guests until Mr. and Mrs. Phillips arrived at the farm."

Hmmm...if that could be proven, it would eliminate their having premeditated murder by palytoxin. I'm sure that's what Ballenger is trying to convey. Parrott looked from Marshall to Julia, both of whom wore the looks of cherubs.

"During the weekend of December thirteenth through fifteenth, they had no specific, private conversations with Mr. Phillips. Except for a chance encounter that Julia had with Mr. Phillips on the afternoon of December fourteenth, neither of them was alone with Mr. Phillips at any time during the weekend. When the birthday party on that evening broke up after midnight, Mr. Phillips appeared to be in good health. The next day when Mr. Phillips failed to appear at the informal brunch, Mrs. Campbell went to his room and found him unresponsive. Paramedics and police were called and arrived promptly. After being briefly questioned by the police, Mr. and Mrs. Winthrop were given clearance to leave. They went directly to their home in Rye, New York." Ballenger folded the document and placed it inside the alligator brief-case.

He's not even going to give me a copy, Parrott marveled. *If these people think they're going to get away without answering my questions—*

Parrott sucked in a pint of air before responding. He chose his words and his tone with care. "I appreciate your proffer, Mr. Ballenger, Mr. Winthrop, Mrs. Winthrop. It certainly opens up some of the necessary conversation in this investigation." He drew in another breath, arming both lungs and body with the strength he needed in this three-against-one meeting. "It doesn't, however, suffice. The West Brandywine Police Department is charged with investigating Mr. Phillips' murder. As lifelong acquaintances and members of the group of party guests at the Campbells' home, you are subject to questioning. I'll grant that you have anticipated and answered some of the questions I have, but there are others, and I need your respons-es, just as those of all of the other party guests."

Parrott watched the Winthrops as he spoke, look-ing for body language or facial expressions that would give away the feelings hidden behind the proffer. While Marshall sat still, looking straight ahead, Julia shifted in her seat, just enough to indi-cate discomfort.

Ballenger noted the nonverbal exchange of in-formation and took over, "If you submit your list of questions, Detective, my clients will review them with me, and perhaps we will provide a supplemental proffer in the next couple of days."

"With all due respect, this investigation cannot wait another couple of days. There is pressure from high levels to solve the case, and we all know time is of the essence. We can go the subpoena route, or, since we are all here now, we—can—answer—the—questions—today." Parrott couldn't hold back the irritation in his voice anymore. He was growing weary of driving back and forth to New York for tiny tidbits of information.

Exuding the essence of self-control, Ballenger looked at his clients before saying, "Why don't you excuse us for a few minutes, Detective, while I confer with the Winthrops about your request?"

Is it my imagination, or did this self-important creep place undue emphasis on the word, "request"? Parrott reminded himself to show restraint. Little would be gained by getting into a shouting match with these people. He slowly uncrossed his legs and stood, staring at Ballenger the whole time. He would give them their privacy, but he would not retreat like a beaten dog. He had worked too hard and come too far with this case to do that.

೮ೞೞ

Ten minutes later, Parrott was invited back into the office, the puffers circling in the aquarium somehow bolstering his confidence. He resumed his place at the table and opened his iPad, as he had earlier.

Ballenger cleared his throat. "My clients have decided to have a look at your questions. We will go over them in private, and we will draft another proffer. Would you be so kind as to leave us with a copy? Give us an hour or so, have lunch here in Manhattan. Come back around one, and we will meet again."

Luckily, Parrott had made several copies of his questions. Wordlessly, he removed the top copy from the pocket of his notebook and handed it across the table to Ballenger. He nodded to the group and withdrew from the room, dragging his ugly, impatient thoughts with him. He had questions, all right, and after this morning's shenanigans, he had added a few more. For example, what transpired when Julia and Preston conversed alone on December fourteenth?

CHaPtER 47

Parrott had no appetite for food. The Winthrops' proffer had left him with a bad taste in his mouth. Besides, his dress shoes were pinching his feet, and he felt the weight of the homicide on the back of his neck. He brushed the snow from a bench outside of a restaurant, sat on the chilly steel, and called Chief Schrik.

"Checking in. Winthrops lawyered up, just as we thought."

"Get anything out of them?"

"Not much. Statement by proffer. Told them I needed more. Would go the subpoena route if I had to. Of course, that's an idle threat, since they'd probably just take the Fifth. They've got my questions. Told me to come back at one for more proffering." Glancing at the diners eating and talking inside the restaurant, Parrott felt empty, isolated. He shivered.

"Glad you didn't back down. Hang tough, Parrott. Oh, by the way, you missed a phone call from another guest at the Campbell party."

"Yeah? Who?"

"Andrea Baker. Says she knew you were busy interviewing others, but there was something she'd just thought of that you should know."

"I'll call her. Thanks." A glimmer of hope that Andrea's call might prove worthwhile ignited a tiny flame inside Parrott's mind.

"Stay in touch."

❧❧❧

When Parrott returned to Winthrop's office, he was impervious to the comfortable indoor temperature, the light fragrance of Trudy's perfume, and the pitying look on the secretary's face. Parrott recognized, but ignored them, not wanting to acknowledge his huge disadvantage. "Are they ready for me?" he asked, looking at his watch.

"Yes, Detective," Trudy replied, her voice betraying a warmth absent before. "You can go right in."

Parrott strode past the secretary's desk and into the Fed President's office with the grace that football players seem to maintain for life, comfortable moving before an audience. The three-person audience was sitting in the same chairs, looking as if they had not moved since the last round had ended. Parrott took the same seat across from Ballenger. "I'm back," he announced simply. "What now?"

"Unfortunately," Ballenger stated then cleared his throat, "Mr. and Mrs. Winthrop have declined to address the rest of your questions at this time. They feel they have provided you with sufficient information in the proffer, and they have no further information to add."

"That's outrageous," Parrott said, finally unable to hold back his temper. He focused his dark gaze on Marshall and then on Julia. "Of course, it is within your legal right to hide behind the woodpile like wild rabbits, but it just makes you look suspicious." He slapped the table with the palm of his hand, so hard that the papers in front of Ballenger jumped. "This is no game of hide-and-seek we are playing. A man has been murdered, and we *will* find his killers, with or without your cooperation."

Julia's hand flew to cover her mouth, barely eclipsing a squeal.

Marshall's eyes flew from Parrott to Ballenger, as if to say, "Do you believe this guy, talking to us this way?"

Before his anger completely got the best of him, Parrott rose, placed his notebook under his arm, and headed back through the door and past Ms. Cunningham. *If they think I lack the manners of the one-percent, so be it.*

ↄ⃝ↄ

Before his next appointment, a meeting with Libby and Les Bloom, Parrott stopped by LaVilla Pizzeria for a quick bite to eat. The deep dish personal pizza would fill the bill. While he waited to be served, he punched up the station's number.

Schrik answered halfway through the first ring. "Parrott?"

"Yeah. I'm in a restaurant, so can't say much. They won't talk, and I lost my temper. You'll probably have to deal with complaints, but I'm not sorry for what I did."

Schrik hesitated before replying. "Finish your lunch and interview with the Blooms, and then we'll talk. Thanks for the heads up. I'd hate to be blindsided by these guys."

Parrott clicked off and dialed Andrea Baker's number. Three long rings, a voicemail, and a beep later, he left a message. "Parrott returning your call. Hope to talk soon." He gave his cell phone number and clicked off. *When a door closes, a window opens,* he thought. *I sure could use a roomful of open windows.*

He reviewed his list of questions for the Blooms. He added a new one: Were you aware that Julia Winthrop had an unpleasant encounter with the victim on Saturday afternoon? He knew the Blooms' connection to the Campbells was different from the others'. They were younger and didn't share the college background. Still, Libby was Margo's sister, and the granddaughter of Sterling Martin, founder of one of the most prestigious Wall Street firms, so these were one percenters in their own right. While they weren't high on the list of suspects, they still might bring some fresh light to the case. Parrott rubbed his hands in anticipation.

When he arrived at the condo at Fifteen William Street, a formal, but friendly doorman greeted him. Parrott showed his badge and was directed to the elevator behind the mahogany desk. The high ceilings and fragrances of opulent floral arrangements in New York lobbies had begun to fade into the woodwork, so focused was Parrott on the case.

A round-bellied Libby greeted Parrott at the door. *No servants in sight, maybe these younger people were less dependent on help, or maybe it was the maid's day off.* Parrott remembered Nicole's Rosa and decided having servants still must be in vogue.

"Come right in, Detective," Libby said. "It's Francesca's day off. Let me take your coat."

A door opened, and Libby's husband entered from the adjoining room, taking Parrott's coat and the heavy wooden hanger from his wife's hand. "I appreciate your scheduling this meeting for the afternoon, after the markets close," Les said.

"No problem," Parrott replied.

"Let's sit in the dining room, shall we?" Les led the way to a formal dining room with large windows on one wall, a burning fireplace on the opposite wall. Above the mantle, a museum-quality oil painting showed a green meadow in the spring.

The sturdy chairs and table were more comfortable than the ones in Marshall Winthrop's office.

Parrott hoped the meeting would be, too.

"Would you like something to drink?" Libby asked.

"No, thanks," Parrott replied. "I'm good." He opened his iPad.

"I expect you have some questions for us," Les pre-empted. "But before you start, I just want to make a statement."

The Winthrops' proffer stood fresh in Parrott's mind, but he maintained a friendly expression.

Les went on. "Libby and I were invited to the Campbells' party because of my relationship with John E. He was my teacher at Princeton, and he mentored my career. He also introduced me to Libby, so he and Caro are very special to us. We are not part of their usual social group, and we have no connection to Preston Phillips, beyond the fact that Libby's sister Margo was engaged to him forty years ago. We are both shocked and saddened to have been on the premises where Preston died, but neither of us has any idea of who might have killed him."

Sensing Les was leading up to a complete brush-off, Parrott interjected. "I understand, and I appreciate your meeting with me. Do you remember the old Rubik's cube puzzle? A murder investigation is a lot like that. Often people think they can't turn the plastic the right way, but when we talk with them, ask the right questions, a pattern develops.

Your input, as guests at the Campbells' is very valuable."

"Okay," Les answered, seeming to weigh Parrott's words. "We'll help any way we can." He made eye contact with Libby, who nodded.

Parrott glanced at his list of questions, although he had mostly committed them to memory. "You two slept on the third floor at Bucolia, while Phillips had the room on the fourth floor, correct?" When they nodded, Parrott asked, "Did either of you hear or see any activity, anyone going to or from the fourth floor other than the Phillipses on Friday night?"

Libby answered, "I didn't. But our room opened on a side hallway, and besides, I'm a pretty heavy sleeper with this pregnancy and all. Did you, Les?"

"No. I was really tired Friday night, after working, traveling to the farm in that heavy snow, and eating and drinking. The beds were so comfortable, I fell asleep the minute my head hit the pillow."

"How about during the afternoon or evening before the dinner Saturday night?"

Again the couple claimed not to have seen or heard anything unusual.

Parrott asked the same question a third time. "We know Mrs. Phillips was injured and resting in the family room after the horse accident on Saturday. Is there anything at all you may have seen or heard to indicate that anyone besides Mr. Phillips went up to the fourth floor on Saturday night or early Sunday morning?"

Les echoed his earlier comment. "It was so late when we all went to bed Saturday night. We were tired and slept soundly."

Parrott made eye contact with Libby while Les was speaking. Her green eyes shifted upward, as if she were remembering something. *What?* "Mrs. Bloom?"

"I—uh, I slept soundly, as well. I got up a few times to go to the bathroom, but the house was quiet, and I didn't notice anything out of the ordinary."

Parrott knew there was more to it than that, but he went on. "Were either of you aware of any animosity between Mr. Phillips and anyone else in the group?"

Libby and Les exchanged glances but remained silent.

"I'll come back to that question. What, did you think, was the state of the relationship between Mr. and Mrs. Phillips?"

Libby answered, "They were newlyweds, you know. Nicole skipped going shopping with the ladies so she could be with Preston when the guys went riding. She was sort of clingy."

Parrott turned toward Les. "Did Mr. Phillips seem to cling to her?"

"I don't think so. I got the impression that he thought she was being juvenile, that he was a little embarrassed. But then again, maybe he was flattered."

"Mr. Phillips was once engaged to your sister, Mrs. Bloom."

Libby's complexion grew pink, and she moved her hand from her belly to her forehead. "Yes, that's true."

"What was your impression of how Mr. Phillips and your sister were getting along during the weekend?"

"You'll have to ask my sister, Detective. I can't say." She twisted an antique diamond bracelet around on her wrist.

"Just your impressions."

"I think it may have been difficult for Margo to be at the same party with Preston after all those years, but again, you need to ask her."

"You weren't part of the Campbells' college group, so I'm curious to know what you thought about the conversation, particularly among the men, throughout the weekend, during cocktails, at the dinner party. What did they talk about? Would you characterize the conversation as friendly? Did you feel that they were friends, enemies, rivals?"

Les responded this time. "It was typical social chatter. Some reminiscing, some sarcastic digs. Everybody likes John E. and wanted him to have a good birthday, so the conversation was basically positive."

"Anything that struck you as strange?"

"Not really. At one point they were talking about fraternity pranks they'd pulled, kidnapping a guy and tying him to a tree somewhere, letting a greased pig loose in the frat house, putting laxatives into one another's drinks. It all seemed pretty ridiculous to me."

Parrott's brain fired with the mention of laxatives, and he thought about the Metamucil in Phillips' toiletry kit, but he kept on.

"Let's get back to the question I asked earlier. Do you think anyone held a grudge against Mr. Phillips?"

Libby answered this one. "I don't think Preston was very popular with the group. He and Caro were cousins, and that's probably why he was invited. Otherwise, he really didn't fit in."

Parrott needed more of an answer than that. "Do you think there was animosity, for example, between Mr. Phillips and Mr. Winthrop?"

"Rumor has it that Winthrop was about to sue Phillips. Something having to do with mismanagement of funds. But none of that came up over the weekend," Les said.

"How about Mrs. Winthrop?"

"Oh, Julia wasn't a card-carrying member of the Preston Phillips Fan Club. She didn't go all goo-goo-eyed over him like Kitty, but I can't see her killing him, either. Julia's sort of all out for Julia. Not in a mean way."

"Did you overhear or hear about an encounter

Mrs. Winthrop had with Mr. Phillips on Saturday afternoon?"

"No, but Julia is the type of person who tells you just what's on her mind. If Preston ticked her off, I can imagine she gave him an earful."

Parrott changed subjects. "I'd like the two of you to think back over the weekend. Was there anything you ate or drank that smelled or tasted odd or made you sick?"

Les looked at Libby before answering. "We've talked to each other about that. Everyone ate the same food all weekend, and no one else got sick."

"Well, I wasn't feeling that great, but I have a reason," Libby said, patting her stomach.

Parrott asked, "Was there ever a time when Mr. Phillips had something to eat or drink that no one else did?"

Les shook his head and glanced at Libby again. "I don't think so. We all had the same catered dinner. Except for Vicki's truffles, which were all different."

"What do you mean, different?" Parrott asked. The ones Leon had given him to analyze looked all the same.

"Different flavors, different decorations."

"How were the truffles served?"

"Vicki passed them out herself," Les replied.

"Come to think of it," Libby added, "I think I heard Vicki say Preston was allergic to chocolate, and she had made a white chocolate one for him."

Interesting, Parrott thought. *There weren't any white chocolate truffles in the batch I analyzed.*

"Anything else you can think of that Preston may have had that no one else did?"

Les looked thoughtful. "The men all had cigars on the porch after dinner Saturday night. You don't think there was poison in the cigar, do you?"

"How were the cigars served?" Parrott asked, his voice thick.

"They were a birthday gift for John E., passed out by the person who brought them."

"And that was?" Parrott asked.

"Marshall Winthrop."

Chapter 48

Chief Schrik was masticating his paper clip double-time as he listened to former President Dalton's drawl over the telephone. Dalton had been shouting for several minutes without giving Schrik an opening to reply. The diatribe centered on Parrott's lack of progress on the case, though the real matter, Schrik suspected, had more to do with Parrott's losing his temper while meeting with the Winthrops and Rodney Ballenger. Words and phrases such as "unheard of," "impertinent," "disrespectful," and "out of line" peppered Dalton's language.

Schrik tuned in and out, as he considered how to respond to this powerful politician without becoming impertinent himself. If he were totally honest, he would have to say he could understand Parrott's frustrations with the Winthrops and their high-powered attorney, who had pushed the limits of the law to evade answering what amounted to first-round questions in a murder investigation. But total honesty would intensify the situation, and it was his job to keep things as calm as possible.

"Yes, I understand what you are saying, Mr. President. Of course, I do…yes, I'm aware that the Winthrops are solid citizens—"

"Maybe I was foolish to think such a small police department could handle a case of this magnitude. If Parrott's the best you have, then maybe I should make a call to the FBI Director."

Schrik took out the paper clip and took in a breath. "On the basis of what federal crime? Now, listen, Mr. President, we are well on our way to solving the case. Calling in the FBI now would mean starting all over."

"It's been almost a month since Preston's death, and your man Parrott is just getting around to interviewing some of the most important figures in America, and insulting them, too."

"I'm not making excuses, but don't forget the holidays have intervened in this investigation, and the important figures, as you say, have been unavailable for interview. We're trying to be sensitive."

"Listen, there's no getting around Parrott's behavior with the Winthrops. It was unprofessional and offensive."

"I'm sorry you feel that way, Mr. President. I'll make sure it doesn't happen again, but I ask you not to bring the feebies into this case. Give us a few more days, and we'll give you the murderer."

"Okay, Schrik. You have one week, but do me a favor. Keep Parrott away from the Winthrops."

"I'll keep it in mind, Mr. President, but Parrott is the chief investigator, and the Winthrops *are* on the suspect list. Just so you know."

Andrea entered her home office after a glorious afternoon ride on Mustafa. She shed her outerwear and riding boots and warmed her hands and sock-clad feet in front of the fireplace, where a cinnamon-scented log burned black and orange. She felt energized, healthy, and lucky, very, very lucky. The events of the past three weeks had shown her just how precarious life could be. She promised herself for the millionth time never to take the good things in her life for granted.

Moving from the fireplace to the desk, she glanced at her cell phone. *I wonder if Detective Parrott tried to reach me.* She pressed the side button, and the screen lit up. Three voicemails. As she pushed the voicemail icon, the phone rang, and Caro's number appeared.

Andrea answered the incoming call, cancelling the former operation. "Caro? Hi."

"Bad news," Caro said, her voice almost a whisper. "It's Gerald."

"Oh, no. What's happened?"

"Another stroke, and it's very bad. Kitty could hardly talk, she was so choked up. She had to put Lexie on the phone."

"Poor Gerald. Poor Kitty." Her voice oozed with sincere pity.

"He's on a ventilator. If he does make it, who knows how much brain damage he will have?

Maybe it would just be better for him to go peacefully."

"Well, we don't get to choose these things," Andrea said.

"Kitty doesn't want company, at least not tonight. We'll see what tomorrow brings. Oh, Andrea, ever since John E.'s party there's been a curse on us. I can't get it out of my head that Preston's death was the trigger for all of this sorrow—Gerald's stroke, Vicky's rehab, and now maybe Gerald's death, too." She burst into sobs. "Who—whoever killed Preston—you might say he or she was responsible for all of it."

Andrea wished she could give her friend a hug through the phone. "Take some deep breaths, Caro. You'll make yourself sick blaming your party for every bad thing that happens. Gerald might have had these strokes anyway, and Vicky's rehab is probably a good thing, after all."

Caro took several inhales and exhales. "I know you're right. I think I'm still in shock from the whole thing. I mean, I've been going along from year to year, thinking that sixty-five is the new forty-five, and all that, and suddenly it doesn't matter how good we look or how comfortable our lives are, we are completely vulnerable, defenseless against illness and death. I'm almost afraid to get out of bed in the morning for fear another bad thing will happen."

"Have you discussed this with John E.?"

"Not really. I think he's suffering from guilty feelings of his own. That, plus whatever feelings he has about his own mortality after turning sixty-five. I'm trying not to lay anything else on him."

"I understand how you feel, but as long as you two have been together, he can probably see through your protective screen, and you'd probably feel better if you shared it with him. Just saying."

"You're probably right. Maybe I'll talk to him when he gets back from New York tonight. He had a late afternoon meeting with Marshall."

"Good idea. And if you want me to go with you to the hospital tomorrow morning, I'll be glad to. The only plans I have are to complete some revisions. They can wait, though."

"Thanks, Andrea. I really appreciate you. I'll call you in the morning."

⌘

Andrea hung up the phone and called her voicemail. Three new messages, two from Parrott, and one from her editor. Ordinarily, her writing came first, but everything had seemed topsy-turvy since December fourteenth. She pushed 88 to return Parrott's second call.

"Parrott speaking," the deep voice answered after a single ring.

"Andrea Baker." Her voice remained in neutral. Contacting police officers during investigations could be dicey. Some welcomed her expertise and ideas, but some resented layperson interference. Parrott could go either way.

"Yes, Mrs. Baker. I was returning your call."

It sounds like he is driving. "I wondered if you might have time to meet with me. I've been thinking about Preston's death, and there is something I want to share with you. It might be important."

"Of course. I'm on my way back to the station now. I could come there this evening or first thing tomorrow morning."

Andrea thought about Gerald and decided to leave her morning free in case she had to go into New York with Caro. "How about I'll come to the station to meet with you tonight? Would eight p.m. be okay?"

"Sure. Eight p.m. And thank you."

Andrea disconnected the call and thought about what she had to tell Parrott. Maybe it would turn out to be nothing, but she didn't think so. *He does sound genuinely interested. And maybe if this all pans out, it will help Caro get her life together again, as well.*

⌾⌾⌾

It was only six p.m. when Parrott pulled into the station parking lot, shifted into park, and killed the ignition. It was cold and dark. The lights shining from the station windows beckoned him inside, though he yearned to go home instead. The day had been difficult.

Chief Schrik's car sat in its parking space. Parrott readied himself to face his superior officer. It wasn't that he was afraid. Schrik couldn't have been more supportive of him if he were his own family member. Remembering how he had left the Winthrops and their smooth-talking attorney still singed the edges of his psyche. It wasn't like him to lose his cool that way, but even now, with hints of regret simmering inside, he remembered the smug looks on their faces and wanted to punch their lights out, one and all. He shook his head as if to clear out the cinders, as he strode into the station and directly to Schrik's office.

The cleaning crew had just been through, so a pleasant minty fragrance greeted him. Chief Schrik was bent over an open file of papers, black-framed glasses pushed down the slope of his nose, his signature paper clip resting between generous lips. He looked up as Parrott's tall frame filled the doorway. "Oh, hi, Parrott. Come on in."

Parrott noted the weariness in his voice. "Anything new?"

"Nothing except for the ultimatum issued by our favorite ex-pres. We have a week to solve the case, or the Feebies will come in and relieve us. So, make my day, and tell me we can put this baby away in a week."

Parrott rubbed his head with both hands, the

springy growth of hair reminding him it would soon be time for another haircut. He couldn't remember the last time he had done anything personal, not related to the case. He sighed. "I'd like to say we're close. I was hoping for more information from the Winthrops, but I got some good info from the Blooms. Andrea Baker is coming here at eight tonight, and I meet with Margo Rinaldi tomorrow, so the picture is filling in with details. I guess you could say I'm optimistic."

"Are you still leaning toward the widow?"

"Yeah, but Marshall Winthrop is high on my suspect list, too, especially after today."

"Don't let the lawyer's fancy footwork prejudice you against Winthrop. That's just how most of those rich guys are. We're lucky *all* of the party-goers didn't lawyer up."

"I know," Parrott replied, biting off the bitterness in his voice. "But Winthrop had a money motive, he's got an aquarium full of corals in his office, he was about to file a lawsuit against Phillips, and, get this, he brought and passed out the cigars to the guys on Saturday night. What if he gave Phillips a poisoned cigar?"

"Hard to prove now that the cigar's been consumed. And then there's the Metamucil."

"Yeah, I know." Parrott pondered the facts and innuendoes of the case thus far. "I'm hoping Mrs. Baker's visit will give us some new insights. She's a crime writer, you know. I don't think she'd be wasting her time coming in if she didn't think she had something important."

"Well, I'm going to head for home now. The wife's cooking a pot roast tonight, my favorite." He grabbed his lined trench coat from the coatrack behind his desk and thrust one arm and then the other into it. He turned back to look Parrott in the eye. "I'm behind you a hundred percent, but keep in mind that the clock is ticking."

CHapteR 49

With two hours to kill, Parrott grabbed a makeshift meal from a package of ramen noodles in the bottom drawer of his desk, a blueberry muffin he found in the break room, and a cup of coffee left in the pot since morning. It would have to do. He microwaved the entrée and ate at his desk while flipping through his notes. As he read, he made a mental list of which of the fourteen party guests could be eliminated from consideration as the killer. The Blooms were out. A full generation younger, their only connection to the victim was the fact that he had hurt her sister back when they were young kids. Caro and John E. Campbell appeared to be lacking in motive, as well. The Bakers, likewise, seemed innocent, and the fact that they did not stay at Bucolia overnight limited their opportunity. He was less sure of the Kelleys, but having spent so much time with Kitty at the hospital, he had a gut feeling she was clear as well.

He drew a stack of index cards and a felt-tip pen from his top drawer and designed a neat list of suspects, one name per card He then began listing details that implicated each person.

412

When he was finished, this is what he had:

1. Nicole Phillips
Inherits $350 million if married to PP when
he dies
Cremates body, hiding evidence?
Has aquarium
Computer search history shows palytoxin
Has possession of Metamucil contain-
er/poison
Bartosh?
Jealousy over Margo?
2. Marshall Winthrop/Julia
Trust broken, giving MW control of $
Wife argues with PP Saturday afternoon
Brought cigars to party/passed them out
Has aquarium
Has New Year's Eve party, cover?
Lawyers up, refuses to answer questions

3. Vicky Spiller/Leon
Revenge for son's death
Alcoholic drinking, loss of control?
Truffles made and passed out, white choco-
late for PP?
Has aquarium
Goes to rehab after PP's death, guilt?

4. Gerald Kelley
Revenge for PP's appointment as treas secy

Jealous of Kitty's attention to PP
Stroke after PP's death, guilt?

5. Margo Rinaldi
Revenge for desertion at altar
Flirting on Friday night, afterward?

Sometimes it helped to make lists. Parrott stared at the cards for a while, shuffling through them several times. *No matter how I look at it, the strongest suspect is Nicole. Certainly, the one-percenters would be relieved if she were prosecuted for her husband's murder. So much cleaner if it wasn't one of them.*

Parrott gathered the trash from his food and drink and threw it in the wastebasket. *My job is not about politics. It's to discover the truth and then prove it. I wish Tonya were here. I could sure use a woman's point of view. Or maybe just a hug or two.* He glanced at the clock on the wall. *Enough time to make a few phone calls.*

❦❦❦

When the phone rang at Bucolia, Caro gave a startled cry and grabbed at the pearl choker around her neck. Right away she thought of Gerald, so she was relieved to see *West Brandywine PD* on her caller ID.

After exchanging pleasantries with the detective,

she asked, "What can I do for you?"

"I wanted to ask you a few questions about the invitations to the birthday party. When did you tell me they went out?"

"November thirteenth, one month before the party."

"All sent on the same day?"

"Yes."

"So all of the guests were invited at the same time?"

"Yes. But remember, I didn't send an invitation to Margo. I wasn't aware she was back in the US until Libby called to RSVP. Libby asked if Margo could come, and, of course, I said yes."

"Did the other guests know Mr. Phillips would be at the party?"

"Oh, I don't know. I suppose they would have guessed so, since Preston was my cousin, and he usually comes to our parties."

"At any time before the party, did anyone ask you whether he was going to be there?"

"No—o—o, not that I can remember."

"Okay, thanks, Mrs. Campbell. I appreciate your help."

"No problem." Caro disconnected the call, but held the receiver in her hand, a pensive look on her face. *I know what he's getting at. He's trying to figure out who had a month to premeditate Preston's murder.* She imagined mug shots of each of the party guests, parading before her eyes like a black and white silent movie. As she considered the possibility of each one of her dear friends being a murderer, a pain stabbed her belly.

∽∾∽

The next call went to Leon, who was putting in a few hours at his office.

"Mr. Spiller, Detective Parrott. Do you have a minute?"

"Sure. What's up?"

Parrott took the diplomatic route. "I wanted to ask your wife a few questions about her truffles, but perhaps you can help me, since she may be hard to reach."

"I'll try."

"Do you know whether the truffles she took to the party were freshly made or frozen?"

"That I know. Vicki spent the whole day the Thursday before the party making those truffles. She wanted them to be fresh. That was our birthday gift to John E."

Parrott detected the pride in his voice. "Do you know how she goes about making all of the different fillings? Does she make one type at a time and start all over, or does she have all of the fillings out in the kitchen at the same time?"

"I've seen her making candy for years. She usually makes one type at a time and freezes them, but since this batch was special, she probably had all the shells and all the fillings in the kitchen at the same time. It would have been an all-day process."

"What if a person was allergic to chocolate—or nuts—or some other ingredient? Would she do anything different in preparing the truffles?"

"Vicky has a variety of shells and fillings, so anyone who is allergic can avoid exposure. The white chocolate ones are for people allergic to chocolate. She's especially careful about nuts."

Parrott played with his moustache, thinking. "So there's no chocolate in white chocolate?"

"No. White chocolate doesn't have any chocolate—unless you consider cocoa butter chocolate. But most people don't react to that."

"One more question, please. Who cleans your home aquarium?"

Leon sounded perplexed as he answered, "Uh, I do."

ဢჄ

In the few minutes left before Andrea's appointment, Parrott called Maria Rodriguez, the medical examiner. He wanted to know whether freezing palytoxin would alter it. He really didn't think Vicki's truffles were the murder weapon, but the ones he had analyzed had been frozen, while the ones served at the party were not.

"Interesting question. Don't know, but I'll find out. Palytoxin is so new, there are lots of things we don't know about it."

"Give me a buzz when you find out, please." *That's the kind of minute detail that could make or break a case. After all of this time and effort, I'm going to adopt "Thorough" as my middle name.*

✑✑

Wearing a black hooded shearling coat, fuzzy mittens, cashmere scarf, and black suede Ugg boots, Andrea breezed into Parrott's office. *Expensive, but simple,* Parrott thought. *This woman doesn't flaunt her wealth. I respect that.*

"Thanks for letting me come," she began, as she took off the coat and sat opposite Parrott.

"I should be the one thanking you."

"Some detectives I've worked with didn't want anything to do with the opinions of lay observers. They especially didn't want authors snooping around, polluting the case."

Parrott gave an indulgent smile and leaned forward on his elbows. "Well, this detective appreciates your coming out here in the cold, dark evening."

Andrea unwrapped the scarf from around her throat and folded it on her lap. She seemed to be considering just where to start. "I don't know whether you've heard. Gerald Kelley has had another stroke. It's looking bad, and everyone is worried for him and Kitty."

"I'm very sorry to hear that," Parrott replied. He

418

thought of how open Kitty had been with him at the hospital, and he realized that he truly was sorry.

"That's not the reason I've come, of course." Andrea paused to pick a piece of lint from her lapel. "I've been doing a lot of thinking about Preston's death. Funny how different it feels to think about a murder investigation when you are actually involved in it. Anyway, what I want to talk to you about is Nicole."

Parrott's heart skipped a beat, but he kept his face in neutral. "What about her?"

"You know, I spent a fair amount of time with her that Saturday, both before and after she was thrown from the horse. I don't mean to brag, but I have good instincts about people. And, while I'm sure Nicole is a prime suspect in the case, I just don't think she is intelligent or sophisticated enough to have killed Preston."

"Let me remind you, Mrs. Baker, Lizzie Borden was neither intelligent nor sophisticated, yet she was suspected of a vicious murder."

"Yes, I know, but this is different. Preston was a very astute man, but let's face it. Nicole was a trophy wife, pure and simple. Besides that, I was there when they took him out of the house. If he was poisoned, it wasn't with cyanide or arsenic or strychnine, or any of those common poisons. There was no blood or vomit, no telltale complexion change. I just can't see Nicole being scientific enough to pull something like that off."

"Nowadays anybody can learn about poisons on the Internet," Parrott responded, thinking of the search history for palytoxin on the Phillips computer.

"That's just it," Andrea replied, "Nicole doesn't know anything about computers, either. I know it sounds unbelievable in this day and age, but I think she's telling the truth. She told me she'd signed up for a beginning computer class that started that Monday, and she guessed she would be missing it because of her broken ankle. I was surprised she wasn't computer literate like so many people her age, but she said she'd never needed it in any of her jobs, and now that she had time to learn, she felt it was important."

Parrott felt a bubble burst. If this were true, he would have an even harder time proving a case against the young widow. He made eye contact with Andrea and asked, "Since you don't think Mrs. Phillips killed her husband, who *do* you think did it?"

Andrea looked at the scarf in her lap. She hesitated as though climbing a tall fence, about to go over, but unsure of what awaited her on the other side. Parrott knew her friendship with Caro and John E. tugged at her to remain on one side. She took a deep breath. "I'm not privy to all of the facts in the case."

"But you do have an opinion," Parrott prompted.

"All along, I have suspected Marshall Winthrop," Andrea said in a quiet voice. "A friend told me he was about to file a lawsuit against Preston."

"Then why kill him? Why not let the legal system do its work?"

"Good point. Maybe he didn't have the stomach for the adverse publicity." Her voice trailed off, and she appeared to be lost in thought. "Marshall certainly has the intellect to research and use a poison, though I hate to think the President of the New York Federal Reserve Bank is so unscrupulous." She rearranged the scarf around her neck. "Well, that's what I wanted to tell you, about Nicole and Marshall, and I hope it helps."

She rose and reached her arms into the shearling. As she buttoned the coat, she said, "I don't know whether Marshall is the one who killed Preston or not, but I'll bet Preston would have liked to kill Marshall. If that lawsuit had been filed, it would've dragged Preston through the mud. In fact, if Marshall had been the one killed, my first suspect would have been Preston."

Chapter 50

Margo's stomach had been acting up all night, probably in anticipation of the next morning's meeting with that black detective from West Brandywine. Caro had told her he was very polite, very professional, but having never had much to do with police before, she took little comfort. If she were honest with herself, though, it wasn't the detective making her stomach so jumpy. It was Preston.

How ironic that she had spent forty years getting him out of her system, and in just one weekend, he had taken up permanent residence in her heart. She had revisited those miraculous moments from the weekend at Bucolia, analyzing every word, every gesture, every touch. She'd critiqued the events from the lenses of Preston the Lover, Preston the Liar, and Preston the Other Woman's Husband.

Then she began all over again, this time looking at her own behavior: Margo the Strong, Margo the Smitten, Margo the Wounded. Each time she hoped for a different ending. In the three weeks since his death, she had tried everything to distract herself from the constant string of "what ifs." She'd indulged in shopping trips, romance novels, dry martinis, bubble baths, sleeping pills. Nothing worked.

Was Nicole having these problems? Margo considered calling her, making a date to get together, just to see if the suffering was any different for the legitimate widow. What held her back was the encounter with Nicole on the stairs in the wee hours of the morning of December fifteenth. *Everyone thinks Nicole had the best alibi because of her broken ankle, but I know different. She must have been the one who killed Preston. Nobody in our crowd would have done it, no matter how much they disliked him.* For the umpteenth time, she considered how much to tell the detective.

Now, after a miserable night of little sleep and much pain, both physical and emotional, she looked at the bedside clock. *Five thirty. I might as well get up and start getting ready.* She started to rub her eyes before remembering her plastic surgeon's warning against it. She climbed out of her spongy memory-foam bed and stumbled to the bathroom. The mirror confirmed it had been a bad night. Her hair was jumbled, and those persistent wrinkles she had spent so much money to erase were threatening to creep back onto the sides of her eyes. *Too much crying,* she admonished herself.

Margo opened the door to her closet and peered inside. She looked for something comfortable to wear for the meeting with the detective. The lime green silk lounge suit peeked at her from behind her fluffy bathrobe. She hadn't worn it since Bucolia, hadn't even had it cleaned. It would always remind her of Preston and those last intimate moments. On impulse, she took it from the hanger and laid it on the velvet bench. Maybe this would give her the strength she needed for the interview. She viewed it as a form of armor, the closest thing she could think of to wrapping her body with the essence of Preston, himself.

❧❦❧

Andrea's exit line had echoed in Parrott's ears for the rest of the evening and into the next morning. What she came to tell Parrott about Nicole's lack of computer skills was a droplet in an ocean compared to the roaring waters set loose by her chance remark about Preston and Marshall. Parrott felt infused with a new vitality in the case. This could be the break he had been hoping for. When the alarm buzzed at four-forty-five a.m., he was ready to embark on the day's journey.

Despite this new energy, Parrott wasn't exactly looking forward to his eight a.m. interview at Margo's residence within the AKA Central Park. There were more important people to talk to. Yet, as the last guest to be interviewed, Margo was a necessary part of the investigation. He smiled at the memory of having thought of himself as "thorough" just yesterday. "Thorough" meant questioning every witness with the same skill and determination. He resolved to closet his thoughts about Winthrop and carry through with the Rinaldi interview as efficiently as possible. Before he left New York, he would pay Nicole another visit, too.

He ate a bowl of oatmeal with raisins, followed by a cup of scalding coffee, and fed Horace. Dressing in Dockers, a button-down shirt, and a navy sports jacket, he threw a solid burgundy tie around his neck, intending to complete the outfit after his long drive to New York. He glanced at Tonya's picture. "Miss you, baby. Finally, I feel this case is about to crack open. Wish you were here."

Horace called, "Oh, dear," as Parrott hugged the picture to his chest.

ⱥↄⱥↄ

No servant ushered Parrott into Margo's condo at the AKA. No lawyers stood there with proffers, either. Just a sixty-something auburn-haired woman who looked like an ex-model, but whose under-eye circles and hand-wringing mannerisms gave her a worried appearance. The lime green of her outfit did little to enhance her pale complexion, either. Parrott took in these details in a single glance, before realizing with a start, *Lime green! The thread on the chair in the fourth floor bedroom.*

"May I take your coat and hat, Detective?" Margo asked in a voice flavored by her years in Italy. "I've given my housekeeper the day off. No one needs to know my business with you."

Parrott doffed his outerwear and stamped his feet on the thick, cream-colored rug. He transferred the coat and hat to Margo, who set them on a tawny velvet bench. A serious-faced gentleman gazed at him from an oil painting hung over a mantle, as if to warn him off.

It was not lost on him that this was the grand-daughter of the late, great Sterling Martin, founder of Sterling Martin Financial. Had there been mists and whooshing sounds, the atmosphere could not have been more surreal. But then the whole case had been.

"Let's sit here," Margo said, pointing toward the parallel love seats in the glass-walled living room. The view of sunny Manhattan with its spiky buildings and dots of moving traffic below was impressive.

Margo sat, but remained on the edge of the love seat, as if she might bolt at any moment.

Perched across from her, Parrott wondered why she was so nervous. Maybe she'd left more than a lime green thread in that room on the fourth floor. "Mrs. Rinaldi," he began.

"You can call me Margo. Mrs. Rinaldi seems no longer accurate, now that I am divorced, and I haven't been Ms. Martin in a very long time. I guess I will have to rename myself."

"Okay, Margo," Parrott started again, uncomfortable with the informality, but wanting to help the witness relax. "You know I'm investigating the Phillips murder, and as a guest at Bucolia that weekend, you are on my interview list."

At the mention of the name Phillips, Margo's eyes grew wet. Parrott 'd have to proceed gingerly. An emotional witness could flood the case with irrelevant and misleading evidence, or, even worse, de-rail it completely. "These are routine interviews, you understand," he said, his baritone voice as soothing as warm butterscotch.

Margo nodded. She looked as though she didn't trust herself to speak.

"And do you remember I read you your rights at Bucolia the day of Mr. Phillips' death?"

"Yes. Right to remain silent, right to an attorney. I remember."

"And you waive those rights to speak with me today?"

"Yes, yes, of course. I'm not a suspect, am I?"

"At this point, everyone is a person of interest, Mrs.—Margo." Parrott went on, "Could you explain to me your relationship with the Campbells?"

"Certainly. Caro and I were pledge sisters, Kappa Kappa Gamma sorority. We both majored in English, roomed together senior year. We've been close all these years, even when I lived in Italy. And John E.? He and Caro started dating freshman year, so he's been a part of the mix forever."

"So it was logical that you would be invited to Mr. Campbell's birthday party."

"Yes. Well, I didn't actually receive my invitation until late. My decision to move back to New York was a sudden one. I was staying with my sister, Libby, who received an invitation in the mail. When she told Caro I was here, Caro invited me to come, as well."

"Did you know Mr. Phillips was going to be in attendance at the party?" Parrott watched for more tears, but this time all he saw was a flinch.

"I assumed he would, and I almost declined to attend. I really didn't care to see him again." Margo pinched a piece of silk between thumb and forefinger and began to rub the fabric.

"You were once engaged to him, I understand."

"Yes, a horrible time in my life. Better forgotten." More rubbing of fabric.

"So why did you attend a party where you felt sure you'd see him?"

Margo stopped the fabric-rubbing and sat up straighter. "I decided that forty years ago was ancient history. Why shouldn't I be there for my dear friend's birthday? Besides, I was curious about Preston. Had he aged? Had he changed?"

"And had he changed?" Parrott asked, hoping to keep her talking.

"In some ways, yes, and some ways no. He was older, of course, and wore his success in his face, his manner. But he still had that air of superiority that rubbed people the wrong way. I used to think of it as super-confidence, and I envied him for it."

"So, during the weekend of the party, were you able to reconnect with Mr. Phillips?"

Margo flinched again, and her hand returned to the seam of her pants leg. "What do you mean, 'reconnect'?"

"You know—talk, catch up—whatever old friends do when they meet up again."

A pained expression fluttered across Margo's attractive features. She looked upward, as if for divine inspiration, before responding. "Look, I'm sure others have told you. Preston glommed onto me Friday night and didn't let up until—until he turned up dead on Sunday. I didn't kill him, though."

"What do you mean 'glommed onto you'?"

"You know, chased me, followed me around, engaged me in conversation."

"How did Mrs. Phillips feel about that, do you think?"

"Nicole? I don't think she was happy. I wouldn't have been in her place. I *was* in her place once, you know, well, almost."

"You and Mr. Phillips were engaged."

"Yes, and he left me the day of our wedding. To marry one of my best friends. Very painful."

"So apparently Mr. Phillips was a womanizer."

"That, Detective, is an understatement." Margo's laugh sounded like a dry cough. She stood up and asked, "Can I get you something to drink? Coffee or tea?"

"I hate to put you out," Parrott replied.

"Not a problem. I'm going to make some for myself anyway. What do you prefer?"

"Coffee. Black. Mind if I come with you?"

Margo walked into the kitchenette, the swishing of the lime green silk not lost on Parrott.

As Margo brewed the single cup of coffee and another of tea for herself, Parrott gathered his thoughts. This interview was turning out to be more interesting than he'd expected, and he didn't want to pass up any opportunities for information.

"Here you are," Margo said. "One coffee, black." She uttered another dry cough laugh, as if embarrassed to say the word "black" to someone who was.

"Let's sit here, shall we?" Margo said, pointing to the breakfast room furniture.

Parrott gazed at the glass sculpture hanging over the table. It cast gemstone-colored light in every direction, serving as both light source and art.

"That's a Chihuly. Do you like it?"

"Beautiful," he mumbled, though he thought it rather extravagant for the space, and it probably cost a fortune.

"I suppose you have more questions," she said, stirring her tea with a constant rhythmic motion.

"Yes. Let's get back to the party weekend. You say Mr. Phillips glommed onto you. What, specifically, does that mean? Did he say or do anything inappropriate?"

"Inappropriate for Preston, or inappropriate for the rest of the world? Preston had his own moral code, and it was not atypical of him to act impulsively. Like many rich and powerful men, he felt the rules didn't apply to him."

"Rules?"

"Rules, like how to behave when you are at a party with your new wife, and your old fiancée shows up."

"How did he behave, then?"

"Like an overgrown teenager. Showing off. Flirting." Her voice carried a trace of disdain, but also of something pleasant, as if she were simultaneously repelled and attracted by the victim's attentions toward her.

"How did that make you feel?" Parrott asked.

Margo thought for a long moment before responding. When she finally spoke, the words came out with the speed of thick syrup. "I guess, conflicted. As much as I'd convinced myself I hated his guts, I was flattered by his attention, particularly when he had a beautiful twenty-something wife hanging on his every word. And there is something about one's first true love that...that never dies. Oh."

"What did you think about his relationship with his wife?" Parrott asked, hoping to divert her attention from death.

"Well, obviously, it must not have been much of a relationship if he was flirting with me so soon after their wedding." Margo appeared to realize how she sounded, because she quickly said, "I'm sorry. That was catty of me." She took a sip of tea.

"Did you spend any time alone with Mr. Phillips during the weekend?" Mentally, Parrott crossed his fingers.

"You know you are asking a loaded question, Detective."

"Yes, I know, but an important one."

"Well, the answer is yes."

"I appreciate your honesty. And, of course, I need details."

"And if I refuse to provide them?"

"You will be subpoenaed. This is a murder investigation."

"And I am not the killer. But I would rather not have to testify publicly, if I can avoid it. I'm really a very shy person."

"Look, I can't promise you that you won't have to testify eventually, but right now I'm just conducting interviews with each of the party guests. What you have to tell me may or may not turn out to be important in the overall scheme of things. But it sounds like you did have some feelings for Mr. Phillips. If I'm right, you must want his murderer to be discovered and justice to be done." Parrott was rolling the dice, but he hoped it would unlock something inside Margo's brain and then her mouth.

Margo stood up and began pacing. Parrott could

almost hear the alarm bells in her mind. He gave her time. After about three minutes, she returned to sit down next to him.

"Okay, Detective. On Friday night during dinner, I left the table to use the bathroom. When I came out, Preston was waiting for me. He told me he had made a big mistake not marrying me, that he had suffered for it all of those years. He pinned me against the wall and kissed me."

"How did you react to that?"

"I was stunned by the unexpectedness of it. I broke away from him and returned to the table. I think I said something like, 'Good. I'm glad you suffered, too.' That dredged up a lot of feelings for me, and I was upset. I vowed to myself that I would ignore him the rest of the weekend."

"But you didn't—"

"No. Saturday, after Nicole broke her ankle and came back from the hospital, she was on the sofa in the den, which left Preston free to chase after me. He persuaded me to come to his room on the fourth floor, just to talk."

"Can you remember what you were wearing when you went to his room?"

Margo looked at Parrott sideways. She stood up and moved back to her original seat, where Parrott could see her facial expressions much better. "Why, I—I was wearing the same outfit I have on now."

Parrott nodded as the clue of the thread clicked

into place in his brain. "Go on."

"All we did was talk, though Preston wanted more. I was trying to play it cool. I knew better than to trust him, and I kept pushing him away. Still, there was a certain vindication in having the upper hand with him. He had hurt me so, and I hated him for it. But then I saw another side of him, a vulnerable side. He flashed those dimples at me, and I felt myself being dragged in as if a merciless undertow had me in its grip."

Parrott lowered his voice to say, "I am sorry, but I have to ask—"

"Did I sleep with him? No, not then. I reminded him that he was a married man and had no business propositioning me that way."

"But he didn't give up?"

"No, he told me he wanted to make things right with me, to marry me. He promised he would tell Nicole that night, so we could be together."

Parrott thought of his conversations with Nicole. She had never indicated Preston was about to divorce her. *But why would she? That would be tantamount to painting a big "M" on her own face.* He held his breath as he asked, "*Did* he tell Nicole he wanted a divorce?"

"I'm not sure. He led me to believe he had. It was a whirlwind twenty-four hours. I've gone over it again and again, but I'm not sure."

"Were you and Mr. Phillips intimate, then?"

Before Parrott could utter the last syllable, Margo burst into wailing sobs and hid her face in her hands. The sobs seemed to emanate from a place in her core and were so loud, he wondered if the chandelier would crack.

Parrott remained silent, allowing the emotional outburst to play itself out. The irony of this woman's grief as compared to that of the widow nibbled at his consciousness. After a while, the wails transitioned into hiccups, and Margo regained a measure of composure. Her expression, however, remained tormented.

Finally, she spoke, though her voice was a hoarse whisper. "I still loved him, Heaven help me! I still loved him, and I slept with him that night. After the dinner, after everyone went to bed for the evening, I went to his room, and we made love."

Parrott resisted the impulse to pat her on the hand, to show sympathy for her anguish. He reminded himself that she had just risen on the suspect list, despite her protestations to the contrary, and it wouldn't do to touch one of the suspects.

Instead, he asked, "What time was it when you left Mr. Phillips' room that night?"

Between hiccups, Margo replied, "Around three."

"And he was alive?"

"Very much so. He was alive and happy." Fresh sobs threatened to rush forth, but Margo took deep breaths.

"And there was no sign that he was feeling ill?"

"No, nothing. I was probably the most shocked of everyone the next day when he was found unresponsive."

"There was no indication that Mr. Phillips left his room on the fourth floor between three a.m. and noon the next day?"

"None. I had the room next to the hallway on the third floor, so I think I would have heard him if he had."

Silence blanketed the room for many seconds, as Parrott thought of other questions. His suspicions roamed from one face to another in a bizarre mental line-up. Was Nicole the murderer, after all, having suspected that Preston had set his sights on divorce and marriage to Margo? Was Margo telling the truth that she didn't kill Preston in those wee hours of the morning? Or were the Winthrops somehow still in the mix, possibly having administered the poison via cigar, and it didn't kick in until after the Phillips-Rinaldi rendezvous? And then there were the truffles and Gerald Kelley's reaction to the word, "palytoxin."

"What if Phillips had told his wife he wanted a divorce? That may have given her the idea to kill him," Parrott thought aloud, watching Margo's face as he spoke. "The only thing is, Nicole's ankle. She was too incapacitated to go up the stairs to the fourth floor that night."

Margo cleared her throat. The time had come to tell what only she knew. "Uh, Detective. I may have some important information for you about that."

"Okay," he replied with caution, "let's hear it."

"Nicole was not too incapacitated. In fact, around three-thirty a.m., I heard her on the stairs and confronted her on the third floor on her way up to see Preston."

Chapter 51

As he was leaving Margo's place, his mind churning with details about the case, Parrott felt the vibration of his cell phone. Rushing to pull it from his pants pocket before losing the call, he fumbled, but not before he saw who was calling, Schrik.

"Chief," he answered, a bit out of breath.

"Gerald Kelley just died. I just heard it on MSNBC."

"Sorry to hear that," Parrott muttered, shifting the cell phone to his other ear, so he could grab his car keys from his right pocket. He thought of Kitty and her needlepoint, the long hospital vigil, now over.

"Thought you'd want to know in case it comes up in your interviews. How'd the Rinaldi interview go?"

"Much more productive than I expected. I'm going to pop in on the Widow Phillips while I'm here. De-brief in a few hours."

"Okay, Parrott, but, remember, the clock is ticking. I wouldn't be surprised if I got another call from Dalton today, what with all this publicity about Kelley in the news. People might connect the dots."

"I'm going as fast as I can, Chief. And for the first time, I believe I'm making progress."

"Good to hear."

છ૭છ૭

On second thought, Parrott returned the car keys to his pocket, deciding to walk the mile and a half from the AKA to Nicole's. He needed the exercise, and moving the car on the Upper West Side was such a hassle. Besides, he had always been a kinesthetic learner, thinking best when moving. The day was cold and crisp. Tiny particles of snow dust hovered in the air, gracing the scene with floating glitter. The routine sounds and smells of traffic provided wallpaper for Parrott's short journey, both the physical and the mental.

There were two areas of interest he wanted to explore with Nicole. Was she aware of her husband's flirtation and affair with Margo? He would need to tread delicately over this path if he wanted honest answers to the multiple questions associated with that. The second area had to do with Preston's own motivations. Was he worried about the lawsuit Winthrop was about to file? Enough to do something drastic? Ever since Andrea's offhand remark, synapses had been firing in Parrott's brain. Today he intended to find out once and for all. And he hoped Billy Bartosh was nowhere around to muddle things up, either.

By the time Parrott arrived at One West Seventy-Second Street, he had the outline of a plan in mind. The doorman greeted him with an unexpected handshake, and before he could take out his badge, the security officer greeted him with a friendly, "Is Mrs. Phillips expecting you, sir?"

"Not today, Doc. Just in the neighborhood and thought I'd drop by." *Are the Dakota employees always this nice, or are they intrigued by having a resident suspected of killing her husband?*

"Ringing her for you...Mrs. Phillips, Detective Parrott is here to see you, ma'am. No, he says he was in the neighborhood...Yes, of course, ma'am." Stanley, as his name badge read, hung up the phone and reported to Parrott, "You can go upstairs. Mrs. Phillips asked you to give her five minutes, though."

"Sure. No problem. Thanks, man." Parrott shook hands with Stanley and started to turn toward the elevator.

"Must be a tough case," Stanley commented, drawing Parrott back to the desk. "All them rich people."

"They're all tough," Parrott replied. "Murders are bad, no matter who the victims are."

"Sure seems strange without Mr. Phillips 'round here."

"Was he well-liked by the staff?"

"Big tipper." Stanley grinned. "That makes for 'well-liked.' Sure did miss him at Christmas this year."

"Well, at least you still have Mrs. Phillips here."

"*Her?* She's got a lot to learn about tipping—that's for sure."

Parrott was surprised by the guard's candor, but he wasn't going to look a gift horse in the mouth. "So, I wonder if she'll stay here permanently, now Mr. Phillips is gone."

"Just between you and me," Stanley replied *sotto voce*, "I don't think she would have been here too long anyway."

"What makes you think that?"

"I been here twenty-seven years, seen 'em come and go. Miz Phillips, she was a short timer if I ever saw one. Beautiful babe, but…"

"Not someone to get old with, eh?"

"Yeah. That's what I mean. But poor Mr. Phillips. He ain't never gonna get old."

~~~

Apparently, Rosa was back from vacation, because she let Parrott in with her usual formal efficiency, taking his coat and then leading him into the living room, where Nicole was seated on a sofa, her ankle propped up on a firm, slanted pillow and surrounded by a blue padded ice pack.

"Forgive me for not standing, Detective. I've just

had physical therapy, and my ankle is throbbing." She was wearing an eggplant-colored velour warmup suit, expensive-looking, but with the lower right leg cut off. Her hair was in a ponytail, and she was wearing no makeup.

"I apologize for coming without calling first, but—"

"You were in the neighborhood. I heard." The look on Nicole's face was halfway between bored and disgusted.

"Yes, and I wanted to discuss some things with you." It felt weird looking down at her, but Parrott waited until he was invited to sit.

"*Discuss?* Sorry for sounding so abrupt, but I hardly think we have anything to *discuss.*"

"Is it something I said?" Parrott offered. He could see he would get nowhere fast with this attitude.

"No, I'm—I'm sorry. I'm just crabby. It seems everything is such a struggle. I'm afraid I've been wallowing in self-pity." She patted the sofa next to her.

Parrott took his familiar seat across from her instead. He preferred to have full view of her face. "You're entitled, I guess. You've been through a lot these past few weeks."

A film of tears glossed Nicole's velvet brown eyes, but she shook off the show of emotion. "Yes, but I was never much for crying over spilt milk. I don't know why I should start now." She brushed her palms against one another as if to signal that the pity party had ended. "Now, what would you like to discuss?"

"A few things. The last time I was here—"

"New Year's Day. We didn't really talk because Billy was here. Well, don't worry, Detective, you won't see Billy here anymore."

"Oh?" Parrott's eyebrows rose.

"I broke up with him. I shouldn't have let him come here…so soon after Preston. I guess I was lonely, and Billy and I had some good times together once."

"But not anymore?"

"He was all sweet at first, but then he started bossing me around too much. He was just after my money. I know that now."

"Good that you saw that when you did and acted on it."

"Yeah. But it's still lonely. All the money in the world is not worth a damn if you don't have anyone to share your life with."

Parrott thought of Tonya and knew that was true. "By the way, you met both Bartosh and Mr. Phillips while you were working at the Lamborghini dealership. Correct?"

"True. I actually miss those days at the dealership. Everyone was friendly and happy. Not stuffy."

"Yes. Well, what exactly was your job there?"

"Receptionist."

"I mean, what did you do as a receptionist?"

"Basically I greeted people. Put shoppers with sales staff. Offered coffee and snacks. Sometimes phone duty, too."

"No computer work?"

"No. Actually, I am sure it surprises you, but I am a total klutz on the computer. It's something I plan to work on as soon as all *this* is better." She pointed to her ice-wrapped ankle.

Parrott nodded and shifted gears. "Well, Mrs. Phillips, I want to ask you some more questions about Mr. Phillips. I don't mean to make you uncomfortable."

"I'm about as uncomfortable as a person can be already."

"Okay. I'm sure you're aware that you are Mr. Phillips' fourth wife, and that he has had many girlfriends over the years."

Nicole's eyes widened, and her mouth formed an O, as if she were about to step into a dark hole in the midst of a frozen lake. "Of course, I know that. You can't date and marry a guy like Preston Phillips without knowing that you'll be living with ghosts. Everywhere you go, it feels like people are comparing you, like you can never measure up to this one or that one. It's not easy, trust me."

"So, when you were invited to Mr. Campbell's birthday party, you must have had some trepidation about going."

"Oh, you don't know the half of it." Nicole

shuddered, as if to emphasize the horror of it all. "As much as I miss Preston, I do not miss that."

"Are you aware that one of the guests at the party was once engaged to Mr. Phillips?"

"Yes. Margo. And she was flirting with him all weekend, too. That was another thing about Preston. It was like potato chips. Once you loved him, you couldn't stop. It totally pissed me off."

"Did her flirting concern you?"

"Concern me? Sure. Nobody likes having another woman chasing after her husband. But let's say it wasn't the first time, and I figured it wouldn't be the last—Oh, but it did turn out to be the last, didn't it? Well, to tell you the truth, I was in no position to do much about it. I was in an incredible amount of pain, taking oxycodone, mostly out of it."

"Speaking of your injury, once you broke your ankle, you were pretty much confined to the downstairs. Is that correct?"

"Yes, pretty much."

"So Mr. Phillips continued to sleep in the bedroom on the fourth floor, while you slept on the sofa in the den?"

"Yes."

"Did you make an attempt to go up to the fourth floor at any time following your injury?"

Nicole sighed. "I suppose Ms. Margo Snoop told you. Yes, I tried to go upstairs late Saturday night, more like early Sunday morning. She saw me on the stairs and convinced me to go back down-stairs."

"Did you go back upstairs later?"

"No, it was too painful and difficult. I decided to wait till the next morning to see Preston. Now, of course, I wish I'd ignored Margo and gone up."

"Why did you want to see your husband then?"

A crease appeared in her otherwise-smooth fore-head. "It's hard to put into words. There I was, ba-sically a stranger in the house, hurting and feeling sorry for myself. My anchor was on the fourth floor."

Parrott was beginning to think Nicole might not be as much of an airhead as everyone thought. "Had anything occurred during the day or evening to cause you to feel that way?"

"Nothing, really. Just a bad feeling I had when Preston told me good night and went upstairs."

"Did this feeling have anything to do with the fact that you felt Margo was flirting with your hus-band?"

"M—Maybe it did. Though I must say that it wasn't the first time I felt shut out by Preston. He was a very closed-up person. It was something I struggled with."

Parrott shifted on the sofa. "Let's talk about Mr. Phillips for a moment. Were you aware he was about to be sued by Marshall Winthrop?"

Nicole's countenance changed from worried to shocked. "No. Sued? For what?"

"Apparently Mr. Winthrop believed that Mr. Phillips had mismanaged the Winthrop estate."

Frowning, Nicole replied, "See what I mean? Preston never told me anything about that. He apparently was a man of many secrets." She fiddled with the zipper of her warmup suit, touched a spot inside of her upper arm. Standing, she caused the ice pack to fall to the floor. Using her cane to walk around the living room, she appeared to be engrossed with the ramifications of this new concept. Parrott gave her the time and space. After a few laps, she plopped down in the exact spot and said, "So do you think Marshall is the one who killed him?"

"I can't answer your question, but I have another question for you. Do you think Mr. Phillips, knowing of the pending lawsuit, might have been angry with Mr. Winthrop?"

"Oh, ho, probably not angry. Probably furious. Maybe that's why Preston was so cranky the weeks before the party. Lots of times he would close himself up in his office at night, leaving me alone to wonder what was wrong."

Pleased with the way the interview was going, Parrott pressed on. "In your experience with Mr. Phillips, both before and after you were married, what was he like when he became angry?"

Nicole jerked her head upward, so her eyes met Parrott's. It was as if she were confronting a part of her husband and her marriage that she had completely suppressed until now. Her voice, when it came, was a whisper. "It was not good to be on Preston's bad side. He didn't get angry often, but when he did, just stay away."

"Do you mean he became explosive?"

"Cold, mean, yeah, I guess 'explosive' works. Maybe cruel."

"Did he ever become explosive with you?"

Holding eye contact, Nicole used her cane to stand. She removed her zippered jacket and began removing her right arm from the pink shell she was wearing. Parrott could see glimpses of shoulder, bra, elbow, and midriff, but the mini-strip was happening so fast, he was dumbfounded. Finally, Nicole stopped, her shell still covering her left side. She rotated her arm outward to expose the inside of her bicep, where an angry red scar in the shape of a lightning bolt was imprinted. It looked to be a few months old.

"Did he do that to you?" Parrott mumbled. The vivid mark just didn't jibe with the act of a former secretary of the treasury, a billionaire, a member of high society.

"He hit me with a granite paperweight. He threw it at my face, but I raised my arms to shield myself. Better to have the scar there, don't you think?"

"When did this occur?"

"May. He overheard a voicemail from Billy and went off the deep end."

"Before you were married?"

"Yes. We were married on June fifth."

"And knowing that he had a violent temper, you married him anyway?"

"I know. I should have seen this as a sign, big time. But he apologized profusely, promised never to hurt me again, told me he loved me and that thinking of me with Billy made him temporarily insane. I wanted to believe him, and I did."

"And did he ever hurt you again after that?"

"No. He kept his word. And, now, I know for sure he'll never hurt me again."

Chapter 52

Ignited with fresh ideas and leads in the case, Parrott phoned Officer Barton as he drove back to Brandywine. He wanted some quick information from the Lamborghini dealership. Was Bill Bartosh still employed in the shop there? Did he show up at work today? Parrott's instincts told him Nicole was telling the truth about breaking up with Bartosh, but it was worth checking to make sure there wasn't foul play involved, and there might be a need to interview him at some point in the future. Next, he wanted to verify Nicole's story about having no computer skills. It had been less than a year since she worked there, and someone in personnel should be able to corroborate.

Also, it wouldn't hurt to check Nicole's phone records for the period since her husband's death. He wanted to make sure that the breakup with Billy was legit.

When Parrott arrived back at the station, dusk was hovering over the crimson roof. He hoped Schrik was still there.

His hopes were realized when he saw the brawny chief pacing around the hallway, hands clasped behind his back and chewing on his paper clip. The thought passed through Parrott's mind that this iconic image of Schrik would be implanted in his brain forever.

When Schrik noticed Parrott, he broke stride and greeted the detective with a combination hand-shake-hug. "Glad you made it back before I had to leave for the day. We need to talk."

"Something ominous, Chief?"

"Been a long day. Lots of pressure from the top on this case. Local, state and national." He led Parrott toward his office and motioned for him to sit. "Tell me something good, something real good."

Parrott summarized his interviews with Margo and Nicole, pinpointing specific details pertinent to the case. He started with Margo's affair with Phillips, her nervousness and repeated claims not to have killed him, and her encounter with Nicole on the third floor hallway, confirmed by Nicole. He continued with Nicole's break with Bartosh, her lack of computer skills, and her comments about Phillips' brooding, likely fury with Winthrop, and fiery temper—including the spousal abuse.

Schrik listened, the paper clip moving around in his mouth. Parrott could tell by his lack of eye contact that the new information was doing little to appease the fireball of impatience roiling about inside. Parrott's short-lived feeling of efficacy was evaporating as he delivered each detail. When he finished, he said, "That's it."

Usually, at the end of Parrott's reports, Schrik

would praise Parrott's good work, but today there was just silence as the words settled around them both. After an uncomfortable quiet, Schrik said, "So, where are we, Parrott? Who is our perp, and where's the evidence to convict him?"

Parrott knew better than to beat around the bush. "I've narrowed the list of suspects, and I'm closing in on the killer. I just need a little more time."

"More time? It's January sixth for Pete's sake. It's been almost four weeks. You know as well as I do that this case is growing icier than a Popsicle at the North Pole." Schrik began storming back and forth in the short space between desk and chair. "What makes you think you are closing in?"

"Andrea Baker made a passing remark the other day—"

"The crime writer? What did *she* have to say?"

"She said with the threat of a lawsuit being filed by Winthrop against Phillips, it wouldn't surprise her if Phillips had wanted to kill Winthrop. Something like that."

Schrik sat down and looked at Parrott with an inscrutable expression.

"So I started thinking, what if Phillips is the one who researched palytoxin on his computer? He might have used his own aquarium to harvest the deadly stuff, and took it to Bucolia in a Metamucil container to poison Winthrop. Maybe he planned to put it in Winthrop's CPAP machine somehow."

"Then why didn't he go through with it?"

"I don't know. Maybe he got distracted by the Rinaldi woman and decided it wasn't worth pursuing."

"So the Metamucil container full of palytoxin was just sitting in his bathroom, unused, and he forgot what was in it and ingested it himself. Is that your thinking?"

"No, Chief."

Schrik was toying with him now. Parrott sighed. "I'm thinking somehow someone else administered the poison to Phillips early Sunday morning. That narrows the suspect list considerably."

"Where's the Metamucil container now?"

"In the property room. Crime lab dusted for prints and found multiples."

"Look, Parrott. Nothing against you. I know you've broken your back for this case, but the Board of Supervisors is on my case. Our little department is just not equipped to handle such a high profile case. I think it's time to turn the case over to the state police.

Parrott gasped and bent over, covering his face with both hands. He felt as though he were slipping down the face of a mountain after a long, hard climb. After several seconds he replied, "Please, Chief. Give me one more shot at this. I have an idea that might just work. We've come too far to give up now."

Shaking his head, with a wry smile, Schrik said, "Parrott, you remind me so much of me when I was your age. You're just a dog with a bone. Okay, twenty-four hours. That's it. Bring me the killer and the evidence by tomorrow night, or, Wednesday morning, I'll roll this case over on its back. Okay?"

"Deal."

They shook hands, and Parrott left Schrik in his office, mumbling unintelligibly through the paper clip.

✍✍

By this time, six-thirty, Parrott's stomach was rumbling with a ferocity that demanded action. He hadn't eaten since breakfast, but the sand in the hourglass was sifting with equal ferocity. He had come too far with this case to let someone else solve it. He took a chance that Maria Rodriguez was working late at the coroner's office. Sometimes she had such a backload she would stay till midnight. If so, he would pay her an after-hours visit.

Just as he developed this plan, his cell phone rang.

"Maria? You must have ESP. I was just thinking about coming over to see you, if you're going to be there awhile longer."

"Yeah, I'm still here. The new year is off to a hectic start. It's taken me longer than expected to find the answer to your question. Frozen palytoxin is still lethal. Tested in the kitchens of yours truly under controlled conditions." When she didn't hear the expected laughter, she continued, "Just kidding. State lab did the testing. Hope it helps."

"Perfect. Thanks for your help, as always."

"Always here to serve."

"Okay if I come by? I've got some other things to run past you."

"Sure."

"Have you eaten? I can pick up some sandwiches en route."

"Best offer I've had all day."

ᏇᎧᏇᎧ

On the way to the Chester County Coroner's Office, Parrott stopped at Capriotti's for two of their famous sandwiches. The urgency of his mission was directly proportional to the heaviness of his right foot on the accelerator. Luckily the to-go line at the highly regarded restaurant was short and the service swift.

It was also convenient that his Skype-visit with Tonya had been postponed for some reason, usually on Sunday or Monday night at eight (and six-thirty the next morning in Kabul). He needed to give his full attention to this case for the next twenty-four hours. He wasn't about to let it go.

As he entered Maria's office, the aroma oozing from the warm foil-wrapped sandwiches caused the deputy coroner to inhale with a moan of pleasure. "Mmm, Parrott. Your presence and your presents both hit the spot tonight." She removed her gloves and washed her hands with a gritty antibacterial soap then led Parrott out of the autopsy room and into her small office. "Mind if we eat first, talk second?"

Parrott set two places at Maria's desk, using paper towels and napkins. The steamy pastrami, Swiss cheese, Russian dressing, and coleslaw sandwiches and cold bottles of water seemed like a royal feast. After a ceremonial touching of the water bottles, the two diners gave their energy to chewing and swallowing.

Maria spoke first. "Delicious. I'd forgotten how much I love Capriotti's."

"Let me do the dishes," Parrott teased, crumpling up the paper remains and tossing them in the wastebasket.

"Okay," Maria said, putting the plastic cap back on her water bottle. "I'm not hungry anymore." Her expression turned serious. "How's the Phillips case going?"

"I wish I could say 'well,' but it's anything but. Too much political pressure and the characters are difficult—rich, well-connected, crafty. I've got some solid theories, but no hard evidence, and the chief is giving me one day to solve before turning it over to the state." Parrott tapped his heel on the floor with nervous energy.

Maria touched his forearm with sympathy. "Tell me how I can help."

"Okay. The Metamucil container was filled with palytoxin, the substance that killed Phillips."

Maria nodded.

"And whoever brought it and used it, left it there to be discovered after Phillips' death."

Another nod.

"The container had multiple fingerprints, whole and partial, so it was handled by several people."

"Yes, I believe we were able to identify fingerprints of Mr. Phillips, Mrs. Phillips, and the housekeeper, as well as other unknowns."

"Well, my theory is that Phillips manufactured the palytoxin himself and brought it in the Metamucil container in order to poison someone else."

"And ended up taking it himself? Are you saying it was a suicide?" Maria's voice rose an octave.

"Not necessarily. Someone might have taken advantage of its being there and used it to poison Phillips."

"But that would require the other person to know what was in the container."

"Maybe or maybe not." Parrott used a blank sheet of computer paper to draw a diagram of the bathroom counter as he remembered it from the day of the murder. "I wish we'd been more thorough in gathering evidence from the bathroom that first day. At the time we didn't know it was a murder, and we were tiptoeing around the fancy farm-house." His picture included the sink, the open Dopp kit, the bottles of pills, the victim's tooth-brush and toothpaste, and a water glass, about a quarter full of clear liquid. "I'd give anything to have that water glass."

"If there were traces of palytoxin in it, it would have been dangerous for anyone to handle. If any-one touched it and touched his mouth, we would have had another death on our hands."

Parrott liked the way Maria said, "We." It was one of the reasons he enjoyed working with her. "Maria, let's go over the toxicity of palytoxin again. How quickly does it take effect, and what does it do to the person ingesting it?"

"Okay, but remember, this is a fairly new toxin, so information about it is scarce. What makes it a so-called 'designer' poison is that it is naturally oc-curring, and it doesn't cause the typical symptoms that other poisons do, like lividity or bleeding. It essentially acts quickly to bring about cell death. The victim doesn't suffer much, and it leaves al-most no traces."

"If it leaves no traces, how did you discover it?"

"Almost by accident. I had just read an article in a medical journal about some people who died cleaning their fish tanks. One guy boiled the water and inhaled the poison in gas form. Another guy ingested it after handling the toxin. Our victim ap-peared to have been poisoned, but there were no traces of poison in his system. So I took skin samples from his lips, gums and inside his mouth. Bingo—palytoxin. Maybe the killer read the same article that I did."

"So Phillips pretty much died in his sleep."

"Right. He may have awakened and had the sense that something was wrong, difficulty breathing or moving, but by the time that occurred, it was too late to call for help or do anything about it. And don't forget, he had taken lots of drugs and alcohol prior to going to sleep."

"Can you help me narrow down the time of death? I have a witness who last saw him around three a.m. and said he was fine."

"And the body was found just after noon. I would say he might have been poisoned between three-thirty and six-thirty, and his organs shut down approximately one to two hours afterward."

"Could you testify to that?"

"Sure." Maria shook her head as if trying to loosen a sticky problem. "Can I ask *you* a question, though?" Without waiting for permission, she went on. "If Phillips brought the palytoxin in the Metamucil container and knew it was there, wouldn't he have been careful not to take the poison, himself? I'm just not picturing how it got from the container into his system."

"That, my dear Ms. Rodriguez, is exactly the answer I am seeking." He looked at his watch. "And I only have about twenty hours to find it."

CHAPTER 53

B y the time Parrott left the coroner's office, it was almost eight. He checked for messages and was surprised to find one from Caro. "Did you hear about Gerald? It's just awful." Her voice caught, and she took a few seconds before going on. "First Preston and now Gerald. It made me wonder if you've made progress on the case. I'm still so torn up about Preston's death. Maybe it would help me heal if I knew that you had found the killer. Anyway, please call me if you have a chance."

Delighted at his good fortune, Parrott returned the call. After the preliminaries, he said, "If you're at Bucolia, I wonder if I might come over for a short while this evening."

"Tonight?" He guessed Caro was not expecting a police visit at such short notice or at such an hour. "Well, I suppose it would be okay. Do you have news for us?"

Considering how much he would be able to share with the victim's cousin at this point, he said, "The case is progressing. We may have some news in the very near future, but mostly I wanted to revisit the fourth floor suite where Mr. Phillips was staying."

The long, winding approach to the farmhouse made Parrott think of the twists and turns of the case. He had come such a long way since the quick cremation and funeral, the early interviews and learning that just about everyone had a motive to kill Phillips, checking out the cigars and truffles, the widow's eager boyfriend, the victim's mother, and all those fish tanks. There was a certain symmetry in returning to the scene of the crime in these last hours. Parrott knew in his heart this was the best use of his time.

John E. opened the door and ushered Parrott inside, where a pine-scented fire lit up the family room with warmth and fragrance. Caro was needlepointing, sitting on the sofa where Nicole had slept after breaking her ankle. When Parrott came in, she put down the fabric to shake his hand. The large house seemed otherwise empty and quiet, especially in comparison to the first time Parrott was there.

"Would you like to sit down? Have something to drink?" Caro offered.

"No, ma'am, as I told you over the phone, I'd like to see the upstairs. And if you could accompany me, I'd appreciate it." He looked at John E. to make sure he understood he was included.

"Okay, let's go up," John E. replied. He led the way to the staircase and started climbing. At the second floor hallway, he paused. "This is where our bedroom is."

"Also where the Spillers and Winthrops stayed, if I remember correctly," Parrott said.

Looking impressed, John E. asked, "Is there anything you want to see on this floor?"

"Just to confirm, the Winthrops had the bedroom closest to the staircase, correct?"

"Yes, that's right," Caro said. "They were the closest to the staircase."

The threesome continued up the stairs to the third floor. "This is where the Kelleys, the Blooms, and Ms. Rinaldi stayed," Parrott stated, "with Ms. Rinaldi in the outside bedroom." He looked around, imagining how simple it was for Margo to sneak up the stairs to the fourth floor without anyone noticing.

Passing by the antiques and expensive-looking oil paintings on the landing, Parrott said, "Let's go on." The stairs to the fourth floor were narrower, and the area smaller and less ornate. The room to the bedroom suite was closed, as if to block off what had happened there.

"Here you go," John E. said, as he turned and pushed the porcelain doorknob and turned on the light. The bedroom had been straightened and cleaned, the scent of furniture polish still in the air. Parrott walked about the small room, imagining the exchanges between the victim and Margo that had happened there. He wondered whether it was possible for someone to enter the room after Phillips had gone to sleep without waking him.

The Campbells were standing at the doorway in silence, watching as Parrott moved around the room.

"Mrs. Campbell, would you mind going outside of the room and closing the door then opening the door as quietly as possible?"

Caro did as requested. The turning of the knob, the movement of the door, and the release of the doorknob—all went smoothly and soundlessly.

"Has the door been oiled since December fifteenth?" Parrott asked.

"No, I don't think so," Caro replied. "But if it was, it would have been part of routine maintenance. All of the doors are kept in good working order. That's one of the chores for the help in a home like this."

John E. broke in. "So that establishes that someone could have sneaked in and poisoned Preston without waking him. But we already knew that."

Parrott ignored the comment and moved into the attached bathroom. The tile and appliances were gleaming, and the countertop accessories were arranged in perfect order. "Is this the same drinking glass that was here the night of the murder?" Parrott asked, although he doubted there would be a duplicate of the glass that matched the gold and black harlequin-decorated wastebasket and toothbrush holder.

Saralyn Richard

"Yes. It's been washed, of course," Caro replied. She took in a quick breath and bit her lip.

Parrott examined the shiny knobs and pulls, wondering if it would be beneficial to dust them for prints at this late date. They looked as if they'd been scrubbed and polished, and, anyway, there probably wouldn't be time, given Schrik's tight deadline.

"Okay, folks. I think I've seen enough here. There's just one more thing I'd like you to help me with." Parrott led the way out of the bedroom into the hallway and started down the stairs.

"What is it?" John E. asked.

When he landed on the third floor, Parrott turned to face the Campbells. "I'd like for you to go down to the second floor, wait until I call to you, and then come back up the stairs to the third floor."

John E. and Caro looked at each other, and then John E. nodded. "Okay."

They started down the stairs, and Parrott went into the bedroom that had been occupied by Margo. He closed the door, noting how quietly the hinges and the latch operated. He seated himself on the bed and shouted, "Okay, come on up."

Immediately, he could hear the sounds of footsteps on the stairs. There was no doubt Margo would have heard Nicole as she climbed the stairs with her ankle in that metal contraption, and especially if she hadn't gone to sleep yet. Also, Margo may have heard anyone else who came up the stairs

464

to go to the fourth floor, so the Winthrops or Spillers would have had a bigger risk. He jumped up, smoothed out the comforter of the bed, then opened the door to meet the Campbells outside the door.

"Thank you for conducting those little experiments with me," Parrott said. "I think we can go downstairs now."

On the way down, Parrott wondered whether the Winthrops had heard Nicole on the stairs. Maybe the white noise of the CPAP machines covered for her, or maybe they were sleeping soundly by the time she ventured up. *Anyway, I think I know what my next step is going to be.*

Parrott shook hands with John E. and Caro and thanked them again for their assistance. They ushered him out into the dark, cold night and closed the door silently behind him.

Then John E. turned to Caro and said, "I'm very afraid for Margo."

Caro replied, "Me, too."

❧

By the time he returned home from Bucolia, Parrott was feeling exhausted. It had been a full day, and the time pressure was giving him a headache. The sandwich that had tasted so good hours ago had left him thirsty. He opened the refrigerator and contemplated opening a Heineken, but decided he needed to keep his head clear for a few more hours at least. He grabbed a two-liter of Mountain Dew instead. The fizz he heard when opening it reminded him of champagne. He'd have to get some real champagne tomorrow night to celebrate solving the case.

Drinking from the plastic bottle, he walked over to Tonya's picture. He wondered why she had had to cancel their Skype date. "I miss you so much, my love," he crooned to her smiling face. Wish you were here to help me deal with these crazy people." He imagined her standing behind him, arms wrapped around his waist, head resting on his back. "Only thirteen more weeks till you'll be here for good," he whispered. He could almost feel the warmth soaking into his skin and comforting him, encouraging him.

Parrott opened Horace's cage and carried the little guy to the kitchen table, where his notes, charts, drawings, a fresh pen, and a legal pad awaited. Today's visits with Margo, Nicole, Maria, and the Campbells had given him what he needed to figure out who'd killed Preston Phillips. What he did now was to reconstruct the killing, putting all of the information he had into a neat concept map. Before he went to bed, he had a good idea of how he would prove it, too.

☙❧

The next morning Parrott leaped out of bed, energized by adrenalin. He had dreamed of Tonya, holding a trophy just out of his reach. He was running toward her, the wind blasting against the sides of his face. He was within ten feet of his goal, but he knew he couldn't slow down yet. Then the alarm woke him. It was show time.

The first leg of his day's journey was to call Schrik. Depending on the outcome of his trip to New York, he would need Schrik to manage the necessary paperwork entailed in closing a Pennsylvania case in New York. This could become quite complicated, especially when dealing with the potential arrest of a prominent citizen. Nevertheless, Schrik was delighted with Parrott's hypothesis and plan. "Good work, Parrott, and good luck. I'll be ready to jump into action as soon as you call."

The sun blazed through the windshield as Parrott drove his usual path into New York. His plan was to drop in on Margo without calling first. She had been so distressed the last time he was there, and he knew this visit wouldn't be easy either.

It was almost nine-thirty when he arrived at the AKA, and the desk clerk called to announce him. This time Margo had a personal assistant there, a polite young woman, wearing a starched uniform with "Elena" embroidered on the shirt pocket, and beckoning him inside with a finger to her lips. "Ms. Rinaldi is not feeling well this morning. She asks that we not make noise." She led him into the kitchenette. He sat under the Chihuly chandelier, where a kaleidoscope of colorful patterns danced on the table. "I'll just take Ms. Rinaldi her coffee, and she'll be with you in a few minutes."

Parrott nodded. He needed her to be awake when he met with her. The smell of strong coffee assailed his nose. Maybe he could get some, too.

Another twenty minutes and a robust cup of coffee later, Parrott watched Margo make her grand entrance into the room, as if she were a runway model. She was dressed in a rust-colored cashmere sweater and tan pants. Except for the obvious purple half-moons beneath her eyes, she had the face of an angel. Not for the first time, Parrott marveled at Phillips' taste for beautiful women.

"I'm sorry to keep you waiting, Detective, but I didn't know you were coming back." The dig at Parrott's lack of manners was subtle but did not go unnoticed.

"I apologize for not calling first. My day requires me to be in New York, and I have some follow-up questions for you."

"Just let me—Elena," Margo said to the housekeeper, "could you give us some privacy, please?"

"Surely," Elena replied. "I'll be back in the laundry room if you need me."

"I see Elena gave you some coffee. Would you like a refill?"

"No, ma'am. One's my limit, thank you. Let me get down to business." He fiddled with his iPad to stall for time. "You do remember that I read you your Miranda rights at Bucolia and reminded you of them yesterday?"

"Yes, yes. I didn't kill Preston, so I'm sure I don't have anything to worry about."

"Yes, ma'am. Well, I've done some investigating since we met yesterday, and I have a few more questions. We also have some evidence taken from the bedroom occupied by Mr. Phillips." Parrott gave Margo a penetrating look.

"Ask. Let's get this over with." She massaged the pressure points on her forehead.

"Yesterday, you told me that Nicole Phillips attempted to go to her husband on the fourth floor after three a.m. on the night in question, correct?"

"Yes." Margo appeared to relax a little.

"And you convinced her to go back downstairs and wait until the next day to see Mr. Phillips."

"Yes, I helped her go back down the stairs and get resettled on the sofa, as well."

"Why did you intervene?"

"Well, I would think that would be obvious. I had just had sex with her husband. I wasn't sure how much she knew about our relationship, and I didn't want to expose Preston to her scrutiny. Besides, I have more respect for Caro and John E. than to have risked having a brouhaha in their home at three a.m."

Parrott nodded. "You also told me Mr. Phillips had indicated to you that he had told his wife he wanted a divorce."

469

"Yes, it was a condition for our sleeping together." Margo began rubbing the fabric of her sweater between thumb and forefinger, just as she had the day before.

"Did it seem to you that Mrs. Phillips had been told such a thing when you saw her on her way upstairs?"

"I don't know. I know *I* wouldn't be climbing three flights of stairs with a broken ankle to see a scoundrel who had just broken up with me, but maybe the younger generation is different. Maybe she was going to plead with him to change his mind."

"How did it make you feel to think that Mr. Phillips might not have told her, that he slept with you under false pretenses?" Parrott was pushing some hot buttons, but he pressed on.

"Okay, I admit it. I was furious. The whole weekend had been a roller coaster with my feelings for Preston going up, down, up, down, and at that moment I just wanted to get off."

Parrott noticed tears forming in Margo's eyes, but he had to go forward. "So you went back into Phillips' bedroom to confront him."

Margo's eyes opened wide with something that might have been fear. She gasped. "How did you know that?"

"It fits with the facts of the case. What I need to know from you is how you found Mr. Phillips when you went back to his room."

"How did I find him? I found him asleep. He didn't hear me open the door or enter the room, didn't wake up at all." Her voice had taken on a shrill quality.

"Did you go over to the bed? Could you tell if he was still alive at that time?"

"He was still alive. He was snoring. Mad as I was, I stood there and watched him sleep. He looked as innocent as a baby."

"So what did you do next?"

"I just stood there for what seemed like a long time, watching. He was smiling in his sleep, as if he were dreaming about something happy."

"And then you went into the bathroom?"

"How did—yes, yes, I did. I had to go to the bathroom, and I didn't want to go back downstairs yet. Maybe I was hoping the flush would wake Preston up, and we could have it out."

"Why didn't you just wake him up if you wanted to have it out with him?"

"Okay, to be totally honest, I *did* try to wake him up. I stood over him and spoke as loudly as I could without shouting and waking up the whole house, but he didn't budge. I shook him and shook him, but he just kept that silly smile on his face and rolled over. I know he'd had a lot to drink that night, and maybe he took some pills that interacted with the alcohol. He just wouldn't wake up."

"While you were in the bathroom, you noticed the Metamucil container there." Parrott gambled, though his voice sounded as if it were an established fact. "Your fingerprint was left on the label."

"Yes. It was strange. The guys had been talking at dinner about fraternity pranks they had committed with Metamucil. It occurred to me that I could get even with Preston by pulling the same prank on him. It was childish, I know, but I thought it would be a way to let him know that I knew he hadn't told Nicole, and ultimately it would be harmless."

"So what did you do next?"

"I mixed some Metamucil with water in the drinking cup next to the sink. That's all. I just mixed it and left it there, and then I went back to my room and went to sleep.

"How did you measure the Metamucil? Was there a measuring spoon?"

Margo's eyes narrowed, as if she were reading between the lines of Parrott's questions. "I—I don't think so. I think I just poured a small amount of Metamucil into the water and rolled it around in the glass to dissolve it." She moved her hand in circles, as if holding an imaginary brandy snifter.

"Did you wash your hands after mixing the Metamucil with the water?"

Now, Margo stood and paced around the room. "Washed my hands? I'm sure I did. I always wash my hands thoroughly before leaving the restroom. It's a lifelong habit."

"A lucky one for you, as it turns out. So you washed your hands and left the Metamucil mixture for Mr. Phillips to drink, hoping it would loosen his bowels, as a prank."

Margo sat again. "Yes, I did. As I say, it wasn't the most mature way to handle my anger, but as it turned out, Preston probably never even drank it."

"Unfortunately, you are wrong about that, Ms. Rinaldi. Mr. Phillips must have awakened after you left. Perhaps the alcohol had left his mouth very dry. He drank the mixture you prepared and went back to bed. But it wasn't Metamucil in the container. It was a deadly poison called palytoxin. It was your actions, Ms. Rinaldi, that killed Preston Phillips."

"Killed him? *I* didn't kill Preston. I *loved* him." Margo began shrieking and gasping. Elena came running into the room, and Parrott instructed her to call for the paramedics. Margo was hyperventilating and moaning, "No—o—o, n—o—o," as her color changed from cream to paper.

Afraid she would lose consciousness and hit the ceramic floor, Parrott moved her into the living room, where he placed her on the sofa with an ice pack behind her neck.

☙❧☙

Margo was taken to Mount Sinai Hospital, the same place where Gerald had been taken after his stroke. Parrott followed the ambulance, and Libby was there to meet it when it pulled into the driveway. While in the emergency room, Margo refused to cooperate. Her agitation and incoherent outbursts led to restraints and an interview with a psychiatrist. When her hysteria included the expression of suicidal ideation, she was given a heavy dose of Lorazepam. Parrott left while Libby was making arrangements to have her transported to the Haven of Westchester, a private facility in White Plains. She would be placed in a close-observation unit, stripped of everything but a hospital gown, with an attendant, who would become her shadow for the foreseeable future.

On the way back to the station, Parrott called Schrik and brought him up-to-date. An hour and a half later, Parrott pulled into his parking space. He was well within the twenty-four-hour limit, but that didn't seem to matter much anymore. When Schrik, standing at the window on the second floor, saw him, he went downstairs to greet the detective at the front door. Parrott opened the door to his boss's applause.

"Thanks, Chief," Parrott said, modestly. "Let's go sit down. We have a lot to talk about."

഻഻഻

Schrik handed a stack of messages across the desk to Parrott. "So the Widow checked out," he said, referring to Barton's reports about Bartosh, Nicole's lack of computer skills, and her phone records. She was playing straight with you, after all."

"This was some case, Chief. I'm sorry I can't give you an arrest and conviction, after all this work, but—"

"I know, it was an accidental death, at best. Rinaldi had no idea she was killing her boyfriend. She just thought she was playing a prank on him. What's so strange is just about everyone there had a motive to kill Phillips. At one point, I even thought it might be a conspiracy."

"Don't forget Phillips' own role in setting the whole thing up. He went to a lot of trouble to bring that palytoxin in the Metamucil container. Ironic that the one who ended up dying was him."

"Yeah. I'm convinced he intended to kill Winthrop. That was the one person who presented the biggest threat to him with that messy lawsuit," Parrott said.

"Why do you think he didn't go through with it?"

"Oh, I've thought that through. I think he planned to wait until Sunday morning, when everyone was downstairs having brunch. He would have stayed upstairs, so he could sneak into Winthrop's room and coat his CPAP machine with palytoxin. Sunday night, when Winthrop was back at home, he would have inhaled the poison in his sleep and died. By that time, Phillips would be far away, and he would have dumped the palytoxin. It was an ingenious plan, actually."

"Well," Schrik said, rolling the paper clip around in his mouth, "I'll be taking the evidence to the district attorney and recommending we wrap this up as an accidental death."

Parrott nodded. "How does Dalton feel about that?"

"I offered to bring murder charges, but he knew it would come out at trial that Phillips had brought the poison with mal-intent. Dalton said, 'Let it go.'" Schrik took out his paper clip and laid it on his desk. "Man, these one-percenters are really something, aren't they? I guess they think they're invulnerable. They're just used to having things go their way all of the time."

"You could say that, but if you think about it, they aren't the happiest bunch. Phillips and Kelley are dead, Vicki Spiller is in a rehab hospital, and Margo Rinaldi might never recover from her nervous breakdown. The Winthrops will always feel cheated by Phillips, no matter how much other money they have, and the Blooms will have major worries over Margo. The Campbells will probably never find peace at Bucolia after this, either."

"You left out the Bakers," Schrik said.

"Yeah, thank goodness for Andrea. It was her comment about Phillips' wanting to kill Winthrop that turned my thinking around."

"And the wealthy Widow Phillips."

"Aside from her broken ankle and physical and

mental scars from poor choices in men, I guess she'll be the only one who comes out ahead in all this."

Parrott rubbed his eyes, suddenly realizing how depleted he felt. "After this case, I think I need a vacation."

"Hmm, hmm," came a sound from behind Parrott.

When he turned to see Tonya standing in the doorway, wearing her uniform and holding a bottle of champagne, his mouth opened in shock.

"A vacation? How about a honeymoon, Detective?"

ACKNOWLEDGMENTS

I am deeply indebted to the following people who assisted with authenticating information for this novel: Scott Richard and Edward Richard; Drs. Howard Rubin, Kerri Halfant, and Andy Kahn; Chief of Police, Henry Porretto; the staff at West Brandywine Township Hall; Curtiss Brown; Mike Hoover; Jamie Hennigan; and my writers' critique group: Irene Amiet, Susan Baker, Shannon Caldwell, Michael Hennen, Gary Hoffman, Dan McKeithan, and Richard Peake. If the story rings true, it is to their credit. If not, the fault is mine.

Thanks also to editors, Joyce H., Faith C., and Lauri Wellington; cover artists, Rebecca Evans and Jack Jackson; author photographer, Jennifer Reynolds; and publicist, Caitlin Hamilton Marketing. Their expertise and professionalism, along with their belief in the value of this book, provide its wings.

Most of all, thanks to you, Readers. You are the ones who have made this dream come true.

~ Saralyn Richard

About the Author

Award-winning mystery and children's books author, Saralyn Richard, has been a teacher who wrote on the side. Now she is a writer who teaches on the side. Some of her poems and essays have won awards and contests from the time she was in high school. Her children's picture book, *Naughty Nana*, has reached thousands of children in five countries. *Murder in the One Percent* pulls back the curtain on the privileged and powerful. Set on a gentleman's farm in Pennsylvania and in the tony areas of New York, the book shows what happens when someone comes to a party with murder in his heart and poison in his pocket.

A member of Mystery Writers of America and International Thriller Writers, Richard has completed a stand-alone mystery, Murder at Lincoln High, and is working on another Oliver Parrott mystery. Her website is www.saralynrichard.com.

Made in the USA
San Bernardino, CA
28 February 2020